John Keats, Harry Buxton Forman

Poetical works and other writings, now first brought together, including poems and numerous letters not before published

Edited with notes and appendices by Harry Buxton Forman. Vol. 1

John Keats, Harry Buxton Forman

Poetical works and other writings, now first brought together, including poems and numerous letters not before published
Edited with notes and appendices by Harry Buxton Forman. Vol. 1

ISBN/EAN: 9783337114978

Printed in Europe, USA, Canada, Australia, Japan

Cover: Foto ©Andreas Hilbeck / pixelio.de

More available books at **www.hansebooks.com**

From a miniature of Keats in the Editor's possession.

THE POETICAL WORKS

AND OTHER WRITINGS

OF

JOHN KEATS

NOW FIRST BROUGHT TOGETHER

INCLUDING POEMS AND NUMEROUS LETTERS ·

NOT BEFORE PUBLISHED

EDITED

WITH NOTES AND APPENDICES

BY

HARRY BUXTON FORMAN

IN FOUR VOLUMES

VOLUME I

LONDON
REEVES & TURNER 196 STRAND

CONTENTS OF VOLUME I.

ILLUSTRATIONS TO VOLUME I.

ix

PREFACE.

BY THE EDITOR.

THE volumes now laid before the public have occupied
the leisure hours of some years, and have been delayed
by various circumstances which need not be detailed.
The most gratifying of these was an interruption of
several months during which my leisure had to be devoted to the preparation of two new editions of Shelley's
Poetical Works, to meet a demand consequent on the
favourable reception of the former edition. The only
other cause of delay that concerns the public is the frequent discovery of fresh material; and in this respect I
hope that Keats's many readers will find compensation.

Partly by the knowledge that much unused material
existed, and partly by the feeling that the editions
of Keats's writings current up to the present time left
room for one on the lines of my library edition of
Shelley, I was led to undertake this work ; and in carrying it out I have followed the same principles of revision
as in the other case, namely to gather together everything I could find from the hand of the poet, to establish
the text as nearly as possible in accordance with what the

poet wrote or meant to write, to make no changes without record,[1] and to elucidate and illustrate from such
printed and manuscript sources as were open to me.

The three volumes of poetry printed during Keats's
life have been reproduced upon this plan ; and their
contents have been collated with all available manuscripts and printed issues of authority, variations being
given in foot-notes. The posthumous poems in order
of date follow the three printed volumes ; and the
chronology has only been interrupted wittingly in the
matter of *Otho the Great, King Stephen,* and *The Cap
and Bells.* Here it was impossible to preserve the real
order, because Keats had other things in progress at
the same time as *Otho,* and these, if strict chronological
order were followed, would have to be interspersed
among the acts and scenes of the tragedy. It seemed
better therefore to set the dramatic attempts apart as
a kind of appendix, to be completed by the less happy
experiment *The Cap and Bells,* and to leave the real
poetical work of Keats to close characteristically with
La Belle Dame sans Merci and the beautiful sonnet
which was really the last thing he wrote in verse.

The literary fragments and notes in prose naturally
follow the posthumous poetry ; and the letters come

---

[1] Not to detain the reader at the outset with details of a tech-
nical kind, I have set apart among the Addenda to the Preface
some notes relating to spelling, inflexion, &c., and some lists of
altered words.

last, in order of date,—those to Fanny Brawne last of all and apart.

Each volume has its appendix of matters related to its own particular contents ; and the general appendix in Volume IV consists of personal recollections, criticisms, &c., not related to any particular volume, but to the life and works of Keats generally.

The materials used for the present edition, besides what are generally known through published volumes, include, I believe, all that is most important. Whatever may remain in the hands of the American section of the Keats family is likely to be of minor importance, seeing how largely Lord Houghton was supplied with material from that source. His Lordship kindly offered to let me go over again the papers at Fryston Hall which served as the basis of his many editions ; and I regret that circumstances have prevented me from availing myself of that privilege ; but, as I have made full use of Lord Houghton's valuable series of books, the needs of the case should be fulfilled. Sir Charles Dilke's collections include many things of the utmost consequence, both to the text of the writings of Keats and to the completeness of illustrative detail. Letters from the poet, books formerly possessed by him, numerous letters from George Keats, Severn, and Brown, and a great mass of related documents, have been placed unreservedly in my hands by Sir Charles Dilke, and figure conspicuously throughout

the volumes. The most important of the papers of
Severn fell into the hands of Mr. Henry Sotheran of
Piccadilly; and I have had the advantage of going
over them all and making full collations, either by
Mr. Sotheran's kindness or by that of later owners of
such as passed from the Piccadilly establishment before
I examined the collection. The numerous letters to
and from Haydon, preserved in the journals of the
painter, have largely enhanced the value of the edition,
filling up important blanks and supplying a great
number of additions and corrections. The manuscripts
of *Endymion*, *Lamia*, *The Eve of St. Agnes*, and a
portion of *Isabella* should be mentioned as especially
fruitful of various readings and cancelled passages;
and not the least of the fortunate chances attending my
efforts to complete my work for Keats's lovers was the
unexpected discovery of Richard Woodhouse's copy of
Endymion, in which were noted, not only the variations of the final manuscript from the printed text,
but also those of the first draft, which had not itself
come to the surface. Woodhouse seems to have been
an ardent admirer of Keats and an enthusiastic student
of his works, as well as a capital scholar; for his copy
of *Endymion* was interleaved, seemingly while Keats
was still alive, and the textual differences above referred
to were noted down in the most business-like and
elaborate manner, while the pages bear many remarks
and hints of a learned and acute kind, whereof I

have not scrupled to avail myself. I think he must have meant to edit Keats's writings at some time. So far as regards the largest of Keats's poems, this book has been of more service than either of the other printed copies of *Endymion* I have used, namely Sir Charles Dilke's copy and one in my own possession with a number of autograph corrections. But Sir Charles Dilke's copy has a quantity of manuscript poems bound up at the end ; and these have yielded a good deal of assistance in textual work.

The letters of Keats to his sister, which form so large a proportion of the letters now first published, throw a flood of new light on his character. We knew him in nearly all relations except that of a protecting brother to a younger sister ; and it is this hiatus in his delightful personality that these charming letters fill.

The beautiful couplets which I have gathered in from *The Indicator* and placed as a rejected passage of *Endymion*, at page 221 of the present volume, appeared with the signature "XXX"; and I am obliged to confess that, although that signature may be very readily reconciled with the authorship assigned to the passage, it was on purely internal evidence that I placed the couplets where they are. Their manner is absolutely identical with that of the best parts of the poem ; and, if Keats did not write it, there were two men living at the time who might, as far as manner goes, have written any page of *Endymion*—a conclusion which few critics if any will be prepared to adopt.

The number of *The Indicator* in which the lines appeared opened with a paper on the Spirit of the Ancient Mythology, the close of which is a paragraph about Wordsworth, illustrated by the insertion of the sonnet "The world is too much with us," a sonnet which on another occasion (Volume IV, page 281) Hunt brought into juxtaposition with Wordsworth's description of the Hymn to Pan as a "pretty piece of paganism." At the end of this mythological number of *The Indicator* appear our couplets under the title of *Vox et prœterea nihil*, introduced by the following paragraph :—

"It does not enter within the plan, or perhaps we should rather say, the understood promises, of this little weekly publication, to relieve the Editor with *much* correspondence; but he is glad when he can indulge himself, in proportion ; and he inserts with pleasure the following piece of poetry, which is very much to his heathenish taste."

Not to rest on my own judgment alone in connecting these verses with *Endymion*, I sent them to the late Dante Gabriel Rossetti, who was much interested in the scheme and progress of these volumes ; and in reply to my enquiry what he thought about the extract he wrote to me thus :—

"I remember setting eyes in my earliest days on

the passage you send me, and doubtless came to the conclusion that it must be by Keats, though it had for me no such charm as attached to the wondrous *Belle Dame sans Merci* ... I can well understand Keats's rejecting this passage ; since, though replete with a general luscious beauty, it is quite without such supreme value in imaginative treatment as (despite some Cockney syllabification) the passage which I suppose to have preceded it. Is there any language in which X is called anything like *Keat?* In such case the XXX might represent Keats."

The riddle of the meaning of this signature held out during the exchange of several letters; and later on Rossetti wrote to me :

" I should think that triple X almost certainly stands for *Triplex* in relation to Diana — Luna — Hecate. Keats's text-book was of course Lemprière, and much bearing that way is to be found under those headings there. Keats speaks of the triple character of Diana at the end of the Sonnet to Homer."

To this it should be added that Endymion (Volume I, page 286), when his heart is divided between his Goddess as known to him and the fair Indian in whose form she disguises herself, exclaims " I have a triple soul"; and that Keats himself had certainly three public names, to wit, John Keats, Caviare, and Lucy Vaughan Lloyd, though how far he had mentally adopted the two pen-names by January 1820, I have no knowledge. Such an explanation as Rossetti's corresponds precisely in idea with a name applied by Keats's schoolfellow Cowper to Charles Cowden Clarke, in whose *Recollections*, speaking of Cowper, he says :—— "His jocular school-name for me was 'Three hundred,' in allusion to my initials C. C. C." As regards the actual fabric of the couplets, the difficulty is, not to find something there particularly like Keats's work, but to find a single turn or phrase that is not redolent of him. If one particular point is better to rest on than another, I incline to the couplet

> Like the low voice of Syrinx, when she ran
> Into the forests from Arcadian Pan :

which is identical in manner and phrase with a less excellent couplet retained in the early sketch meant to have been called *Endymion* (page 13 of this volume) :——

> Telling us how fair, trembling Syrinx fled
> Arcadian Pan, with such a horrid dread.

Of work attributed to Keats in former editions and rejected from the present volumes there is very little ; but of such rejection as has been necessary an account should be rendered. The poem and sonnet given in Lord Houghton's Aldine edition (and others) as of doubtful authenticity are both omitted because I cannot bring myself to think that Keats had anything more to do with the poem than with the sonnet, which is to be found among Laman Blanchard's works, and

is assigned to that author in more than one anthology.[1]
Lord Houghton has recorded his belief that the sonnet
was "one of George Byron's forgeries" (Aldine edition,
page 493); but at page 326, the poem commencing
with the words "What sylph-like form before my eyes,"
is introduced by a suggestion that there were genuine
pieces among the forgeries sold at the George Byron
"autograph" auction.   My own belief is that, so far
as the actual documents are concerned, all were forged ;
but that many of them were copies, in assumed hands,
of genuine documents.   Some of the Shelley letters
certainly were; and I think it is only a question of
time how soon this particular piece of verse shall be
traced to the source outside Keats's work from which
George Byron copied it.   The letter beginning "My
dear Spencer" which was printed at pages 27 and 28
of the edition of Keats's Life and Letters published in
1867, and the letter beginning "My dear Haydon,"
printed at pages 49-51 of the same volume, are omitted
on similar grounds.   Both seem to me unlike Keats in
all respects ; and both are from the George Byron sale,
the Haydon one being moreover addressed to "W.
Haydon" instead of "B. R. Haydon."   The song
"Stay, ruby-breasted warbler, stay," given at page

---

[1] As for instance in Leigh Hunt's *Book of the Sonnet*, Dr.
Mackay's *A Thousand and One Gems of English Poetry*, and Mr.
John Dennis's *English Sonnets*.

VOL. I.   *b*

6 of the Aldine edition, was probably sent to Lord
Houghton from America, where people go so far
as to print fac-similes of George Keats's writing
for fac-similes of John's—although there is not the
faintest likeness between them.   I omit the song because, in a scrap-book in my possession containing a
mass of transcripts by George Keats [1] from his brother's
poetry, I find this poem not only written in George's
hand but signed "G. K." instead of "J. K."; and I
confess I think it more likely to be one of the effu-
sions which George is recorded to have produced than
an early poem by John.

It is impossible to read Keats's poetry closely without
being struck by the earnest single-heartedness of his devotion to his art.   It is the most salient moral quality
which his writings display, and contributes more than
any cultivation of thought, study of philosophy, or
adherence to the spirit of the Greek mythology, to

---

[1] This curious volume was originally used for writing fair copies
of poems in—poems from various hands.   At a later stage it was
converted into a scrap-book,—newspaper cuttings and other curiosities being stuck over pages of George Keats's writing; and in one
part several of George's copies from John's poems are inserted, having
at their head the autograph manuscript of the sonnet to Mrs.
George Keats (when Miss Wylie), whom I suppose to have been
the owner of the book, seeing that it contains among its curiosities
the original parchment commission of James Wylie, as adjutant of
the Fifeshire Regiment of Fencible Infantry, signed by George III.
in 1794.

give to his works that stability which made certain from the first what he half doubtingly ventured to "think" in writing to his brother,—that he should be "among the English poets" after his death. It was perhaps this great earnestness, over-straining his super-sensitive nature, that led to most of the faults of his more youthful productions. The line of his reading was from early times the best calculated to invigorate and inspire his style ; and although he fell at first into some of the laxities of early English poets, the small damage here and there effected in this way is insignificant when compared with the good he got from his studies. Spenser very soon gained a great influence over him, as the notes to *Endymion* will tend to indicate ; but curiously enough the early poem called an *Imitation of Spenser* has very little that is directly Spenserian, and is much more like an imitation of Thomson —an echo from the Spenserian galleries of *The Castle of Indolence*. In the opening of "I stood tip-toe upon a little hill," Keats makes good use of a mental phase inspired by the earlier poem *The Floure and the Lefe*, and if, in the same line of reading, he caught the trick of writing such a couplet as

> And glides into a bed of water lillies :
> Broad leav'd are they and their white canopies

the balance is still very clearly in our favour. Now and then the debt to classic literature is a little too evident ; but as a rule Keats's works are remarkably free from other men's thoughts. It is quite exceptional to come upon such a household word as was reset for us in the lines

> To where the hurrying freshnesses aye preach
> A natural sermon o'er their pebbly beds ;

which we cannot help placing at a disadvantage beside the lines from *As You Like It* (Act II, Scene 1)

> And this our life exempt from public haunt
> Finds tongues in trees, books in the running brooks,
> Sermons in stones and good in every thing.

But the real wonder about Keats is what a little way into the land of his poetry the reader carries with him the sense of shortcomings of this kind. *Endymion* bears us along in a whirl of imaginative creation ; and the beauties with which it is lavishly strewn scarcely leave time for the thought that the construction wants perspicacity—a thought which will intrude at last. In work later than *Endymion* there are probably more passages wherein the thought or feeling, whatever it may be, is expressed with an almost absolute felicity than will be found in the like bulk of work by any other modern English poet. The Odes to a Nightingale, on a Grecian Urn and on Indolence, *The Eve of St. Mark* and *La Belle Dame sans Merci*, may be named among the most sustained examples of this lofty felicity. Perhaps it will be objected that the opening of the Ode to a Nightingale is not really clear,—that it is not

made evident at a glance how the poet's numbness
arose from being too happy in the bird's happiness,—
too happy that the bird sang "of summer in full-
throated ease"; but I am not sure that the tremulous
thickness of utterance arising from intense emotion is not
better rendered by the means employed, even if uncon-
sciously employed and unintentionally rendered, than
it would have been if the thought had undergone a
little more chastening; while the prismatic line

No hungry generations tread thee down

is Dantesque in its weird vigour,—a touch of the
highest genius, bringing before us visions of many ter-
rible things, and chiefly of multitudinous keen and cruel
faces more awful in the relentless oppressiveness of
their onset upon the sensitive among men than anything
in the mighty visions of damnation and detestableness
seen five hundred years ago in Italy. The unphilo-
sophic obliqueness of the analogy drawn—the comparison between the lot of the *individual* man and that of
the *general* nightingale — scarcely detracts from the
value, as it certainly does not from the supreme beauty,
of the poem—while we know not how much the pathos
is enhanced by this very obliqueness of analogy.

It was late in Keats's short life before he began to
give birth to grand thoughts such as those just glanced
at.   The mythology and poetry of the moon were
perhaps longer uppermost in his thoughts than in any
other poet's.   Beside the *Endymion* that he speaks of

in his letter to Clarke of the 17th of December 1816, a poem now identified with " I stood tip-toe upon a little hill," there are what we may term lunar traces throughout the early volume of Poems. Even in the poor little poem *To Some Ladies*, which is not even carefully finished up to its own Tom Moorish standard, seeing that the second quatrain lacks a rhyme,— even in this we have talk of "Cynthia's face, the enthusiast's friend." In the Epistle to George Felton Mathew we read

> in happy hour
> Came chaste Diana from her shady bower,

and in the Epistle to George Keats there are the really admirable verses about the poet and what he sees beside the mere moon in heaven—

> Ah, yes ! much more would start into his sight—
> The revelries and mysteries of night :
> And should I ever see them, I will tell you
> Such tales as needs must with amazement spell you.

Again in the Epistle to Clarke—

> When Cynthia smiles upon a summer's night,
> And peers among the cloudlet's jet and white,
> As though she were reclining in a bed
> Of bean blossoms, in heaven freshly shed.

Once more in the Sonnet to George Keats—

> Cynthia is from her silken curtains peeping
> So scantly, that it seems her bridal night,
> And she her half-discover'd revels keeping.

And the Hecate character of the moon is clearly enough

alluded to in the two lines closing the Sonnet to
* * * * * *

> And when the moon her pallid face discloses,
> I'll gather some by spells, and incantation.

Indeed Keats may almost be said to have made the
moon and her lover his own,—so much so that Browning, in one of his two tributes to Keats, conveys a
whole romanceful of meaning in a word, the word
even in those glorious trochaics from *One Word More*:—

> What, there's nothing in the moon note-worthy?
> Nay—for if that moon could love a mortal,
> Use, to charm him (so to fit a fancy)
> All her magic ('tis the old sweet mythos)
> She would turn a new side to her mortal,
> Side unseen of herdsman, huntsman, steersman—
> Blank to Zoroaster on his terrace,
> Blind to Galileo on his turret,
> Dumb to Homer, dumb to Keats—him, even!

Had Keats never passed out of the lunar phase he
would still have produced a book far more remarkable
than Chamberlayne's *Pharonnida*, a poem which bears
a certain resemblance to *Endymion*, and which, I think,
had been read by the modern poet (see page 265 of
this volume); and much of even the 1817 volume
must perforce have been remembered; but it is the
volume published in 1820 that assures him a seat
among the immortals.

Mr. Francis Turner Palgrave refers in his *Golden
Treasury* to Keats as "a poet deserving the title 'mar-

vellous boy' in a much higher sense than Chatterton,"
and says that Shakespeare, Milton, and Wordsworth
would have left "poems of less excellence and hope"
than Keats has left "had their lives been closed at
twenty-five." Such was Keats's enthusiasm for Chatterton that I feel sure he would have been the first to
wish Mr. Palgrave to be reminded that the Bristol boy
really was a boy in the strictest sense, having won for
himself at the hands of Keats the proud title of "the
most English of poets except Shakespeare" by a truly
prodigious mass of work all done before he was
eighteen years old—an age he never attained. The
comparison with Shakespeare, Milton, and Wordsworth
holds; but it is only fair to ask on behalf of Chatterton what Keats would have left had he failed to
attain eighteen instead of twenty-six years. I think
the real marvel of Keats is best touched on by Mrs.
Browning in Book I of *Aurora Leigh*:

> By Keats's soul, the man who never stepped
> In gradual progress like another man,
> But, turning grandly on his central self,
> Ensphered himself in twenty perfect years
> And died, not young,—(the life of a long life,
> Distilled to a mere drop, falling like a tear
> Upon the world's cold cheek to make it burn
> For ever ;) by that strong excepted soul,
> I count it strange and hard to understand
> That nearly all young poets should write old ; ...

What is really notable is that he who had produced
practically nothing as a boy, who between the ages of

twenty and twenty-five had been through so much sorrow and anguish tending to stop his work, should yet have written within those five years such a body of poetry, so suddenly rising to the highest excellence of expression and the most startling imaginative capacity, and this out of poetic beginnings scarcely removed from the common-place.

That Keats himself was always at the very antipodes of common-place, we have ample evidence in the various recollections of his childhood, boyhood, and youth ; in the facts of his life; and in the excellently recorded physiognomy. In every authentic portrait, he is a marked man [1]; and there is scarcely an act on record that does not express individuality and character.

By all who really knew Keats he seems to have been greatly beloved,—one of the surest proofs of the nobility of his character. His devotion to his mother and his brothers, taking practical forms, his paternal solicitude for his young orphan sister, his readiness to assist friends from his own slender resources, his promptness to protect the weak and oppressed, his enthusiasm for the good, the beautiful, and the true, and his contempt for everything that was mean, sordid, or hollow, are all qualities which find, more or less, a balanced expression in his writings and his acts. His words and his life

---

[1] See Addenda to the Preface for remarks on the portraits of Keats.

speak for him fully in the following volumes; for the
reminiscences which follow his own writings form a bio-
graphy of the most vivid kind taken in connexion with
his own letters; and truly of a more lovable character it
would be hard indeed to find living records such as
these. The fluctuation of his nobler qualities under
premature physical decay is one of the saddest spectacles in the history of literature; but, although his
friends had all somewhat to bear with when the hand
of death was upon him, the main stream of his life
remained noble and beautiful to the last. In the records
that relate to the times when he was between twenty
and twenty-three years of age, and in his letters even
later than those times, there is a splendid elasticity corresponding with the "fine compactness of person" which
he is said to have had. That his forces were rather
volcanic and intermittent than sustained and resistant
the melancholy result showed; and however much or
little prophetic truth may have been in Coleridge's well-
known utterance "there is death in that hand," the final
verdict will probably be that this noble nature, with all
its male vigour, had not the due proportion of patient
stolid resistance to make head against a dire combina-
tion of misfortunes.

Hunt in his admirable remarks upon *The Eve of St.
Agnes* points to the fainting of Porphyro at sight of
Madeline as the one flaw in the poem, and apologizes
for it on the score of the poet's enfeebled state of health

at the time. But I think this is rather hard on all three
—poem, poet, and disease. If it be so important a fault,
I fear we must acquit bodily disease of any part or lot
in it, for Keats's young people always had a way of
fainting, whether conceived in his more vigorous or in his
less vigorous period. Endymion after the visit of Diana
(Volume I, page 222) is described as having "Swoon'd
drunken from pleasure's nipple"; and he swoons at the
thought of Diana's voice when he is in the palace of
Neptune, at the end of Book III of the poem: at
the end of Book IV he is represented as kneeling
before the goddess "in a blissful swoon," which however may not be meant quite literally; and again, in
Book IV, lines 745-7, the disguised Diana tells how
as a child she gave kisses "to the void air," and how
when she imagined

> the warm tremble of a devout kiss
> Even then, that moment, at the thought of this,
> Fainting I fell into a bed of flowers,
> And languish'd there three days.

Lycius faints when he meets with Lamia at the road-
side; Lamia had previously fallen "into a swooning love
of him"; and the idea of swooning lovers was so
familiar to the poet that, when his own time came, he
wrote to his lady (Volume IV, page 134), "all I can
bring you is a swooning admiration of your beauty."

To me it has always seemed that Keats's attitude towards women was that of impassioned chivalry not

wholly free from a hysterical element. The line in
"Woman! when I behold thee"

> E'en then, elate, my spirit leaps and prances,

is not inapt; and

> My ear is open like a greedy shark,
>   To catch the tunings of a voice divine

expresses the exaggeration of sentiment perfectly.

> Light feet, dark violet eyes, and parted hair;
>   Soft dimpled hands, white neck, and creamy breast,
>   Are things on which the dazzled senses rest
> Till the fond fixed eyes forget they stare.

This is all more or less hysterical; and, with all its
obvious charm for young people, so, very much so, is

> God! she is like a milk white lamb that bleats
> For man's protection.

In one of his letters Keats describes the reactionary
converse of this exaggerated sentiment, in a passage
which is an anticipation of the *Ode on Indolence* (Volume
III, page 280), and in which the phase of feeling is described as "a delightful sensation, about three degrees
on this side of faintness"; and even in the carefully
finished *Ode to Psyche*, we have the line

> And on the sudden, fainting with surprise,

applied to the mere vision of Cupid and Psyche.

This default of male robustness in one particular is a
contradiction in Keats's manly and even pugnacious
character; but I do not think it ought to be regarded

with intolerance, even though it helped so valuable a life to fall into a hereditary consumption. The fact of the matter is that, somehow or other, an Oriental as well as a Greek strain had passed into the child of Finsbury parents; and if we have the supreme advantage of a romantic colour and warmth throughout a great part of the poetry left by this wondrously gifted youth, we must be content to take with it the prevalent temperament of the lovers in oriental romances and tales, who faint as a matter of course under due provocation, very much to the surprise of a northerly reader not previously acquainted with their customs. Strange and occult things happen now and again in the building up of men of genius; but I do not know that the presence, in a London child of unremarkable parents, of clear emanations from the spirit of Greek mythology and the spirit of Eastern romance is more wonderful than the transfusion of the sublimated essence of the French revolution into the veins of Shelley, the scion of a long line of Sussex squires, or the perfect intuition of medieval romance life displayed by Thomas Chatterton, the descendant of a line of Bristol sextons.

For want of a better opportunity, I am fain to add here some stray items gathered in the course of enquiries among Keats's friends. Miss Charlotte Reynolds tells me that he was passionately fond of music, and would sit for hours while she played the piano to him. It was to a Spanish air which she used to play that the song

"Hush, hush! tread softly!" was composed; and so sensitive was he to proper execution, that, when a wrong note has been played in a public performance, he has been known to say that he would like to "go down into the orchestra and smash all the fiddles."

One of Mr. Dilke's reminiscences of Keats, the tradition of which has been kept alive by Mr. John Snook of Belmont Castle, has a curious bearing on the poet's faith in immortality, and indicates a belief at one time even in metempsychosis. After the death of Thomas Keats, a white rabbit came into the garden of Mr. Dilke, who shot the creature. Keats declared that the poor thing was his brother Tom's spirit; and so earnest was he in this view, impressing it upon others of the circle, that when the rabbit was put on table, no one could look at it, and it was immediately ordered to be removed.

The following document is said to have been sent by Keats to a friend in August 1820, just before his departure for Italy, with the intention that, in the worst event, it should have effect as his last will and testament. I find it transcribed among the papers of Sir Charles Dilke, but without any indication of the source, or of the authority on which it rests; but it has an air of genuineness; and Sir Charles Dilke does not doubt its authenticity.

"My share of books divide amongst my friends. In case of my death this scrap of paper may be serviceable in your possession.

"All my estate real and personal consists in the hopes of the sale of books, published or unpublished. Now I wish —— and you to be the first paid Creditors—the rest is *in nubibus*; but in case it should shower, pay —— the few pounds I owe him."

It only remains to record my acknowledgments for help of all kinds received during the progress of my work. Not only have I been very largely assisted with the loan and use of original documents by and about Keats, and with free permissions to avail myself of various copyright works both principal and related; but I have found all those who knew Keats or who are related to members of his circle willing to render assistance by corresponding with me on moot points; and several friends and correspondents have given me material help by making references, copies, and enquiries for me during occasional absences from town,—by reading proofs, and even in some instances by making translations from various languages by way of illustration. Numerous instances of help in one or another of the afore-mentioned kinds will be found named in their particular places in these volumes; but it is fitting to set down here my hearty sense of the kindnesses I have experienced; and I beg that if, through mischance, any kind friend or correspondent is omitted from the list, he will believe that he has my cordial thanks none the less. Those, then, to whom I desire to record my obligations are, Señora Fanny Keats de Llanos and her son Señor

Juan Keats y Llanós, the late Joseph Severn, the Right
Honourable Sir Charles Dilke, Baronet, M.P., the Right
Honourable Lord Houghton, the late Dante Gabriel
Rossetti, Frank Scott Haydon, Esq., Frederick Words-
worth Haydon, Esq., John Taylor, Esq., John Metivier,
Esq., of the British Museum, Richard Garnett, Esq.,
Frederick Locker, Esq., John Payne, Esq., Messrs.
Henry Sotheran & Co., William Dilke, Esq., of
Chichester, John Snook, Esq., of Belmont Castle, Miss
Charlotte Reynolds, Mrs. Charles Cowden Clarke,
Messrs. Smith, Elder & Co., R. C. Day, Esq., J. Dykes
Campbell, Esq., Captain Clark, of Holland House, my
brother Alfred Forman, Philip Bourke Marston, Esq.,
R. F. Sketchley, Esq., the Venerable Archdeacon Hessey,
the Rev. G. R. Gleig, late Chaplain General of the
Forces, Alexander Ireland, Esq., Dr. Reinhold Köhler,
R. A. Potts, Esq., W. B. Scott, Esq., J. George Wilmot,
Esq., Miss Violet Paget, and Miss Emma Lazarus.

H. BUXTON FORMAN.

46 MARLBOROUGH HILL, ST. JOHN'S WOOD,
October 1883.

ADDENDA TO THE PREFACE.

NOTE ON THE PORTRAITS OF KEATS.

THE portraits of Keats reproduced in the present edition have been chosen as characteristic and valuable representations of the poet in different aspects, done from the life. The number here given does not exhaust the list of portraits for which Keats actually sat, nor does it include any of the reminiscent compositions of which so many were produced after his death.

The most important of the portraits is unquestionably the miniature painted by Severn and exhibited at the Royal Academy in 1819. This Severn repeated several times; and Sir Charles Dilke has had no less than three examples of the miniature, of which he still possesses two. The first, that for which Keats actually sat, was given by the poet to Fanny Brawne before his departure for Italy, and eventually passed into the hands of Sir Charles Dilke's grandfather. This is to all intents and purposes the portrait which appeared in the *Life, Letters* &c. of 1848, which forms the frontispiece to more than one of Lord Houghton's editions of Keats's poetry, and which is given in Volume I of the present edition. The plate used by Lord Houghton was actually engraved from a copy which Severn made for Mr. Dilke; and the plate used for the present edition has been done by the photo-intaglio process from a miniature in my own possession executed in a more transparent medium than the original in Sir Charles Dilke's hands,—a medium lending itself peculiarly to the method employed. Severn also painted the same composition in oils, half life-size, for Mr. Moxon, of course long after Keats's death; and this picture is now the property of Mr. George P. Boyce.

The charcoal sketch which forms the frontispiece to Volume III of this edition was the earliest of Severn's drawings of Keats from the life. It was engraved as long ago as 1828 for Leigh Hunt's *Lord Byron and Some of his Contemporaries*; but, as Severn wrote to me that he considered the plate used by Hunt a caricature, I was glad of the opportunity to give a fac-simile by the photo-intaglio process from the original drawing now in the Forster Collection at the South Kensington Museum. I have had it printed on paper like that of the original; and if the oval were surrounded by a mount instead of an engraved line and plate-mark, it would need an expert to discover that he had not the original drawing before him.

Severn's last sketch of Keats was that drawn in Indian ink on the 28th of January 1821, given as a frontispiece to Volume IV, from a plate etched by Mr. W. B. Scott. The drawing is, I believe, in the hands of Mr. Edgar Drummond.

The frontispiece to Volume II is from a chalk drawing by Hilton, which was published by Messrs. Taylor and Walton of Upper Gower Street in 1841. It was unquestionably done from the life; and it is possible that Hilton may have done other life sketches of Keats, whom he was in the habit of meeting at the house of their mutual friend John Taylor, Keats's publisher.

The large profile head given opposite page 44 of Volume III is a sketch for the portrait of Keats intro-

duced by Haydon into his great picture of Christ's Entry
into Jerusalem, now in the Museum at Philadelphia.
This pen sketch was drawn in Haydon's Journal in
November 1816; and the lower part of another page of
the Journal, of which a fac-simile is given opposite page
64 of Volume III, shows the attitude of the figure which
the head was intended to surmount, and explains the
meaning of the line passing diagonally from the chin in
the large profile,—a line which would scarcely otherwise
be taken for that of the shoulder and upper part of the
arm.

Besides these portraits there is a mask of Keats believed to have been moulded from the life by Haydon,
and certainly taken in plaster by some one, during
Keats's life-time. Mrs. Llanos considers it a more satisfactory representation of her brother than any of the
portraits; and in some respects it has certainly a far
higher value and interest. Notwithstanding the constraint of the muscles under the discomfort of the operation, and the loss of expression through the closing of
the eyes, this cast is priceless as recording the actual
bone and muscle structure of Keats's face and forehead.
The low forehead we have heard so much about turns
out to be a forehead of splendid capacity and modelling
—low, it is true, and receding, but broad and massive,
and showing a fine and expressive arch. The structure
of the face is altogether extremely fine; and I regret
that I have not been able on the present occasion to
give a perfect representation of it. The late Dante
Gabriel Rossetti had one of the casts from the mask, and
had promised to place it at my disposal for the purposes
of this edition; but his premature death intervened.
I am indebted to Señor Juan Keats y Llanos, the poet's
nephew, for a beautiful painting in grisaille done from the

mask in Spain, disposed in a favourable light; but this painting does not lend itself to mechanical reproduction. At a late stage in the preparation of my volumes, I obtained the loan of another example of the mask from Mr. Philip Bourke Marston; and have been able to get some reproductions that serve certain purposes of illustration, while rendering the original in a somewhat unsympathetic manner and not preserving the higher beauties of it as seen in the round.

The purpose which the mask serves for the present is that of testing the outline value of the several portraits, to which end I have had it reproduced in their respective positions.

Taking it first in the position of the Haydon profile of November 1816, it will be found that that bold and masterly sketch stands the test well, although the mask corrects the angularity of the upper lip in the pen-sketch, and shows a more marked massiveness of nose, while of course giving no sign of the intense eagerness of the fixed eye which is the central idea of Haydon's conception.

Hilton's chalk sketch, given in Volume II, doubtless renders the general appearance and expression of Keats in a moment of sickness and something of constraint, and has its own particular charm; but the mouth and hair are conventionalized, the chin a little exaggerated, and the nose pinched. This last point of comparison with the mask is not to be accounted for on the ground that Keats was out of condition; for he was clearly in much better health than when Severn did the last sketch, in which the nose of the dying man is not nearly so pinched.

Severn's charcoal sketch probably has more of the spirit and general expression of Keats in or about 1817:

certainly it was not drawn later than the beginning of
1818, for it was done in England in the presence of
Shelley, who never was in England after that time. But
this sketch, when set beside a reproduction of the mask
in the same position, loses more than the Haydon profile
does. The eyes and the hair are charmingly rendered ;
but the upper lip has something of the same angularity
which the mask refuses to confirm in the profile ; the
forehead is too straight and high, the chin not massive
enough, and the general appearance less masculine.
Still, it must not be lightly esteemed ; for it is beautiful
in itself; and Charles Cowden Clarke considered it the
best of the portraits of Keats.

In the miniature the build of the face is much more
faithfully rendered : chin, mouth, nose, brows, all answer
as fully to the massive and masculine bone-structure as
a minature could well answer to the lines of a life-sized
plaster cast. It will be seen from the reduced rendering
that the one is in almost entire harmony with the other,
while the miniature has a play and beauty of expression
impossible to a mask, not to mention the far-seeing eyes
that always render unintelligible to me Clarke's description of this as " an every-day and of the ' earth, earthy '
likeness."

But Severn's last sketch, the frontispiece to Volume
IV, harmonizes more completely with the mask than the
miniature does, and is a most valuable record. The main
structural point of superiority is the forehead. That of
the miniature tends to a perpendicularity of expression ;
but that of the final sketch does not look any more per-
pendicular than the forehead of the actual mask.

The authenticity of the mask is beyond question. It
is well known as the cast of Keats's face both to his
sister and to Miss Reynolds; and the only thing wanting

is the actual record when, where, and by whom, it was moulded. Rossetti told me, when first showing it to me, that it was recorded to have been made by Haydon, whose son, however, finds no entry on the subject in the journals : nevertheless, I have little doubt that Haydon made it, first because, with his habit (a very uncommon one) of making plaster casts of men of parts known to him, it was most unlikely that he would have omitted Keats, for whom he had so high an admiration and so great an affection ; and secondly because there is a reference in Keats's correspondence tending in this direction. At page 96 of Volume III he writes to Bailey that he has not succeeded in seeing Haydon, " nor been able to ex- purgatorize more masks for" Bailey. The meaning is not clear ; but at all events it connects the ideas of Haydon, Keats, and mask-making, with something of a purgatorial kind, which may or may not have been the necessary embedding of the poet's face in wet plaster of Paris.

At page 380 of Volume IV it will be seen that Severn speaks of " the beautiful profile of Girometti's " as a por- trait which he wishes to have on Keats's monument. This I presume to be the medallion from which a wood- cut was executed by Mr. Scharf for the illustrated edition of Keats's Poems published by Messrs. Moxon & Co. in 1854,—a cut reproduced at page lvi of the present volume. Sir Charles Dilke has a plaster cast of the medallion in fine preservation. It has much artistic merit, though apparently a posthumous portrait ; and it is right to record that John Hamilton Reynolds thought this medallion the best likeness of his friend.

The portrait forming the frontispiece of Lord Hough- ton's Aldine edition renders a portion of a large picture in his Lordship's possession,—one of Severn's many posthumous oil-paintings of his friend. Another of these, and one of high merit and interest, is in the National Portrait Gallery, from the Catalogue of which collection I may as well give the following extract :—

"John Keats 1795-1821. Painted at Rome, in 1821, by Joseph Severn.... Description. An upright square picture. A full-length figure, on a small scale, seated on a cane-bottomed chair to the right, with his head bent forward, reading a book open across his knee. He rests his left elbow on the back of a second chair placed beside him. The youthful poet is dressed in a plain dark suit with a small shirt-collar and neck-tie. On the wall of the apartment hangs an engraving of Shakspeare in a black frame, and to the right through a window opening to the ground, is a view into a garden. The face, seen in profile to the right, is almost entirely in shadow, light being admitted through the open window behind. The face is boyish and close shaven. The hair is a deep rich yellow-brown colour. Signed, on the carpeted floor to the right, ' J. Severn, Rome 1823'.

"A letter written by Mr. Severn December 22nd 1858 contains the following particulars :—' The room, the open window, the carpet, chairs, are all portraits, even to the mezzotinto portrait of Shakspeare, given him by his old landlady in the Isle of Wight. On the morning of my visit to Hampstead (1819) I found him sitting with the two chairs, as I have painted him. After this time he lost his cheerfulness, and I never saw him like himself again.'

" Presented January 1859 by S. Smith Travers, Esq."

The discrepancy between the statement at the head, "painted at Rome in 1821," and the evidence of the signature, "J. Severn, Rome 1823," is presumably to be reconciled by the supposition that this picture, mentioned by Severn to Brown in a letter partly printed at page 365 of Volume IV, was not finished till 1823, though already begun in the summer of 1821.

It is to be regretted that the National Portrait Gallery should possess only posthumous portraits of Keats; and one of them totally uninteresting. The large oil painting by Hilton has no claim whatever to a place in the national collection. The forbidding and lowering young man there depicted is not Keats; and the work is a mere posthumous parody of Severn's miniature, done with little skill, less taste, and still less feeling.

It would be interesting to know what became of a bust of Keats exhibited at the Royal Academy in 1822, of which there is a notice in *The London Magazine* for May of that year. Referring to Frederick Smith, "a pupil of Chantrey," it is said, "There is a bust, by the same hand, of John Keats the poet, which strongly recals the gifted author of Endymion to our remembrance." Of course the probability is that the bust was executed after Keats's death by the aid of the mask; but I have no knowledge on the subject.

H. B. F.

Note on the Spelling, Inflexions, &c. found in Keats's Writings, and adopted in this Edition.

In the minor matters of orthography, punctuation, &c., I have thought it proper to let the author have the principal voice, rather than to apply any external standard. To ascertain Keats's delibe-rate preferences as far as possible, and carry them out consistently, seems to me the best procedure. In applying such a principle to those works which were printed in his life-time, it is necessary to record all deviations from the text even when they are in pursu-ance of the poet's own rules; but in reprinting the posthumous works it is allowable to move a little more freely, because the text of those works is certain to have been revised in minor detail from a different point of view. I have therefore endeavoured to accommodate the orthography &c. of the posthumous poems to that of the others without recording the particular forms adopted in previous editions.

In many instances Keats adopted, no doubt deliberately, the orthography of Spenser,—as in *lilly, ballance, pavillion*, and I have not thought it advisable to interfere with a preference of this kind. Even for *but* instead of *butt* he had the authority of elder writers ; and I presume no one will dispute the orthography *chace*, seeing that Somerville, to whom the word belongs of right, spelt it so.

These are but samples of a great many words which Keats used with a different spelling from that commonly employed ; but there is no occasion to discuss the vocabulary further.

The most difficult matter to deal with from the point of view of the poet's intention has been that of words inflected in the past participle. There is evidence both internal and external that Keats attached importance to the way in which his past participles in *ed* or *'d* were printed. The external evidence takes the form of an instruction for the printer, written upon the manuscript of *Endymion* in his own handwriting :

" Attend to the punctuation in general as marked, and to the Elisions in the last syllables of the participles as they are written."

This makes it abundantly clear that he had a serious intention in regard to the participles ; and there is ample internal evidence that that intention, expressed broadly, was to print *ed* when that syllable was to be pronounced and to replace the *e* by an apostrophe in the opposite case. This sounds at first quite simple ; and Keats himself had clearly no notion how difficult a task he had set himself, and how very partially the ardent mood of poetic composition admits of carrying out any such rule in detail. The three books which he got printed all betray the intention to follow this rule ; and each is inconsistent in itself as to the carrying out of the rule ; while the manuscripts of Keats which I have examined in connexion with this edition are naturally still more wayward. The difficulty of now carrying the poet's own rule out for him arises from several circumstances. In regard to the great majority of words ending with *ed* in his works there is no doubt whatever, upon metrical grounds, that the syllable is to be pronounced. But in many instances the *e* in the final *ed* is left standing, both in manuscript and in print, when metrical considerations make it absolutely certain that it was meant to be replaced by an apostrophe ; while in a not

inconsiderable number of cases, where the question is rather rhythmical than metrical, it is by no means certain whether the *e* was
left in by accident or on purpose. Cases in which an apostrophe
replaces an *e* that is peremptorily wanted for rhyme or metre or
rhythm are comparatively uncommon ; but they exist ; and in one
or two passages the author's manuscript shows a curious exception,—
an *è* (accented in a manner beyond all dispute) when the verse is such
that the real need was an apostrophe instead of an *e*. If these were
all the points one had to consider the matter would still be a simple
one enough to settle : one would say without hesitation, " leave the
e in when it is quite clear it is to be sounded ; replace it by an apostrophe when it is quite clear it is mute ; and when there is a doubt
give it the benefit of the doubt and leave it in."   For it is obviously
of little consequence whether we read (*Endymion*, Book I, line
10)

> Of all the unhealthy and o'erdarkenèd ways

or

> Of all the unhealthy and o'erdarken'd ways :

the rhythm is easy and noble in either case : if we sound the *e*, the
richness of the redundant second foot has an echo of redundancy
in the fifth foot : if we leave the *e* out, it has not ; and in the manuscript and first edition of *Endymion* the *e* stands,—according to
the rule, to be pronounced.   Similarly, it is of no great moment
whether we read (*Sonnet to* * * * * *)

> Be echoèd swiftly through that ivory shell

or

> Be echo'd swiftly through that ivory shell.

On the other hand it is of some consequence whether we read
(*Endymion*, Book I, line 111)

> Who gathering round the altar seemèd to pry

or

> Who gathering round the altar seem'd to pry :

the *e* has clearly no business there ; but there it is both in the
manuscript and in the first edition,—to be pronounced, according to
the rule, and therefore to be expelled for an apostrophe by an editor
desirous of carrying the poet's rule into effect for him.   Just as important is it that we should read in the Sonnet *On First looking
into Chapman's Homer*

> That deep-brow'd Homer rul'd as his demesne ;

and not

> That deep-brow'd Homer rulèd as his demesne ;

but *ruled* Keats wrote and printed, though in the same sonnet he wrote and printed *star'd* and not *stared*.   And unfortunately the words ending in *ed* are not all or nearly all of a class thus easy to deal with : there is a host of words which are inflected, not by the addition of *ed*, but by the addition of *d* to an *e* which they have already, as *place, face, love, move, range, change, pile, wile, charge, force, rouse, twine, use, scare, dance, pulse, picture* ; and many of these, especially those in which the *e* has an influence upon the value of the consonant it follows, have a disguised, I had almost said an emasculated look, when the *e* is replaced by an apostrophe : you take something away from them that was theirs ; and this is not the same thing as withholding something that you might or might not give them in inflecting them.   Then again there are the words which change a letter when inflected with *ed*, such as *bury, marry, tarry, dry, descry, reply* ; and these are the hardest of all to deal with.   *Dried* according to Keats's rule is a dissyllable ; the elision of the *e* makes an ugly word enough, *dri'd* ; and I have not met with it in Keats's poetry ; but I do find in his manuscript *dry'd*, and I also find *descry'd* ; and this, I take it, would have been his way of settling the number of syllables to be given to each of the words of that class.   *Honied*, he writes for a dissyllable ; but he would doubtless have put *honey'd*, had he thought about the spelling of the uninflected word.¡ As regards the words which change their feature and complexion when written with an apostrophe instead of an *e*, I can only say thus much,—Keats wrote and printed, often over and over again, *puls'd, danc'd, rang'd, increas'd, discours'd, shar'd, unconfin'd, rais'd, arous'd, disguis'd, smil'd, surcharg'd, heav'd, lov'd, pin'd, clos'd, seiz'd, convuls'd*, and even *pictur'd* ; but that he treated these words thus with some compunction, even were it an unconscious or slumbering undercurrent of compunction, may perhaps be fairly deduced from the fact that he very often left them with the *e*, in cases in which it was of precisely the same importance to excise that vowel as it was in the cases in which he did excise it.

" Therefore 'tis " not " with full happiness that I " have set hand to the task of carrying out in detail the rule which Keats evidently meant to follow.   It is a stern duty, from which one must not shrink, to disfeature several more words in order to conform to the practice of an author who has found such disfeaturement generally necessary.   With a living author one would argue in the hope of persuading him to leave every *e* in and put an accent or two dots on every one that is to be sounded, if the reader cannot be trusted to sound them for himself.   But for one who is among the immortals we must work as far as may be after his proper fashion. It is necessary to make the text consistent with its own rules,—to consider the ease of the reader in the manner in which the poet intended to consider it, and no other. So much by way of apology to the many lovely words printed in this edition otherwise than one would wish to see them printed. The following lists of altered words have been made with the view of relieving the foot-notes.

H. B. F.

LISTS OF WORDS ALTERED SO AS TO CONSIST WITH KEATS'S RULE OR PRACTICE.

In the 1817 Volume

	Page and line of this edition	
ancles	23	82
lily	50	89
honour	57	128
laurel'd	61	3
shewn	94	167
smoothiness	101	377

In ENDYMION

honour   Preface

	Book	Line
Latmos	I	63
valley-lilies	,,	157
owlets	,,	182
honour	,,	226
pavilion	,,	628
balances	,,	644
tease	,,	745
crystaline	,,	793
pavilions	II	56
lilies	,,	100
,,	,,	115
farewel	,,	129
lily	,,	408
honour	,, .	436
ay	,,	555
tease	,,	602
farewel	,,	626
,,	,,	669

In ENDYMION—continued

	Book	Line
lily	II	946
tease	,,	954
shew	,,	990
sphery	III	33
splendor	,,	91
gulf	,,	94
lily	,,	103
blithly	,,	156
shew	,,	209
farewel	,,	275
shew	,,	388
shewing	,,	502
lily	,,	577
chase	,,	590
shew	,,	851
lily	IV	118
water-lily	,,	186
shewing	,,	376
Shew	,,	588
ay	,,	626
farewel	,,	651
river-lily	,,	664
miscal	,,	942
lily	,,	980

In the 1820 Volume

lily	LAMIA	Pt. I	24
fairily	,,	,,	200

In the 1820 volume—continued

			Line				Line
Fairies	LAMIA	Pt. I	329	fairily EVE OF ST.			
ay	„	II	45		AGNES	St. V	3
Ay	„	„	55	lily	„	VI	7
honour	„	„	127	fairies	„	XIX	6
gray	„	„	287	ay	„	XLII	1
lilies	ISABELLA	St. XIX	5	lilies	FANCY		49
ay	„	XXIV	1	gray HYPERION		Bk. III	114
lily	„	XLVI	6				

WORDS ENDING IN *ed.*

In the 1817 Volume

	Page in this edition	Line of poem			Page in this edition	Line of poem
passed	5	1	honied		32	24
leaved	7	5	broidered		32	45
played	8	25	placed		32	49
overtwined	8	35	reclined		37	18
scattered	9	45	tried		37	32
inspired	13	163	loved		38	14
delayed	15	212	fine-eyed		44	35
turned	15	213	intertwined		44	43
soothed	15	224	black-eyed		46	87
eyed	15	225	tired		50	84
turned	17	9	Lured		51	101
prepared	21	29	required		56	105
bright-eyed	23	73	strayed		66	9
large-eyed	24	127	ruled		78	6
turned	24	129	Smoothed		91	57
arched	24	130	chequered		91	77
Embroidered	29	14	Bared		95	190
listened	30	30	blasphemed		95	202
glistened	30	32	dared		98	300

In ENDYMION

	Book	Line			Book	Line
finished	I	55	used		I	134
strayed	„	69	trailed		„	145
unsullied	„	97	piled		„	183
seemed	„	111	paled		„	189
died	„	116	Eyed		„	194

In ENDYMION—continued

	Book	Line		Book	Line
fire-tailed	I	367	unaccustomed	III	90
used	"	433	Lashed	"	111
Dried	"	439	chaced	"	138
used	"	546	died	"	139
dazed	"	601	dried	"	144
used	"	728	dived	"	351
died	"	733	tried	"	390
moved	"	897	ceased	"	423
preserved	"	904	phantasied	"	506
magnified	II	19	emptied	" 510 & 515	
dared	"	36	poisoned	"	602
reached	"	84	Moved	"	606
clear-eyed	"	109	reached	"	671
Descried	"	245	applied	"	781
exclaimed	"	295	eyed	"	803
Medicined	"	484	Moved	"	822
used	"	553	cried	"	832
zoned	"	569	uninspired	IV	25
exhaled	"	663	replied	"	125
endued	"	707	imbrued	"	212
ashamed	"	787	gazed	"	293
self-doomed	"	843	full-veined	"	400
pursued	"	928	yawned	"	464
honied	"	997	tamed	"	591
blear-eyed	III	11	duped	"	629
bared	"	35	entered	"	951
Couched	"	58	dark-eyed	"	977

In the 1820 Volume

LAMIA	Part	Line	LAMIA—continued	Part	Line
Striped	I	49	arrived	I	378
Eyed	"	50	unsullied	"	383
penanced	"	55	mused	II	38
robed	"	76	subdued	"	82
Cried	"	168	canopied	"	132
Flared	"	358	paced	"	134
corniced	"	360	insphered	"	183
robed	"	365	placed	"	196
replied	"	374	cried	"	261-271

In the 1820 Volume—continued

LAMIA—continued	Part	Line
soft-toned	II	261
fair-spaced	„	273

ISABELLA	St.	Line
rich-ored	XIV	8
Paled	XVII	4
pined	LXIII	1

EVE OF ST. AGNES		
eager-eyed	IV	7
unespied	XIX	4
sleepy-eyed	„	7
gazed	XXVIII	2
ceased	XXXIII	7
dyed	XXXVIII	3
saved	„	6

NIGHTINGALE	St.	Line
leaden-eyed	3	8

PSYCHE		
inspired	—	43

FANCY		
Dulcet-eyed	—	81

" Bards of Passion"		
Double-lived		4
„		40

HYPERION	Book	Line
unpractised	I	62
lank-eared	„	230
keen-eyed	„	278
cried	II	293
„	„	295
lilies	III	35

LIST OF PERSONS COMPOSING THE KEATS CIRCLE, WITH DATES OF BIRTH AND DEATH.[1]

JOHN KEATS, born 31 October 1795, died 23 February 1821.

Thomas Keats, father of the poet, died 16 April 1804.

Frances Keats, born Jennings, mother of the poet, died 1807.

George Keats, brother of the poet, born Spring of 1797, died 1842.

Thomas Keats, brother of the poet, born 18 November 1798, died December 1818.

Fanny Keats, sister of the poet, born 3 June 1803.

Frances (or Fanny) Brawne, born 9 August 1800, died, Mrs. Lindon, 1865.

---

[1] The Family Bible in which were recorded the births and deaths of the Keats family was, among other books belonging to Keats's sister, seized by the Custom House officers in Spain many years ago, and never restored. Mrs. Llanos thinks the intervals between the births of her three brothers covered a space of three years, and that Thomas was nearly six years older than herself. Her own birth is recorded in the register of baptisms at the church of St. Botolph, Bishopsgate, where I have also had the good fortune to find an entry of the birth of the poet, though not of the births of his brothers. As we know the day of Thomas Keats's birth, the other data leave no doubt, I think, as to the year ; and George's birth must have been about midway between John's and Thomas's —April or May probably, as he had lately come of age when he went to America in June 1818.

Charles Cowden Clarke, born 1787, died 13 March 1877.

James Henry Leigh Hunt, born 19 October 1784, died 28 August 1859.

Benjamin Robert Haydon, born 26 January 1786, died 22 June 1846.

John Hamilton Reynolds, born 9 September 1796, died 15 November 1852.

Charlotte Reynolds, mother of the last-named, born 15 November 1761, died 13 May 1848.

Jane Reynolds, daughter of the last-named, born 6 November 1794, died, Mrs. Hood, 4 December 1846.

Mariane Reynolds, sister of the last-named, born 23 February 1793, died, Mrs. Green, 7 January 1874.

Charlotte Reynolds, sister of the last-named, born 12 May 1802.

Charles Wells, born 1802, died 17 February 1879.

Charles Wentworth Dilke of Chichester, born 25 November 1742, died 25 March 1826.

Charles Wentworth Dilke, Keats's friend, son of the last-named, born 8 December 1789, died 10 August 1864.

Charles Wentworth Dilke, afterwards first Baronet of the name, son of Keats's friend, born 18 February 1810, died 11 May 1869.

William Dilke, younger brother of Keats's friend, born 16 August 1796.

John Snook, born 7 October 1780, died 29 January 1863.

Lætitia Snook, wife of John Snook, born Dilke 4 April 1784, died 9 March 1865.

John Taylor, born 31 July 1781, died 5 July 1864.

James Augustus Hessey, born 28 July 1785, died 7 April 1870.

Benjamin Bailey, born about 1794, died 1852.

James Rice, not living in December 1833.

Joseph Severn, born 1793, died 3 August 1879.

Charles Armitage Brown, died about 1842.

William Wordsworth, born 7 April 1770, died 23 April 1850.

Percy Bysshe Shelley, born 4 August 1792, died 8 July 1822.

I should have been glad to add particulars of birth and death in regard to Richard Woodhouse, George Felton Mathew, Thomas Richards, and some others, concerning whom, up to the time of going to press, I have not learnt the required details.

INDEX OF FIRST LINES.

INDEX OF FIRST LINES.

Poems.

.

[Keats's first volume, published early in 1817, is a foolscap octavo worked in half sheets. It was issued in drab boards, with a back label *Keats's Poems*, and consists of a blank leaf, fly-title *Poems* in heavy black letter, with imprint on verso, "PRINTED BY C. RICHARDS, NO. 18, WARWICK STREET, GOLDEN SQUARE, LONDON", title-page as given opposite, Dedication with note on verso as reproduced, and pages 1 to 121 including the fly-titles to the Epistles, Sonnets, and *Sleep and Poetry*, all as reproduced in the following pages. There are head-lines in Roman capitals running throughout each section, recto and verso alike, (1) *Poems*, (2) *Epistles*, (3) *Sonnets*, and (4) *Sleep and Poetry*. Leigh Hunt, reviewing with characteristic boldness, loyalty, and insight this volume, dedicated to him, laid his finger unerringly on its weak and strong points. His review appeared in *The Examiner* for the 1st of June and 6th and 13th of July 1817, and will be found reprinted as an Appendix in the present edition of Keats's Works; but I have not hesitated to snatch a line from it now and then by way of appropriate foot-note to these early poems.—H. B. F.]

𝔓𝔬𝔢𝔪𝔰,

BY

JOHN KEATS.

" What more felicity can fall to creature,
" Than to enjoy delight with liberty."

Fate of the Butterfly.—SPENSER.

LONDON:

PRINTED FOR

C. & J. OLLIER, 3, WELBECK STREET,

CAVENDISH SQUARE.

1817.

DEDICATION.

TO LEIGH HUNT, ESQ.

G<small>LORY</small> and loveliness have pass'd away;
   For if we wander out in early morn,
   No wreathed incense do we see upborne
Into the east, to meet the smiling day:
No crowd of nymphs soft voic'd and young, and gay,
   In woven baskets bringing ears of corn,
   Roses, and pinks, and violets, to adorn
The shrine of Flora in her early May.
But there are left delights as high as these,
   And I shall ever bless my destiny,.
That in a time, when under pleasant trees
   Pan is no longer sought, I feel a free
A leafy luxury, seeing I could please
   With these poor offerings, a man like thee.

Readers of Charles Cowden Clarke's Recollections of Keats, printed in the present edition, will remember the statement, still appropriate here, that, "on the evening when the last proof sheet [of the 1817 volume] was brought from the printer, it was accompanied by the information that if a 'dedication to the book was intended it must be sent forthwith.' Whereupon he withdrew to a side table, and in the buzz of a mixed conversation (for there were several friends in the room) he composed and brought to Charles Ollier, the publisher, the Dedication Sonnet to Leigh Hunt." The first of the three Sonnets to Keats in Hunt's *Foliage* forms a fitting reply to this; and the three will be found in the Appendix.

[THE Short Pieces in the middle of the Book, {as well as some of the Sonnets, were written at an earlier period than the rest of the Poems.]

POEMS.

" Places of nestling green for Poets made."

STORY OF RIMINI.

I STOOD tip-toe upon a little hill,
The air was cooling, and so very still,
That the sweet buds which with a modest pride
Pull droopingly, in slanting curve aside,
Their scantly leav'd, and finely tapering stems,   5
Had not yet lost those starry diadems
Caught from the early sobbing of the morn.
The clouds were pure and white as flocks new shorn,
And fresh from the clear brook; sweetly they slept
On the blue fields of heaven, and then there crept   10
A little noiseless noise among the leaves,
Born of the very sigh that silence heaves:
For not the faintest motion could be seen
Of all the shades that slanted o'er the green.

(1) Leigh Hunt tells us in *Lord Byron and Some of his Contemporaries* that "this poem was suggested to Keats by a delightful summer's-day, as he stood beside the gate that leads from the Battery on Hampstead Heath into a field by Caen Wood."

(12) Hunt calls this (see Appendix) "a fancy, founded, as all beautiful fancies are, on a strong sense of what really exists or occurs."

There was wide wand'ring for the greediest eye,   15
To peer about upon variety ;
Far round the horizon's crystal air to skim,
And trace the dwindled edgings of its brim ;
To picture out the quaint, and curious bending
Of a fresh woodland alley, never ending ;   20
Or by the bowery clefts, and leafy shelves,
Guess where the jaunty streams refresh themselves.
I gazed awhile, and felt as light, and free
As though the fanning wings of Mercury
Had play'd upon my heels : I was light-hearted,   25
And many pleasures to my vision started ;
So I straightway began to pluck a posey
Of luxuries bright, milky, soft and rosy.

A bush of May flowers with the bees about them ;
Ah, sure no tasteful nook would be without them ;   30
And let a lush laburnum oversweep them,
And let long grass grow round the roots to keep them
Moist, cool and green ; and shade the violets,
That they may bind the moss in leafy nets.

A filbert hedge with wild briar overtwin'd,   35
And clumps of woodbine taking the soft wind
Upon their summer thrones ; there too should be
The frequent chequer of a youngling tree,
That with a score of light green brethren shoots
From the quaint mossiness of aged roots :   40

(37-41) Of this passage Hunt says, " Any body who has seen a
throng of young beeches, furnishing those natural clumpy seats at
the root, must recognize the truth and grace of this description."
He adds that the remainder of the poem, especially verses 47 to 86,
" affords an exquisite proof of close observation of nature as well as
the most luxuriant fancy."

Round which is heard a spring-head of clear waters
Babbling so wildly of its lovely daughters
The spreading blue bells : it may haply mourn
That such fair clusters should be rudely torn
From their fresh beds, and scatter'd thoughtlessly   45
By infant hands, left on the path to die.

Open afresh your round of starry folds,
Ye ardent marigolds !
Dry up the moisture from your golden lids,
For great Apollo bids   50
That in these days your praises should be sung
On many harps, which he has lately strung ;
And when again your dewiness he kisses,
Tell him, I have you in my world of blisses :
So haply when I rove in some far vale,   55
His mighty voice may come upon the gale.

Here are sweet peas, on tip-toe for a flight :
With wings of gentle flush o'er delicate white,
And taper fingers catching at all things,
To bind them all about with tiny rings.   60

Linger awhile upon some bending planks
That lean against a streamlet's rushy banks,
And watch intently Nature's gentle doings :

(61-80) Clarke says Keats told him this passage was the recollection of the friends' "having frequently loitered over the rail of a
foot-bridge that spanned . . . a little brook in the last field upon
entering Edmonton." Keats, he says, "thought the picture correct,
and acknowledged to a partiality for it." Lord Houghton prints
the following alternative reading of the passage beginning with line
61 :—
> "Linger awhile among some bending planks
> That lean against a streamlet's daisied banks,

They will be found softer than ring-dove's cooings.
How silent comes the water round that bend ;   65
Not the minutest whisper does it send
To the o'erhanging sallows : blades of grass
Slowly across the chequer'd shadows pass.
Why, you might read two sonnets, ere they reach
To where the hurrying freshnesses aye preach   70
A natural sermon o'er their pebbly beds ;
Where swarms of minnows show their little heads,
Staying their wavy bodies 'gainst the streams,
To taste the luxury of sunny beams
Temper'd with coolness.   How they ever wrestle   75
With their own sweet delight, and ever nestle
Their silver bellies on the pebbly sand.
If you but scantily hold out the hand,
That very instant not one will remain ;
But turn your eye, and they are there again.   80
The ripples seem right glad to reach those cresses,
And cool themselves among the em'rald tresses ;
The while they cool themselves, they freshness give,
And moisture, that the bowery green may live :
So keeping up an interchange of favours,   85
Like good men in the truth of their behaviours.
Sometimes goldfinches one by one will drop
From low hung branches ; little space they stop ;
But sip, and twitter, and their feathers sleek ;
Then off at once, as in a wanton freak :   90
Or perhaps, to show their black, and golden wings,
Pausing upon their yellow flutterings.
Were I in such a place, I sure should pray

And watch intently Nature's gentle doings :
That will be found as soft as ringdoves' cooings.
The inward ear will hear her and be blest,
And tingle with a joy too light for rest."

That nought less sweet, might call my thoughts away,
Than the soft rustle of a maiden's gown   95
Fanning away the dandelion's down;
Than the light music of her nimble toes
Patting against the sorrel as she goes.
How she would start, and blush, thus to be caught
Playing in all her innocence of thought.   100
O let me lead her gently o'er the brook,
Watch her half-smiling lips, and downward look;
O let me for one moment touch her wrist;
Let me one moment to her breathing list;
And as she leaves me may she often turn   105
Her fair eyes looking through her locks auburne.
What next?   A tuft of evening primroses,
O'er which the mind may hover till it dozes;
O'er which it well might take a pleasant sleep,
But that 'tis ever startled by the leap   110
Of buds into ripe flowers; or by the flitting
Of diverse moths, that aye their rest are quitting;
Or by the moon lifting her silver rim
Above a cloud, and with a gradual swim
Coming into the blue with all her light.   115
O Maker of sweet poets, dear delight
Of this fair world, and all its gentle livers;

---

(96) Mr. F. Locker possesses a single leaf of the autograph manuscript of this poem, beginning with line 96 and ending with line 182. It seems to have been preserved by Haydon, who has written upon it, "Given me by my Dear Friend Keats—B. R. Haydon". The verbal variations are given below.

(99) The manuscript reads *will* for *would*.

(106) In the manuscript, *peeping* for *looking*.

(115) Lord Houghton notes, presumably from some other manuscript, the following variation:—

> Floating through space with ever-living eye,
> The crowned queen of ocean and the sky.

Spangler of clouds, halo of crystal rivers,
Mingler with leaves, and dew and tumbling streams,
Closer of lovely eyes to lovely dreams,   120
Lover of loneliness, and wandering,
Of upcast eye, and tender pondering !
Thee must I praise above all other glories
That smile us on to tell delightful stories.
For what has made the sage or poet write   125
But the fair paradise of Nature's light ?
In the calm grandeur of a sober line,
We see the waving of the mountain pine ;
And when a tale is beautifully staid,
We feel the safety of a hawthorn glade :   130
When it is moving on luxurious wings,
The soul is lost in pleasant smotherings :
Fair dewy roses brush against our faces,
And flowering laurels spring from diamond vases ;
O'er head we see the jasmine and sweet briar,   135
And bloomy grapes laughing from green attire ;
While at our feet, the voice of crystal bubbles
Charms us at once away from all our troubles :
So that we feel uplifted from the world,
Walking upon the white clouds wreath'd and curl'd. 140
So felt he, who first told, how Psyche went
On the smooth wind to realms of wonderment ;
What Psyche felt, and Love, when their full lips

---

(128) In the manuscript we read *a mountain Pine.*
(141) Compare *Endymion*, final couplet :—

> Peona went
> Home through the gloomy wood in wonderment.

(144) This was originally written in the manuscript, *What fondle-
ing and amourous nips;* but the words are marked to be trans-
posed.

First touch'd ; what amorous, and fondling nips
They gave each other's cheeks ; with all their sighs, 145
And how they kist each other's tremulous eyes :
The silver lamp,—the ravishment,—the wonder—
The darkness,—loneliness,—the fearful thunder ;
Their woes gone by, and both to heaven upflown,
To bow for gratitude before Jove's throne. 150
So did he feel, who pull'd the boughs aside,
That we might look into a forest wide,
To catch a glimpse of Fauns, and Dryades
Coming with softest rustle through the trees ;
And garlands woven of flowers wild, and sweet, 155
Upheld on ivory wrists, or sporting feet :
Telling us how fair, trembling Syrinx fled
Arcadian Pan, with such a fearful dread.
Poor nymph,—poor Pan,—how he did weep to find,
Nought but a lovely sighing of the wind 160
Along the reedy stream ; a half heard strain,
Full of sweet desolation—balmy pain.

What first inspir'd a bard of old to sing
Narcissus pining o'er the untainted spring ?
In some delicious ramble, he had found 165
A little space, with boughs all woven round ;
And in the midst of all, a clearer pool
Than e'er reflected in its pleasant cool,

---

(151) Cancelled manuscript reading, *So do they feel who pull* ;
and in the next line, *may* for *might*.

(153) In the manuscript, and in the original edition, *Fawns* for
Fauns.

(155) Cancelled manuscript reading, *And curious garlands of
flowers* &c.

(156) The manuscript has *sportive* for *sporting*.

(159) In the manuscript, *how did he weep*.

The blue sky here, and there, serenely peeping
Through tendril wreaths fantastically creeping.   170
And on the bank a lonely flower he spied,
A meek and forlorn flower, with naught of pride,
Drooping its beauty o'er the watery clearness,
To woo its own sad image into nearness:
Deaf to light Zephyrus it would not move;   175
But still would seem to droop, to pine, to love.
So while the poet stood in this sweet spot,
Some fainter gleamings o'er his fancy shot;
Nor was it long ere he had told the tale
Of young Narcissus, and sad Echo's bale.   180

Where had he been, from whose warm head out-flew
That sweetest of all songs, that ever new,
That aye refreshing, pure deliciousness,
Coming ever to bless
The wanderer by moonlight? to him bringing   185
Shapes from the invisible world, unearthly singing
From out the middle air, from flowery nests,
And from the pillowy silkiness that rests
Full in the speculation of the stars.
Ah! surely he had burst our mortal bars;   190
Into some wond'rous region he had gone,
To search for thee, divine Endymion!

He was a Poet, sure a lover too,
Who stood on Latmus' top, what time there blew
Soft breezes from the myrtle vale below;   195
And brought in faintness solemn, sweet, and slow
A hymn from Dian's temple; while upswelling,
The incense went to her own starry dwelling.

---

(174) We read *fair* for *sad* in the manuscript.

But though her face was clear as infant's eyes,
Though she stood smiling o'er the sacrifice,   200
The Poet wept at her so piteous fate,
Wept that such beauty should be desolate :
So in fine wrath some golden sounds he won,
And gave meek Cynthia her Endymion.

Queen of the wide air ; thou most lovely queen   205
Of all the brightness that mine eyes have seen !
As thou exceedest all things in thy shine,
So every tale, does this sweet tale of thine.
O for three words of honey, that I might
Tell but one wonder of thy bridal night !   210

Where distant ships do seem to show their keels,
Phœbus awhile delay'd his mighty wheels,
And turn'd to smile upon thy bashful eyes,
Ere he his unseen pomp would solemnize.
The evening weather was so bright, and clear,   215
That men of health were of unusual cheer ;
Stepping like Homer at the trumpet's call,
Or young Apollo on the pedestal :
And lovely women were as fair and warm,
As Venus looking sideways in alarm.   220
The breezes were ethereal, and pure,
And crept through half closed lattices to cure
The languid sick ; it cool'd their fever'd sleep,
And sooth'd them into slumbers full and deep.
Soon they awoke clear ey'd : nor burnt with thirsting, 225
Nor with hot fingers, nor with temples bursting :
And springing up, they met the wond'ring sight
Of their dear friends, nigh foolish with delight ;
Who feel their arms, and breasts, and kiss and stare,
And on their placid foreheads part the hair.   230

Young men, and maidens at each other gaz'd
With hands held back, and motionless, amaz'd
To see the brightness in each other's eyes ;
And so they stood, fill'd with a sweet surprise,
Until their tongues were loos'd in poesy.   235
Therefore no lover did of anguish die :
But the soft numbers, in that moment spoken,
Made silken ties, that never may be broken.
Cynthia ! I cannot tell the greater blisses,
That follow'd thine, and thy dear shepherd's kisses : 240
Was there a poet born ?—but now no more,
My wand'ring spirit must no farther soar.—

---

(233) In the original edition, *others'*.

(242) The publication of *Endymion* in the following year gives
an additional interest to this concluding passage, beginning at line
181. That the subject was already, as early as the summer of
1816, commending itself to Keats as one worth his ambition appears
from this, for the book was out so early in 1817 that the sale was
said to have " dropped " by the 29th of April (see the publishers'
letter of that date in the Appendix). Thus, the delightful summer's
day mentioned by Hunt (see page 7) cannot have been in 1817 ;
but there is an extant letter to Charles Cowden Clarke, which will
be found among the letters in this edition, and which mentions,
under date 17 December 1816, a work entitled *Endymion*, as to be
finished in " one more attack." Perhaps this points to a rejected
draft on a small scale, to which the foregoing poem was the introduction.

SPECIMEN

OF AN

INDUCTION TO A POEM.

Lo! I must tell a tale of chivalry ;
For large white plumes are dancing in mine eye.
Not like the formal crest of latter days :
But bending in a thousand graceful ways ;
So graceful, that it seems no mortal hand,   5
Or e'en the touch of Archimago's wand,
Could charm them into such an attitude.
We must think rather, that in playful mood,
Some mountain breeze had turn'd its chief delight,
To show this wonder of its gentle might.   10
Lo! I must tell a tale of chivalry ;
For while I muse, the lance points slantingly

Hunt speaks confidently of this and the next composition as connected—" The *Specimen of an Induction to a Poem*, and the fragment of the Poem itself entitled *Calidore*" (see Appendix) ; and this view is borne out, not only by internal evidence, but by the fact that in a volume of transcripts made in a copy-book of Tom Keats's these two compositions are written continuously, the first headed simply *Induction*, and the second *Calidore*. Several passages are marked in the margin ; and at the end of *Calidore* is written, " Marked by Leigh Hunt—1816." Hunt's marking resulted in the disappearance of one bad rhyme, for in the transcript line 17 stands thus :

And now no more her anxious grief remembring

and the last word in line 18 is underlined by Hunt. Some minor

Athwart the morning air: some lady sweet,
Who cannot feel for cold her tender feet,
From the worn top of some old battlement   15
Hails it with tears, her stout defender sent:
And from her own pure self no joy dissembling,
Wraps round her ample robe with happy trembling.
Sometimes, when the good Knight his rest would take,
It is reflected, clearly, in a lake,   20
With the young ashen boughs, 'gainst which it rests,
And th' half seen mossiness of linnets' nests.
Ah! shall I ever tell its cruelty,
When the fire flashes from a warrior's eye,
And his tremendous hand is grasping it,   25
And his dark brow for very wrath is knit?
Or when his spirit, with more calm intent,
Leaps to the honors of a tournament,
And makes the gazers round about the ring
Stare at the grandeur of the ballancing?   30
No, no! this is far off:—then how shall I
Revive the dying tones of minstrelsy,
Which linger yet about lone gothic arches,
In dark green ivy, and among wild larches?
How sing the splendour of the revelries,   35
When buts of wine are drunk off to the lees?
And that bright lance, against the fretted wall,
Beneath the shade of stately banneral,
Is slung with shining cuirass, sword, and shield?
Where ye may see a spur in bloody field.   40
Light-footed damsels move with gentle paces
Round the wide hall, and show their happy faces;

---

variations are: *say* for *think* in line 8, *his* for *its* in lines 9 and 10,
grandeur for *splendour* in line 35, *this bright spear* for *that bright
lance* in line 37, and *you* for *ye* in line 40.

Or stand in courtly talk by fives and sevens :
Like those fair stars that twinkle in the heavens.
Yet must I tell a tale of chivalry :   45
Or wherefore comes that steed so proudly by ?
Wherefore more proudly does the gentle knight,
Rein in the swelling of his ample might ?

Spenser! thy brows are arched, open, kind,
And come like a clear sun-rise to my mind ;   50
And always does my heart with pleasure dance,
When I think on thy noble countenance :
Where never yet was ought more earthly seen
Than the pure freshness of thy laurels green.
Therefore, great bard, I not so fearfully   55
Call on thy gentle spirit to hover nigh
My daring steps : or if thy tender care,
Thus startled unaware,
Be jealous that the foot of other wight
Should madly follow that bright path of light   60
Trac'd by thy lov'd Libertas ; he will speak,
And tell thee that my prayer is very meek ;
That I will follow with due reverence,
And start with awe at mine own strange pretence.
Him thou wilt hear ; so I will rest in hope   65
To see wide plains, fair trees and lawny slope :
The morn, the eve, the light, the shade, the flowers ;
Clear streams, smooth lakes, and overlooking towers.

---

(44) The transcript reads *which* for *that*.

(46) In previous editions, *knight;* but in a copy of the 1817 volume bearing on the title-page an inscription in Keats's writing, the word *steed* is substituted in manuscript for *knight.* The transcript also reads *steed.*

(57) The transcript reads *gentle* for *tender.*

(59) The transcript has *living* in place of *other.*

(61) *Libertas* means Leigh Hunt.   See page 54.

CALIDORE.

𝔄 𝔉ragment.

═══

Young Calidore is paddling o'er the lake;
His healthful spirit eager and awake
To feel the beauty of a silent eve,
Which seem'd full loath this happy world to leave;
The light dwelt o'er the scene so lingeringly.   5
He bares his forehead to the cool blue sky,
And smiles at the far clearness all around,
Until his heart is well nigh over wound,
And turns for calmness to the pleasant green
Of easy slopes, and shadowy trees that lean   10
So elegantly o'er the waters' brim
And show their blossoms trim.
Scarce can his clear and nimble eye-sight follow
The freaks, and dartings of the black-wing'd swallow,
Delighting much, to see it half at rest,   15
Dip so refreshingly its wings, and breast
'Gainst the smooth surface, and to mark anon,
The widening circles into nothing gone.

And now the sharp keel of his little boat
Comes up with ripple, and with easy float,   20

In the transcript in Tom Keats's copy-book we read *clear* for *cool* in line 6, *was* for *is* in line 8, *which* for *that* in line 10, *his* for *its* in line 16.

And glides into a bed of water lillies :
Broad leav'd are they and their white canopies
Are upward turn'd to catch the heavens' dew.
Near to a little island's point they grew ;
Whence Calidore might have the goodliest view   25
Of this sweet spot of earth.   The bowery shore
Went off in gentle windings to the hoar
And light blue mountains : but no breathing man
With a warm heart, and eye prepar'd to scan
Nature's clear beauty, could pass lightly by   30
Objects that look'd out so invitingly
On either side.   These, gentle Calidore
Greeted, as he had known them long before.

The sidelong view of swelling leafiness,
Which the glad setting sun, in gold doth dress ;   35
Whence ever, and anon the jay outsprings,
And scales upon the beauty of its wings.

The lonely turret, shatter'd, and outworn,
Stands venerably proud ; too proud to mourn
Its long lost grandeur : fir trees grow around,   40
Aye dropping their hard fruit upon the ground.

The little chapel with the cross above
Upholding wreaths of ivy ; the white dove,
That on the window spreads his feathers light,

---

(28) In the transcript, line 28 reads—

    And light blue Mountains.   But sure no breathing man

and in line 29 *an* stands in place of *and*.

    (40) In the transcript this and the next line stand thus :—

        Its long lost grandeur.   Laburnums grow around
        And bow their golden honors to the ground.

    (42) In the transcript, *its cross.*
    (44) The transcript reads *window*; the first edition, *windows.*

And seems from purple clouds to wing its flight.　　45
Green tufted islands casting their soft shades
Across the lake ; sequester'd leafy glades,
That through the dimness of their twilight show
Large dock leaves, spiral foxgloves, or the glow
Of the wild cat's eyes, or the silvery stems　　50
Of delicate birch trees, or long grass which hems
A little brook.　The youth had long been viewing
These pleasant things, and heaven was bedewing
The mountain flowers, when his glad senses caught
A trumpet's silver voice.　Ah ! it was fraught　　55
With many joys for him : the warder's ken
Had found white coursers prancing in the glen :
Friends very dear to him he soon will see ;
So pushes off his boat most eagerly,
And soon upon the lake he skims along,　　60
Deaf to the nightingale's first under-song ;
Nor minds he the white swans that dream so sweetly :
His spirit flies before him so completely.

And now he turns a jutting point of land,
Whence may be seen the castle gloomy, and grand :　65
Nor will a bee buzz round two swelling peaches,
Before the point of his light shallop reaches
Those marble steps that through the water dip :
Now over them he goes with hasty trip,
And scarcely stays to ope the folding doors :　　70
Anon he leaps along the oaken floors
Of halls and corridors.

---

(48) *Which* for *That* in the transcript.
(57) In the transcript we read *seen* for *found.*
(60) In the transcript, *across the lake.*
(69) The transcript reads *flies* for *goes.*
(70) *And scarcely stops,* in the transcript.

Delicious sounds! those little bright-ey'd things
That float about the air on azure wings,
Had been less heartfelt by him than the clang   75
Of clattering hoofs; into the court he sprang,
Just as two noble steeds, and palfreys twain,
Were slanting out their necks with loosened rein;
While from beneath the threat'ning portcullis
They brought their happy burthens.   What a kiss,   80
What gentle squeeze he gave each lady's hand!
How tremblingly their delicate ankles spann'd!
Into how sweet a trance his soul was gone,
While whisperings of affection
Made him delay to let their tender feet   85
Come to the earth; with an incline so sweet
From their low palfreys o'er his neck they bent:
And whether there were tears of languishment,
Or that the evening dew had pearl'd their tresses,
He feels a moisture on his cheek, and blesses   90
With lips that tremble, and with glistening eye,
All the soft luxury
That nestled in his arms.   A dimpled hand,
Fair as some wonder out of fairy land,
Hung from his shoulder like the drooping flowers   95
Of whitest Cassia, fresh from summer showers:
And this he fondled with his happy cheek
As if for joy he would no further seek;
When the kind voice of good Sir Clerimond
Came to his ear, like something from beyond   100
His present being: so he gently drew
His warm arms, thrilling now with pulses new,

---

(78) In the transcript, *from loosened rein.*
(85) The transcript reads *pretty feet.*
(101) *This present being*, in the transcript.

From their sweet thrall, and forward gently bending,
Thank'd heaven that his joy was never ending;
While 'gainst his forehead he devoutly press'd   105
A hand heaven made to succour the distress'd;
A hand that from the world's bleak promontory
Had lifted Calidore for deeds of Glory.

Amid the pages, and the torches' glare,
There stood a knight, patting the flowing hair   110
Of his proud horse's mane : he was withal
A man of elegance, and stature tall:
So that the waving of his plumes would be
High as the berries of a wild ash tree,
Or as the winged cap of Mercury.   115
His armour was so dexterously wrought
In shape, that sure no living man had thought
It hard, and heavy steel : but that indeed
It was some glorious form, some splendid weed,
In which a spirit new come from the skies   120
Might live, and show itself to human eyes.
'Tis the far-fam'd, the brave Sir Gondibert,
Said the good man to Calidore alert;
While the young warrior with a step of grace
Came up,—a courtly smile upon his face,   125
And mailed hand held out, ready to greet
The large-ey'd wonder, and ambitious heat
Of the aspiring boy; who as he led
Those smiling ladies, often turn'd his head
To admire the visor arch'd so gracefully   130
Over a knightly brow; while they went by
The lamps that from the high-roof'd hall were pendent,
And gave the steel a shining quite transcendent.

---

(103) The transcript reads *meekly bending*.

Soon in a pleasant chamber they are seated ;
The sweet-lipp'd ladies have already greeted   135
All the green leaves that round the window clamber,
To show their purple stars, and bells of amber.
Sir Gondibert has doff'd his shining steel,
Gladdening in the free, and airy feel
Of a light mantle ; and while Clerimond   140
Is looking round about him with a fond,
And placid eye, young Calidore is burning
To hear of knightly deeds, and gallant spurning
Of all unworthiness ; and how the strong of arm
Kept off dismay, and terror, and alarm   145
From lovely woman : while brimful of this,
He gave each damsel's hand so warm a kiss,
And had such manly ardour in his eye,
That each at other look'd half staringly ;
And then their features started into smiles   150
Sweet as blue heavens o'er enchanted isles.

Softly the breezes from the forest came,
Softly they blew aside the taper's flame ;
Clear was the song from Philomel's far bower ;
Grateful the incense from the lime-tree flower ;   155
Mysterious, wild, the far heard trumpet's tone ;
Lovely the moon in ether, all alone :
Sweet too the converse of these happy mortals,
As that of busy spirits when the portals
Are closing in the west ; or that soft humming   160
We hear around when Hesperus is coming.
Sweet be their sleep. * * * * * * * *

(139) In the transcript, *free and easy.*
(147) The transcript reads, *sweet* for *warm.*
(158) In the transcript, *those* for *these.*

TO

SOME LADIES.

———

W HAT though while the wonders of nature exploring,
    I cannot your light, mazy footsteps attend ;
Nor listen to accents, that almost adoring,
    Bless Cynthia's face, the enthusiast's friend :

Yet   over   the   steep,   whence   the   mountain   stream
       rushes,   5
    With you, kindest friends, in idea I rove ;
Mark the clear tumbling crystal, its passionate gushes,
    Its spray that the wild flower kindly bedews.

Why linger you so, the wild labyrinth strolling ?
    Why breathless, unable your bliss to declare ?   10
Ah ! you list to the nightingale's tender condoling,
    Responsive to sylphs, in the moon-beamy air.

'Tis morn, and the flowers with dew are yet drooping,
    I see you are treading the verge of the sea :
And now ! ah, I see it—you just now are stooping   15
    To pick up the keep-sake intended for me.

If a cherub, on pinions of silver descending,
   Had brought me a gem from the fret-work of heaven ;
And smiles, with his star-cheering voice sweetly blending,
   The blessings of Tighe had melodiously given ;   20

It had not created a warmer emotion
   Than the present, fair nymphs, I was blest with from
       you,
Than the shell, from the bright golden sands of the
      ocean
   Which the emerald waves at your feet gladly threw.

For, indeed, 'tis a sweet and peculiar pleasure,   25
   (And blissful is he who such happiness finds,)
To possess but a span of the hour of leisure,
   In elegant, pure, and aerial minds.

---

(20) The reference to Mrs. Tighe, the authoress of the now almost forgotten poem of *Psyche,* is significant as an indication of the poet's taste in verse at this period.

On receiving a curious Shell, and a Copy of Verses, from the same Ladies.

⸻

H AST thou from the caves of Golconda, a gem
Pure as the ice-drop that froze on the mountain ?
Bright as the humming-bird's green diadem,
    When it flutters in sun-beams that shine through a
    fountain ?

The title of this poem has generally stood distributed between this and the preceding composition ; though Lord Houghton, in his latest (Aldine) edition, restores the arrangement of the 1817 volume. Hunt calls these verses (see Appendix), a " string of magistrate-in-terrogatories about a shell and a copy of verses." In Tom Keats's book of transcripts, already mentioned, the poem is headed merely " On receiving a curious shell and a copy of verses " ; but an-other transcript, in the hand-writing of George Keats, is subscribed (not headed) " Written on receiving a copy of Tom Moore's Golden Chain,' and a most beautiful Dome shaped shell from a Lady." The reference is no doubt to *The Wreath and the Chain* ; and this small revelation is satisfactory as accounting for the Tom Moorish triviality of the two pieces. In the last-named copy, in line 6 we read *full* for *right*, in line 7 *wrought* for *mark'd*, in line 9 *his mane thickly*, in line 10 *which* for *that*. Line 17 reads—

Ah courteous Sir Eric ! with joy thou art crown'd :

In line 19 we have *I too have my blisses*, and line 23 is

And lo ! it possesses this property rare.

In line 29, George Keats's transcript has *soft-speaking* for *soft sigh-ing*, and line 31 is

The Hymns of the wondering Spirits were mute !

Hast thou a goblet for dark sparkling wine ?   5
    That goblet right heavy, and massy, and gold ?
And splendidly mark'd with the story divine
    Of Armida the fair, and Rinaldo the bold ?

Hast thou a steed with a mane richly flowing ?
    Hast thou a sword that thine enemy's smart is ?   10
Hast thou a trumpet rich melodies blowing ?
    And wear'st thou the shield of the fam'd Britomartis ?

What is it that hangs from thy shoulder, so brave,
    Embroider'd with many a spring peering flower ?
Is it a scarf that thy fair lady gave ?   15
    And hastest thou now to that fair lady's bower ?

Ah ! courteous Sir Knight, with large joy thou art
        crown'd ;
    Full many the glories that brighten thy youth !
I will tell thee my blisses, which richly abound
    In magical powers to bless, and to sooth.   20

On this scroll thou seest written in characters fair
    A sun-beamy tale of a wreath, and a chain ;
And, warrior, it nurtures the property rare
    Of charming my mind from the trammels of pain.

This canopy mark : 'tis the work of a fay ;   25
    Beneath its rich shade did King Oberon languish,
When lovely Titania was far, far away,
    And cruelly left him to sorrow, and anguish.

In line 37 we have *And* for *So*, and in line 39 *song* for *tale*. None
of these variations are shown by the other copy, which corresponds
almost exactly with the volume of 1817, but reads line 31 thus :
        The wandering spirits of Heaven are mute.

There, oft would he bring from his soft sighing lute
    Wild strains to which, spell-bound, the nightingales
       listen'd ;   30
The wondering spirits of heaven were mute,
    And tears 'mong the dewdrops of morning oft glisten'd.

In this little dome, all those melodies strange,
    Soft, plaintive, and melting, for ever will sigh ;
Nor e'er will the notes from their tenderness change ;   35
    Nor e'er will the music of Oberon die.

So, when I am in a voluptuous vein,
    I pillow my head on the sweets of the rose,
And list to the tale of the wreath, and the chain,
    Till its echoes depart ; then I sink to repose.   40

Adieu, valiant Eric ! with joy thou art crown'd ;
    Full many the glories that brighten thy youth,
I too have my blisses, which richly abound
    In magical powers, to bless and to sooth.

TO * * * *

———

Hadst thou liv'd in days of old,
O what wonders had been told
Of thy lively countenance,
And thy humid eyes that dance
In the midst of their own brightness ;   5
In the very fane of lightness.
Over which thine eyebrows, leaning,
Picture out each lovely meaning :
In a dainty bend they lie,
Like to streaks across the sky,   10
Or the feathers from a crow,
Fallen on a bed of snow.
Of thy dark hair that extends
Into many graceful bends :
As the leaves of Hellebore   15
Turn to whence they sprung before.
And behind each ample curl
Peeps the richness of a pearl.
Downward too flows many a tress
With a glossy waviness ;   20
Full, and round like globes that rise
From the censer to the skies

Through sunny air.   Add too, the sweetness
Of thy honey'd voice ; the neatness
Of thine ankle lightly turn'd :   25
With those beauties, scarce discern'd,
Kept with such sweet privacy,
That they seldom meet the eye
Of the little loves that fly
Round about with eager pry.   30
Saving when, with freshening lave,
Thou dipp'st them in the taintless wave ;
Like twin water lillies, born
In the coolness of the morn.
O, if thou hadst breathed then,   35
Now the Muses had been ten.
Couldst thou wish for lineage higher
Than twin sister of Thalia ?
At least for ever, evermore,
Will I call the Graces four.   40

Hadst thou liv'd when chivalry
Lifted up her lance on high,
Tell me what thou wouldst have been ?
Ah ! I see the silver sheen
Of thy broider'd, floating vest   45
Cov'ring half thine ivory breast ;
Which, O heavens ! I should see,
But that cruel destiny
Has plac'd a golden cuirass there ;
Keeping secret what is fair.   50
Like sunbeams in a cloudlet nested
Thy locks in knightly casque are rested :
O'er which bend four milky plumes
Like the gentle lilly's blooms
Springing from a costly vase.   55

See with what a stately pace
Comes thine alabaster steed ;
Servant of heroic deed !
O'er his loins, his trappings glow
Like the northern lights on snow.　　　60
Mount his back ! thy sword unsheath !
Sign of the enchanter's death ;
Bane of every wicked spell ;
Silencer of dragon's yell.
Alas ! thou this wilt never do :　　　65
Thou art an enchantress too,
And wilt surely never spill
Blood of those whose eyes can kill.

TO

HOPE.

―――

When by my solitary hearth I sit,
  And hateful thoughts enwrap my soul in gloom ;
When no fair dreams before my " mind's eye " flit,
  And the bare heath of life presents no bloom ;
    Sweet Hope, ethereal balm upon me shed,   5
    And wave thy silver pinions o'er my head.

Whene'er I wander, at the fall of night,
  Where woven boughs shut out the moon's bright ray,
Should sad Despondency my musings fright,
  And frown, to drive fair Cheerfulness away,   10
    Peep with the moon-beams through the leafy roof,
    And keep that fiend Despondence far aloof.

Should Disappointment, parent of Despair,
  Strive for her son to seize my careless heart ;
When, like a cloud, he sits upon the air,   15
  Preparing on his spell-bound prey to dart :
    Chace him away, sweet Hope, with visage bright,
    And fright him as the morning frightens night !

Whene'er the fate of those I hold most dear
  Tells to my fearful breast a tale of sorrow,   20

O bright-eyed Hope, my morbid fancy cheer ;
　Let me awhile thy sweetest comforts borrow :
　　Thy heaven-born radiance around me shed,
　　And wave thy silver pinions o'er my head !

Should e'er unhappy love my bosom pain,　　25
　From cruel parents, or relentless fair ;
O let me think it is not quite in vain
　To sigh out sonnets to the midnight air !
　　Sweet Hope, ethereal balm upon me shed,
　　And wave thy silver pinions o'er my head !　　30

In the long vista of the years to roll,
　Let me not see our country's honour fade :
O let me see our land retain her soul,
　Her pride, her freedom ; and not freedom's shade.
　　From thy bright eyes unusual brightness shed—　　35
　　Beneath thy pinions canopy my head !

Let me not see the patriot's high bequest,
　Great liberty ! how great in plain attire !
With the base purple of a court oppress'd,
　Bowing her head, and ready to expire :　　40
　　But let me see thee stoop from heaven on wings
　　That fill the skies with silver glitterings !

And as, in sparkling majesty, a star
　Gilds the bright summit of some gloomy cloud ;
Brightening the half veil'd face of heaven afar :　　45
　So, when dark thoughts my boding spirit shroud,
　　Sweet Hope, celestial influence round me shed,
　　Waving thy silver pinions o'er my head.

February, 1815.

IMITATION OF SPENSER.

* * * * * * *

Now Morning from her orient chamber came,
And her first footsteps touch'd a verdant hill;
Crowning its lawny crest with amber flame,
Silv'ring the untainted gushes of its rill;
Which, pure from mossy beds, did down distill,   5
And after parting beds of simple flowers,
By many streams a little lake did fill,
Which round its marge reflected woven bowers,
And, in its middle space, a sky that never lowers.

There the king-fisher saw his plumage bright   10
Vieing with fish of brilliant dye below;

The copy of these stanzas in Tom Keats's copy-book has a reading in line 12 which ought perhaps to supersede the printed text
of 1817, namely, *golden scalès light*. It seems highly likely that
Keats really meant to carry his archaism to the extent of making
scales a dissyllable, especially as the metre is thus corrected. Lord
Houghton states on the authority of the notes of Charles Armitage
Brown, given to his lordship in 1832, that this is the earliest known
composition of Keats, and was written while he was living at
Edmonton.

Whose silken fins, and golden scales' light
Cast upward, through the waves, a ruby glow :
There saw the swan his neck of arched snow,
And oar'd himself along with majesty ;   15
Sparkled his jetty eyes ; his feet did show
Beneath the waves like Afric's ebony,
And on his back a fay reclin'd voluptuously.

Ah ! could I tell the wonders of an isle
That in that fairest lake had placed been,   20
I could e'en Dido of her grief beguile ;
Or rob from aged Lear his bitter teen :
For sure so fair a place was never seen,
Of all that ever charm'd romantic eye :
It seem'd an emerald in the silver sheen   25
Of the bright waters ; or as when on high,
Through clouds of fleecy white, laughs the cœrulean sky.

And all around it dipp'd luxuriously
Slopings of verdure through the glossy tide,
Which, as it were in gentle amity,   30
Rippled delighted up the flowery side ;
As if to glean the ruddy tears, it try'd,
Which fell profusely from the rose-tree stem !
Haply it was the workings of its pride,
In strife to throw upon the shore a gem   35
Outvieing all the buds in Flora's diadem.

* * * * * * *

---

(29) In line 29 the transcript reads *glassy* for *glossy* ; and this is
likely enough to be right.

Woman! when I behold thee flippant, vain,
   Inconstant, childish, proud, and full of fancies ;
   Without that modest softening that enhances
The downcast eye, repentant of the pain
That its mild light creates to heal again :   5
   E'en then, elate, my spirit leaps, and prances,
   E'en then my soul with exultation dances
For that to love, so long, I've dormant lain :
But when I see thee meek, and kind, and tender,
   Heavens ! how desperately do I adore   10
Thy winning graces ;—to be thy defender
   I hotly burn—to be a Calidore—
A very Red Cross Knight—a stout Leander—
   Might I be lov'd by thee like these of yore.

Light feet, dark violet eyes, and parted hair ;   15
   Soft dimpled hands, white neck, and creamy breast,
   Are things on which the dazzled senses rest
Till the fond, fixed eyes, forget they stare.
From such fine pictures, heavens ! I cannot dare
   To turn my admiration, though unpossess'd   20
   They be of what is worthy,—though not drest
In lovely modesty, and virtues rare.

Yet these I leave as thoughtless as a lark ;
  These lures I straight forget,—e'en ere I dine,
Or thrice my palate moisten : but when I mark   25
  Such charms with mild intelligences shine,
My ear is open like a greedy shark,
  To catch the tunings of a voice divine.

Ah ! who can e'er forget so fair a being ?
  Who can forget her half retiring sweets ?   30
  God ! she is like a milk-white lamb that bleats
For man's protection.   Surely the All-seeing,
Who joys to see us with his gifts agreeing,
  Will never give him pinions, who intreats
  Such innocence to ruin,—who vilely cheats   35
A dove-like bosom.   In truth there is no freeing
One's thoughts from such a beauty ; when I hear
  A lay that once I saw her hand awake,
Her form seems floating palpable, and near ;
  Had I e'er seen her from an arbour take   40
A dewy flower, oft would that hand appear,
  And o'er my eyes the trembling moisture shake.

EPISTLES.

―――――――

"Among the rest a shepheard (though but young
"Yet hartned to his pipe) with all the skill
"His few yeeres could, began to fit his quill."

Britannia's Pastorals.—BROWNE.

―――――――

EPISTLES.

TO

GEORGE FELTON MATHEW.

———

Sweet are the pleasures that to verse belong,
And doubly sweet a brotherhood in song ;
Nor can remembrance, Mathew ! bring to view
A fate more pleasing, a delight more true.
Than that in which the brother Poets joy'd,   5
Who with combined powers, their wit employ'd
To raise a trophy to the drama's muses.
The thought of this great partnership diffuses
Over the genius loving heart, a feeling
Of all that's high, and great, and good, and healing.   10

Too partial friend ! fain would I follow thee
Past each horizon of fine poesy ;
Fain would I echo back each pleasant note
As o'er Sicilian seas, clear anthems float
'Mong the light skimming gondolas far parted,   15
Just when the sun his farewell beam has darted :

But 'tis impossible ; far different cares
Beckon me sternly from soft " Lydian airs,"
And hold my faculties so long in thrall,
That I am oft in doubt whether at all   20
I shall again see Phœbus in the morning :
Or flush'd Aurora in the roseate dawning !
Or a white Naiad in a rippling stream ;
Or a rapt seraph in a moonlight beam ;
Or again witness what with thee I've seen,   25
The dew by fairy feet swept from the green,
After a night of some quaint jubilee
Which every elf and fay had come to see :
When bright processions took their airy march
Beneath the curved moon's triumphal arch.   30

But might I now each passing moment give
To the coy muse, with me she would not live
In this dark city, nor would condescend
'Mid contradictions her delights to lend.
Should e'er the fine-ey'd maid to me be kind,   35
Ah ! surely it must be whene'er I find
Some flowery spot, sequester'd, wild, romantic,
That often must have seen a poet frantic ;
Where oaks, that erst the Druid knew, are growing,
And flowers, the glory of one day, are blowing ;   40
Where the dark-leav'd laburnum's drooping clusters
Reflect athwart the stream their yellow lustres,
And intertwin'd the cassia's arms unite,
With its own drooping buds, but very white.
Where on one side are covert branches hung,   45
'Mong which the nightingales have always sung
In leafy quiet : where to pry, aloof,
Atween the pillars of the sylvan roof,
Would be to find where violet beds were nestling,

And where the bee with cowslip bells was wrestling.   50
There must be too a ruin dark, and gloomy,
To say "joy not too much in all that's bloomy."

Yet this is vain—O Mathew lend thy aid
To find a place where I may greet the maid—
Where we may soft humanity put on,   55
And sit, and rhyme and think on Chatterton ;
And that warm-hearted Shakspeare sent to meet him
Four laurell'd spirits, heaven-ward to intreat him.
With reverence would we speak of all the sages
Who have left streaks of light athwart their ages :   60
And thou shouldst moralize on Milton's blindness,
And mourn the fearful dearth of human kindness
To those who strove with the bright golden wing
Of genius, to flap away each sting
Thrown by the pitiless world.   We next could tell   65
Of those who in the cause of freedom fell ;
Of our own Alfred, of Helvetian Tell ;
Of him whose name to ev'ry heart's a solace,
High-minded and unbending William Wallace.
While to the rugged north our musing turns   70
We well might drop a tear for him, and Burns.

Felton ! without incitements such as these,
How vain for me the niggard Muse to tease :
For thee, she will thy every dwelling grace,
And make "a sun-shine in a shady place :"   75
For thou wast once a flowret blooming wild,
Close to the source, bright, pure, and undefil'd,
Whence gush the streams of song : in happy hour
Came chaste Diana from her shady bower,
Just as the sun was from the east uprising ;   80
And, as for him some gift she was devising,

Beheld thee, pluck'd thee, cast thee in the stream
To meet her glorious brother's greeting beam.
I marvel much that thou hast never told
How, from a flower, into a fish of gold   85
Apollo chang'd thee; how thou next didst seem
A black-ey'd swan upon the widening stream;
And when thou first didst in that mirror trace
The placid features of a human face:
That thou hast never told thy travels strange,   90
And all the wonders of the mazy range
O'er pebbly crystal, and o'er golden sands;
Kissing thy daily food from Naiad's pearly hands.

November, 1815.

TO

MY BROTHER GEORGE.

F ULL many a dreary hour have I past,
My brain bewilder'd, and my mind o'ercast
With heaviness ; in seasons when I've thought
No spherey strains by me could e'er be caught
From the blue dome, though I to dimness gaze   5
On the far depth where sheeted lightning plays ;
Or, on the wavy grass outstretch'd supinely,
Pry 'mong the stars, to strive to think divinely :
That I should never hear Apollo's song,
Though feathery clouds were floating all along   10
The purple west, and, two bright streaks between,
The golden lyre itself were dimly seen :
That the still murmur of the honey bee
Would never teach a rural song to me :
That the bright glance from beauty's eyelids slanting   15
Would never make a lay of mine enchanting,
Or warm my breast with ardour to unfold
Some tale of love and arms in time of old.

But there are times, when those that love the bay,

This epistle seems to have been composed at Margate, for a very
careful transcript of it in George Keats's hand-writing is subscribed
" Margate, August 1816 ".   In line 11 of this copy we read *strokes*
for *streaks*, and in line 12 *faintly* for *dimly*.

Fly from all sorrowing far, far away ;   20
A sudden glow comes on them, nought they see
In water, earth, or air, but poesy.
It has been said, dear George, and true I hold it,
(For knightly Spenser to Libertas told it,)
That when a Poet is in such a trance,   25
In air he sees white coursers paw, and prance,
Bestridden of gay knights, in gay apparel,
Who at each other tilt in playful quarrel,
And what we, ignorantly, sheet-lightning call,
Is the swift opening of their wide portal,   30
When the bright warder blows his trumpet clear,
Whose tones reach nought on earth but Poet's ear.
When these enchanted portals open wide,
And through the light the horsemen swiftly glide,
The Poet's eye can reach those golden halls,   35
And view the glory of their festivals :
Their ladies fair, that in the distance seem
Fit for the silv'ring of a seraph's dream ;
Their rich brimm'd goblets, that incessant run
Like the bright spots that move about the sun ;   40
And, when upheld, the wine from each bright jar
Pours with the lustre of a falling star.
Yet further off, are dimly seen their bowers,
Of which, no mortal eye can reach the flowers ;
And 'tis right just, for well Apollo knows   45
'Twould make the Poet quarrel with the rose.

---

(24) See note to line 44, page 54.

(37) The transcript reads *bright* for *fair*.

(42) Hunt (see Appendix) notes this comparison of poured wine
to a falling star as an instance of Keats's early "tendency to notice
everything too indiscriminately and without an eye to natural proportion and effect ;" and the comparison in verses 48-50 is charged
with the same fault.

All that's reveal'd from that far seat of blisses,
Is, the clear fountains' interchanging kisses,
As gracefully descending, light and thin,
Like silver streaks across a dolphin's fin,   50
When he upswimmeth from the coral caves,
And sports with half his tail above the waves.

These wonders strange he sees, and many more,
Whose head is pregnant with poetic lore.
Should he upon an evening ramble fare   55
With forehead to the soothing breezes bare,
Would he naught see but the dark, silent blue
With all its diamonds trembling through and through?
Or the coy moon, when in the waviness
Of whitest clouds she does her beauty dress,   60
And staidly paces higher up, and higher,
Like a sweet nun in holy-day attire?
Ah, yes! much more would start into his sight—
The revelries, and mysteries of night:
And should I ever see them, I will tell you   65
Such tales as needs must with amazement spell you.

These are the living pleasures of the bard:
But richer far posterity's award.
What does he murmur with his latest breath,
While his proud eye looks through the film of death? 70

---

(48) In the transcript,

     Is, the clear fountains, interchanging kisses,

perhaps the right reading.

  (51) *When he upspringeth*, in the transcript.
  (60) The transcript reads *doth* instead of *does*.
  (65-6) The transcript reads—

     And should I ever view them, I will tell ye
     Such Tales, as needs must with amazement spell ye.

" What though I leave this dull, and earthly mould,
" Yet shall my spirit lofty converse hold
" With after times.—The patriot shall feel
" My stern alarum, and unsheath his steel ;
" Or, in the senate thunder out my numbers   75
" To startle princes from their easy slumbers.
" The sage will mingle with each moral theme
" My happy thoughts sententious ; he will teem
" With lofty periods when my verses fire him,
" And then I'll stoop from heaven to inspire him.   80
" Lays have I left of such a dear delight
" That maids will sing them on their bridal night.
" Gay villagers, upon a morn of May,
" When they have tir'd their gentle limbs with play,
" And form'd a snowy circle on the grass,   85
" And plac'd in midst of all that lovely lass
" Who chosen is their queen,—with her fine head
" Crowned with flowers purple, white, and red :
" For there the lilly, and the musk-rose, sighing,
" Are emblems true of hapless lovers dying :   90
" Between her breasts, that never yet felt trouble,
" A bunch of violets full blown, and double,
" Serenely sleep :—she from a casket takes
" A little book,—and then a joy awakes
" About each youthful heart,—with stifled cries,   95
" And rubbing of white hands, and sparkling eyes :
" For she's to read a tale of hopes, and fears ;
" One that I foster'd in my youthful years :
" The pearls, that on each glist'ning circlet sleep,
" Gush ever and anon with silent creep,   100

---

(77) In the transcript, *the moral theme.*
(86) The transcript reads—

    Placing in midst thereof, that happy lass.

" Lur'd by the innocent dimples.   To sweet rest
" Shall the dear babe, upon its mother's breast,
" Be lull'd with songs of mine.   Fair world, adieu !
" Thy dales, and hills, are fading from my view :
" Swiftly I mount, upon wide spreading pinions,   105
" Far from the narrow bounds of thy dominions.
" Full joy I feel, while thus I cleave the air,
" That my soft verse will charm thy daughters fair,
" And warm thy sons ! " Ah, my dear friend and brother,
Could I, at once, my mad ambition smother,   110
For tasting joys like these, sure I should be
Happier, and dearer to society.
At times, 'tis true, I've felt relief from pain
When some bright thought has darted through my brain :
Through all that day I've felt a greater pleasure   115
Than if I'd brought to light a hidden treasure.
As to my sonnets, though none else should heed them,
I feel delighted, still, that you should read them.
Of late, too, I have had much calm enjoyment,
Stretch'd on the grass at my best lov'd employment   120
Of scribbling lines for you.   These things I thought
While, in my face, the freshest breeze I caught.
E'en now I'm pillow'd on a bed of flowers
That crowns a lofty clift, which proudly towers
Above the ocean-waves.   The stalks, and blades,   125
Chequer my tablet with their quivering shades.
On one side is a field of drooping oats,
Through which the poppies show their scarlet coats ;
So pert and useless, that they bring to mind
The scarlet coats that pester human-kind.   130

---

(118) The transcript reads *will* for *should*.
(125) The transcript reads, *ocean's waves.*

And on the other side, outspread, is seen
Ocean's blue mantle streak'd with purple, and green.
Now 'tis I see a canvass'd ship, and now
Mark the bright silver curling round her prow.
I see the lark down-dropping to his nest,   135
And the broad winged sea-gull never at rest ;
For when no more he spreads his feathers free,
His breast is dancing on the restless sea.
Now I direct my eyes into the west,
Which at this moment is in sunbeams drest :   140
Why westward turn ?   'Twas but to say adieu !
'Twas but to kiss my hand, dear George, to you !

August, 1816.

---

(139) The transcript reads *towards the west.*

TO

CHARLES COWDEN CLARKE.

OFT have you seen a swan superbly frowning,
And with proud breast his own white shadow crowning ;
He slants his neck beneath the waters bright
So silently, it seems a beam of light
Come from the galaxy : anon he sports,—   5
With outspread wings the Naiad Zephyr courts,
Or ruffles all the surface of the lake
In striving from its crystal face to take
Some diamond water drops, and them to treasure
In milky nest, and sip them off at leisure.   10
But not a moment can he there insure them,
Nor to such downy rest can he allure them ;
For down they rush as though they would be free,
And drop like hours into eternity.
Just like that bird am I in loss of time,   15
Whenc'er I venture on the stream of rhyme ;
With shatter'd boat, oar snapt, and canvass rent,
I slowly sail, scarce knowing my intent ;
Still scooping up the water with my fingers,

Charles Cowden Clarke was born at Enfield on the 15th of
December 1787 ; so that he was in his twenty-ninth year when the
young poet addressed this epistle to him. He died at Villa Novello,
Genoa, on the 13th of March 1877, in his ninetieth year.

In which a trembling diamond never lingers.   20
By this, friend Charles, you may full plainly see
Why I have never penn'd a line to thee :
Because my thoughts were never free, and clear,
And little fit to please a classic ear ;
Because my wine was of too poor a savour   25
For one whose palate gladdens in the flavour
Of sparkling Helicon :—small good it were
To take him to a desert rude, and bare,
Who had on Baiæ's shore reclin'd at ease,
While Tasso's page was floating in a breeze   30
That gave soft music from Armida's bowers,
Mingled with fragrance from her rarest flowers :
Small good to one who had by Mulla's stream
Fondled the maidens with the breasts of cream ;
Who had beheld Belphœbe in a brook,   35
And lovely Una in a leafy nook,
And Archimago leaning o'er his book :
Who had of all that's sweet tasted, and seen,
From silv'ry ripple, up to beauty's queen ;
From the sequester'd haunts of gay Titania,   40
To the blue dwelling of divine Urania :
One, who, of late, had ta'en sweet forest walks
With him who elegantly chats, and talks—
The wrong'd Libertas,—who has told you stories
Of laurel chaplets, and Apollo's glories ;   45
Of troops chivalrous prancing through a city,
And tearful ladies made for love, and pity :
With many else which I have never known.

---

(44) Mrs. Charles Cowden Clarke, speaking from knowledge de-
rived from her husband, tells me there is no doubt whatever about
Libertas being, as one would naturally imagine, a name for Leigh
Hunt.

Thus have I thought ; and days on days have flown
Slowly, or rapidly—unwilling still   50
For you to try my dull, unlearned quill.
Nor should I now, but that I've known you long ;
That you first taught me all the sweets of song :
The grand, the sweet, the terse, the free, the fine ;
What swell'd with pathos, and what right divine :   55
Spenserian vowels that elope with ease,
And float along like birds o'er summer seas ;
Miltonian storms, and more, Miltonian tenderness ;
Michael in arms, and more, meek Eve's fair slender-
      ness.
Who read for me the sonnet swelling loudly   60
Up to its climax and then dying proudly ?
Who found for me the grandeur of the ode,
Growing, like Atlas, stronger from its load ?
Who let me taste that more than cordial dram,
The sharp, the rapier-pointed epigram ?   65
Show'd me that epic was of all the king,
Round, vast, and spanning all like Saturn's ring ?
You too upheld the veil from Clio's beauty,
And pointed out the patriot's stern duty ;
The might of Alfred, and the shaft of Tell ;   70
The hand of Brutus, that so grandly fell
Upon a tyrant's head.   Ah ! had I never seen,
Or known your kindness, what might I have been ?
What my enjoyments in my youthful years,
Bereft of all that now my life endears ?   75
And can I e'er these benefits forget ?
And can I e'er repay the friendly debt ?
No, doubly no ;—yet should these rhymings please,
I shall roll on the grass with two-fold ease :
For I have long time been my fancy feeding   80
With hopes that you would one day think the reading

Of my rough verses not an hour misspent ;
Should it e'er be so, what a rich content !
Some weeks have pass'd since last I saw the spires
In lucent Thames reflected :—warm desires   85
To see the sun o'erpeep the eastern dimness,
And morning shadows streaking into slimness
Across the lawny fields, and pebbly water ;
To mark the time as they grow broad, and shorter ;
To feel the air that plays about the hills,   90
And sips its freshness from the little rills ;
To see high, golden corn wave in the light
When Cynthia smiles upon a summer's night,
And peers among the cloudlets jet and white,
As though she were reclining in a bed   95
Of bean blossoms, in heaven freshly shed.
No sooner had I stepp'd into these pleasures
Than I began to think of rhymes and measures :
The air that floated by me seem'd to say
"Write! thou wilt never have a better day."   100
And so I did.   When many lines I'd written,
Though with their grace I was not oversmitten,
Yet, as my hand was warm, I thought I'd better
Trust to my feelings, and write you a letter.
Such an attempt requir'd an inspiration   105
Of a peculiar sort,—a consummation ;—
Which, had I felt, these scribblings might have been
Verses from which the soul would never wean :
But many days have past since last my heart
Was warm'd luxuriously by divine Mozart ;   110
By Arne delighted, or by Handel madden'd ;
Or by the song of Erin pierc'd and sadden'd :
What time you were before the music sitting,

(82 & 94) The first edition reads *mispent* and *cloudlet's*.

And the rich notes to each sensation fitting.
Since I have walk'd with you through shady lanes   115
That freshly terminate in open plains,
And revel'd in a chat that ceased not
When at night-fall among your books we got :
No, nor when supper came, nor after that,—
Nor when reluctantly I took my hat ;   120
No, nor till cordially you shook my hand
Mid-way between our homes :—your accents bland
Still sounded in my ears, when I no more
Could hear your footsteps touch the grav'ly floor.
Sometimes I lost them, and then found again ;   125
You chang'd the footpath for the grassy plain.
In those still moments I have wish'd you joys
That well you know to honor :—" Life's very toys
" With him," said I, "will take a pleasant charm ;
" It cannot be that ought will work him harm."   130
These thoughts now come o'er me with all their might :—
Again I shake your hand,—friend Charles, good night.

September, 1816.

---

(130) Hunt says (see Appendix), in evident allusion to Keats's
prowess as a boxer and readiness to back his friends—" we can
only add, without any disrespect to the graver warmth of our young
poet, that if Ought attempted it, Ought would find he had stout
work to do with more than one person." The student will probably
turn to the posthumous poems and compare these epistles with that
to John Hamilton Reynolds written in 1818.

SONNETS.

SONNETS.

I.

TO MY BROTHER GEORGE.

MANY the wonders I this day have seen:
  The sun, when first he kist away the tears
  That fill'd the eyes of morn ;—the laurell'd peers
Who from the feathery gold of evening lean ;—

Among the late Joseph Severn's Keats relics were a few leaves torn from a small oblong pocket note-book, bearing pencilled sketches by Keats of rude figures &c., and what seem to be the first drafts (in pencil also) of this sonnet and the two quatrains of the sonnet *To my Brothers*. The erasures are not such as to indicate any want of fluency. I have collated this draft with a careful transcript made by George Keats himself, and with another in Tom Keats's copy-book. This last does not vary from the printed text, and bears no date ; but the other transcript, like that of the Epistle to George Keats, is subscribed " Margate, August, 1816 ". In the draft, line 3 at first stood unfinished—

    That trembled on the morning's eye
and then—
    That trembled in the eye of Morn
and finally—
    That hung on Morning's cheek—the laurell'd Peers,
which is the reading of George Keats's transcript. In line 4 we

The ocean with its vastness, its blue green,   !
   Its ships, its rocks, its caves, its hopes, its fears,—
   Its voice mysterious, which whoso hears ˅
Must think on what will be, and what has been.
E'en now, dear George, while this for you I write,
   ˄Cynthia is from her silken curtains peeping
So scantly, that it seems her bridal night,
   And she her half-discover'd revels keeping.
But what, without the social thought of thee,
Would be the wonders of the sky and sea?

---

have *That* for *Who* in the transcript ; while the draft reads *That in the Paleing* (altered to *feathery*) *gold.* In line 6 of the draft, *Dangers* stands cancelled in favour of *Rocks.*   Line 8 in both draft and transcript is—

    Must muse on what's to come and what has been.

In line 10 the draft reads *silver* for *silken*, and there is a cancelled line 11 :—
    Giving the world such snatches of delight,

for which the reading of the text is substituted.   The final couplet was originally—

    The Sights have warmed me but without thy love,
    What Joy in Earth or Sea or Heaven above?

This is cancelled in the draft in favour of the reading of the text. In line 13 the transcript has *thoughts* for *thought.*   Even the small beginning of lunar impersonation that we see in lines 10 to 12 has its interest in the mental history of one who was born to luxuriate through such a harvest of luscious thought and imagery as *Endymion.*

II.

TO * * * * * *

H AD I a man's fair form, then might my sighs
　　Be echoed swiftly through that ivory shell
　　Thine ear, and find thy gentle heart ; so well
Would passion arm me for the enterprize :
But ah ! I am no knight whose foeman dies ;
　　No cuirass glistens on my bosom's swell ;
　　I am no happy shepherd of the dell
Whose lips have trembled with a maiden's eyes.
Yet must I dote upon thee,—call thee sweet,
　　Sweeter by far than Hybla's honied roses
　　　When steep'd in dew rich to intoxication.
Ah ! I will taste that dew, for me 't is meet,
　　And when the moon her pallid face discloses,
　　　I'll gather some by spells, and incantation.

Tom Keats's copy-book contains a transcript of this sonnet showing
no variation in the text, except by a copyist's error at the end,—the
last word being *incantations*. There is no heading beyond the word
Sonnet, no date, and no clue to the identity of the person addressed.

III.

Written on the day that Mr. Leigh Hunt left Prison.

———

WHAT though, for showing truth to flatter'd state,
Kind Hunt was shut in prison, yet has he,
In his immortal spirit, been as free
As the sky-searching lark, and as elate.

———

The Hunts left prison on the 2nd of February 1815, according to Leigh Hunt's own account, though Thornton Hunt says the 3rd at page 99, Volume I, of the *Correspondence* (1862). The expressions employed towards Leigh Hunt in this sonnet are not, one would say, intemperate ; and yet, adding the innocuous phrase in *Sleep and Poetry* (lines 354-5),

> It was a poet's house who keeps the keys
> Of pleasure's temple,

and the fact that the little volume was dedicated to Hunt, Professor Wilson, well described by Horne as "the clown of *Blackwood's Magazine*," found sufficient ground for one of the unseemliest of the coarse pleasantries delivered in the character of "Christopher North"—to wit the allegation that Keats fed Hunt "on the oil cakes of flattery" till he became "flatulent of praise." Keats's real offence in the eyes of Wilson was of course his friendship with such a radical as Hunt, and his venturing to characterize as "showing truth to flatter'd state" the article in *The Examiner* for which Hunt and his brother were imprisoned for two years and fined a thousand pounds. What Hunt had written *was* the truth, no doubt ; but it was unfortunate for Keats, at his start in literature, to subscribe to such truth-

Minion of grandeur! think you he did wait?
Think you he nought but prison walls did see,
Till, so unwilling, thou unturn'dst the key?
Ah, no! far happier, nobler was his fate!

---

telling as this, for instance, in which Hunt translated *The Morning Post's* "language of adulation into that of truth":

"What person, unacquainted with the true state of the case, would imagine, in reading these astounding eulogies, that this 'Glory of the people' was the subject of millions of shrugs and reproaches!— . . . that this 'Exciter of desire' [bravo! Messieurs of the *Post!*]—this 'Adonis in loveliness' was a corpulent man of fifty! —in short, this *delightful, blissful, wise, pleasurable, honourable, virtuous, true,* and *immortal* prince, was a violator of his word, a libertine over head and ears in disgrace, a despiser of domestic ties, the companion of gamblers and demireps, a man who has just closed half a century without one single claim on the gratitude of his country, or the respect of posterity!"

Even towards such a ruthless polemic as Professor Wilson one must seek to be just; and I do not doubt that he felt called upon to oppose the Hunt set with every pulsation of "a heart as rough as Esau's hand," but loyal enough to those politicians whom Keats called the Prince Regent's "wretched crew." It was really, I take it, from this poor little sonnet that the animus of the predominant press party against Keats originated. An article celebrating "The Departure of the Proprietors of this Paper from Prison" occupied the first page of *The Examiner* for Sunday, the 5th of February 1815. The opening is as follows :—

"The two years' imprisonment inflicted on the Proprietors of this Paper for differing with the *Morning Post* on the merits of the PRINCE REGENT, expired on Thursday last; and on that day accordingly we quitted our respective Jails." On the subject of how they felt on the occasion, Hunt excuses himself from particularity, but observes with characteristic pleasantness, "there is a feeling of space and of airy clearness about everything, which is alternately delightful and painful." The greater part of the article is far from being in Hunt's best manner; but the end should stand on record here: "We feel that we have driven another nail or two into the old oaken edifice of English Liberty; and if we have rapped our fingers a little in the operation, it is only a laugh and a wring of the hands, and all is as it should be."

VOL. I.　　　　　　　F

In Spenser's halls he stray'd, and bowers fair,
   Culling enchanted flowers; and he flew
With daring Milton through the fields of air :
   To regions of his own his genius true
Took happy flights.   Who shall his fame impair
   When thou art dead, and all thy wretched crew ?

IV.

—

Hᴏᴡ many bards gild the lapses of time !
  A few of them have ever been the food
  Of my delighted fancy,—I could brood
Over their beauties, earthly, or sublime :
And often, when I sit me down to rhyme,
    These will in throngs before my mind intrude :
    But no confusion, no disturbance rude
Do they occasion ; 't is a pleasing chime. ╱
So the unnumber'd sounds that evening store ;
    The songs of birds—the whisp'ring of the leaves—
    The voice of waters—the great bell that heaves
With solemn sound,—and thousand others more,
    That distance of recognizance bereaves,
Make pleasing music, and not wild uproar.

Hunt adduces the first line (see Appendix) as an example of Keats's "sense of the proper variety of versification without a due consideration of its principles", and very justly adds, "by no contrivance of any sort can we prevent this from jumping out of the heroic measure into mere rhythmicality." Clarke records that when this and one or two other early poems of Keats were first shown by him to Hunt, Horace Smith, being present, remarked on the 13th line, " What a well-condensed expression for a youth so young !"

V.

To a Friend who sent me some Roses.

As late I rambled in the happy fields,
  What time the sky-lark shakes the tremulous dew
  From his lush clover covert;—when anew
Adventurous knights take up their dinted shields:
I saw the sweetest flower wild nature yields,
  A fresh-blown musk-rose; 't was the first that threw
  Its sweets upon the summer: graceful it grew
As is the wand that queen Titania wields.

This sonnet was addressed to Charles Wells, the author of *Stories after Nature, Joseph and his Brethren,* and a few fugitive compositions. His great dramatic poem, *Joseph and his Brethren,* probably came out late in 1823, for though the title-page is dated 1824, the label at the back is dated 1823. The book was left in oblivion till within the last few years. Wells, however, lived to find himself famous in 1876, on the issue of a revised edition, which I had the pleasure of fitting for and seeing through the press for him. He died at Marseilles on the 17th of February 1879, in his 78th year, having finally corrected and interpolated a copy of the new edition of his great work for some future re-edition. A single sentence from one of his last letters to me gives more insight into his character than anything of many times greater extent that could be added here :—

"In stopping Joe" (latterly he wrote of *Joseph and his Brethren* in this familiar way as a rule, and under the term *stop* he included the whole work of revision and seeing through the press)—" In stopping Joe—if another fifty years does not (and it will not) stop

And, as I feasted on its fragrancy,
  I thought the garden-rose it far excell'd :
But when, O Wells ! thy roses came to me
  My sense with their deliciousness was spell'd :
Soft voices had they, that with tender plea
  Whisper'd of peace, and truth, and friendliness un-
      quell'd.

---

him—get rid of all the dones and dids and thou and thines you
possibly can.
              " For ever and a day yours
                     " Joseph."

In Tom Keats's copy-book this sonnet is headed " To Charles
Wells on receiving a bunch of roses," and dated " June 29, 1816."
In this heading the word *full-blown* stands cancelled before *roses*.
The only variation beyond spelling and pointing is in the last line,
which is

  Whispered of truth, Humanity and Friendliness unquell'd.

VI.

To G. A. W.

Nɴʏᴍᴘʜ of the downward smile and sidelong glance,
  In what diviner moments of the day
  Art thou most lovely ?—when gone far astray
Into the labyrinths of sweet utterance,
Or when serenely wand'ring in a trance
  Of sober thought ?—or when starting away
  With careless robe to meet the morning ray
Thou spar'st the flowers in thy mazy dance ?
Haply 'tis when thy ruby lips part sweetly,
  And so remain, because thou listenest:
But thou to please wert nurtured so completely
  That I can never tell what mood is best.
I shall as soon pronounce which Grace more neatly
  Trips it before Apollo than the rest.

The subject of this sonnet was Miss Georgiana Augusta Wylie,
afterwards the wife of Keats's brother George, and now (1881) Mrs.
Jeffrey. I should not have connected the sonnet positively with this
lady had I not seen the manuscript in Keats's writing, headed " To
Miss Wylie." The manuscript corresponds verbatim with the
sonnet as published in 1817; but in the two quatrains the better
punctuation is that of the manuscript; and I have followed it in the
text. The thirteenth line shows one correction : *Nymph* was originally written where *Grace* now stands. In a transcript in Tom
Keats's copy-book we read *what grace* ; and the sonnet is headed
" Sonnet to a Lady ", and dated " Dec. 1816 ".

VII.

O SOLITUDE! if I must with thee dwell,
Let it not be among the jumbled heap
Of murky buildings; climb with me the steep,—
Nature's observatory—whence the dell,
Its flowery slopes, its river's crystal swell,
May seem a span; let me thy vigils keep
'Mongst boughs pavillion'd, where the deer's swift
leap
Startles the wild bee from the fox-glove bell.
But though I'll gladly trace these scenes with thee,
Yet the sweet converse of an innocent mind,
Whose words are images of thoughts refin'd,
Is my soul's pleasure; and it sure must be
Almost the highest bliss of human-kind,
When to thy haunts two kindred spirits flee.

This Sonnet, published in *The Examiner* for the 5th of May 1816,
signed "J. K.", is stated by Charles Cowden Clarke (*Gentleman's
Magazine* for February 1874) to be "Keats's first *published* poem."
In Tom Keats's copy-book it is headed "Sonnet to Solitude", and
undated. The only variation is in line 9,—*I'd* for *I'll*. *The Examiner* reads *rivers* for *river's* in line 5, and lines 9 and 10 stand
thus—

> Ah! fain would I frequent such scenes with thee;
> But the sweet converse of an innocent mind.

VIII.

TO MY BROTHERS.

SMALL, busy flames play through the fresh laid coals,
   And their faint cracklings o'er our silence creep
   Like whispers of the household gods that keep
A gentle empire o'er fraternal souls.

In Tom Keats's copy-book this sonnet is headed "Written to his
Brother Tom on his Birthday," and dated " Nov. 18, 1816." In the
last line the transcript reads *place* for *face*. The sonnet seems to
have been originally written in pencil in the note-book referred to at
page 61, immediately after the sonnet to George Keats ; but the two
quatrains, which fill one page, are all that I found of this sonnet
among the Keats relics of Severn. The quatrains stand finally thus
in the draft :—

   Small flames are peeping through the fresh laid coals
      And their faint Crackling o'er our Silence creeps
      Like Whispers of the Household God that keeps
   A gentle empire o'er fraternal Souls
   And while for Rhymes I search around the Poles
      Your Eyes are fixéd as in poetic sleep
      Upon the Pages Voluble and deep
   That aye at fall of Night our care condoles.

There is a cancelled reading at line 2, unfinished—

   With a faint Crackling head distract...

and another at line 5—

   And while I am thinking of a Rhyme ;

and here *searching* was substituted for *thinking of*, before the
whole was cancelled in favour of the reading of the text.

And while, for rhymes, I search around the poles,
  Your eyes are fix'd, as in poetic sleep,
  Upon the lore so voluble and deep,
That aye at fall of night our care condoles.
This is your birth-day Tom, and I rejoice
  That thus it passes smoothly, quietly.
Many such eves of gently whisp'ring noise
  May we together pass, and calmly try
What are this world's true joys,—ere the great voice,
  From its fair face, shall bid our spirits fly.

November 18, 1816.

IX.

K EEN, fitful gusts are whisp'ring here and there
  Among the bushes half leafless, and dry ;
  The stars look very cold about the sky,
And I have many miles on foot to fare.
Yet feel I little of the cool bleak air,
  Or of the dead leaves rustling drearily,
  Or of those silver lamps that burn on high,
Or of the distance from home's pleasant lair :
For I am brimfull of the friendliness
  That in a little cottage I have found ;
Of fair-hair'd Milton's eloquent distress,
  And all his love for gentle Lycid drown'd ;
Of lovely Laura in her light green dress,
  And faithful Petrarch gloriously crown'd.

Clarke records that this sonnet was written on the occasion of
Keats's first becoming acquainted with Leigh Hunt at the Cottage
in the Vale of Health, Hampstead.

X.

To one who has been long in city pent,
  'Tis very sweet to look into the fair
  And open face of heaven,—to breathe a prayer
Full in the smile of the blue firmament.
Who is more happy, when, with heart's content,
  Fatigued he sinks into some pleasant lair
  Of wavy grass, and reads a debonair
And gentle tale of love and languishment?

In a transcript in the hand-writing of George Keats this sonnet is subscribed as " Written in the Fields—June 1816 ". The variations shown by this manuscript, no doubt correctly copied from the original, are,—in line 2, *upon* for *into* ; in line 4 *bright* for *blue* ; in line 5 *heart's* is written correctly, though *hearts* is wrongly printed in the 1817 volume ; in line 6 *upon a* for *into some* ; in line 7 *some* for *a* ; in line 9 *Returning, thoughtful, homeward* for *Returning home at evening* ; line 11 is

    Following the wafted Cloudlet's light career ;

and line 14 is

    That droppeth through the Æther silently.

In Tom Keats's copy-book the only variation from the printed text of 1817 is in line 4, *bright* for *blue*. It is clear the sonnet was carefully revised for the 1817 volume ; and it is curious Keats did not find out that he was indebted to Milton for his "prosperous opening". Compare *Paradise Lost*, IX, 445,

    As one who long in populous City pent...

Returning home at evening, with an ear
  Catching the notes of Philomel,—an eye
Watching the sailing cloudlet's bright career,
  He mourns that day so soon has glided by :
E'en like the passage of an angel's tear
  That falls through the clear ether silently.

XI.

On first looking into Chapman's Homer.

MUCH have I travell'd in the realms of gold,
And many goodly states and kingdoms seen ;
Round many western islands have I been
Which bards in fealty to Apollo hold.

Charles Cowden Clarke says, in the article in *The Gentleman's Magazine* referred to at page 71, that this sonnet was sent to him by Keats so as to reach him at 10 o'clock one morning when they two had parted "at day-spring" after a night encounter with a copy of Chapman's Homer belonging to Mr. Alsager of *The Times.* Mr. F. Locker possesses an undated manuscript of the sonnet in Keats's writing, headed "On the first looking into Chapman's Homer"; while in Tom Keats's copy-book the heading is " Sonnet on looking into Chapman's Homer," and the date " 1816." In that book, though not in Mr. Locker's manuscript, line 5 opens with *But* instead of *Oft.* In the manuscript line 6 originally read *Which low-brow'd Homer*; but *deep* is substituted for *low*; and for line 7 we read both in the manuscript and in the copy-book

Yet could I never judge what men could mean.

In line 11 the autograph manuscript reads *wond'ring eyes* for *eagle eyes.* The variation in line 7 is of value in connexion with one of the reminiscences of Clarke, who says the seventh line originally stood thus:

Yet could I never tell what men could mean

and that Keats substituted the reading of the text because he considered the first reading "bald, and too simply wondering." But he may have been actuated by another reason also, as thus : in an article headed "Young Poets" in *The Examiner* for the 1st of De-

Oft of one wide expanse had I been told
  That deep-brow'd Homer rul'd as his demesne ;
  Yet did I never breathe its pure serene
Till I heard Chapman speak out loud and bold :

---

cember 1816, Hunt had spoken in high praise of a set of Keats's manuscript poems shown to him, and had printed this one as given in Tom Keats's copy-book, with the remark that it contained "one incorrect rhyme." The only disputable rhyme is that of *mean* and *demesne*, and that is got rid of by the revision. "The rest of the composition," says Hunt, "with the exception of a little vagueness in calling the regions of poetry 'the realms of gold', we do not hesitate to pronounce excellent, especially the last six lines. The word *swims* is complete ; and the whole conclusion is equally powerful and quiet." He appears to have become reconciled to "the realms of gold" in later years, to judge from the close of that charming work *Imagination and Fancy*. Speaking of this sonnet he says at page 345 (I quote the third edition, dated 1846),—"'Stared' has been thought by some too violent, but it is precisely the word required by the occasion. The Spaniard was too original and ardent a man either to look, or to affect to look, coldly superior to it. His 'eagle eyes' are from life, as may be seen by Titian's portrait of him." Of the last line, which ends the poetry of *Imagination and Fancy*, Hunt says "We leave the reader standing upon it, with all the illimitable world of thought and feeling before him, to which his imagination will have been brought, while journeying through these 'realms of gold.'"

The last four lines seem to be a reminiscence of Robertson's History of America, recorded by Clarke as among Keats's later school reading; but, as Mr. Tennyson pointed out to Mr. Palgrave (*Golden Treasury*, 1861, page 320) the reference should really be to Balboa. From Hunt's remark about the portrait it is clear this was no mere slip of the pen : Cortez was the man whom Keats's imagination saw in the situation, and it is to be presumed that his memory betrayed him, for it seems unlikely that he met with the story elsewhere, told of Cortez. The passage in Robertson's History of America (Works, edition of 1817, Volume VIII, page 287) is as follows :

"At length the Indians assured them, that from the top of the next mountain they should discover the ocean which was the object of their wishes. When, with infinite toil, they had climbed up the greater part of that steep ascent, Balboa commanded his men to

Then felt I like some watcher of the skies
    When a new planet swims into his ken ;
Or like stout Cortez when with eagle eyes
    He star'd at the Pacific—and all his men
Look'd at each other with a wild surmise—
    Silent, upon a peak in Darien.

---

halt, and advanced alone to the summit, that he might be the first
who should enjoy a spectacle which he had so long desired. As
soon as he beheld the South Sea stretching in endless prospect below him, he fell on his knees, and lifting up his hands to heaven,
returned thanks to God, who had conducted him to a discovery so
beneficial to his country, and so honourable to himself. His fol-
lowers, observing his transports of joy, rushed forward to join in his
wonder, exultation, and gratitude."

An account of this incident will also be found in Washington
Irving's *Voyages and Discoveries of the Companions of Columbus.*
The reader will of course turn to the Sonnet to Homer among
the posthumous Poems of 1818, and read it in connexion with this
one published by Keats. It is not difficult to decide which is the
finer ; but that, though not so great a sonnet as this, has some lines
that are hardly indeed to be surpassed.

XII.

On leaving some Friends at an early Hour.

GIVE me a golden pen, and let me lean
  On heap'd up flowers, in regions clear, and far ;
  Bring me a tablet whiter than a star,
Or hand of hymning angel, when 't is seen
The silver strings of heavenly harp atween :
  And let there glide by many a pearly car,
  Pink robes, and wavy hair, and diamond jar,
And half discovered wings, and glances keen.
The while let music wander round my ears,
  And as it reaches each delicious ending,
    Let me write down a line of glorious tone,
And full of many wonders of the spheres :
  For what a height my spirit is contending !
    'Tis not content so soon to be alone.

This sonnet also belongs to the Cottage in the Vale of Health, as we are led to infer from Clarke's mention of it in connexion with No. IX and No. XV.

XIII.

ADDRESSED TO HAYDON.

———

Highmindedness, a jealousy for good,
 A loving-kindness for the great man's fame,
 Dwells here and there with people of no name,
In noisome alley, and in pathless wood :
And where we think the truth least understood,
 Oft may be found a "singleness of aim,"
 That ought to frighten into hooded shame
A money-mong'ring, pitiable brood.
How glorious this affection for the cause
 Of stedfast genius, toiling gallantly !
What when a stout unbending champion awes
 Envy, and Malice to their native sty ?
Unnumber'd souls breathe out a still applause,
 Proud to behold him in his country's eye.

———

Benjamin Robert Haydon, historical painter, was born on the 26th of January 1786, and died by his own hand on the 22nd of June 1846.

XIV.

ADDRESSED TO THE SAME.

———

GREAT spirits now on earth are sojourning ;
   He of the cloud, the cataract, the lake,
   Who on Helvellyn's summit, wide awake,
Catches his freshness from Archangel's wing :
He of the rose, the violet, the spring,
   The social smile, the chain for Freedom's sake :
   And lo !—whose stedfastness would never take
A meaner sound than Raphael's whispering.
And other spirits there are standing apart
   Upon the forehead of the age to come ;
These, these will give the world another heart,
   And other pulses.   Hear ye not the hum
Of mighty workings ?———
   Listen awhile ye nations, and be dumb.

———————————————

In Tom Keats's copy-book this Sonnet is headed simply " Sonnet "
and is dated 1816 merely.   There are no variations.   It is almost
superfluous to identify the two men referred to in the first six lines
—Wordsworth and Leigh Hunt.

XV.

On the Grasshopper and Cricket.

THE poetry of earth is never dead :
When all the birds are faint with the hot sun,
And hide in cooling trees, a voice will run
From hedge to hedge about the new-mown mead ;
That is the Grasshopper's—he takes the lead
In summer luxury,—he has never done
With his delights ; for when tired out with fun
He rests at ease beneath some pleasant weed.
The poetry of earth is ceasing never :
On a lone winter evening, when the frost
Has wrought a silence, from the stove there shrills
The Cricket's song, in warmth increasing ever,
And seems to one in drowsiness half lost,
The Grasshopper's among some grassy hills.

December 30, 1816.

Clarke records that this sonnet was written at Leigh Hunt's cottage, on a challenge from Hunt. See Clarke's account in his Recollections of Keats ; and see Appendix for Hunt's Sonnet. Both Sonnets appeared together in *The Examiner* for the 21st of September 1817 ; but Keats's volume had already appeared in June of that year.

XVI.

TO KOSCIUSKO.

GOOD Kosciusko, thy great name alone
　Is a full harvest whence to reap high feeling ;
　It comes upon us like the glorious pealing
Of the wide spheres—an everlasting tone.
And now it tells me, that in worlds unknown,
　The names of heroes, burst from clouds concealing,
　And changed to harmonies, for ever stealing
Through cloudless blue, and round each silver throne.
It tells me too, that on a happy day,
　When some good spirit walks upon the earth,
　　Thy name with Alfred's, and the great of yore
　Gently commingling, gives tremendous birth
To a loud hymn, that sounds far, far away
　　To where the great God lives for evermore.

This sonnet was published in *The Examiner* for the 16th of
February 1817. The punctuation differs slightly from that of the
1817 volume; and in the eighth line we read *around* for *and round*.
The date " Dec. 1816 " and the initials " J. K." appear under the
sonnet in *The Examiner.*

XVII.

Happy is England! I could be content
  To see no other verdure than its own ;
  To feel no other breezes than are blown
Through its tall woods with high romances blent :
Yet do I sometimes feel a languishment
  For skies Italian, and an inward groan
  To sit upon an Alp as on a throne,
And half forget what world or worldling meant.
Happy is England, sweet her artless daughters ;
  Enough their simple loveliness for me,
    Enough their whitest arms in silence clinging :
  Yet do I often warmly burn to see
    Beauties of deeper glance, and hear their singing,
And float with them about the summer waters.

SLEEP AND POETRY.

"As I lay in my bed slepe full unmete
"Was unto me, but why that I ne might
"Rest I ne wist, for there n'as erthly wight
"[As I suppose] had more of hertis ese
"Than I, for I n'ad sicknesse nor disese."

CHAUCER.

SLEEP AND POETRY.

WHAT is more gentle than a wind in summer?
What is more soothing than the pretty hummer
That stays one moment in an open flower,
And buzzes cheerily from bower to bower?
What is more tranquil than a musk-rose blowing   5
In a green island, far from all men's knowing?
More healthful than the leafiness of dales?
More secret than a nest of nightingales?
More serene than Cordelia's countenance?
More full of visions than a high romance?   10
What, but thee Sleep?   Soft closer of our eyes!
Low murmurer of tender lullabies!
Light hoverer around our happy pillows!
Wreather of poppy buds, and weeping willows!
Silent entangler of a beauty's tresses!   15
Most happy listener! when the morning blesses
Thee for enlivening all the cheerful eyes
That glance so brightly at the new sun-rise.

But what is higher beyond thought than thee?
Fresher than berries of a mountain tree?   20

Hunt (see Appendix) pronounces this the best poem in the book,
with his usual excellent critical perception.

More strange, more beautiful, more smooth, more regal,
Than wings of swans, than doves, than dim-seen eagle?
What is it? And to what shall I compare it?
It has a glory, and nought else can share it:
The thought thereof is awful, sweet, and holy,   25
Chasing away all worldliness and folly;
Coming sometimes like fearful claps of thunder,
Or the low rumblings earth's regions under;
And sometimes like a gentle whispering
Of all the secrets of some wond'rous thing   30
That breathes about us in the vacant air;
So that we look around with prying stare,
Perhaps to see shapes of light, aerial lymning,
And catch soft floatings from a faint-heard hymning;
To see the laurel wreath, on high suspended,   35
That is to crown our name when life is ended.
Sometimes it gives a glory to the voice,
And from the heart up-springs, rejoice! rejoice!
Sounds which will reach the Framer of all things,
And die away in ardent mutterings.   40

No one who once the glorious sun has seen,
And all the clouds, and felt his bosom clean
For his great Maker's presence, but must know
What 't is I mean, and feel his being glow:
Therefore no insult will I give his spirit,   45
By telling what he sees from native merit.

O Poesy! for thee I hold my pen
That am not yet a glorious denizen
Of thy wide heaven—Should I rather kneel
Upon some mountain-top until I feel   50
A glowing splendour round about me hung,
And echo back the voice of thine own tongue?

O Poesy! for thee I grasp my pen
That am not yet a glorious denizen
Of thy wide heaven; yet, to my ardent prayer,   55
Yield from thy sanctuary some clear air,
Smooth'd for intoxication by the breath
Of flowering bays, that I may die a death
Of luxury, and my young spirit follow
The morning sun-beams to the great Apollo   60
Like a fresh sacrifice; or, if I can bear
The o'erwhelming sweets, 'twill bring to me the fair
Visions of all places: a bowery nook
Will be elysium—an eternal book
Whence I may copy many a lovely saying   65
About the leaves, and flowers—about the playing
Of nymphs in woods, and fountains; and the shade
Keeping a silence round a sleeping maid;
And many a verse from so strange influence
That we must ever wonder how, and whence   70
It came.   Also imaginings will hover
Round my fire-side, and haply there discover
Vistas of solemn beauty, where I'd wander
In happy silence, like the clear Meander
Through its lone vales; and where I found a spot   75
Of awfuller shade, or an enchanted grot,
Or a green hill o'erspread with chequer'd dress
Of flowers, and fearful from its loveliness,
Write on my tablets all that was permitted,
All that was for our human senses fitted.   80
Then the events of this wide world I'd seize
Like a strong giant, and my spirit teaze
Till at its shoulders it should proudly see
Wings to find out an immortality.

---

(74) In the original, *meander* with a small *m*.

Stop and consider ! life is but a day ;   85
A fragile dew-drop on its perilous way
From a tree's summit ; a poor Indian's sleep
While his boat hastens to the monstrous steep
Of Montmorenci.   Why so sad a moan ?
Life is the rose's hope while yet unblown ;   90
The reading of an ever-changing tale ;
The light uplifting of a maiden's veil ;
A pigeon tumbling in clear summer air ;
A laughing school-boy, without grief or care,
Riding the springy branches of an elm.   95

O for ten years, that I may overwhelm
Myself in poesy ; so I may do the deed
That my own soul has to itself decreed.
Then will I pass the countries that I see
In long perspective, and continually   100
Taste their pure fountains.   First the realm I'll pass
Of Flora, and old Pan : sleep in the grass,
Feed upon apples red, and strawberries,
And choose each pleasure that my fancy sees ;
Catch the white-handed nymphs in shady places,   105
To woo sweet kisses from averted faces,—
Play with their fingers, touch their shoulders white
Into a pretty shrinking with a bite
As hard as lips can make it : till agreed,
A lovely tale of human life we'll read.   110
And one will teach a tame dove how it best
May fan the cool air gently o'er my rest ;
Another, bending o'er her nimble tread,
Will set a green robe floating round her head,
And still will dance with ever varied ease,   115
Smiling upon the flowers and the trees :
Another will entice me on, and on

Through almond blossoms and rich cinnamon;
Till in the bosom of a leafy world
We rest in silence, like two gems upcurl'd   120
In the recesses of a pearly shell.

And can I ever bid these joys farewell ?
Yes, I must pass them for a nobler life,
Where I may find the agonies, the strife
Of human hearts: for lo ! I see afar,   125
O'ersailing the blue cragginess, a car
And steeds with streamy manes—the charioteer
Looks out upon the winds with glorious fear :
And now the numerous tramplings quiver lightly
Along a huge cloud's ridge ; and now with sprightly 130
Wheel downward come they into fresher skies,
Tipt round with silver from the sun's bright eyes.
Still downward with capacious whirl they glide ;
And now I see them on a green-hill's side
In breezy rest among the nodding stalks.   135
The charioteer with wond'rous gesture talks
To the trees and mountains ; and there soon appear
Shapes of delight, of mystery, and fear,
Passing along before a dusky space
Made by some mighty oaks: as they would chase   140
Some ever-fleeting music on they sweep.
Lo ! how they murmur, laugh, and smile, and weep :
Some with upholden hand and mouth severe ;
Some with their faces muffled to the ear
Between their arms ; some, clear in youthful bloom, 145
Go glad and smilingly athwart the gloom ;
Some looking back, and some with upward gaze ;
Yes, thousands in a thousand different ways
Flit onward—now a lovely wreath of girls
Dancing their sleek hair into tangled curls ;   150

And now broad wings.   Most awfully intent
The driver of those steeds is forward bent,
And seems to listen : O that I might know
All that he writes with such a hurrying glow!

The visions all are fled—the car is fled   155
Into the light of heaven, and in their stead
A sense of real things comes doubly strong,
And, like a muddy stream, would bear along
My soul to nothingness : but I will strive
Against all doubtings, and will keep alive   160
The thought of that same chariot, and the strange
Journey it went.

         Is there so small a range
In the present strength of manhood, that the high
Imagination cannot freely fly
As she was wont of old ? prepare her steeds,   165
Paw up against the light, and do strange deeds
Upon the clouds ? Has she not shown us all ?
From the clear space of ether, to the small
Breath of new buds unfolding ? From the meaning
Of Jove's large eye-brow, to the tender greening   170
Of April meadows ? Here her altar shone,
E'en in this isle ; and who could paragon
The fervid choir that lifted up a noise
Of harmony, to where it aye will poise
Its mighty self of convoluting sound,   175
Huge as a planet, and like that roll round,
Eternally around a dizzy void ?
Ay, in those days the Muses were nigh cloy'd
With honors ; nor had any other care
Than to sing out and sooth their wavy hair.   180

Could all this be forgotten ? Yes, a scism

Nurtured by foppery and barbarism,
Made great Apollo blush for this his land.
Men were thought wise who could not understand
His glories : with a puling infant's force   185
They sway'd about upon a rocking horse,
And thought it Pegasus.   Ah dismal soul'd !
The winds of heaven blew, the ocean roll'd
Its gathering waves—ye felt it not.   The blue
Bar'd its eternal bosom, and the dew   190
Of summer nights collected still to make
The morning precious : beauty was awake !
Why were ye not awake ? But ye were dead
To things ye knew not of,—were closely wed
To musty laws lined out with wretched rule   195
And compass vile : so that ye taught a school
Of dolts to smooth, inlay, and clip, and fit,
Till, like the certain wands of Jacob's wit,
Their verses tallied.   Easy was the task :
A thousand handicraftsmen wore the mask   200
Of Poesy.   Ill-fated, impious race !
That blasphem'd the bright Lyrist to his face,
And did not know it,—no, they went about,
Holding a poor, decrepid standard out
Mark'd with most flimsy mottos, and in large   205
The name of one Boileau !

                                O ye whose charge
It is to hover round our pleasant hills !
Whose congregated majesty so fills
My boundly reverence, that I cannot trace
Your hallowed names, in this unholy place,   210
So near those common folk ; did not their shames
Affright you ? Did our old lamenting Thames
Delight you ? Did ye never cluster round

Delicious Avon, with a mournful sound,
And weep ? Or did ye wholly bid adieu   215
To regions where no more the laurel grew ?
Or did ye stay to give a welcoming
To some lone spirits who could proudly sing
Their youth away, and die ? 'T was even so :
But let me think away those times of woe :   220
Now 't is a fairer season ; ye have breathed
Rich benedictions o'er us ; ye have wreathed
Fresh garlands : for sweet music has been heard
In many places ;—some has been upstirr'd
From out its crystal dwelling in a lake,   225
By a swan's ebon bill ; from a thick brake,
Nested and quiet in a valley mild,
Bubbles a pipe ; fine sounds are floating wild
About the earth : happy are ye and glad.

These things are doubtless : yet in truth we've had   230
Strange thunders from the potency of song ;
Mingled indeed with what is sweet and strong,
From majesty : but in clear truth the themes
Are ugly cubs, the Poets Polyphemes
Disturbing the grand sea.   A drainless shower   235
Of light is poesy ; 't is the supreme of power ;
'T is might half slumb'ring on its own right arm.
The very archings of her eye-lids charm
A thousand willing agents to obey,
And still she governs with the mildest sway :   240
But strength alone though of the Muses born
Is like a fallen angel : trees uptorn,
Darkness, and worms, and shrouds, and sepulchres
Delight it ; for it feeds upon the burrs,
And thorns of life ; forgetting the great end   245

Of poesy, that it should be a friend
To sooth the cares, and lift the thoughts of man.

   Yet I rejoice : a myrtle fairer than
E'er grew in Paphos, from the bitter weeds
Lifts its sweet head into the air, and feeds   `   250
A silent space with ever sprouting green.
All tenderest birds there find a pleasant screen,
Creep through the shade with jaunty fluttering,
Nibble the little cupped flowers and sing.
Then let us clear away the choaking thorns   255
From round its gentle stem ; let the young fawns,
Yeaned in after times, when we are flown,
Find a fresh sward beneath it, overgrown
With simple flowers : let there nothing be
More boisterous than a lover's bended knee ;   260
Nought more ungentle than the placid look
Of one who leans upon a closed book ;
Nought more untranquil than the grassy slopes
Between two hills.   All hail delightful hopes !
As she was wont, th' imagination   265
Into most lovely labyrinths will be gone,
And they shall be accounted poet kings
Who simply tell the most heart-easing things.
O may these joys be ripe before I die.

Will not some say that I presumptuously   270
Have spoken ? that from hastening disgrace
'T were better far to hide my foolish face ?
That whining boyhood should with reverence bow
Ere the dread thunderbolt could reach ?   How !

(250-1) An idea, says Hunt (see Appendix), "of as lovely and
powerful a nature in embodying an abstraction, as we ever remember to have seen put into words ".

If I do hide myself, it sure shall be   275
In the very fane, the light of Poesy :
If I do fall, at least I will be laid
Beneath the silence of a poplar shade ;
And over me the grass shall be smooth shaven ;
And there shall be a kind memorial graven.   280
But off Despondence! miserable bane!
They should not know thee, who athirst to gain
A noble end, are thirsty every hour.
What though I am not wealthy in the dower
Of spanning wisdom ; though I do not know   285
The shiftings of the mighty winds that blow
Hither and thither all the changing thoughts
Of man : though no great minist'ring reason sorts
Out the dark mysteries of human souls
To clear conceiving : yet there ever rolls   290
A vast idea before me, and I glean
Therefrom my liberty ; thence too I've seen
The end and aim of Poesy. 'T is clear
As anything most true ; as that the year
Is made of the four seasons—manifest   295
As a large cross, some old cathedral's crest,
Lifted to the white clouds.   Therefore should I
Be but the essence of deformity,
A coward, did my very eye-lids wink
At speaking out what I have dar'd to think.   300
Ah! rather let me like a madman run
Over some precipice ; let the hot sun
Melt my Dedalian wings, and drive me down
Convuls'd and headlong!   Stay! an inward frown
Of conscience bids me be more calm awhile.   305
An ocean dim, sprinkled with many an isle,
Spreads awfully before eme.   How much toil!
How many days! what desperate turmoil!

Ere I can have explored its widenesses.
Ah, what a task! upon my bended knees,   310
I could unsay those—no, impossible!
Impossible!

        For sweet relief I 'll dwell
On humbler thoughts, and let this strange assay
Begun in gentleness die so away.
E'en now all tumult from my bosom fades: 315
I turn full hearted to the friendly aids
That smooth the path of honour; brotherhood,
And friendliness the nurse of mutual good.
The hearty grasp that sends a pleasant sonnet
Into the brain ere one can think upon it;   320
The silence when some rhymes are coming out;
And when they're come, the very pleasant rout:
The message certain to be done to-morrow.
'T is perhaps as well that it should be to borrow
Some precious book from out its snug retreat,   325
To cluster round it when we next shall meet.
Scarce can I scribble on; for lovely airs
Are fluttering round the room like doves in pairs;
Many delights of that glad day recalling,
When first my senses caught their tender falling.   330
And with these airs come forms of elegance
Stooping their shoulders o'er a horse's prance,
Careless, and grand—fingers soft and round
Parting luxuriant curls;—and the swift bound
Of Bacchus from his chariot, when his eye   335
Made Ariadne's cheek look blushingly.
Thus I remember all the pleasant flow
Of words at opening a portfolio.

Things such as these are ever harbingers
To trains of peaceful images: the stirs   340

Of a swan's neck unseen among the rushes :
A linnet starting all about the bushes :
A butterfly, with golden wings broad parted,
Nestling a rose, convuls'd as though it smarted
With over pleasure—many, many more,   345
Might I indulge at large in all my store
Of luxuries : yet I must not forget
Sleep, quiet with his poppy coronet :
For what there may be worthy in these rhymes
I partly owe to him : and thus, the chimes   350
Of friendly voices had just given place
To as sweet a silence, when I 'gan retrace
The pleasant day, upon a couch at ease.
It was a poet's house who keeps the keys
Of pleasure's temple.   Round about were hung   355
The glorious features of the bards who sung
In other ages—cold and sacred busts
Smiled at each other.   Happy he who trusts
To clear Futurity his darling fame !
Then there were fauns and satyrs taking aim   360
At swelling apples with a frisky leap
And reaching fingers, 'mid a luscious heap
Of vine-leaves.   Then there rose to view a fane
Of liny marble, and thereto a train
Of nymphs approaching fairly o'er the sward :   365
One, loveliest, holding her white hand toward
The dazzling sun-rise : two sisters sweet

---

(354) Hunt's house, no doubt ; for he it is who tells us in plain
prose (see Appendix) that the poem " originated in sleeping in a
room adorned with busts and pictures,"—"many a bust from Shout",
perhaps, as Shelley says in the *Letter to Maria Gisborne*. Mr.
Cowden Clarke says in *The Gentleman's Magazine* for February
1874, " It was in the library at Hunt's cottage, where an extempo-
rary bed had been made up for him on the sofa ".

Bending their graceful figures till they meet
Over the trippings of a little child :
And some are hearing, eagerly, the wild   370
Thrilling liquidity of dewy piping.
See, in another picture, nymphs are wiping
Cherishingly Diana's timorous limbs ;—
A fold of lawny mantle dabbling swims
At the bath's edge, and keeps a gentle motion   375
With the subsiding crystal : as when ocean
Heaves calmly its broad swelling smoothness o'er
Its rocky marge, and balances once more
The patient weeds ; that now unshent by foam
Feel all about their undulating home.   380

Sappho's meek head was there half smiling down
At nothing ; just as though the earnest frown
Of over thinking had that moment gone
From off her brow, and left her all alone.

Great Alfred's too, with anxious, pitying eyes,   385
As if he always listened to the sighs
Of the goaded world ; and Kosciusko's worn
By horrid suffrance—mightily forlorn.

Petrarch, outstepping from the shady green,
Starts at the sight of Laura ; nor can wean   390
His eyes from her sweet face.   Most happy they !
For over them was seen a free display
Of out-spread wings, and from between them shone
The face of Poesy : from off her throne
She overlook'd things that I scarce could tell.   395
The very sense of where I was might well
Keep Sleep aloof : but more than that there came
Thought after thought to nourish up the flame

Within my breast; so that the morning light
Surprised me even from a sleepless night;   400
And up I rose refresh'd, and glad, and gay,
Resolving to begin that very day
These lines ; and howsoever they be done,
I leave them as a father does his son.

ffinis.

The imprint of the 1817 volume of *Poems* is as follows :—

C. Richards, Printer, 18, Warwick-street, Golden-square, London.

ENDYMION:

A Romance.

ENDYMION:

A Poetic Romance.

BY JOHN KEATS.

"THE STRETCHED METRE OF AN ANTIQUE SONG."

LONDON:

PRINTED FOR TAYLOR AND HESSEY,

93, FLEET STREET.

1818.

[In Woodhouse's copy of *Endymion* (see Preface) there is a note against the passage "so I will begin" &c., line 39, Book I, to the effect that the poem was begun in the spring of 1817 and finished in the winter of 1817-18 ; and in the title-page he has inserted *April* before 1818. The statement corresponds with Keats's own record of May 1817 (see Letters) that he was busying himself at Margate with the commencement of *Endymion.* This reference cannot of course be to the same *Endymion* that he expected to finish in one more attack when he wrote to Clarke in December 1816. Probably the conception referred to by Lord Houghton (Aldine edition, page xvii) as "long germinating in his fancy" really took bodily form and sub-stance, and that substance was ,wholly rejected, when Keats came within the radius of Haydon's heroic art propaganda, for the design on an ambitious scale which the next Spring was to see in print. Woodhouse records that at the end of the first draft is written "Burford Bridge, Nov. 28, 1817". His statement as to the month of issue scarcely does more than confirm the record of the series of documents bearing on this point published by Lord Houghton. Thus, the first book was in the publisher's hands by January 1818, and the last was copied out by the 14th of March ; the original Pre-face, rejected upon the unfavourable verdict of Reynolds and others of Keats's friends, is dated the 19th of March ; the Preface as pub-lished is dated the 10th of April, and went, it seems, in a letter to Reynolds of that date ; and on the 27th of April Keats wrote to Taylor apologizing for giving him "all the trouble" of *Endymion,* and adding, apparently in allusion to that poem, " The book pleased me much. It is very free from faults ; and, although there are one or two words I should wish replaced, I see in many places an improve-ment greatly to the purpose". The measure of Keats's fluency in composition may be judged by observing the alterations recorded in Book I in the following pages. Of that Book there appears to have been but one manuscript, written on sheets of quarto foolscap paper, and considerably altered before going to press. The other three Books were written into a blank book and afterwards copied on quarto foolscap uniform with that used for Book I. Hence the printer's copy (the quarto manuscript) shows much more revision in Book I than elsewhere. With that manuscript I have collated the printed text throughout ; but the variations given in Books II, III, and IV as from the draft, I have taken from Woodhouse's manuscript annotations. The original edition of *Endymion* is a handsome octavo volume, originally issued in thick drab boards labelled at back, *Keats's Endymion. Lond. 1818,* and consisting of fly-title as here reproduced, but with imprint at foot of verso, "*Printed by T. Miller, Noble street, Cheapside"*, title-page (with its motto adapted from Shakespeare's seventeenth Sonnet), and dedication to Chatterton's memory, as given opposite, Preface pages vii to ix, an erratum leaf with sometimes one and sometimes five errata printed on recto, and 207 pages of text including the fly-titles to the four books as given in the present edition. The head-line throughout is *Endymion* in Roman small capitals, the number of the Book being indicated in smaller letters at the inner corners, and the pages in Arabic figures as usual at the outer corners. The full page consists of 22 lines; and the lines are numbered in tens in the margin; not every ten lines of verse, but every ten lines of print, so that when a fresh paragraph begins with a portion of a verse, that particular verse counts for two lines. In numbering the lines in fives I have of course counted by lines of verse.—H. B. F.]

PREFACE.

KNOWING within myself the manner in
which this Poem has been produced, it
is not without a feeling of regret that I
make it public.

What manner I mean, will be quite
clear to the reader, who must soon perceive great inexperience, immaturity,
and every error denoting a feverish attempt, rather than a deed accomplished.
The two first books, and indeed the two
last, I feel sensible are not of such completion as to warrant their passing the
press; nor should they if I thought a

year's castigation would do them any good ;—it will not : the foundations are too sandy. It is just that this youngster should die away : a sad thought for me, if I had not some hope that while it is dwindling I may be plotting, and fitting myself for verses fit to live.

This may be speaking too presumptuously, and may deserve a punishment : but no feeling man will be forward to inflict it : he will leave me alone, with the conviction that there is not a fiercer hell than the failure in a great object. This is not written with the least atom of purpose to forestall criticisms of course, but from the desire I have to conciliate men who are competent to look, and who do look with a zealous eye, to the honor of English literature.

The imagination of a boy is healthy, and the mature imagination of a man is healthy; but there is a space of life between, in which the soul is in a ferment, the character undecided, the way of life uncertain, the ambition thick-sighted: thence proceeds mawkishness, and all the thousand bitters which those men I speak of must necessarily taste in going over the following pages.

I hope I have not in too late a day touched the beautiful mythology of Greece, and dulled its brightness: for I wish to try once more,[1] before I bid it farewell.

Teignmouth,
April 10, 1818.

---

[1] Woodhouse notes—"This alluded to his then intention of writing a poem on the fall of Hyperion.   He commenced this poem: but, thanks to the critics who fell foul of *this* work, he discontinued it. The fragment was published in 1820."

ORIGINAL PREFACE &c., REJECTED
IN FAVOUR OF THE FOREGOING.[1]

In a great nation, the work of an individual is of so little importance; his pleadings and excuses are so uninteresting; his "way of life" such a nothing, that a Preface seems a sort of impertinent bow to strangers who care nothing about it.

A Preface, however, should be down in so many words; and such a one that by an eye-glance over the type the Reader may catch an idea of an Author's modesty, and non-opinion of himself—which I sincerely hope may be seen in the few lines I have to write, notwithstanding many proverbs of many ages old which men find a great pleasure in receiving as gospel.

About a twelvemonth since, I published a little book of verses; it was read by some dozen of my friends who lik'd it; and some dozen whom I was unacquainted with, who did not.

Now, when a dozen human beings are at words with another dozen, it becomes a matter of anxiety to side with one's friends—more especially when excited thereto

---

[1] Reprinted from Lord Houghton's *Life and Letters of John Keats*, 1867.

by a great love of Poetry. I fought under disadvantages.
Before I began I had no inward feel of being able to
finish ; and as I proceeded my steps were all uncertain. So
this Poem must rather be considered as an endeavour than
a thing accomplished ; a poor prologue to what, if I live,
I humbly hope to do. In duty to the Public I should
have kept it back for a year or two, knowing it to be so
faulty: but I really cannot do so,—by repetition my
favourite passages sound vapid in my ears, and I would
rather redeem myself with a new Poem should this one
be found of any interest.

I have to apologize to the lovers of simplicity for
touching the spell of loneliness that hung about Endymion ; if any of my lines plead for me with such people
I shall be proud.

It has been too much the fashion of late to consider
men bigoted and addicted to every word that may chance
to escape their lips ; now I here declare that I have not
any particular affection for any particular phrase, word, or
letter in the whole affair. I have written to please myself, and in hopes to please others, and for a love of fame ;
if I neither please myself, nor others, nor get fame, of
what consequence is Phraseology ?

I would fain escape the bickerings that all Works not
exactly in chime bring upon their begetters—but this is
not fair to expect, there must be conversation of some
sort and to object shows a man's consequence. In case
of a London drizzle or a Scotch mist, the following quotation from Marston may perhaps 'stead me as an um-
brella for an hour or so: "let it be the curtesy of my
peruser rather to pity my self-hindering labours than to
malice me."

One word more—for we cannot help seeing our own
affairs in every point of view—should any one call my

dedication to Chatterton affected I answer as followeth: "Were I dead, sir, I should like a Book dedicated to me."

TEIGNMOUTH,
March 19th, 1818.

[*Title-Page.*]

ENDYMION.

A ROMANCE.

BY JOHN KEATS.

" The stretched metre of an antique song."
Shakspeare's Sonnets.

INSCRIBED,

WITH EVERY FEELING OF PRIDE AND REGRET
AND WITH "A BOWED MIND,"

TO THE MEMORY OF

THE MOST ENGLISH OF POETS EXCEPT SHAKSPEARE,

THOMAS CHATTERTON.

ENDYMION.

BOOK I.

ENDYMION.

BOOK I.

A THING of beauty is a joy for ever: *Amen* '.
Its loveliness increases; it will never
Pass into nothingness; but still will keep
A bower quiet for us, and a sleep
Full of sweet dreams, and health, and quiet breathing. 5
Therefore, on every morrow, are we wreathing
A flowery band to bind us to the earth,

---

(1) The manuscript shows no variation in this renowned opening line; but Dr. B. W. Richardson tells me that his friend the late Mr. Henry Stephens of Finchley, who was a fellow student in medicine with Keats, and lived in the same rooms with him for a time, preserved the recollection of an earlier opening line. Keats is said to have written the line, presumably in some rough draft of his intended opening, thus—

A thing of beauty is a constant joy :

the tradition is that his friend, on hearing this, pronounced the opening line "a fine line, but wanting something", and that Keats pondered it over, and at length broke out with an inspired " I have it ", and set down the household word that now stands at the head of the poem.

Spite of despondence, of the inhuman dearth
Of noble natures, of the gloomy days,
Of all the unhealthy and o'er-darkened ways   10
Made for our searching : yes, in spite of all,
Some shape of beauty moves away the pall
From our dark spirits.   Such the sun, the moon,
Trees old, and young, sprouting a shady boon
For simple sheep ; and such are daffodils   15
With the green world they live in ; and clear rills
That for themselves a cooling covert make
'Gainst the hot season ; the mid forest brake,
Rich with a sprinkling of fair musk-rose blooms :
And such too is the grandeur of the dooms   20
We have imagined for the mighty dead ;
All lovely tales that we have heard or read :
An endless fountain of immortal drink,
Pouring unto us from the heaven's brink.

---

(9) In the manuscript, *ways* stands altered to *days.*

(13) Instead of line 13 there were originally three lines in the manuscript :

> From our dark Spirits, and before us dances
> Like glitter on the points of Arthur's Lances.
> Of these bright powers are the Sun, and Moon...

But before the manuscript went to press Keats's keen perception of fitness rejected the medieval allusion, and supplied the reading of the text.

(15) In the manuscript,
> of these are daffodils
> And the green world, &c.

(20) The manuscript reads—
> Of these too are the grandeur of the dooms...

(21) Compare Thomson's *Seasons* (*Winter*, line 432) :
> And hold high converse with the mighty dead.

(24) In the manuscript,
> Telling us we are on the heaven's brink.

Nor do we merely feel these essences   25
For one short hour; no, even as the trees
That whisper round a temple become soon
Dear as the temple's self, so does the moon,
The passion poesy, glories infinite,
Haunt us till they become a cheering light   30
Unto our souls, and bound to us so fast,
That, whether there be shine, or gloom o'ercast,
They alway must be with us, or we die. *(Wordsworth)*

Therefore, 'tis with full happiness that I
Will trace the story of Endymion.   35
The very music of the name has gone
Into my being, and each pleasant scene
Is growing fresh before me as the green
Of our own vallies: so I will begin
Now while I cannot hear the city's din;   40
Now while the early budders are just new,
And run in mazes of the youngest hue
About old forests; while the willow trails
Its delicate amber; and the dairy pails
Bring home increase of milk. And, as the year   45
Grows lush in juicy stalks, I'll smoothly steer
My little boat, for many quiet hours,
With streams that deepen freshly into bowers.
Many and many a verse I hope to write,
Before the daisies, vermeil rimm'd and white,   50

---

(29) In the manuscript,

     And passion, poetry, glories infinite, ...

(50) Keats originally wrote this word *vermil* both here and in line 696 of this Book. Whether he adopted it from Spenser or some other writer I know not; but in Spenser it is *vermell*: see *Faerie Queene*, Book II, Canto X, stanza 24.

Hide in deep herbage ; and ere yet the bees
Hum about globes of clover and sweet peas,
I must be near the middle of my story.
O may no wintry season, bare and hoary,
See it half finish'd : but let Autumn bold,   55
With universal tinge of sober gold,
Be all about me when I make an end. Ɣ꜀ ꜀ ꜀
And now at once, adventuresome, I send
My herald thought into a wilderness :
There let its trumpet blow, and quickly dress   60
My uncertain path with green, that I may speed
Easily onward, thorough flowers and weed.

   Upon the sides of Latmus was outspread
A mighty forest ; for the moist earth fed
So plenteously all weed-hidden roots   65
Into o'er-hanging boughs, and precious fruits.
And it had gloomy shades, sequestered deep,
Where no man went ; and if from shepherd's keep
A lamb stray'd far a-down those inmost glens,
Never again saw he the happy pens   70
Whither his brethren, bleating with content,
Over the hills at every nightfall went.
Among the shepherds, 'twas believed ever,
That not one fleecy lamb which thus did sever
From the white flock, but pass'd unworried   75
By angry wolf, or pard with prying head,
Until it came to some unfooted plains

---

(58) In the manuscript there is a comma after *now* and none
after *adventuresome*.
   (71) The manuscript reads *To which* for *Whither*.
   (74) In the manuscript, *fleecy* is altered to *fleecing*, which, in turn,
is altered back to *fleecy*.

Where fed the herds of <u>Pan</u>: aye great his gains
Who thus one lamb did lose.   Paths there were many,
Winding through palmy fern, and rushes fenny,   80
And ivy banks ; all leading pleasantly
To a wide lawn, whence one could only see
Stems thronging all around between the swell
Of turf and slanting branches : who could tell
The freshness of the space of heaven above,   85
Edg'd round with dark tree tops ? through which a dove
Would often beat its wings, and often too
A little cloud would move across the blue.

　　Full in the middle of this pleasantness
There stood a <u>marble altar</u>, with a tress   90
Of flowers budded newly ; and the dew
Had taken fairy phantasies to strew
Daisies upon the sacred sward last eve,
And so the dawned light in pomp receive.
For 'twas the morn : Apollo's upward fire   95
Made every eastern cloud a silvery pyre
Of brightness so unsully'd, that therein
A melancholy spirit well might win
Oblivion, and melt out his essence fine
Into the winds : rain-scented eglantine   100

---

(78) In the manuscript,
　　　　　　　　　　　　　　　　aye great his gains
　　　Who thus but one did lose.

The reading of the text is supplied, as an alternative, in pencil.
In the first edition *ay* is printed for *aye*.
　　(83) This line originally stood a foot short in the manuscript,
thus—
　　　Stems thronging round between the swell...

　　(94) Cancelled manuscript reading, *coming light* for *dawned light*.
　　(99) Cancelled manuscript reading, *pure* for *fine*.

Gave temperate sweets to that well-wooing sun ;
The lark was lost in him ; cold springs had run
To warm their chilliest bubbles in the grass ;
Man's voice was on the mountains ; and the mass
Of nature's lives and wonders puls'd tenfold,   105
To feel this sun-rise and its glories old.

Now while the silent workings of the dawn
Were busiest, into that self-same lawn
All suddenly, with joyful cries, there sped
A troop of little children garlanded ;   110
Who gathering round the altar, seem'd to pry
Earnestly round as wishing to espy
Some folk of holiday : nor had they waited
For many moments, ere their ears were sated
With a faint breath of music, which ev'n then   115
Fill'd out its voice, and di'd away again.
Within a little space again it gave
Its airy swellings, with a gentle wave,
To light-hung leaves, in smoothest echoes breaking
Through copse-clad vallies,—ere their death, o'ertaking
The surgy murmurs of the lonely sea.   121

And now, as deep into the wood as we
Might mark a lynx's eye, there glimmered light
Fair faces and a rush of garments white,

---

(107) In the manuscript, originally, *these silent workings*, altered
to *the*, seemingly in consequence of a marginal query in another
handwriting, but finally changed back again to *these*. I presume
Keats was eventually convinced that *these silent workings* might
seem to include man's voice on the mountains.

(115) In the manuscript the contraction for *even* is clearly *e'en*, not
ev'n as in the printed text.

(119) Cancelled manuscript reading, *and* for *in*.

Plainer and plainer showing, till at last   125
Into the widest alley they all past,
Making directly for the woodland altar.
O kindly muse! let not my weak tongue faulter
In telling of this goodly company,
Of their old piety, and of their glee: 130
But let a portion of ethereal dew   .
Fall on my head, and presently unmew -
My soul; that I may dare, in wayfaring,
To stammer where old Chaucer us'd to sing.

  Leading the way, young damsels danced along, 135
Bearing the burden of a shepherd song;

---

(125) The manuscript has *showing*, Keats's usual orthography, the first edition *shewing*.

(128) In the manuscript Keats had cancelled the whole of this invocation, sacrificing with it the lovely line 127; but the passage was finally restored by means of a pencilled *Stet*.

(132) The word *unmew*, in the sense of enfranchise, may probably be a relic of Shakespearean study. Compare *Romeo and Juliet*, Act III, Scene IV, line 11—

   To-night she is mew'd up to her heaviness.

(135) This and the next two lines exercised the poet's fastidious taste greatly. They stood originally thus :

   In front some pretty Damsels danced along,
   Bearing the Burden of a shepherd Song;
   And each with handy wicker over brimmed...

and even then he had begun to write *may day Song* instead of *shepherd Song*. Then there is an intermediate reading for line 135, before that of the text is supplied—

   And in the front young Damsels danced along,

while two rejected marginal readings for line 137 are—

   Each bringing a white wicker over brimmed
and
   Each brought a little wicker over brimmed.

Each having a white wicker over brimm'd
With April's tender younglings : next, well trimm'd,
A crowd of shepherds with as sunburnt looks
As may be read of in Arcadian books ;   140
Such as sat listening round Apollo's pipe,
When the great deity, for earth too ripe,
Let his divinity o'er-flowing die
In music, through the vales of Thessaly :
Some idly trail'd their sheep-hooks on the ground,   145
And some kept up a shrilly mellow sound
With ebon-tipped flutes : close after these,
Now coming from beneath the forest trees,
A venerable priest full soberly,
Begirt with ministring looks : alway his eye   150
Stedfast upon the matted turf he kept,
And after him his sacred vestments swept.
From his right hand there swung a vase, milk-white,
Of mingled wine, out-sparkling generous light ;

---

(144) A lovely allusion to the lovely story of Apollo's nine years'
sojourn on earth as the herdsman of Admetus, when banished
from Olympus for killing the Cyclops who had forged the thunder-
bolts wherewith Æsculapius had been slain.

(150) *Begirt with ministring looks* is perhaps somewhat licen-
tiously elliptical ; but there is no doubt that was what Keats wrote,
and I presume there can be none as to the meaning—surrounded
by people whose looks showed their eagerness to do their minister-
ing part.

(153) This couplet originally stood thus—

> From his right hand there swung a milk white vase
> Of mingled wines, outsparkling like the Stars—

the less vigorous reading of the text being evidently supplied to get
rid of the false rhyme. It is to be noted, however, that the bare
idea of rhyming *vase* and *stars* shows that Keats no longer pronounced *vase* as if it rhymed with *pace*, as at page 32 of this
volume.

And in his left he held a basket full   155
Of all sweet herbs that searching eye could cull :
Wild thyme, and valley-lillies whiter still
Than Leda's love, and cresses from the rill.
His aged head, crowned with beechen wreath,
Seem'd like a poll of ivy in the teeth   160
Of winter hoar.   Then came another crowd
Of shepherds, lifting in due time aloud
Their share of the ditty.   After them appear'd,
Up-followed by a multitude that rear'd
Their voices to the clouds, a fair wrought car,   165
Easily rolling so as scarce to mar
The freedom of three steeds of dapple brown :
Who stood therein did seem of great renown
Among the throng.   His youth was fully blown,
Showing like Ganymede to manhood grown ;   170
And, for those simple times, his garments were
A chieftain king's : beneath his breast, half bare,
Was hung a silver bugle, and between
His nervy knees there lay a boar-spear keen.
A smile was on his countenance ; he seem'd,   175
To common lookers on, like one who dream'd
Of idleness in groves Elysian :

---

(157) The motive of amending the rhyme was probably not the
only one for the next erasure.   Lines 157 and 158 were originally—

  Wild thyme, and valley lillies white as Leda's
  Bosom, and choicest strips from mountain Cedars.

Then *blossoms from the rill* has place in the manuscript before
the final *cresses from the rill* is supplied.   *Whiter than Leda's love*
(Jupiter in the form of a swan) is an obviously better comparison
than *white as Leda's bosom.*

  (163) In the manuscript, *o' the Ditty.*
  (168) In the manuscript, *sat* is here cancelled in favour of *stood.*
  (170) In the first edition *Shewing.*

But there were some who feelingly could scan
A lurking trouble in his nether lip,
And see that oftentimes the reins would slip   180
Through his forgotten hands : then would they sigh,
And think of yellow leaves, of owlets' cry,
Of logs pil'd solemnly.—Ah, well-a-day,
Why should our young ⟨Endymion⟩ pine away !

    Soon the assembly, in a circle rang'd,   185
Stood silent round the shrine : each look was chang'd
To sudden veneration : women meek
Beckon'd their sons to silence ; while each cheek
Of virgin bloom pal'd gently for slight fear.
Endymion too, without a forest peer,   190
Stood, wan, and pale, and with an awed face,
Among his brothers of the mountain chace.
In midst of all, the venerable priest
Ey'd them with joy from greatest to the least,
And, after lifting up his aged hands,   195
Thus spake he : " Men of Latmos ! shepherd bands !
Whose care it is to guard a thousand flocks :
Whether descended from beneath the rocks
That overtop your mountains ; whether come
From vallies where the pipe is never dumb ;   200
Or from your swelling downs, where sweet air stirs
Blue hare-bells lightly, and where prickly furze
Buds lavish gold ; or ye, whose precious charge
Nibble their fill at ocean's very marge,
Whose mellow reeds are touch'd with sounds forlorn 205

---

(191) Cancelled manuscript reading, *a bowed face* for *an awed face*.
(192) In the first edition *chase* here, though *chace* in line 532 of the same Book. The manuscript gives *chace* in both instances, as at page 34 of the present volume.

By the dim echoes of old Triton's horn:
Mothers and wives! who day by day prepare
The scrip with needments, for the mountain air;
And all ye gentle girls who foster up
Udderless lambs, and in a little cup   210
Will put choice honey for a favoured youth:
Yea, every one attend! for in good truth
Our vows are wanting to our great god Pan.
Are not our lowing heifers sleeker than
Night-swollen mushrooms? Are not our wide plains 215
Speckled with countless fleeces? Have not rains
Green'd over April's lap? No howling sad
Sickens our fearful ewes; and we have had
Great bounty from Endymion our lord.
The earth is glad: the merry lark has pour'd   220
His early song against yon breezy sky,
That spreads so clear o'er our solemnity."

---

(208) The writer in the *Quarterly Review* whom Shelley apostrophized as

> Thou noteless blot on a remembered name!

accused Keats of inventing (or as he put it "spawning") certain words, among which was *needments*. Had the "noteless blot's" reading extended far enough, he might have found this word in almost the same context in Spenser's *Faerie Queene* (Book I, Canto VI, stanza 35):

> and eke behind,
> His scrip did hang, in which his needments he did bind.

In Canto I of the same Book, stanza 6, the same word occurs in connexion with *bag* instead of *scrip*:

> Behind her farre away a Dwarfe did lag,
> That lazie seem'd in beeing euer last,
> Or wearied with bearing of her bag
> Of needments at his back.

Oddments and *needments* are not wholly obsolete even yet in some parts of England.

Thus ending, on the shrine he heap'd a spire
Of teeming sweets, enkindling sacred fire ;
Anon he stain'd the thick and spongy sod   225
With wine, in honor of the shepherd-god.
Now while the earth was drinking it, and while
Bay leaves were crackling in the fragrant pile,
And gummy frankincense was sparkling bright
'Neath smothering parsley, and a hazy light   230
Spread greyly eastward, thus a chorus sang :

"O THOU, whose mighty palace roof doth hang
From jagged trunks, and overshadoweth
Eternal whispers, glooms, the birth, life, death
Of unseen flowers in heavy peacefulness ;   235
Who lov'st to see the hamadryads dress
Their ruffled locks where meeting hazels darken ;
And through whole solemn hours dost sit, and hearken
The dreary melody of bedded reeds—
In desolate places, where dank moisture breeds   240
The pipy hemlock to strange overgrowth ;

---

(232) It was the Hymn to Pan beginning here that the young poet when engaged in the composition of *Endymion* was induced to recite in the presence of Wordsworth, on the 28th of December 1817, at Haydon's house. Leigh Hunt records that the elder poet pronounced it "a very pretty piece of paganism," though his own magnificent sonnet,

The world is too much with us,

shows that he was not always in a mood to contemn the poetic-imaginative aspects of nature open to "a Pagan suckled in a creed outworn." It is worth while to note in this connexion the coincidence between the couplet in the text, lines 205-6, and the end of that sonnet :

So might I, standing on this pleasant lea,
  Have glimpses that would make me less forlorn ;
Have sight of Proteus rising from the sea ;
  Or hear old Triton blow his wreathed horn.

Bethinking thee, how melancholy loth
Thou wast to lose fair Syrinx—do thou now,
By thy love's milky brow !
By all the trembling mazes that she ran,   245
Hear us, great Pan !

   " O thou, for whose soul-soothing quiet, turtles
Passion their voices cooingly 'mong myrtles,

---

(246) Cancelled manuscript reading—
> Listen great Pan !

The beautiful tale of Syrinx seems to have entered into Keats's
soul, and not unnaturally. Compare this with the tender passage,
> Telling us how fair, trembling Syrinx fled
> Arcadian Pan,

and so on (page 13 of the present volume), and above all with the
exquisite couplet
> Like the low voice of Syrinx, when she ran
> Into the forests from Arcadian Pan

in the rejected passage of Book II, which was published in *The Indicator*. See note after line 853, Book II.

(248) The verb to passion is another of the words which the
" noteless blot " in the *Quarterly Review* accused Keats of inventing. Spenser, as we have seen, was a sealed book to him ; so that
it is not strange he ignored the passage in *The Faerie Queene*
(Book II, Canto IX, stanza 41),
> Great wonder had the knight to see the maid
> So strangely passioned.

But Shakespeare seems to have been a sealed book too, at all
events during those seasons in which he took the liberty accorded
by Shelley of spilling the overflowing venom from his fangs : otherwise he might have discovered such passages as
> Madam, 'twas Ariadne passioning
> For Theseus' perjury and unjust flight ;
> *Two Gentlemen of Verona*, Act IV, Scene IV, lines 172-3.
> And shall not myself . . . passion as they
>   *Tempest*, Act V, Scene I, lines 22-4.
> Dumbly she passions, franticly she doteth
>   *Venus and Adonis*, line 1059.

What time thou wanderest at eventide
Through sunny meadows, that outskirt the side   250
Of thine enmossed realms : O thou, to whom
Broad leaved fig trees even now foredoom   *·
Their ripen'd fruitage ; yellow girted bees
Their golden honeycombs ; our village leas
Their fairest blossom'd beans and poppied corn ;   255
The chuckling linnet its five young unborn,
To sing for thee ; low creeping strawberries
Their summer coolness ; pent up butterflies
Their freckled wings ; yea, the fresh budding year
All its completions—be quickly near,   260
By every wind that nods the mountain pine,
O forester divine !

  " Thou, to whom every faun and satyr flies
For willing service ; whether to surprise
The squatted hare while in half sleeping fit ;   265
Or upward ragged precipices flit
To save poor lambkins from the eagle's maw ;
Or by mysterious enticement draw
Bewildered shepherds to their path again ;
Or to tread breathless round the frothy main,   270
And gather up all fancifullest shells
For thee to tumble into Naiads' cells,
And, being hidden, laugh at their out-peeping ;
Or to delight thee with fantastic leaping,
The while they pelt each other on the crown   275
With silvery oak apples, and fir cones brown—

---

(263) In the manuscript and in the first edition we read *fawn*
for *faun*.
  (272) Cancelled manuscript reading—
        To tumble them into fair Naiads Cells.

By all the echoes that about thee ring,
Hear us, O satyr king!

"O Hearkener to the loud clapping shears,
While ever and anon to his shorn peers　　　280
A ram goes bleating: Winder of the horn,
When snouted wild-boars routing tender corn
Anger our huntsmen: Breather round our farms,
To keep off mildews, and all weather harms:
Strange ministrant of undescribed sounds,　　　285
That come a swooning over hollow grounds,
And wither drearily on barren moors:
Dread opener of the mysterious doors
Leading to universal knowledge—see,
Great son of Dryope,　　　290
The many that are come to pay their vows
With leaves about their brows!

"Be still the unimaginable lodge
For solitary thinkings; such as dodge
Conception to the very bourne of heaven,　　　295
Then leave the naked brain: be still the leaven,
That spreading in this dull and clodded earth
Gives it a touch ethereal—a new birth:
Be still a symbol of immensity;
A firmament reflected in a sea;　　　300

---

(283) The manuscript reads *Huntsmen*, the first edition *huntsman*; but it is most unlikely that Keats made this slight change in a wrong direction.

(290) Of the various parentages assigned to Pan by the ancients Keats seems to have preferred the Homeric.

(293) The quotation-marks here and at the close of the hymn are not in the first edition, nor in the manuscript; but they are in the corrected copy.

An element filling the space between ;
An unknown—but no more : we humbly screen
With uplift hands our foreheads, lowly bending,
And giving out a shout most heaven rending,
Conjure thee to receive our humble Pæan,   305
Upon thy Mount Lycean ! "

Even while they brought the burden to a close,
A shout from the whole multitude arose,
That lingered in the air like dying rolls
Of abrupt thunder, when Ionian shoals   310
Of dolphins bob their noses through the brine.
Meantime, on shady levels, mossy fine,
Young companies nimbly began dancing
To the swift treble pipe, and humming string.
Aye, those fair living forms swam heavenly   315
To tunes forgotten—out of memory :
Fair creatures ! whose young childrens' children bred
Thermopylæ its heroes—not yet dead,
But in old marbles ever beautiful.
High genitors, unconscious did they cull   320
Time's sweet first-fruits—they danc'd to weariness,

---

(307) The contraction *E'en* is in the manuscript ; but the first edition reads *Even*.

(311) The verb to *bob* seems to have been considered open to question : *push* and *raise* stand as marginal suggestions in the manuscript.

(313) The accentuation of the final syllable of dancing is not a piece of original licentiousness, but a reminiscence of a rhythmical way of Spenser's : compare *Faerie Queene*, Book II, Canto VII, stanza 23—

> The hateful messengers of heavy things,
> Of death and dolor telling sad tidings.

(315) The manuscript shows a marginal suggestion of *mov'd* for *swam* here.

(319) Doubtless meant to refer specially to the Elgin marbles.

And then in quiet circles did they press
The hillock turf, and caught the latter end
Of some strange history, potent to send
A young mind from its bodily tenement.   325
Or they might watch the quoit-pitchers, intent
On either side ; pitying the sad death
Of Hyacinthus, when the cruel breath
Of Zephyr slew him,—Zephyr penitent,
Who now, ere Phœbus mounts the firmament,   330
Fondles the flower amid the sobbing rain.
The archers too, upon a wider plain,
Beside the feathery whizzing of the shaft,
And the dull twanging bowstring, and the raft
Branch down sweeping from a tall ash top,   335
Call'd up a thousand thoughts to envelope
Those who would watch.   Perhaps, the trembling knee
And frantic gape of lonely Niobe,
Poor, lonely Niobe ! when her lovely young
Were dead and gone, and her caressing tongue   340
Lay a lost thing upon her paly lip,
And very, very deadliness did nip
Her motherly cheeks.   Arous'd from this sad mood
By one, who at a distance loud halloo'd,
Uplifting his strong bow into the air,   345
Many might after brighter visions stare :
After the Argonauts, in blind amaze

---

(335) The manuscript gives no help to this somewhat ailing line.
It stands there precisely as in Keats's printed text. It seems more
likely that he meant the heavy monosyllable *Branch* to do duty for
a whole foot or time-beat than that he accidentally let drop the
second syllable of *downward* for example.

(339) This line is punctuated as in Keats's edition : the manuscript gives no stops whatever in it.

(347) The reference here is to the passage from the second Book

Tossing about on Neptune's restless ways,
Until, from the horizon's vaulted side,
There shot a golden splendour far and wide,   350
Spangling those million poutings of the brine
With quivering ore : 'twas even an awful shine
From the exaltation of Apollo's bow ;
A heavenly beacon in their dreary woe.
Who thus were ripe for high contemplating,   355
Might turn their steps towards the sober ring
Where sat Endymion and the aged priest
'Mong shepherds gone in eld, whose looks increas'd
The silvery setting of their mortal star.
There they discours'd upon the fragile bar   360
That keeps us from our homes ethereal ;
And what our duties there : to nightly call
Vesper, the beauty-crest of summer weather ;

---

of the *Argonautica* of Apollonius Rhodius, beginning at verse 674
(τοῖσι δὲ Λητοῦς υἰὸς, κ.τ.λ.), which Shelley had in mind when (Prose
Works, Volume III, page 56) he alluded to the Apollo "so finely
described by Apollonius Rhodius when the dazzling radiance of his
beautiful limbs suddenly shone over the dark Euxine."

> Right glorious before their wondering sight
> Appeared the child of Leto, travelling swift
> From Libya northwards to the boundless realms
> Of men that dwell beyond the northern wind.
> The bright curls clustered round about his cheeks
> Like streaming gold : he bore a silver bow
> In his left hand, and o'er his shoulder slung
> A quiver : and beneath his feet divine
> The island trembled, and great waves came up
> Out of the sea and broke upon the shore.

The passage has been kindly rendered for me as above by Mr.
R. C. Day, who has thus saved me the necessity of giving it in
prose or in the stiff and not very accurate rendering of Green or
one of the still poorer translators of Apollonius Rhodius.

   (352) In Keats's edition *even* is here printed in full ; but in the
manuscript it is contracted to *e'en*.

To summon all the downiest clouds together
For the sun's purple couch ; to emulate   365
In ministring the potent rule of fate
With speed of fire-tail'd exhalations ;
To tint her pallid cheek with bloom, who cons
Sweet poesy by moonlight : besides these,
A world of other unguess'd offices.   370
Anon they wander'd, by divine converse,
Into Elysium ; vieing to rehearse
Each one his own anticipated bliss.
One felt heart-certain that he could not miss
His quick gone love, among fair blossom'd boughs, 375
Where every zephyr-sigh pouts, and endows
Her lips with music for the welcoming.
Another wish'd, mid that eternal spring,
To meet his rosy child, with feathery sails,
Sweeping, eye-earnestly, through almond vales :   380
Who, suddenly, should stoop through the smooth wind,
And with the balmiest leaves his temples bind ;
And, ever after, through those regions be
His messenger, his little Mercury.
Some were athirst in soul to see again   385
Their fellow huntsmen o'er the wide champaign
In times long past ; to sit with them, and talk
Of all the chances in their earthly walk ;
Comparing, joyfully, their plenteous stores
Of happiness, to when upon the moors,   390
Benighted, close they huddled from the cold,
And shar'd their famish'd scrips.   Thus all out-told
Their fond imaginations,—saving him

---

(368) In the manuscript, *pretty cheek*, with *pallid* and *waning* as
marginal alternatives.
(386) In the manuscript, *campaign*.
(389) Cancelled manuscript reading, *present* for *plenteous*.

Whose eyelids curtain'd up their jewels dim,
Endymion : yet hourly had he striven   395
To hide the cankering venom, that had riven
His fainting recollections.   Now indeed
His senses had swoon'd off: he did not heed
The sudden silence, or the whispers low,
Or the old eyes dissolving at his woe,   400
Or anxious calls, or close of trembling palms,
Or maiden's sigh, that grief itself embalms :
But in the self-same fixed trance he kept,
Like one who on the earth had never stept.
Aye, even as dead-still as a marble man,   405
Frozen in that old tale Arabian.

(405-6) There are several episodes in *The Thousand and One* ·
Nights that might possibly be cited in connexion with this couplet ;
but there can hardly be any reasonable doubt that the allusion is
to the tale generally associated with the name of Zobeide, its nar-
rator,—that is to say the Eldest Lady's Story in *The Porter and the
Three Ladies of Baghdad*. Although the story is almost too well
known for an extract to be needed, English scholars have yet to
desire a version of *The Thousand and One Nights* at once complete, scholarly, and characteristic in language. No apology is
therefore necessary for inserting the following extract from a version
on a sumptuous scale, by Mr. John Payne, now mainly in manuscript, but in course of private issue by subscription :
"We sailed days and nights, till the captain missed the true
course and the ship went astray with us and entered a sea other
than that we aimed at.   We knew not of this awhile and the wind
blew fair for us ten days, at the end of which time the look-out man
ascended to the mast-head to look out and cried 'Good news !'
Then he came down, rejoicing, and said 'I see a city afar off, as
it were a dove.' At this we rejoiced, and before an hour of the day
was past, the city appeared to us in the distance. So we said to the
captain 'What is the name of the city to which we are drawing
near ?' 'By Allah,' replied he, 'I know not, for I have never before seen it, nor have I ever sailed this sea in my life ! But, since
the affair has ended in safety, nought remains for you but to land
and display your goods, and if an opportunity offer sell or barter

Who whispers him so pantingly and close?
Peona, his sweet sister: of all those,
His friends, the dearest.   Hushing signs she made,
And breath'd a sister's sorrow to persuade   410
A yielding up, a cradling on her care.

---

as may be; but if the occasion serve not, we will rest here two days, then re-victual and depart.' So we entered the harbour and the captain landed and was absent awhile, after which he returned to us and said 'Arise go up into the city and marvel at God's dealings with His creatures and seek refuge from His wrath.' So we went up to the city and saw at the gate men with staves in their hands; but when we drew near them, behold, they had been stricken by the wrath of God and were become stones! Then we entered and found all the town-folk changed into black stones; there was not a live soul left therein, no, not a blower of the fire. At this we were confounded and traversed the streets and markets, where we found the merchandise and gold and silver exposed in their places, and rejoiced saying 'Doubtless, there is some mystery in this.' Then we all dispersed about the streets of the city, distracted each from his fellow by the lust of gain and the stuffs and riches; whilst I went up to the citadel and found it rare and skilful in fashion. I entered the king's palace, where I found all the vessels of gold and silver and saw the king himself seated in the midst of his chamberlains and lieutenants and viziers, and clad in raiment that amazed the wit. As I drew near him, I saw that he was seated on a throne inlaid with pearls and jewels, and arrayed in a robe of cloth of gold embroidered with jewels, each one of which shone like a star, whilst there stood about him fifty white slaves, dressed in various kinds of silks and bearing drawn swords in their hands. I was struck with amazement at the sight, but went on and entered the saloon of the harem, whose walls were covered with hangings of silk, striped with gold. Here I found the queen lying on a couch and clad in a robe covered with fresh pearls. On her head was a crown diademed with divers sorts of jewels, and round her neck collars and necklaces. All her apparel and ornaments were unchanged, but she herself had been smitten of God, and was a black stone."

In line 406 the manuscript shows a cancelled reading, *Sitting* for *Frozen*; and immediately after this line the following passage is obliterated in favour of what now stand as lines 407 to 412:

Her eloquence did breathe away the curse :
She led him, like some midnight spirit nurse
Of happy changes in emphatic dreams,
Along a path between two little streams,—   415
Guarding his forehead, with her round elbow,
From low-grown branches, and his footsteps slow
From stumbling over stumps and hillocks small ;
Until they came to where these steamlets fall,
With mingled bubblings and a gentle rush,   420
Into a river, clear, brimful, and flush
With crystal mocking of the trees and sky.
A little shallop, floating there hard by,
Pointed its beak over the fringed bank ;
And soon it lightly dipt, and rose, and sank,   425
And dipt again, with the young couple's weight,—
Peona guiding, through the water straight,
Towards a bowery island opposite ;
Which gaining presently, she steered light

  Now happily, there sitting on the grass
  Was fair Peona, a most tender Lass,
  And his sweet sister ; who, uprising, went
  With stifled sobs, and o'er his shoulder leant.
  Putting her trembling hand against his cheek
  She said : ' My dear Endymion, let us seek
  A pleasant bower where thou may'st rest apart,
  And ease in slumber thine afflicted heart :
  Come my own dearest brother : these our friends
  Will joy in thinking thou dost sleep where bends
  Our freshening River through yon birchen grove :
  Do come now !' Could he gainsay her who strove,
  So soothingly, to breathe away a Curse ?

Sweet and tender as this passage is, no one will doubt the excellence of the self-criticism which led to the substitution of the six
exquisite lines now standing in place of it ; but it was a sad mis-
carriage of fine intention that, in making the change, the poet left
line 411 rhymeless.

Into a shady, fresh, and ripply cove,   430
Where nested was an arbour, overwove
By many a summer's silent fingering ;
To whose cool bosom she was us'd to bring
Her playmates, with their needle broidery,
And minstrel memories of times gone by.   435

      So she was gently glad to see him laid
Under her favourite bower's quiet shade,
On her own couch, new made of flower leaves,
Dry'd carefully on the cooler side of sheaves
When last the sun his autumn tresses shook,   440
And the tann'd harvesters rich armfuls took.
Soon was he quieted to slumbrous rest :
But, ere it crept upon him, he had prest

---

(432) In the manuscript, *With* is here struck out in favour of *By*.

(440) Keats has here sacrificed, no doubt properly, a very pretty picture, consisting of eleven lines struck out of the manuscript. The whole passage originally stood thus :

On her own couch, new made of flower leaves,
Dry'd carefully on the cooler side of sheaves
When last the Harvesters rich armfuls took.
She tied a little bucket to a Crook,
Ran some swift paces to a dark wells side,
And in a sighing-time return'd, supplied
With spar cold water ; in which she did squeeze
A snowy napkin, and upon her knees
Began to cherish her poor Brother's face ;
Damping refreshfully his forehead's space,
His eyes, his Lips : then in a cupped shell
She brought him ruby wine ; then let him smell,
Time after time, a precious amulet,
Which seldom took she from its cabinet.
Thus was he quieted to slumbrous rest :

In supplying the couplet that now stands for this cancelled passage, Keats altered the initial *And* of line 441 to *While*, and back again to *And*.

Peona's busy hand against his lips,
And still, a sleeping, held her finger-tips   445
In tender pressure.   And as a willow keeps
A patient watch over the stream that creeps
Windingly by it, so the quiet maid
Held her in peace : so that a whispering blade *or to autumn.*
Of grass, a wailful gnat, a bee bustling   *or*   450
Down in the blue-bells, or a wren light rustling
Among sere leaves and twigs, might all be heard.

    O magic sleep ! O comfortable bird,
That broodest o'er the troubled sea of the mind
Till it is hush'd and smooth ! O unconfin'd   455
Restraint ! imprisoned liberty ! great key
To golden palaces, strange minstrelsy,
Fountains grotesque, new trees, bespangled caves,
Echoing grottos, full of tumbling waves
And moonlight ; aye, to all the mazy world   460
Of silvery enchantment !—who, upfurl'd
Beneath thy drowsy wing a triple hour,
But renovates and lives ?—Thus, in the bower,
Endymion was calm'd to life again.
Opening his eyelids with a healthier brain,   465

(450-1) The manuscript corresponds with the printed text in regard to this couplet ; but the *or* in line 451 was an afterthought.
Perhaps Keats meant to remedy in the same way line 450, and read
or a bee bustling ; but the roughness of metre may have been intentional.   The licence of framing a couplet so that a rhyming dissyllable must be accentuated on the second syllable in one line and
on the first in the other should have been intolerable to his exquisite and cultivated ear ; but this was of course no innovation of his :
he must have met with it over and over again in his studies of
earlier English poets.
    (454) The manuscript reads *o' the mind* for *of the mind.*

He said : " I feel this thine endearing love
All through my bosom : thou art as a dove
Trembling its closed eyes and sleeked wings
About me; and the pearliest dew not brings
Such morning incense from the fields of May,   470
As do those brighter drops that twinkling stray
From those kind eyes,—the very home and haunt
Of sisterly affection.   Can I want
Aught else, aught nearer heaven, than such tears ?
Yet dry them up, in bidding hence all fears   475
That, any longer, I will pass my days
Alone and sad.   No, I will once more raise
My voice upon the mountain-heights ; once more
Make my horn parley from their foreheads hoar :
Again my trooping hounds their tongues shall loll   480
Around the breathed boar : again I'll poll
The fair-grown yew tree, for a chosen bow :

---

(466) This line is the remnant of five which originally stood for it in the manuscript :

> A cheerfuller resignment, and a smile
> For his fair Sister flowing like the Nile
> Through all the channels of her piety,
> He said : ' Dear Maid, may I this moment die,
> If I feel not this thine endearing Love...

(470) In the manuscript, line 469 was originally followed by the three lines—

> From woodbine hedges such a morning feel,
> As do those brighter drops, that twinkling steal
> Through those pressed lashes, from the blossom'd plant...

which Keats rejected for the three lines in the text. In line 472 he had altered *those* to *thy* in pencil ; and it is at least probable that the adoption of *those* in the printed text was an oversight.

(480) Compare Thomson's *Seasons*, *Winter*, lines 816-17 :—

>   the trooping deer
> Sleep on the new fallen snow.

And, when the pleasant sun is getting low,
Again I'll linger in a sloping mead
To hear the speckled thrushes, and see feed   485
Our idle sheep. So be thou cheered sweet,
And, if thy lute is here, softly intreat
My soul to keep in its resolved course."

    Hereat Peona, in their silver source,
Shut her pure sorrow drops with glad exclaim,   490
And took a lute, from which there pulsing came
A lively prelude, fashioning the way
In which her voice should wander. 'Twas a lay
More subtle cadenced, more forest wild
Than Dryope's lone lulling of her child ;   495
And nothing since has floated in the air
So mournful strange. Surely some influence rare
Went, spiritual, through the damsel's hand ;
For still, with Delphic emphasis, she spann'd
The quick invisible strings, even though she saw   500
Endymion's spirit melt away and thaw

    (494-5) This couplet is marginally substituted in the manuscript
for the following six lines :

        More forest-wild, more subtle-cadenced
        Than can be told by mortal : even wed
        The fainting tenors of a thousand shells
        To a million whisperings of Lilly bells ;
        And mingle too the Nightingale's complain
        Caught in its hundredth echo ; 'twould be vain :...

Strikingly characteristic as this is of the ruling mood of Keats,
one cannot regret the liberality of rejection which threw it aside for
the incomparable reference to Pan's mother in the couplet of the
text. It is just conceivable that the passage given in the foot-note
to line 853 of Book II was a part of the original conception of this
episode, but hardly probable.

    (496) In the manuscript, this line begins with *For*, *And* being
jotted as a suggestion in the margin.

Before the deep intoxication. 502

But soon she came, with sudden burst, upon

Her self-possession—swung the lute aside,

---

(502) The use of this word *intoxication* as a full five-syllable word accented on the final syllable, and a similar use of many words terminating in *ion*, has been a topic of frequent censure with Keats's critics ; but I presume no one at the present day needs to be told that this was merely another Elizabethan licence reproduced. Here is one of many instances from Shakespeare (*Romeo and Juliet,* Act III, Scene V, line 29) :

> Some say the lark makes sweet division,

and one from Spenser (*Faerie Queene,* Book III, Canto VIII, stanza I) :

> Lo oft as I this history record
> My heart doth melt with meere compassion,
> To think how causelesse, of her owne accord,
> This gentle damzell whom I write upon,
> Should plonged be in such affliction...

Spenser, indeed, availed himself so often and so unsparingly of this facile way of rhyming and scanning that it may well have happened that Keats's ardent admiration for the elder poet led him to think even this a beauty to be imitated. Here are fourteen consecutive lines in *The Faerie Queene* (Book III, Canto VI, stanzas 8 and 9), which would be considered very deficient in executive invention nowadays :

> Miraculous may seeme to him that reades
> So straunge ensample of conception ;
> But reason teacheth that the fruitfull seades
> Of all things living, through impression
> Of the sunbeames in moyst complexion,
> Doe life conceiue and quickned are by kynd :
> So, after Nilus inundation,
> Infinite shapes of creatures men doe fynd
> Informed in the mud on which the Sunne hath shynd.

> Great father he of generation
> Is rightly cald, th' authour of life and light ;
> And his faire sister for creation
> Ministreth matter fit, which tempered right
> With heate and humour, breedes the living wight.

And earnestly said : " Brother, 'tis vain to hide   505
That thou dost know of things mysterious,
Immortal, starry ; such alone could thus
Weigh down thy nature.   Hast thou sinn'd in aught
Offensive to the heavenly powers ? Caught
A Paphian dove upon a message sent ?   510
Thy deathful bow against some deer-herd bent,
Sacred to Dian ? Haply, thou hast seen
Her naked limbs among the alders green ;
And that, alas ! is death.   No, I can trace
Something more high perplexing in thy face ! "   515

   Endymion look'd at her, and press'd her hand,
And said, " Art thou so pale, who wast so bland
And merry in our meadows ? How is this ?

-----

(513) Cancelled manuscript reading, *on flags and rushes* for *among
the alders.*

(514) Compare *Romeo and Juliet*, Act II, Scene II, line 64 :

    And the place death, considering who thou art.

(515) This speech of Peona's was originally much longer : the
manuscript shows the following lines, struck out for the reading of
the text :

    And I do pray thee by thy utmost aim
    To tell me all.   No little fault or blame
    Canst thou lay on me for a teasing Girl ;
    Ever as an unfathomable pearl
    Has been thy secrecy to me : but now
    I needs must hunger after it, and vow
    To be its jealous Guardian for aye.

      Uttering these words she got nigh and more nigh,
    And put at last her arms about his neck :
    Nor was there any   , ungentle check,
    Nor any frown, or stir dissatisfied,
    But smooth compliance, and a tender slide
    Of arm in arm, and what is written next.

     ' Doubtless, Peona, thou hast been perplex'd,
    And pained oft in thinking of the change...

Tell me thine ailment : tell me all amiss !—
Ah ! thou hast been unhappy at the change   520
Wrought suddenly in me. What indeed more strange ?
Or more complete to overwhelm surmise ?
Ambition is no sluggard : 'tis no prize,
That toiling years would put within my grasp,
That I have sigh'd for : with so deadly gasp   525
No man e'er panted for a mortal love.
So all have set my heavier grief above
These things which happen.   Rightly have they done :
I, who still saw the horizontal sun
Heave his broad shoulder o'er the edge of the world, 530
Out-facing Lucifer, and then had hurl'd
My spear aloft, as signal for the chace—
I, who, for very sport of heart, would race
With my own steed from Araby ; pluck down
A vulture from his towery perching ; frown   535
A lion into growling, loth retire—
To lose, at once, all my toil breeding fire,
And sink thus low ! but I will ease my breast
Of secret grief, here in this bowery nest.

---

(530) In the manuscript we read *o' the world* for *of the world*.
Compare Thomson, *Winter*, lines 780-1,

> the horizontal sun,
> Broad o'er the south, hangs at his utmost noon.

(531) The last of the stars to disappear before the rising sun.
Ovid says (*Metamorphoses*, Book II, verses 114-15),

> Diffugiunt stellæ ; quarum agmina cogit
> Lucifer, et cœli statione novissimus exit.

(536) In the manuscript, *grumbling* is cancelled for *growling*.
(539) This couplet is substituted in the manuscript for the erased
couplet—

> And come to such a Ghost as I am now !
> But listen, Sister, I will tell the how.

Probably *the* was meant for *thee* ; but perhaps not.

"This river does not see the naked sky,   540
Till it begins to progress silverly
Around the western border of the wood,
Whence, from a certain spot, its winding flood
Seems at the distance like a crescent moon :
And in that nook, the very pride of June,   545
Had I been us'd to pass my weary eves ;
The rather for the sun unwilling leaves
So dear a picture of his sovereign power,
And I could witness his most kingly hour,
When he doth tighten up the golden reins,   550
And paces leisurely down amber plains
His snorting four.   Now when his chariot last
Its beams against the zodiac-lion cast,
There blossom'd suddenly a magic bed
Of sacred ditamy, and poppies red :   555

---

(545) Instead of this and the following line, the manuscript
originally had six lines—

> And in this spot the most endowing boon
> Of balmy air, sweet blooms, and coverts fresh
> Has been outshed ; yes, all that could enmesh
> Our human senses—make us fealty sware
> To gadding Flora.   In this grateful lair
> Have I been used to pass my weary eaves ;

and before these lines were cancelled they evidently gave Keats
much anxiety.   In the first of them *this* was altered to *that* : the
second and third he worked upon in pencil, transposing and erasing ;
but the intention is not now to be made out : *sware* in the fourth
stands presumably for *swear* : in the fifth *gadding Flora* is struck
through in pencil, while *In* is changed to *To* and back again to *In*.

(550) In the first edition, *lighten* for *tighten*.

(555) In the manuscript and in the first edition we read *ditamy*.
I have not succeeded in finding the orthography elsewhere ; but I
see no reason for doubting that Keats met with it somewhere and
preferred it to *dittany*.   In Philemon Holland's Pliny, where it might
have been expected to occur, I can find no more English equivalent

At which I wondered greatly, knowing well
That but one night had wrought this flowery spell ;
And, sitting down close by, began to muse
What it might mean.   Perhaps, thought I, Morpheus,
In passing here, his owlet pinions shook ;   560
Or, it may be, ere matron Night uptook
Her ebon urn, young Mercury, by stealth,
Had dipt his rod in it : such garland wealth
Came not by common growth.   Thus on I thought,
Until my head was dizzy and distraught.   565
Moreover, through the dancing poppies stole
A breeze, most softly lulling to my soul ;
And shaping visions all about my sight
Of colours, wings, and bursts of spangly light ;
The which became more strange, and strange, and dim,
And then were gulph'd in a tumultuous swim :   571
And then I fell asleep.   Ah, can I tell
The enchantment that afterwards befel ?
Yet it was but a dream : yet such a dream
That never tongue, although it overteem   575
With mellow utterance, like a cavern spring,
Could figure out and to conception bring
All I beheld and felt.   Methought I lay

---

for *dictamnus* than *dictamne*; but it is worth noting that three
modern languages drop the *n* and not the *m*—thus, Italian *dittamo*,
Spanish *dictamo*, and French *dictame* ; and in times when spelling
was more or less optional some classical English writer may well
have done the same.

(561) This line first stood in the manuscript thus—

> Or it may be that, ere still Night uptook...

(573) This line is given as in the manuscript and in Keats's
edition.   That its haltness was felt is perhaps indicated by the fact
that something has been written over it in pencil and rubbed out
again.   I suppose we are to accentuate *enchantment* on the first
syllable.

Watching the zenith, where the milky way
Among the stars in virgin splendour pours ; 580
And travelling my eye, until the doors
Of heaven appear'd to open for my flight,
I became loth and fearful to alight
From such high soaring by a downward glance :
So kept me stedfast in that airy trance, 585
Spreading imaginary pinions wide.
When, presently, the stars began to glide,
And faint away, before my eager view :
At which I sigh'd that I could not pursue,
And dropt my vision to the horizon's verge ; 590
And lo ! from opening clouds, I saw emerge
The loveliest moon, that ever silver'd o'er
A shell for Neptune's goblet : she did soar
So passionately bright, my dazzled soul
Commingling with her argent spheres did roll 595
Through clear and cloudy, even when she went
At last into a dark and vapoury tent—
Whereat, methought, the lidless-eyed train
Of planets all were in the blue again.
To commune with those orbs, once more I rais'd 600
My sight right upward : but it was quite daz'd
By a bright something, sailing down apace,
Making me quickly veil my eyes and face :

---

(582) Cancelled manuscript reading *seemed* for *appear'd*.

(596) Compare Thomson's *Seasons, Spring*, line 332,

  From clear to cloudy tossed.

(599) Cancelled manuscript reading, *were all*, for *all were*.

(600-1) This couplet stood thus in the manuscript originally—

  And to commune with them once more I rais'd
  My eyes right upward : but they were quite dazed...

but it is altered to correspond with the printed text.

Again I look'd, and, O ye deities,
Who from Olympus watch our destinies! 605
Whence that completed form of all completeness?
Whence came that high perfection of all sweetness?
Speak, stubborn earth, and tell me where, O where
Hast thou a symbol of her golden hair?
Not oat-sheaves drooping in the western sun; 610
Not—thy soft hand, fair sister! let me shun
Such follying before thee—yet she had,
Indeed, locks bright enough to make me mad;
And they were simply gordian'd up and braided,
Leaving, in naked comeliness, unshaded, 615
Her pearl round ears, white neck, and orbed brow;
The which were blended in, I know not how,
With such a paradise of lips and eyes,
Blush-tinted cheeks, half smiles, and faintest sighs,
That, when I think thereon, my spirit clings 620
And plays about its fancy, till the stings
Of human neighbourhood envenom all.
Unto what awful power shall I call?
To what high fane?—Ah! see her hovering feet,
More bluely vein'd, more soft, more whitely sweet 625
Than those of sea-born Venus, when she rose
From out her cradle shell. The wind out-blows
Her scarf into a fluttering pavillion;
'Tis blue, and over-spangled with a million
Of little eyes, as though thou wert to shed, 630

---

(621) In the manuscript, *fawns* is here struck out and *plays* inserted.

(624) This transition into the present and seeming-actual as Endymion relates the vision that seems to him such a desperate reality may perhaps be selected as one of the things of highest imaginative value in the poem.

(630) Cancelled manuscript reading, *wast* for *wert*.

Over the darkest, lushest blue-bell bed,
Handfuls of daisies."—" Endymion, how strange !
Dream within dream !"—" She took an airy range,
And then, towards me, like a very maid,
Came blushing, waning, willing, and afraid,   635
And press'd me by the hand : Ah ! 'twas too much ;
Methought I fainted at the charmed touch,
Yet held my recollection, even as one
Who dives three fathoms where the waters run
Gurgling in beds of coral: for anon,   640
I felt upmounted in that region
Where falling stars dart their artillery forth,
And eagles struggle with the buffeting north
That ballances the heavy meteor-stone ;—
Felt too, I was not fearful, nor alone,   645
But lapp'd and lull'd along the dangerous sky.
Soon, as it seem'd, we left our journeying high,
And straightway into frightful eddies swoop'd ;
Such as aye muster where grey time has scoop'd
Huge dens and caverns in a mountain's side :   650
There hollow sounds arous'd me, and I sigh'd
To faint once more by looking on my bliss—

---

(632) Cancelled manuscript reading, *bud-stars* for *daisies*.

(638) In this instance the contracted form *e'en* was deliberately altered to *even* in the manuscript. It is *even* in the first edition.

(641) See note to verse 502.

(646) This line stood differently in the manuscript at first, and was followed by two others, now struck out,—thus :

> But lapp'd and lull'd in safe deliriousness ;
> Sleepy with deep foretasting, that did bless
> My Soul from Madness, 'twas such certainty.

(648) Cancelled manuscript reading, *fearful* for *frightful*.

(649) The manuscript reads *aye*, the first edition *ay*.

(651) In this line the more violent expression *died* is judiciously superseded by *sigh'd*.

I was distracted ; madly did I kiss
The wooing arms which held me, and did give
My eyes at once to death: but 'twas to live,   655
To take in draughts of life from the gold fount
Of kind and passionate looks ; to count, and count
The moments, by some greedy help that seem'd
A second self, that each might be redeem'd
And plunder'd of its load of blessedness.   660
Ah, desperate mortal ! I e'en dar'd to press
Her very cheek against my crowned lip,
And, at that moment, felt my body dip
Into a warmer air: a moment more,
Our feet were soft in flowers.   There was store   665

----

(661) In the manuscript, *e'en*, not *ev'n* as in the first edition. The manuscript should rule here, because the presence of the *v* upsets the rhythm.

(662) In the manuscript, *cheeks*, with the *s* struck out.

(665) After *flowers* in this line occurs the following cancelled passage in the manuscript :—

Hurry o'er

O sacrilegious tongue the——best be dumb ;
For should one little accent from thee come
On such a daring theme, all other sounds
Would sicken at it, as would beaten hounds
Scare the elysian Nightingales.

Between these obliterated lines is a chaos of rubbed-out pencillings, of which the sense is so far recoverable that we can safely call them trial lines, and not a continuous passage.   Two fresh starts are made in place of *Hurry o'er*, namely *Sounds past o'er* and *Standing o'er*.   Then there is the whole line

Mingling the whispering of Lily Bells

and then

Came little faintest

Past being substituted for *Came* in the margin : then comes again the variant

Mingled with whisperings of Lily Bells...

Finally in supplying marginally the reading of the text, *There were*

Of newest joys upon that alp.   Sometimes
A scent of violets, and blossoming limes,
Loiter'd around us ; then of honey cells,
Made delicate from all white-flower bells ;
And once, above the edges of our nest,   670
An arch face peep'd,—an Oread as I guess'd.

      "Why did I dream that sleep o'er-power'd me
In midst of all this heaven ?   Why not see,
Far off, the shadows of his pinions dark,
And stare them from me ?   But no, like a spark   675
That needs must die, although its little beam
Reflects upon a diamond, my sweet dream
Fell into nothing—into stupid sleep.
And so it was, until a gentle creep,
A careful moving caught my waking ears,   680
And up I started : Ah ! my sighs, my tears,
My clenched hands ;—for lo ! the poppies hung
Dew-dabbled on their stalks, the ouzel sung
A heavy ditty, and the sullen day
Had chidden herald Hesperus away,   685
With leaden looks : the solitary breeze
Bluster'd, and slept, and its wild self did teaze
With wayward melancholy ; and I thought,
Mark me, Peona ! that sometimes it brought
Faint fare-thee-wells, and sigh-shrilled adieus !—   690
Away I wander'd—all the pleasant hues

---

stores was altered to *There was store.*   The use of *alp* in the singular as a common noun, though unusual, is not peculiar to Keats.
Milton has it in *Paradise Lost*, Book II, line 620—

          O'er many a fiery many a frozen Alp ;

and in *Samson Agonistes*, line 628—

          Nor breath of vernal air from snowy Alp.

Of heaven and earth had faded: deepest shades
Were deepest dungeons; heaths and sunny glades
Were full of pestilent light; our taintless rills
Seem'd sooty, and o'er-spread with upturn'd gills 695
Of dying fish; the vermeil rose had blown
In frightful scarlet, and its thorns out-grown
Like spiked aloe. If an innocent bird
Before my heedless footsteps stirr'd, and stirr'd
In little journeys, I beheld in it 700
A disguis'd demon, missioned to knit
My soul with under darkness; to entice
My stumblings down some monstrous precipice:
Therefore I eager followed, and did curse
The disappointment. Time, that aged nurse, 705
Rock'd me to patience. Now, thank gentle heaven!
These things, with all their comfortings, are given
To my down-sunken hours, and with thee,
Sweet sister, help to stem the ebbing sea
Of weary life." .

    Thus ended he, and both 710
Sat silent: for the maid was very loth
To answer; feeling well that breathed words
Would all be lost, unheard, and vain as swords
Against the enchased crocodile, or leaps
Of grasshoppers against the sun. She weeps, 715
And wonders; struggles to devise some blame;
To put on such a look as would say, *Shame*
On this poor weakness! but, for all her strife,
She could as soon have crush'd away the life
From a sick dove. At length, to break the pause, 720

---

(719) Compare Thomson's *Seasons*, *Winter*, line 374—
 And crushed out lives, by secret barbarous ways.

She said with trembling chance : " Is this the cause ?
This all ? Yet it is strange, and sad, alas !
That one who through this middle earth should pass
Most like a sojourning demi-god, and leave
His name upon the harp-string, should achieve   725
No higher bard than simple maidenhood,
Singing alone, and fearfully,—how the blood
Left his young cheek ; and how he us'd to stray
He knew not where ; and how he would say, *nay*,
If any said 'twas love : and yet 'twas love ;   730
What could it be but love ? How a ring-dove
Let fall a sprig of yew tree in his path ;
And how he di'd : and then, that love doth scathe,
The gentle heart, as northern blasts do roses ;
And then the ballad of his sad life closes   735
With sighs, and an alas !—Endymion !
Be rather in the trumpet's mouth,—anon
Among the winds at large—that all may hearken !
Although, before the crystal heavens darken,
I watch and dote upon the silver lakes   740

---

(722) There is a rejected passage here in the manuscript, which
stands thus :—

> This all ?   Yet it is wonderful—exceeding—
> And yet a shallow dream, for ever breeding
> Tempestuous Weather in that very Soul
> That should be twice content, twice smooth, twice whole,
> As is a double Peach.   'Tis sad Alas !

In altering this for the reading of the text Keats left the line thus,
short by a foot,

> This all ?   Yet it is sad Alas !

The words *strange and* seem to have been put in in proof.

(727) The adjective *young* before *blood* is struck out in the manuscript.

(739) *What though* is here altered in the manuscript to *Although*.

Pictur'd in western cloudiness, that takes
The semblance of gold rocks and bright gold sands,
Islands, and creeks, and amber-fretted strands
With horses prancing o'er them, palaces
And towers of amethyst,—would I so teaze   745
My pleasant days, because I could not mount
Into those regions ? The Morphean fount
Of that fine element that visions, dreams,
And fitful whims of sleep are made of, streams
Into its airy channels with so subtle,   750
So thin a breathing, not the spider's shuttle,
Circled a million times within the space
Of a swallow's nest-door, could delay a trace,
A tinting of its quality : how light   754
Must dreams themselves be ; seeing they're more slight
Than the mere nothing that engenders them !
Then wherefore sully the entrusted gem
Of high and noble life with thoughts so sick ?
Why pierce high-fronted honour to the quick
For nothing but a dream ? " Hereat the youth   760
Look'd up : a conflicting of shame and ruth
Was in his plaited brow : yet, his eyelids
Widened a little, as when Zephyr bids
A little breeze to creep between the fans

(741) In the manuscript, *Pight among* was the first reading here,
then *Pight amid*, and finally *Pictur'd in.*

(747) *That* altered to *The* in the manuscript before *Morphean.*

(756) In the manuscript, *nothingness engendring* for *nothing that
engenders.*

(761) Apparently *conflicting* is meant to be accented on the first
syllable in this place.

(762) In the manuscript *pleated* for *plaited.*

(764) The word *breeze* does not occur here in the manuscript,
which gives *Breath*, that word being written over *Puff*, struck out.

Of careless butterflies : amid his pains   765
He seem'd to taste a drop of manna-dew,
Full palatable ; and a colour grew
Upon his cheek, while thus he lifeful spake.

" Peona ! ever have I long'd to slake
My thirst for the world's praises : nothing base,   770
No merely slumberous phantasm, could unlace
The stubborn canvas for my voyage prepar'd—
Though now 'tis tatter'd ; leaving my bark bar'd
And sullenly drifting : yet my higher hope
Is of too wide, too rainbow-large a scope,   775
To fret at myriads of earthly wrecks.

The expression *fans*, though a little whimsical, is a rich and happy .
designation of the wings of butterflies.

(770) The present Laureate owes to a mere accident this prece-
dent for the term he applies to the coinage of his predecessor—

Of him who uttered nothing base.

In the manuscript the finals of this couplet were originally *mean*
and *unseam* ; and Keats seems to have discovered that those words
do not rhyme, before parting with the manuscript.

(776) The original lines in the manuscript at this point are—

To fret at myriads of earthly wrecks.
Wherein lies happiness?   In that which becks
Our ready minds to blending pleasureable :
And that delight is the most treasureable
That makes the richest Alchymy.   Behold
The clear Religion of Heaven !   Fold
A Rose leaf &c.

This appears to have been next altered to

To fret at sight of this world's losses.   For behold
Wherein lies happiness Peona.   Fold
A Rose leaf &c.

But the words *at sight* are separately cancelled, as if that line had
been set to rights before the whole passage was struck out, and the
six lines of the printed text supplied in the margin.   The reading of

Wherein lies happiness ? In that which becks
Our ready minds to fellowship divine,
A fellowship with essence ; till we shine,
Full alchemiz'd, and free of space.   Behold   780
The clear religion of heaven ! Fold
A rose leaf round thy finger's taperness,
And soothe thy lips : hist, when the airy stress
Of music's kiss impregnates the free winds,
And with a sympathetic touch unbinds   785
Æolian magic from their lucid wombs :
Then old songs waken from enclouded tombs ;
Old ditties sigh above their father's grave ;
Ghosts of melodious prophecyings rave
Round every spot where trod Apollo's foot ;   790
Bronze clarions awake, and faintly bruit,
Where long ago a giant battle was ;
And, from the turf, a lullaby doth pass
In every place where infant Orpheus slept.
Feel we these things ?—that moment have we stept   795
Into a sort of oneness, and our state

the text was supplied in a letter from Keats to Taylor bearing the
postmark "Hampstead, 30 Jan. 1818"; but in that letter line 781
reads
      The clear religion of Heaven—Peona ! fold...

As to the pronunciation of *religion* as four full syllables, see note to
line 502.
  (785) Cancelled line in the manuscript

      And, sympathetically, unconfines

struck out doubtless on account of the false rhyme.
  (786) *Eolian* in the first edition.
  (790) In the manuscript *trod* is substituted for *touch'd*. The first
edition has *were* in place of *where* ; but it is *where* in the manuscript.
  (794) In the manuscript, *spot* is struck out in favour of *place*.
  (796) Unhappily the manuscript gives no trace of the line which

Is like a floating spirit's.   But there are
Richer entanglements, enthralments far
More self-destroying, leading, by degrees,
To the chief intensity : the crown of these   800
Is made of love and friendship, and sits high
Upon the forehead of humanity.
All its more ponderous and bulky worth
Is friendship, whence there ever issues forth
A steady splendour ; but at the tip-top,   805
There hangs by unseen film, an orbed drop
Of light, and that is love : its influence,
Thrown in our eyes, genders a novel sense,
At which we start and fret ; till in the end,
Melting into its radiance, we blend,   810
Mingle, and so become a part of it,—
Nor with aught else can our souls interknit
So wingedly : when we combine therewith,
Life's self is nourish'd by its proper pith,
And we are nurtured like a pelican brood.   815
Aye, so delicious is the unsating food,
That men, who might have tower'd in the van
Of all the congregated world, to fan
And winnow from the coming step of time
All chaff of custom, wipe away all slime   820
Left by men-slugs and human serpentry,
Have been content to let occasion die,
Whilst they did sleep in love's elysium.
And, truly, I would rather be struck dumb,

---

may well have disappeared in transcription and left this one rhymeless.
    (813) In the manuscript, *amalgamate* originally stood in the
place of *combine*.
    (823) Cancelled manuscript reading, *Whiles* for *Whilst*.

Than speak against this ardent listlessness :   825
For I have ever thought that it might bless ·
The world with benefits unknowingly;
As does the nightingale, upperched high,
And cloister'd among cool and bunched leaves—
She sings but to her love, nor e'er conceives   830
How tiptoe Night holds back her dark-grey hood.
Just so may love, although 'tis understood
The mere commingling of passionate breath,
Produce more than our searching witnesseth :
What I know not : but who, of men, can tell   835
That flowers would bloom, or that green fruit would
    swell
To melting pulp, that fish would have bright mail,
The earth its dower of river, wood, and vale,
The meadows runnels, runnels pebble-stones,
The seed its harvest, or the lute its tones,   840
Tones ravishment, or ravishment its sweet
If human souls did never kiss and greet ?

  " Now, if this earthly love has power to make
Men's being mortal, immortal ; to shake
Ambition from their memories, and brim   845
Their measure of content ; what merest whim,
Seems all this poor endeavour after fame,
To one, who keeps within his stedfast aim
A love immortal, an immortal too.

---

  (844) *Man's* instead of *Men's* in the manuscript, but there is an *e*
pencilled over the *a* as if for consideration.
  (847) This line originally began with *Shews*,—altered in the manuscript to *Seems*.
  (849) In the manuscript thus—

            A Love immortal, and immortal too.

The *im* of the first *immortal* is underlined in pencil and the word

Look not so wilder'd ; for these things are true,   850
And never can be born of atomies
That buzz about our slumbers, like brain-flies,
Leaving us fancy-sick.   No, no, I'm sure,
My restless spirit never could endure
To brood so long upon one luxury,   855
Unless it did, though fearfully, espy
A hope beyond the shadow of a dream.
My sayings will the less obscured seem,
When I have told thee how my waking sight
Has made me scruple whether that same night   860
Was pass'd in dreaming.   Hearken, sweet Peona !
Beyond the matron-temple of Latona,
Which we should see but for these darkening boughs,
Lies a deep hollow, from whose ragged brows
Bushes and trees do lean all round athwart,   865
And meet so nearly, that with wings outraught,
And spreaded tail, a vulture could not glide
Past them, but he must brush on every side.
Some moulder'd steps lead into this cool cell,
Far as the slabbed margin of a well,   870
Whose patient level peeps its crystal eye
Right upward, through the bushes, to the sky.

---

both pencilled over ; but it is not clear whether the writing is
Keats's.   In his edition we have *an* for *and*, which appears to be
the right reading, though from the bewilderment of Peona we may
presume that Keats saw his meaning was not very clear.   The
argument seems to be, if a mere earthly love has power to remove
ambition, how much more unworthy an object must fame seem to
him who cherishes an undying love for an immortal being.

(862) Cancelled manuscript reading, *Behind the little Temple.*

(867) The word *spreaded*, notwithstanding the objections of *The
Quarterly Review*, was used again in *Hyperion*, Book I,

> And now, from forth the gloom their plumes immense
> Rose one by one, till all outspreaded were ;...

Oft have I brought thee flowers, on their stalks set
Like vestal primroses, but dark velvet
Edges them round, and they have golden pits :   875
'Twas there I got them, from the gaps and slits
In a mossy stone, that sometimes was my seat,
When all above was faint with mid-day heat.
And there in strife no burning thoughts to heed,
I'd bubble up the water through a reed ;   880
So reaching back to boy-hood : make me ships
Of moulted feathers, touchwood, alder chips,
With leaves stuck in them ; and the Neptune be
Of their petty ocean.   Oftener, heavily,
When love-lorn hours had left me less a child,   885
I sat contemplating the figures wild
Of o'er-head clouds melting the mirror through.
Upon a day, while thus I watch'd, by flew
A cloudy Cupid, with his bow and quiver ;
So plainly character'd, no breeze would shiver   890
The happy chance : so happy, I was fain
To follow it upon the open plain,
And, therefore, was just going ; when, behold !
A wonder, fair as any I have told—
The same bright face I tasted in my sleep,   895
Smiling in the clear well.   My heart did leap

---

(896) This and the following line take the place of twenty which
originally stood in the manuscript.   They are as follows :

> In the green opening smiling. Gods that keep,
> Mercifully, a little strength of heart
> Unkill'd in us by raving, pang and smart ;
> And do preserve it like a lilly root,
> That, in another spring, it may outshoot
> From its wintry prison ; let this hour go
> Drawling along its heavy weight of woe
> And leave me living ! 'Tis not more than need—
> Your veriest help. Ah ! how long did I feed

Through the cool depth.—It mov'd as if to flee—
I started up, when lo! refreshfully,
There came upon my face, in plenteous showers,
Dew-drops, and dewy buds, and leaves, and flowers,   900
Wrapping all objects from my smothered sight,
Bathing my spirit in a new delight.
Aye, such a breathless honey-feel of bliss
Alone preserv'd me from the drear abyss
Of death, for the fair form had gone again.   905
Pleasure is oft a visitant; but pain
Clings cruelly to us, like the gnawing sloth
On the deer's tender haunches: late, and loth,
'Tis scar'd away by slow returning pleasure.
How sickening, how dark the dreadful leisure   910
Of weary days, made deeper exquisite,

> On that crystalline life of Portraiture !
> How hover'd breathless at the tender lure !
> How many times dimpled the watery glass
> With maddest kisses ; and, till they did pass
> And leave the liquid smooth again, how mad !
> O 'twas as if the absolute sisters had
> My Life into the compass of a Nut
> Or all my breathing   and shut
> To a scanty straw.   To look above I fear'd
> Lest my hot eyeballs might be burnt and sear'd
> By a blank naught.   It moved as if to flee—

The first few words of this passage were, intermediately, altered to
Deep in the clear water smiling; and before the two lines of the
printed text appear in the margin we have the trial line

> Was there ⎫ reflected.   How my heart did leap...
> I saw   ⎭

and Keats first wrote *Down* instead of *Through* as the initial word
of line 897.   The only line in the cancelled twenty of which there
are two readings is

> How hover'd breathless at the tender lure !

which is altered to

> How long I hover'd round the tender lure !

By a fore-knowledge of unslumbrous night!
Like sorrow came upon me, heavier still,
Than when I wander'd from the poppy hill:
And a whole age of lingering moments crept   915
Sluggishly by, ere more contentment swept
Away at once the deadly yellow spleen.
Yes, thrice have I this fair enchantment seen;
Once more been tortured with renewed life.
When last the wintry gusts gave over strife   920
With the conquering sun of spring, and left the skies
Warm and serene, but yet with moistened eyes
In pity of the shatter'd infant buds,—
That time thou didst adorn, with amber studs,
My hunting cap, because I laugh'd and smil'd,   925
Chatted with thee, and many days exil'd
All torment from my breast;—'twas even then,
Straying about, yet, coop'd up in the den
Of helpless discontent,—hurling my lance
From place to place, and following at chance,   930
At last, by hap, through some young trees it struck,
And, plashing among bedded pebbles, stuck
In the middle of a brook,—whose silver ramble
Down twenty little falls, through reeds and bramble,
Tracing along, it brought me to a cave,   935
Whence it ran brightly forth, and white did lave
The nether sides of mossy stones and rock,—
'Mong which it gurgled blythe adieus, to mock
Its own sweet grief at parting. Overhead,
Hung a lush screen of drooping weeds, and spread   940

---

(915) Cancelled manuscript reading, *pass'd* for *crept*.
(926) Cancelled manuscript reading, *beguil'd* for *exil'd*.
(933) In the manuscript, the words *In the* are here contracted to *I' th'*.
(940) The misprint of the first edition, *scene* for *screen*, is corrected

Thick, as to curtain up some wood-nymph's home.
"Ah! impious mortal, whither do I roam?"
Said I, low voic'd: "Ah, whither! 'Tis the grot
"Of Proserpine, when Hell, obscure and hot,
"Doth her resign; and where her tender hands   945
"She dabbles, on the cool and sluicy sands:
"Or 'tis the cell of Echo, where she sits,
"And babbles thorough silence, till her wits
"Are gone in tender madness, and anon,
"Faints into sleep, with many a dying tone   950
"Of sadness.   O that she would take my vows,
"And breathe them sighingly among the boughs,
"To sue her gentle ears for whose fair head,
"Daily, I pluck sweet flowerets from their bed,
"And weave them dyingly—send honey-whispers   955
"Round every leaf, that all those gentle lispers
"May sigh my love unto her pitying!
"O charitable echo! hear, and sing
"This ditty to her!—tell her"—so I stay'd
My foolish tongue, and listening, half afraid,   960
Stood stupefied with my own empty folly,
And blushing for the freaks of melancholy.
Salt tears were coming, when I heard my name
Most fondly lipp'd, and then these accents came:

---

in the copy in my possession.   The printer was not much to blame,
for in the manuscript the word is *screne*, an orthography, by the bye,
which the manuscript again shows in Book III, line 425.

(960) In the manuscript, *listening* is contracted to *list'ning*.

(964) There is a cancelled passage here in the manuscript after
Most fondly lipp'd, thus—
                    I kept me still—it came
          Again in passionatest syllables,
          And thus again that voice's tender swells:

and there is another rejected reading of one line—

          Again in passionate syllables: saying:...

"Endymion! the cave is secreter   965
"Than the isle of Delos.   Echo hence shall stir
"No sighs but sigh-warm kisses, or light noise
"Of thy combing hand, the while it travelling cloys
"And trembles through my labyrinthine hair."
At that oppress'd I hurried in.—Ah! where   970
Are those swift moments?   Whither are they fled?
I'll smile no more, Peona; nor will wed
Sorrow the way to death; but patiently
Bear up against it: so farewel, sad sigh;
And come instead demurest meditation,   975
To occupy me wholly, and to fashion
My pilgrimage for the world's dusky brink.
No more will I count over, link by link,
My chain of grief: no longer strive to find
A half-forgetfulness in mountain wind   980
Blustering about my ears: aye, thou shalt see,
Dearest of sisters, what my life shall be;
What a calm round of hours shall make my days.
There is a paly flame of hope that plays
Where'er I look: but yet, I'll say 'tis naught—   985
And here I bid it die.   Have not I caught,
Already, a more healthy countenance?
By this the sun is setting; we may chance
Meet some of our near-dwellers with my car."

This said, he rose, faint-smiling like a star   990
Through autumn mists, and took Peona's hand:
They stept into the boat, and launch'd from land.

---

(969) In the manuscript *labyrinthian* for *labyrinthine.*
(970) The words *At that oppress'd I hurried in* are struck out of
the manuscript, though restored by a *Stet*, and in the margin we have
Since then I never and *I never saw her Beauty more,* both cancelled.
(990) Cancelled manuscript reading, *At this* for *This said.*

ENDYMION.

BOOK II.

ENDYMION.

BOOK II.

O SOVEREIGN power of love! O grief! O balm!
All records, saving thine, come cool, and calm,
And shadowy, through the mist of passed years:
For others, good or bad, hatred and tears
Have become indolent; but touching thine,   5
One sigh doth echo, one poor sob doth pine,
One kiss brings honey-dew from buried days.

---

(1) From this point the various readings are from two separate
manuscripts, as explained in the note at page 107 of this volume. It
is to be understood that, when the word *manuscript* alone is used,
the reading is from the finished copy sent to the press, and that the
term *draft* refers to the copy of the last three Books which was
written into a blank book before being fairly transcribed for the
printer.

(5) The draft reads *but O! for thine* instead of *but touching
thine.*

(7) In the draft, *sends* for *brings.* Compare this line with the
following from Shakespeare—

Enjoy the honey-heavy dew of slumber
(*Julius Cæsar*, Act II, Scene I, line 230);

The woes of Troy, towers smothering o'er their blaze,
Stiff-holden shields, far-piercing spears, keen blades,
Struggling, and blood, and shrieks—all dimly fades   10
Into some backward corner of the brain ;
Yet, in our very souls, we feel amain
The close of Troilus and Cressid sweet.
Hence, pageant history ! hence, gilded cheat !
Swart planet in the universe of deeds !   15
Wide sea, that one continuous murmur breeds
Along the pebbled shore of memory !
Many old rotten-timber'd boats there be
Upon thy vaporous bosom, magnifi'd
To goodly vessels ; many a sail of pride,   20
And golden keel'd, is left unlaunch'd and dry.
But wherefore this ? What care, though owl did fly

A thousand honey secrets shalt thou know :
                    (*Venus and Adonis*, line 16) ;
and with the memorable line in Coleridge's *Kubla Khan*,

    For he on honey-dew hath fed.

(8) The draft reads *crashing* for *smothering* ; and in the next
line *far-reaching spears, clear blades.*
(13-14) In the draft this couplet was written—

    The close of Troilus and Cressida.
    Hence pageant history ! away proud star.

In the final manuscript there is a cancelled reading of line 14,

    Away pageant History ! away proud dull feat.

A doubt appears to have been entertained as to the precise value of
close in this couplet ; for Woodhouse, who, be it observed, dates his
interleaved copy " Nov. 24, 1818," records that he has "learned
that the author meant *embrace.*" He says " This allusion I appre-
hend is to Chaucer's, and not to Shakespeare's work under this
title." But I incline to think the reference more likely to be to
Shakespeare's, albeit both were among Keats's reading.
(19) The rejected reading *misty* for *vaporous* has place in the
draft ; and the finished manuscript reads *vap'rous*, contracted.

About the great Athenian admiral's mast?
What care, though striding Alexander past
The Indus with his Macedonian numbers?   25
Though old Ulysses tortured from his slumbers
The glutted Cyclops, what care?—Juliet leaning
Amid her window-flowers,—sighing,—weaning
Tenderly her fancy from its maiden snow,
Doth more avail than these: the silver flow   30
Of Hero's tears, the swoon of Imogen,
Fair Pastorella in the bandit's den,
Are things to brood on with more ardency
Than the death-day of empires.   Fearfully
Must such conviction come upon his head,   35
Who, thus far, discontent, has dar'd to tread,
Without one muse's smile, or kind behest,
The path of love and poesy.   But rest,

(27-30) In the draft the following lines are cancelled for the
reading of the text :

                    Juliet leans
          Amid her window flowers, sighs,—and as she weans
          Her maiden thoughts from their young firstling snow,
          What sorrows from the melting whiteness grow.

And there is another cancelled reading of line 29,

          Tenderly from their first young snow her maiden breast.

(31) The reference is of course not to the story of Hero and
Leander but to the tears of Hero in *Much Ado about Nothing*, shed
when she was falsely accused; and Imogen must, equally of course,
be Shakespeare's heroine in *Cymbeline*, though she is not the only
Imogen of fiction who has swooned. For Pastorella see *Faerie
Queene*, Book VI, Canto II, stanza I et seq.

(34) The original reading in the draft is—

          Than the death of Empires. How fearfully...

(36) Rejected reading from the draft, *halt and lame* for *discontent*.

(38) The draft affords here a curious comment on the precise
value of the word *rest* as employed on this occasion. What was

In chaffing restlessness, is yet more drear
Than to be crush'd, in striving to uprear   40
Love's standard on the battlements of song.
So once more days and nights aid me along,
Like legion'd soldiers.

                   Brain-sick shepherd prince,
What promise hast thou faithful guarded since
The day of sacrifice? Or, have new sorrows   45
Come with the constant dawn upon thy morrows?
Alas! 'tis his old grief. For many days,
Has he been wandering in uncertain ways :
Through wilderness, and woods of mossed oaks ;
Counting his woe-worn minutes, by the strokes   50
Of the lone woodcutter ; and listening still,

---

originally written was *To rest In chaffing discontent.* Though the
verb *to rest* is a common equivalent for *to remain*, the noun *rest*
has usually a sense of recuperation after labour ; but its meaning
here is probably, considering how it came here, merely inactivity,
without the recuperative *arrière pensée.* The final manuscript and
the printed book both perpetuate the word *chaffing* for *chafing.*
Spenser spells the word with two *f*'s, but with a *u* also, thus (*Faerie
Queene*, Book VI, Canto II, stanza 21) :

    After long search and chauff he turned backe.

(43) In the draft *sturdy* was originally written in the place of
legion'd ; and in the finished manuscript is the cancelled reading
Fainting for *Brain-sick.* Through counting this broken line as
two, the printer numbered line 49 as 50 in the first edition, thus
throwing out the whole of the numbering to the end of Book II ;
and the metrical numbering is further falsified in two similar instances further on.

(44) See the promises recorded in lines 477 *et seq.* and 978 *et seq.*
of Book I.

(49) The words *brittle mossed oaks* occur in the draft for *woods of
mossed oaks.*

(51) Cancelled reading in the draft *distant,* and in the manuscript
lonely, for *lone.*

Hour after hour, to each lush-leav'd rill.
Now he is sitting by a shady spring,
And elbow-deep with feverous fingering
Stems the upbursting cold : a wild rose tree   55
Pavillions him in bloom, and he doth see
A bud which snares his fancy : lo ! but now
He plucks it, dips its stalk in the water : how !
It swells, it buds, it flowers beneath his sight ;
And, in the middle, there is softly pight   60
A golden butterfly ; upon whose wings
There must be surely character'd strange things,
For with wide eye he wonders, and smiles oft.

Lightly this little herald flew aloft,
Follow'd by glad Endymion's clasped hands :   65
Onward it flies.   From languor's sullen bands
His limbs are loos'd, and eager, on he hies
Dazzled to trace it in the sunny skies.

---

(52) This line is precisely according to the manuscript and the
first edition, so that there can be no doubt the word *hour* is to be
scanned first as one syllable and then as two.

(53) *E'en now he's* occurs in the draft in place of *Now he is*.

(56) The draft gives the reading *Bends lightly over him* for
Pavillions him in bloom.

(57) In the draft, *takes* for *snares*.

(58) In the manuscript, *in* was originally contracted to *i'*; but *in*
is inserted as a correction.

(59) Cancelled manuscript reading, *blooms* for *flowers*.

(60) The original reading of the draft was *in its middle*. The
word *pight* (for *pitched*), occurs in *Troilus and Cressida* (V, 10),
Lear (II, 1), and Spenser's *Faerie Queene*, Book III, Canto VII,
stanza 41,—

> Or on the marble Pillour that is pight
> Upon the top of Mount Olympus hight,...

(67-68) The draft gives two rejected readings of this couplet—

It seem'd he flew, the way so easy was ;
And like a new-born spirit did he pass   70
Through the green evening quiet in the sun,
O'er many a heath, through many a woodland dun,
Through buried paths, where sleepy twilight dreams
The summer time away.   One track unseams
A wooded cleft, and, far away, the blue   75
Of ocean fades upon him ; then, anew,
He sinks adown a solitary glen,
Where there was never sound of mortal men,
Saving, perhaps, some snow-light cadences
Melting to silence, when upon the breeze   80
Some holy bark let forth an anthem sweet,
To cheer itself to Delphi.   Still his feet
Went swift beneath the merry-winged guide,
Until it reach'd a splashing fountain's side
That, near a cavern's mouth, for ever pour'd   85
Unto the temperate air : then high it soar'd,
And, downward, suddenly began to dip,

       His limbs are loos'd, and eagerly he paces
       With nimble feet beneath its airy traces—
and
       His limbs are loos'd, and eagerly he traces
       With nimble footsteps all its airy paces.

(69) The draft reads *path* for *way*.
(75) The original reading of the draft is *Thro' woody cleft*.
(80) The draft has *Thawing* in place of *Melting*.
(83) This line was written in the draft—

    Went swift beneath the flutter-loving guide...

The expression *flutter-loving* was struck out; but nothing was substituted till the reading of the text was supplied in the finished
manuscript, in which, in the next line, *he* was originally where *it*
now stands.

    (86) The draft reads *whereat it soar'd*, and begins the next line
with *Then* instead of *And*.

As if, athirst with so much toil, 'twould sip
The crystal spout-head : so it did, with touch
Most delicate, as though afraid to smutch　　　　90
Even with mealy gold the waters clear.
But, at that very touch, to disappear
So fairy-quick, was strange!　Bewildered,
Endymion sought around, and shook each bed
Of covert flowers in vain ; and then he flung　　　95
Himself along the grass.　What gentle tongue,
What whisperer disturb'd his gloomy rest ?
It was a nymph uprisen to the breast
In the fountain's pebbly margin, and she stood
'Mong lillies, like the youngest of the brood.　　　100
To him her dripping hand she softly kist,
And anxiously began to plait and twist
Her ringlets round her fingers, saying : "Youth!
Too long, alas, hast thou starv'd on the ruth,
The bitterness of love : too long indeed,　　　105
Seeing thou art so gentle.　Could I weed

---

(93). At this point the draft has the rejected reading—

　　　　Endymion all around the welkin sped
　　　　His anxious sight,

and a further variation is *Endymion pry'd around.*
　(96-97) In the draft these two lines were written—

　　　　His sullen limbs upon the grass—what tongue,
　　　　What airy whisperer spoilt his angry rest ?

　(99) Here is a further instance of the contracted *I'* being altered
to *In* in the finished manuscript.　In the draft *basin* occurs in the
place of *margin.*
　(102) In the draft is the variation

　　　　And carelessly began to twine and twist
　　　　Her ringlets 'bout her fingers...

　(104) This line originally began with the words *Long hast thou
tasted,* and the next line with *The bitter ruth of love.*

Thy soul of care, by heavens, I would offer
All the bright riches of my crystal coffer
To Amphitrite ; all my clear-ey'd fish,
Golden, or rainbow-sided, or purplish,   110
Vermilion-tail'd, or finn'd with silvery gauze ;
Yea, or my veined pebble-floor, that draws
A virgin light to the deep ; my grotto-sands
Tawny and gold, ooz'd slowly from far lands
By my diligent springs ; my level lillies, shells, 115
My charming rod, my potent river spells ;
Yes, every thing, even to the pearly cup
Meander gave me,—for I bubbled up
To fainting creatures in a desert wild.
But woe is me, I am but as a child   120
To gladden thee ; and all I dare to say,
Is, that I pity thee ; that on this day
I've been thy guide ; that thou must wander far
In other regions, past the scanty bar
To mortal steps, before thou cans't be ta'en 125
From every wasting sigh, from every pain,
Into the gentle bosom of thy love.
Why it is thus, one knows in heaven above :
But, a poor Naiad, I guess not.   Farewell !
I have a ditty for my hollow cell."   130

---

(116) Variation in the draft, *water* for *river*.

(117) In the manuscript, *e'en* for *even*.

(121) The draft reads *all that I may say*.

(128) The reading *some know* for *one knows* occurs in the draft, where the next two lines were first written—

> But, a poor Naiad, I guess not nor tell
> Farewell I must away to my hollow cell—

and then as in the text, but with *I've a new ditty* for *I have a ditty*.

Hereat, she vanished from Endymion's gaze,
Who brooded o'er the water in amaze :
The dashing fount pour'd on, and where its pool
Lay, half asleep, in grass and rushes cool,
Quick waterflies and gnats were sporting still,   135
And fish were dimpling, as if good nor ill
Had fallen out that hour.   The wanderer,
Holding his forehead, to keep off the burr
Of smothering fancies, patiently sat down ;
And, while beneath the evening's sleepy frown   140
Glow-worms began to trim their starry lamps,
Thus breath'd he to himself : " Whoso encamps
To take a fancied city of delight,
O what a wretch is he ! and when 'tis his,
After long toil and travelling, to miss   145

(131-4) These two couplets originally stood in the draft thus—

> Hereat, she vanish'd from the listener's gaze,
> Whose soul kept o'er the water in amaze ;
> The dashing fall pour'd on, and where the pool
> Crept smoothly by fresh grass and rushes cool,...

(139) Rejected reading from the draft, *drowning* for *smothering*.
(140) Cancelled readings, from the draft *gentle*, and from the manuscript *mild*, for *sleepy*.
(143) The manner in which the rhyme to this line was lost appears from the draft, where the passage originally stood thus :

> Whoso encamps
> His soul to take a city of delight
> O what a wretch is he : 'tis in his sight...

Then *'tis in his sight* was struck out in favour of *and when 'tis his*; but nothing was done, in transcribing for the press, to remedy the defect thus produced.

(145) The original reading in the draft was *After long siege and travailing*; but the finished manuscript reads *toil and travelling* as in the text.

The kernel of his hopes, how more than vile :
Yet, for him there's refreshment even in toil ;
Another city doth he set about,
Free from the smallest pebble-bead of doubt
That he will seize on trickling honey-combs :   150
Alas, he finds them dry ; and then he foams,
And onward to another city speeds.
But this is human life : the war, the deeds,
The disappointment, the anxiety,
Imagination's struggles, far and nigh,   155
All human ; bearing in themselves this good,
That they are still the air, the subtle food,
To make us feel existence, and to show
How quiet death is. Where soil is men grow,
Whether to weeds or flowers ; but for me,   160
There is no depth to strike in : I can see
Nought earthly worth my compassing ; so stand
Upon a misty, jutting head of land—
Alone ? No, no ; and by the Orphean lute,
When mad Eurydice is listening to't ;   165
I'd rather stand upon this misty peak,
With not a thing to sigh for, or to seek,

---

(147) The draft reads *e'en* for *even*.

(149) In the first edition, *pebble-head*; but in the manuscript, *pebble-bead*, which reading is restored in the corrected copy in my possession. The draft reads *Without* for *Free from*, and in the next line *there he'll* for *he will*.

(153) In the draft, *acts* for *war*.

(155) *Imaginings and searchings*, in the draft.

(158) In the first edition, *shew*.

(159) *Here is soil to grow* was originally written in the draft.

(164) In the draft, *Alone ? No, heavens !*

(166) Originally written *I'd rather bide*, in the draft.

(167) The original version of this line in the draft is—

     With nought to long for, sigh for, or to seek.

But the soft shadow of my thrice-seen love,
Than be—I care not what.　O meekest dove
Of heaven !　O Cynthia, ten-times bright and fair !   170
From thy blue throne, now filling all the air,
Glance but one little beam of temper'd light
Into my bosom, that the dreadful might
And tyranny of love be somewhat scar'd !
Yet do not so, sweet queen ; one torment spar'd,   175
Would give a pang to jealous misery,
Worse than the torment's self : but rather tie
Large wings upon my shoulders, and point out
My love's far dwelling.　Though the playful rout
Of Cupids shun thee, too divine art thou,   180
Too keen in beauty, for thy silver prow
Not to have dipp'd in love's most gentle stream.
O be propitious, nor severely deem
My madness impious ; for, by all the stars
That tend thy bidding, I do think the bars   185
That kept my spirit in are burst—that I
Am sailing with thee through the dizzy sky !
How beautiful thou art !　The world how deep !
How tremulous-dazzlingly the wheels sweep
Around their axle !　Then these gleaming reins,   190

---

(168) For the three occasions on which Endymion had seen
Diana, refer to the account given to Peona ; beginning with line
540, Book I,—to the passage about the well, line 896, Book I,—
and to the passage in which he hurried into the grotto, line 971,
Book I.

(169) The original reading of the draft was *I know not* in place
of *I care not*.

(181) The word *sharp* occurs in the draft in place of *keen*.

(189) In the draft this line has three tentative openings,—*How
silently and tremulous, How bright and tremulous, How tremulous
and dazzling*.

How lithe ! When this thy chariot attains
Its airy goal, haply some bower veils
Those twilight eyes ? Those eyes !—my spirit fails—
Dear goddess, help ! or the wide-gaping air
Will gulph me—help !"—At this with madden'd stare, 195
And lifted hands, and trembling lips he stood ;
Like old Deucalion mountain'd o'er the flood,
Or blind Orion hungry for the morn.
And, but from the deep cavern there was borne
A voice, he had been froze to senseless stone ;   200
Nor sigh of his, nor plaint, nor passion'd moan
Had more been heard. Thus swell'd it forth: "Descend,
Young mountaineer ! descend where alleys bend
Into the sparry hollows of the world !
Oft hast thou seen bolts of the thunder hurl'd   205
As from thy threshold ; day by day hast been

---

(191) The draft yields the rejected reading, *When this thy silent chariot gains* ; and in the next two lines

> haply thou veilst thine eyes
> In some fresh bower.

In supplying the reading of the text Keats first wrote *Those liquid eyes.*

(195) The draft reads *Oh* for *help !*—and in the next line but one *wondering at* for *mountain'd o'er.*

(198) Here the draft yields the reading—

> Or blind Orion waiting for the dawn—

another evidence of Keats's determination to get rid of the false rhymes where observed. The next line was originally written —

> And, but from the *hollow* cavern there was *born*—

and I am not sure that *born* is not the word intended, though *borne*, the reading of the first edition, must have the preference.

(201) The original reading of the draft is

> Nor sigh of his, nor wild complaint nor moan.

(204) This line originally began in the draft with the word *Spiral.*

A little lower than the chilly sheen
Of icy pinnacles, and dipp'dst thine arms
Into the deadening ether that still charms
Their marble being: now, as deep profound   210
As those are high, descend! He ne'er is crown'd
With immortality, who fears to follow
Where airy voices lead : so through the hollow,
The silent mysteries of earth, descend ! "

    He heard but the last words, nor could contend   215
One moment in reflection : for he fled
Into the fearful deep, to hide his head
From the clear moon, the trees, and coming madness.

    'Twas far too strange, and wonderful for sadness ;
Sharpening, by degrees, his appetite   220
To dive into the deepest. Dark, nor light,
The region ; nor bright, nor sombre wholly,
But mingled up ; a gleaming melancholy ;
A dusky empire and its diadems ;
One faint eternal eventide of gems.   225
Aye, millions sparkled on a vein of gold,
Along whose track the prince quick footsteps told,

---

(208) The draft has the reading *and couldst dip thy palms...*
(210) Cancelled reading of the manuscript, *far* for *deep*.
(211) In the draft

    As those were high, descend ! He ne'er was crown'd...

(214) The draft reads *fearful* for *silent*.
(215) In the manuscript, *But the last words he heard* ; but the
reading of the text is clearly a revision.
(218) The draft reads *night* for *moon*, and in the next line but one
Upwinding for *Sharpening*.
(227-30) In the draft this passage was written as follows :

    Whose track the venturous Latmian follows bold
    Thro' all its lines abrupt and angular :

With all its lines abrupt and angular :
Out-shooting sometimes, like a meteor-star,
Through a vast antre ; then the metal woof,   230
Like Vulcan's rainbow, with some monstrous roof
Curves hugely: now, far in the deep abyss,
It seems an angry lightning, and doth hiss
Fancy into belief : anon it leads
Through winding passages, where sameness breeds   235
Vexing conceptions of some sudden change ;
Whether to silver grots, or giant range
Of sapphire columns, or fantastic bridge
Athwart a flood of crystal.   On a ridge
Now fareth he, that o'er the vast beneath   240
Towers like an ocean-cliff, and whence he seeth
A hundred waterfalls, whose voices come
But as the murmuring surge.   Chilly and numb
His bosom grew, when first he, far away,
Descry'd an orbed diamond, set to fray   245
Old darkness from his throne : 'twas like the sun
Uprisen o'er chaos : and with such a stun
Came the amazement, that, absorb'd in it,
He saw not fiercer wonders—past the wit
Of any spirit to tell, but one of those   250

> And sometimes like a shooting meteor star
> Past a vast antre's gloom.

The reading of the text is in the finished manuscript, where, however, line 230 was first written—

> Past a large Antre ; then the metal woof,...

(231) The draft reads *o'er* for *with*, and in the next line *a* for *the*.
(236) In the draft this line begins with *Dizzy* instead of *Vexing*.
(240) The draft supplies two rejected readings, *Sometimes he
fares* and *Sometimes he went*.
(243) The draft reads *a* in place of *the*.
(248) In the draft we read *this* for *the*.

Who, when this planet's sphering time doth close,
Will be its high remembrancers : who they ?
The mighty ones who have made eternal day
For Greece and England.   While astonishment
With deep-drawn sighs was quieting, he went   255
Into a marble gallery, passing through
A mimic temple, so complete and true
In sacred custom, that he well nigh fear'd
To search it inwards ; whence far off appear'd,
Through a long pillar'd vista, a fair shrine,   260
And, just beyond, on light tiptoe divine,
A quiver'd Dian.   Stepping awfully,
The youth approach'd ; oft turning his veil'd eye
Down sidelong aisles, and into niches old.
And when, more near against the marble cold   265
He had touch'd his forehead, he began to thread
All courts and passages, where silence dead
Rous'd by his whispering footsteps murmured faint :
And long he travers'd to and fro, to acquaint

(253-4) Originally written in the draft—

> The mighty ones who've shone athwart the day
> Of Greece and England.

(256-7) Cancelled reading from the draft—

> Into a marble gallery that near the roof
> Of a fair mimic Temple...

(261-3) Cancelled reading from the draft—

> Thro' a long vist' of columns a fair shrine
> And just beyond lightly diminished
> A Dian quiver'd tiptoe, crescented—.

(264) The draft reads *sideway aisles.*
(266) In the manuscript *tread* stands here altered to *thread.*
(267) The draft reads *The* for *All.*
(269) The words *to acquaint* in the manuscript are contracted to *t'acquaint.*

Himself with every mystery, and awe ;   270
Till, weary, he sat down before the maw
Of a wide outlet, fathomless and dim,
To wild uncertainty and shadows grim.
There, when new wonders ceas'd to float before,
And thoughts of self came on, how crude and sore   275
The journey homeward to habitual self !
A mad-pursuing of the fog-born elf,
Whose flitting lantern, through rude nettle-briar,
Cheats us into a swamp, into a fire,
Into the bosom of a hated thing.   280

What misery most drowningly doth sing
In lone Endymion's ear, now he has raught

(270-2) In the draft,

> Himself with every mystery, until
> His weary legs he rested on the sill
> Of some remotest chamber, outlet dim...

(277) The draft reads *That* for *A*.
(278) The original reading of the draft at this point is—

> Whose flitting Lantern, through rude nettle-beds,
> Cheats us into a bog,—cuttings and shreds
> Of old Vexations plaited to a rope
> Wherewith to haul us from the sight of hope,
> And bind us to our earthly baiting-ring.

These lines were copied into the finished manuscript with the variations *Swamp* for *bog*, *drag* for *haul*, and *bind* for *fix*. The passage
as it stands in the text is supplied in the margin of the manuscript.
The grotesque imagery of the earlier version reminds us, in its rude
vigour, that Keats had actually witnessed, and forcibly described to
Clarke, a bear-baiting.

(282) The final word in this line is clearly *raught* in the manuscript, though *caught* in the first edition. As the obsolete word
occurs often in Shakespeare and makes sense, while the other does
not, we are justified in restoring it, especially seeing that it appears
elsewhere in *Endymion* (see Book I, line 866).

The goal of consciousness? Ah, 'tis the thought,
The deadly feel of solitude : for lo !
He cannot see the heavens, nor the flow   285
Of rivers, nor hill-flowers running wild
In pink and purple chequer, nor, up-pil'd,
The cloudy rack slow journeying in the west,
Like herded elephants ; nor felt, nor prest
Cool grass, nor tasted the fresh slumberous air ;   290
But far from such companionship to wear
An unknown time, surcharg'd with grief, away,
Was now his lot. And must he patient stay,
Tracing fantastic figures with his spear ?
"No!" exclaim'd he, "why should I tarry here ?"   295
No! loudly echoed times innumerable.
At which he straightway started, and 'gan tell
His paces back into the temple's chief ;
Warming and glowing strong in the belief
Of help from Dian : so that when again   300
He caught her airy form, thus did he plain,
Moving more near the while : " O Haunter chaste
Of river sides, and woods, and heathy waste,
Where with thy silver bow and arrows keen

---

(290) In the draft, *the free sleepy air.*
(294) The draft reads *Drawing* for *Tracing.*
(297) The reading of the draft is *roused, and gan to tell,* and in
the next line but one *growing* for *glowing.*
(301) The draft reads—

> thus gan he plain,
> Pacing towards the while.

The finished manuscript reads *Moving towards the while:* The
reading of the text must have been a correction of the proof.
(304) The draft reads—

> Where now with silver bow and arrows keen
> Art thou in covert hid ?

Art thou now forested? O woodland Queen,   305
What smoothest air thy smoother forehead woos?
Where dost thou listen to the wide halloos
Of thy disparted nymphs? Through what dark tree
Glimmers thy crescent? Wheresoe'er it be,
'Tis in the breath of heaven: thou dost taste   310
Freedom as none can taste it, nor dost waste
Thy loveliness in dismal elements ;
But, finding in our green earth sweet contents,
There livest blissfully.   Ah, if to thee
It feels Elysian, how rich to me,   315
An exil'd mortal, sounds its pleasant name!
Within my breast there lives a choking flame—
O let me cool 't the zephyr-boughs among!
A homeward fever parches up my tongue—
O let me slake it at the running springs !   320
Upon my ear a noisy nothing rings—
O let me once more hear the linnet's note !

---

(308) In the draft there is a rejected reading, *From what deep glen...*

(313) In the finished manuscript, *on* for *in.*

(318) In the finished manuscript, *cool't* for *cool it* : otherwise the line is really written as the first edition gives it—

O let me cool it among the zephyr-boughs !

But it seems absolutely certain that *among* was meant to be at the end, to rhyme with *tongue,*—an assurance made doubly sure by the fact that the line was originally written in the draft—

O let me cool't among the waving boughs !

and marked for transposition of *among* to the end. Thus Keats clearly in copying the line altered *waving* to *zephyr* but forgot the transposition.

(319) In the draft this line was written thus—

A fever parches up my suppliant tongue—

and then altered to

An endless fever parches up my tongue.

Before mine eyes thick films and shadows float—
O let me 'noint them with the heaven's light !
Dost thou now lave thy feet and ankles white ?   325
O think how sweet to me the freshening sluice !
Dost thou now please thy thirst with berry-juice?
O think how this dry palate would rejoice !
If in soft slumber thou dost hear my voice,
O think how I should love a bed of flowers !—   330
Young goddess ! let me see my native bowers !
Deliver me from this rapacious deep !"

   Thus ending loudly, as he would o'erleap
His destiny, alert he stood : but when
Obstinate silence came heavily again,   335
Feeling about for its old couch of space
And airy cradle, lowly bow'd his face
Desponding, o'er the marble floor's cold thrill.
But 'twas not long ; for, sweeter than the rill
To its old channel, or a swollen tide   340

---

(325) In the finished manuscript *hands* stands cancelled in favour
of *feet*.

   (327) The draft reads *cherry-juice*.

   (330) In the draft, *would* instead of *should*; *Oh* for *Young* in the
next line ; and the next line but one reads—

        Lift me, oh lift me from this horrid deep !

   (335) In the draft, *cloudily came* is cancelled in favour of *came
heavily* ; and the next couplet originally stood thus—

        Feeling its way to its old couch of space
        And airy cradle he bent down his face.

In the finished manuscript line 335 stands precisely as in the text.

   (339) The draft reads *'Twas not for long.*

   (340) In the draft—

        To its cool channel, the o'erswollen tide...

The finished manuscript reads *cold channel,*—the first edition, *old
channel.*

To margin sallows, were the leaves he spied,
And flowers, and wreaths, and ready myrtle crowns
Up heaping through the slab : refreshment drowns
Itself, and strives its own delights to hide—
Nor in one spot alone ; the floral pride   345
In a long whispering birth enchanted grew
Before his footsteps ; as when heav'd anew
Old ocean rolls a lengthened wave to the shore,
Down whose green back the short-liv'd foam, all hoar,
Bursts gradual, with a wayward indolence.   350

    Increasing still in heart, and pleasant sense,
Upon his fairy journey on he hastes ;
So anxious for the end, he scarcely wastes
One moment with his hand among the sweets :

    (343-4) The reading of the draft is—

        Upswelling through the slab ; refreshment drowns
        Itself, lush tumbling down on every side :

in the finished manuscript, *slap* is written for *slab*, and there is the
cancelled reading,

        Itself, lush-tumbling on every side :

the words *cool fragrance* are inserted and struck out again ; but how
they were to be used is not clear.

    (348-50) The draft shows the original reading to have been as
follows :—

        Old ocean sends a lengthened wave to the shore,
        From whose green head the gentle foam all hoar
        Runs gradual,...

Then we have *O'er whose green back*, and next *Down whose green
back*. The finished manuscript corresponds here precisely with the
printed text ; and there can be no doubt the redundant *the* in line
348 is an intentional undulation. Strictly there are two undulations
in the line, because the final syllable of *lengthened* is to be pronounced, according to Keats's practice.

    (353) The manuscript reads *waits* in place of *wastes*.

Onward he goes—he stops—his bosom beats   355
As plainly in his ear, as the faint charm
Of which the throbs were born.   This still alarm,
This sleepy music, forc'd him walk tiptoe :
For it came more softly than the east could blow
Arion's magic to the Atlantic isles ;   360
Or than the west, made jealous by the smiles
Of thron'd Apollo, could breathe back the lyre
To seas Ionian and Tyrian.

---

(359) In the manuscript, *For it* is contracted into *For't.*

(363) The draft supplies the history of the loss of a rhyme to this line ; but I fear it must remain rhymeless.   The passage was left thus in the draft :

> To seas Ionian and Tyrian.   Dire
> Was the love lorn despair to which it wrought
> Endymion—for dire is the bare thought
> That among lovers things of tenderest worth
> Are swallow'd all, and made a blank—a dearth
> By one devouring flame : and far far worse
> Blessing to them become a heavy curse
> Half happy till comparisons of bliss
> To misery lead them.   'Twas even so with this...

Before this was finished there were the following readings of two of the lines—

> Endymion—for dire to $\left\{ \begin{array}{l} \text{placid} \\ \text{quiet} \end{array} \right\}$ bosoms is the thought,

and

> Half happy will they gaze upon the sky ;

and when the passage was altered in copying out the poem for the press, the first reading (cancelled) of line 365 was—

> Whom, loving, Music slew not,

while, in line 371, *comparisons*, not *comparison*, was written, and line 372 was left thus—

> Is miserable.   'T[was] e'en so with this...

The omission of *was* is curious.   It seems that, in altering line 363 and making line 364 rhyme with it, Keats overlooked the needs of line 362 : there is nothing in the finished manuscript to show that

O did he ever live, that lonely man,
Who lov'd—and music slew not?   'Tis the pest   365
Of love, that fairest joys give most unrest;
That things of delicate and tenderest worth
Are swallow'd all, and made a seared dearth,
By one consuming flame: it doth immerse
And suffocate true blessings in a curse.   370
Half-happy, by comparison of bliss,
Is miserable.   'Twas even so with this
Dew-dropping melody, in the Carian's ear;
First heaven, then hell, and then forgotten clear,
Vanish'd in elemental passion.   375

    And down some swart abysm he had gone,
. Had not a heavenly guide benignant led
To where thick myrtle branches, 'gainst his head

---

he or Taylor had any misgivings on the subject, though it is quite
possible there may have been an intention to introduce some such
line as
      To seas Ionian and seas of Tyre.

The whole passage as it now stands is so superb that both poet and
critic-publisher may be easily pardoned for the oversight. No imagination so delicate in regard to music had been vouchsafed to
poet since Shakespeare wrote, in *Twelfth Night*,

     That strain again! it had a dying fall :
     O, it came o'er my ear like the sweet sound,
     That breathes upon a bank of violets,
     Stealing and giving odour!

The attenuation of sound suggested by the thought that Arion's
lyre-music was wafted by the east wind from the Mediterranean to
the Atlantic, and blown back by Zephyrs, envious of Apollo's approbation, from the Atlantic to the seas about Greece and Tyre, is so
exceeding as to be in some respects preferable to the lovely suggestion in *Twelfth Night*, which brings a second sense into the idea.

    (377) This line originally began (in the draft) with *But that
some*...

Brushing, awakened : then the sounds again
Went noiseless as a passing noontide rain   . 380
Over a bower, where little space he stood ;
For as the sunset peeps into a wood
So saw he panting light, and towards it went
Through winding alleys ; and lo, wonderment !
Upon soft verdure saw, one here, one there,   385
Cupids a slumbering on their pinions fair.

(379-85) This passage stood thus in the draft—
 Brushing awaken'd him : the sounds again
 Came softly as a gentle evening rain,
 Around a bower, where he stay'd harkening
 And through whose tufted shrubby darkening
 Bright starry glimmers came, towards which he went
 Thro' winding alleys, and lo, wonderment !
 Upon soft turf he saw, one here one there...

In the finished manuscript line 380 at first began with *Came* ; but
this was altered to *Went*, and for the rest the passage stands as in the
text. This whole episode should be compared with Spenser's account of "the gardins of Adonis" (*Faerie Queene*, Book III, Canto
VI) which probably suggested to Keats the embodiment of the legend
in his poem. One would think stanzas 44, 46, and 47, at all events,
must have been fresh in his memory :

 And in the thickest covert of that shade
  There was a pleasaunt Arber, not by art
  But of the trees owne inclination made,
  Which knitting their rancke braunches, part to part,
  With wanton yvie twine entrayld athwart,
  And Eglantine and Caprifole emong,
  Fashion'd above within their inmost part,
  That neither Phœbus beams could through them throng,
 Nor Aeolus sharp blast could worke them any wrong.

 There wont fayre Venus often to enjoy
  Her deare Adonis joyous company,
  And reape sweet pleasure of the wanton boy :
  There yet, some say, in secret he does ly,
  Lapped in flowres and pretious spycery,
  By her hid from the world, and from the skill

After a thousand mazes overgone,
At last, with sudden step, he came upon
A chamber, myrtle wall'd, embowered high,
Full of light, incense, tender minstrelsy,   390
And more of beautiful and strange beside :
For on a silken couch of rosy pride,
In midst of all, there lay a sleeping youth
Of fondest beauty ; fonder, in fair sooth,
Than sighs could fathom, or contentment reach :   395
And coverlids gold-tinted like the peach,
Or ripe October's faded marigolds,
Fell sleek about him in a thousand folds—
Not hiding up an Apollonian curve
Of neck and shoulder, nor the tenting swerve   400
Of knee from knee, nor ankles pointing light ;

Of Stygian Gods, which doe her love envy ;
But she her selfe, when ever that she will,
Possesseth him, and of his sweetnesse takes her fill.

And sooth, it seemes, they say ; for he may not
For ever dye, and ever buried bee
In balefull night where all thinges are forgot :
All be he subject to mortalitie,
Yet is eterne in mutabilitie,
And by succession made perpetuall,
Transformed oft, and chaunged diverslie,
For him the Father of all formes they call :
Therfore needs mote he live, that living gives to all.

The word *eterne* (used further on, in Book III, line 42) probably
passed into Keats's vocabulary from this last stanza.
    (396-7) In the draft—

    And draperies mellow-tinted like the peach,
    Or lady peas entwined with marigolds.

    (399) Cancelled manuscript reading, *his* for *an.*
    (400) Woodhouse seems to have been in doubt what *tenting
swerve* meant ; for he notes that Keats told him it meant *in the
form of the top of a tent.*

But rather, giving them to the filled sight
Officiously. Sideway his face repos'd
On one white arm, and tenderly unclos'd,
By tenderest pressure, a faint damask mouth   405
To slumbery pout ; just as the morning south
Disparts a dew-lipp'd rose. Above his head,
Four lilly stalks did their white honours wed
To make a coronal ; and round him grew
All tendrils green, of every bloom and hue,   410
Together intertwin'd and trammel'd fresh :
The vine of glossy sprout ; the ivy mesh,
Shading its Ethiop berries ; and woodbine,
Of velvet leaves and bugle-blooms divine ;
Convolvulus in streaked vases flush ;   415
The creeper, mellowing for an autumn blush ;
And virgin's bower, trailing airily ;
With others of the sisterhood. Hard by,

---

(402) In the manuscript, *gave* instead of *giving*, and in the draft
gazer's instead of *filled*.

(403-4) Compare Sonnet XXII, Livre II, *Amours de Ronsard* (à
Marie de Marquets) :

> Un somme languissant la tenoit mi-penchée
> Dessus le coude droit fermant sa belle bouche.

(405) The draft reads *his* for *a*.

(409) In the draft, *coronet* for *coronal*, and the next line is—

> All tendril green, of pleasant lush and hue.

(412) The draft reads *purply* for *glossy*, and in the next line *dark-
ling* for *Ethiop*.

(414) In the draft—

> With all its honey bugle tufts divine.

(415) Cancelled manuscript reading, *of* for *in*.

(416) In the draft,

> The creeper, blushing deep at Autumn's blush.

Stood serene Cupids watching silently.
One, kneeling to a lyre, touch'd the strings,   420
Muffling to death the pathos with his wings;
And, ever and anon, uprose to look
At the youth's slumber; while another took
A willow-bough, distilling odorous dew,
And shook it on his hair; another flew   425
In through the woven roof, and fluttering-wise
Rain'd violets upon his sleeping eyes.

At these enchantments, and yet many more,
The breathless Latmian wonder'd o'er and o'er;
Until, impatient in embarrassment,   430
He forthright pass'd, and lightly treading went
To that same feather'd lyrist, who straightway,
Smiling, thus whisper'd: "Though from upper day
Thou art a wanderer, and thy presence here
Might seem unholy, be of happy cheer!   435
For 'tis the nicest touch of human honor,

---

(419) This triplet was not originally in the poem. The draft shews
here the reading—

> Stood Cupids holding o'er an upward gaze   ·
> Each a slim wand tipt with a silver blaze
> Each one a silver torch...

The poet's nice taste doubtless rejected this on review as too sug-
gestive of gilt gingerbread cupids such as he may very well have
seen at Edmonton fair.

(424) The draft reads *A myrtle-bough*, and in the next line but
one *In from the branched roof*.

(429) In the draft, Endymion was described as *The mortal Latmian*.

(436) *The nicest touch of human honor* is a curious and not very
perspicuous phrase; but the fact that the original reading of the
draft was *the highest reach of human honor* leaves us in no doubt
that Endymion was given to understand he was receiving the
greatest honour that could be conferred on a human being.

When some ethereal and high-favouring donor
Presents immortal bowers to mortal sense ;
As now 'tis done to thee, Endymion.   Hence
Was I in no wise startled.   So recline   440
Upon these living flowers.   Here is wine,
Alive with sparkles—never, I aver,
Since Ariadne was a vintager,
So cool a purple : taste these juicy pears,
Sent me by sad Vertumnus, when his fears   445
Were high about Pomona : here is cream,
Deepening to richness from a snowy gleam ;
Sweeter than that nurse Amalthea skimm'd
For the boy Jupiter : and here, undimm'd
By any touch, a bunch of blooming plums   450
Ready to melt between an infant's gums :
And here is manna pick'd from Syrian trees,
In starlight, by the three Hesperides.
Feast on, and meanwhile I will let thee know
Of all these things around us."   He did so,   455
Still brooding o'er the cadence of his lyre ;
And thus : " I need not any hearing tire
By telling how the sea-born goddess pin'd
For a mortal youth, and how she strove to bind

---

(442) In the draft the line began with *Sparkling up diamonds.*

(443) It was a peculiarly happy piece of poetic realism to translate
Ariadne's relations with Bacchus into her becoming a vintager ; and
I presume this was Keats's own thought, as well as the idea immediately following, that the God of Orchards conciliated Love with a
gift of pears when paying his addresses to Pomona.

(448) In the draft,

> Even sweet as that which Amalthea skimm'd.

(456-7) This couplet was written thus in the draft—

> Keeping a ravishing cadence with his lyre.
> And thus it was " I'll not thy knowing tire...

Him all in all unto her doting self.   460
Who would not be so prison'd? but, fond elf,
He was content to let her amorous plea
Faint through his careless arms; content to see
An unseiz'd heaven dying at his feet;
Content, O fool! to make a cold retreat,   465
When on the pleasant grass such love, lovelorn,
Lay sorrowing; when every tear was born
Of diverse passion; when her lips and eyes
Were clos'd in sullen moisture, and quick sighs
Came vex'd and pettish through her nostrils small.   470
Hush! no exclaim—yet, justly mightst thou call
Curses upon his head.—I was half glad,
But my poor mistress went distract and mad,
When the boar tusk'd him: so away she flew
To Jove's high throne, and by her plainings drew   475
Immortal tear-drops down the thunderer's beard;
Whereon, it was decreed he should be rear'd
Each summer time to life.   Lo! this is he,
That same Adonis, safe in the privacy
Of this still region all his winter-sleep.   480
Aye, sleep; for when our love-sick queen did weep

(461-4) In the draft thus—

      Who would not be so bound, but, foolish elf,
      He was content to let Divinity
      Slip through his careless arms—content to see
      An unseized heaven sighing at his feet;

and there are the cancelled readings

      He was content to unclasp his...

      He was content to let $\begin{cases} \text{Elysium} \\ \text{a fainting heaven} \end{cases}$
      Faint gradual from his arms.

The finished manuscript corresponds with the printed text.
  (474) In the manuscript, *tush'd*: in the first edition *tusk'd*.
  (479) In the manuscript, *i' the* for *in the*.

Over his waned corse, the tremulous shower
Heal'd up the wound, and, with a balmy power,
Medicin'd death to a lengthened drowsiness:
The which she fills with visions, and doth dress   485
In all this quiet luxury; and hath set
Us young immortals, without any let,
To watch his slumber through.   'Tis well nigh pass'd,
Even to a moment's filling up, and fast
She scuds with summer breezes, to pant through   490
The first long kiss, warm firstling, to renew
Embower'd sports in Cytherea's isle.
Look! how those winged listeners all this while
Stand anxious: see! behold!"—This clamant word
Broke through the careful silence; for they heard   495
A rustling noise of leaves, and out there flutter'd
Pigeons and doves: Adonis something mutter'd,
The while one hand, that erst upon his thigh
Lay dormant, mov'd convuls'd and gradually
Up to his forehead.   Then there was a hum   500
Of sudden voices, echoing, "Come! come!
Arise! awake!   Clear summer has forth walk'd
Unto the clover-sward, and she has talk'd
Full soothingly to every nested finch:

---

(482) In the draft,

       Over this paly corse, the crystal shower...

(487) The draft reads *These* for *Us*, and in the next two lines
winter for *slumber* and *complishing* for *filling up*.

(489) The finished manuscript reads *E'en* for *Even*.

(490) Cancelled reading of the manuscript, *o'er* for *with*.

(491) The draft has *sweet prologue* in place of *warm firstling*.

(495) Cancelled manuscript reading, *and they heard*.

(501) In the draft,

       Of sudden voices, echoing out, "Come! come!

(504) The draft reads *Most* for *Full*.

Rise, Cupids ! or we'll give the blue-bell pinch   505
To your dimpled arms.   Once more sweet life begin ! "
At this, from every side they hurried in,
Rubbing their sleepy eyes with lazy wrists,
And doubling over head their little fists
In backward yawns.   But all were soon alive :   510
For as delicious wine doth, sparkling, dive
In nectar'd clouds and curls through water fair,
So from the arbour roof down swell'd an air
Odorous and enlivening ; making all
To laugh, and play, and sing, and loudly call   515
For their sweet queen : when lo ! the wreathed green
Disparted, and far upward could be seen
Blue heaven, and a silver car, air-borne,
Whose silent wheels, fresh wet from clouds of morn,
Spun off a drizzling dew,—which falling chill   520
On soft Adonis' shoulders, made him still
Nestle and turn uneasily about.
Soon were the white doves plain, with neck stretch'd out,
And silken traces lighten'd in descent ;

---

(505) Cancelled readings,—in the draft,

    Cupids awake ! or black and blue we'll pinch
    Your dimpled arms—for lo ! your Queen, your Queen.

and in the finished copy,

    Cupids awake ! or black and blue we'll pinch
    Your dimpled arms.   Once more sweet life begin !

(509) The draft reads *in the air* for *over head.*
(523) In the draft thus—

    Anon the doves $\left\{ \begin{array}{c} \text{appear'd} \\ \text{were plain} \end{array} \right\}$, with necks stretch'd out.

(524) Woodhouse notes that in the original this line began with
Their instead of *And,* and read *tighten'd* for *lighten'd.*   I presume
both variations are from the draft ; for in the finished manuscript
there is certainly no trace of *Their,* while the other word is certainly

And soon, returning from love's banishment,   525
Queen Venus leaning downward open arm'd :
Her shadow fell upon his breast, and charm'd
A tumult to his heart, and a new life
Into his eyes.   Ah, miserable strife,
But for her comforting ! unhappy sight,   530
But meeting her blue orbs !   Who, who can write
Of these first minutes ?   The unchariest muse
To embracements warm as theirs makes coy excuse.

O it has ruffled every spirit there,

---

written *lighten'd*, even if, as is possible, it was intended to cross the first letter and make a *t* of it. In the line before, Keats wrote the word *out* without crossing the *t* ; and he often omitted that small duty ; but I do not feel safe in altering *lighten'd* to *tighten'd* here, seeing that the first edition reads *lighten'd*, and that it makes the better sense : the traces would be lighter for the doves in descent, one would say, not tighter.

(525) The finished manuscript reads *next* instead of *soon*.

(526) In lieu of the passage extending from line 526 to line 534, the following fifteen lines were originally written in the draft :

Queen Venus bending downward, so o'ertaken,
So suffering sweet, so blushing mad, so shaken
That the wild warmth prob'd the young sleeper's heart
Enchantingly ; and with a sudden start
His trembling arms were out in instant time
To catch his fainting love.—O foolish rhyme
What mighty power is in thee that so often
Thou strivest rugged syllables to soften
Even to the telling of a sweet like this.
Away ! let them embrace alone ! that kiss
Was far too rich for thee to talk upon.
Poor wretch ! mind not those sobs and sighs ! begone !
Speak not one atom of thy paltry stuff,
That they are met is poetry enough.
O this has ruffled every spirit there,...

These lines are struck out of the draft, where their place is not supplied ; but the finished copy corresponds with the printed text.

Saving Love's self, who stands superb to share   535
The general gladness : awfully he stands ;
A sovereign quell is in his waving hands ;
No sight can bear the lightning of his bow ;
His quiver is mysterious, none can know
What themselves think of it ; from forth his eyes   540
There darts strange light of varied hues and dies :
A scowl is sometimes on his brow, but who
Look full upon it feel anon the blue
Of his fair eyes run liquid through their souls.
Endymion feels it, and no more controls   545
The burning prayer within him ; so, bent low,
He had begun a plaining of his woe.
But Vênus, bending forward, said : " My child,
Favour this gentle youth ; his days are wild
With love—he—but alas ! too well I see   550
Thou know'st the deepness of his misery.
Ah, smile not so, my son : I tell thee true,
That when through heavy hours I us'd to rue

---

(535) In the first edition, *love's*, with a small *l* ; but *Love's* in the manuscript.

(538) In the finished manuscript this line stands thus—

His bow no sight can bear for lightning so.

(541) The draft reads first *sundry* and then *changeful* in place of *varied*. The first edition reads *dyes* ; but in the finished manuscript we have *dies* instead of *dyes* : I am pretty confident this is right ; and it is to be regretted that Woodhouse did not record which of the two words was in the draft. Keats was not incapable of applying the word *dyes* to light ; but there is redundancy in *light of varied hues and dyes* ; and the notion of strange light flashing from Love's eyes and dying is in a far higher strain.

(548) The draft reads *leaning* for *bending*.

(552) In the draft *sweet boy !* instead of *my son*, and in the next line but one *mad-brain'd* for *new-born*.

The endless sleep of this new-born Adon',
This stranger aye I pitied.   For upon   555
A dreary morning once I fled away
Into the breezy clouds, to weep and pray
For this my love : for vexing Mars had teaz'd
Me even to tears : thence, when a little eas'd,
Down-looking, vacant, through a hazy wood,   560
I saw this youth as he despairing stood :
Those same dark curls blown vagrant in the wind ;
Those same full fringed lids a constant blind
Over his sullen eyes : I saw him throw
Himself on wither'd leaves, even as though   565
Death had come sudden ; for no jot he mov'd,
Yet mutter'd wildly.   I could hear he lov'd
Some fair immortal, and that his embrace
Had zon'd her through the night.   There is no trace
Of this in heaven : I have mark'd each cheek,   570
And find it is the vainest thing to seek ;
And that of all things 'tis kept secretest.
Endymion ! one day thou wilt be blest :
So still obey the guiding hand that fends
Thee safely through these wonders for sweet ends.   575
'Tis a concealment needful in extreme ;
And if I guess'd not so, the sunny beam
Thou shouldst mount up to with me.   Now adieu !
Here must we leave thee."—At these words upflew
The impatient doves, uprose the floating car,   580
Up went the hum celestial.   High afar
The Latmian saw them minish into nought ;
And, when all were clear vanish'd, still he caught

---

(561) The manuscript reads *yon youth.*
(567) The draft has *madly* in place of *wildly.*

A vivid lightning from that dreadful bow.
When all was darkened, with Ætnean throe   585
The earth clos'd—gave a solitary moan—
And left him once again in twilight lone.

    He did not rave, he did not stare aghast,
For all those visions were o'ergone, and past,
And he in loneliness : he felt assur'd   590
Of happy times, when all he had endur'd
Would seem a feather to the mighty prize.
So, with unusual gladness, on he hies
Through caves, and palaces of mottled ore,
Gold dome, and crystal wall, and turquois floor,   595
Black polish'd porticos of awful shade,
And, at the last, a diamond balustrade,

(584-5) This couplet stood thus in the draft—

    Anon and ever gleams from that dread bow.
    One lightning more—then with Œtnœan throe...

In the manuscript the adjective in line 585 is written *ætnean*, in the first edition Etnean. I presume Keats's intention was to make the first E long by using a diphthong, and that he inadvertently used the wrong one.

(587) The draft reads *shut* for *left*.
(588) In the draft

    Nor did he rave, nor did he $\left\{ \begin{array}{c} \text{feel} \\ \text{stare} \end{array} \right\}$ aghast.

(589) We are to understand *that* after *For*, the sense being doubtless that Endymion did not rave and stare on account of the departure of the visions, and not that the departure of the visions was a sufficient cause for his not raving and staring. Line 590 originally began with *Leaving him solitary*.

(592) The draft reads *joy* for *prize*.
(596) Compare *Sleep and Poetry*, lines 75-6, page 91 :
                and where I found a spot
    Of awfuller shade.

(597-600) The draft reads—
    Then diamond steps and ruby balustrade

Leading afar past wild magnificence,
Spiral through ruggedest loopholes, and thence
Stretching across a void, then guiding o'er   600
Enormous chasms, where, all foam and roar,
Streams subterranean teaze their granite beds;
Then heighten'd just above the silvery heads
Of a thousand fountains, so that he could dash
The waters with his spear; but at the splash,   605
Done heedlessly, those spouting columns rose
Sudden a poplar's height, and 'gan to enclose
His diamond path with fretwork, streaming round
Alive, and dazzling cool, and with a sound,
Haply, like dolphin tumults, when sweet shells   610
Welcome the float of Thetis.   Long he dwells
On this delight; for, every minute's space,
The streams with changed magic interlace:
Sometimes like delicatest lattices,

Leading to fierce and wild magnificence
Spiral by ruggedest loopholes, and thence
Stretching across a void, then leading o'er...

(602) In the draft we have

Streams subterranean $\left\{ \begin{array}{c} \text{rage in} \\ \text{wear their} \end{array} \right\}$ granite beds;

and *hundred* for *thousand* in the next line but one.

(606) The draft reads *He playfully made* in place of *Done heedlessly*.

(607) In the finished manuscript, *'gan enclose*; but *'gan to enclose* in the first edition.

(608) In the draft we read

His mid-air path with fretwork, quivering round...

and in the next line but one *loud* for *sweet*. We must conclude the poet chose, for Thetis' sweet sake, to subdue into sweetness the orthodox clamour of the conchs blown at her approach over the sea.

Cover'd with crystal vines ; then weeping trees,   615
Moving about as in a gentle wind,
Which, in a wink, to watery gauze refin'd,
Pour'd into shapes of curtain'd canopies,
Spangled, and rich with liquid broideries
Of flowers, peacocks, swans, and naiads fair.   620
Swifter than lightning went these wonders rare ;
And then the water, into stubborn streams
Collecting, mimick'd the wrought oaken beams,
Pillars, and frieze, and high fantastic roof,
Of those dusk places in times far aloof   625
Cathedrals call'd.   He bade a loth farewell
To these founts Protean, passing gulph, and dell,
And torrent, and ten thousand jutting shapes,
Half seen through deepest gloom, and griesly gapes,
Blackening on every side, and overhead   630
A vaulted dome like Heaven's, far bespread
With starlight gems : aye, all so huge and strange,
The solitary felt a hurried change
Working within him into something dreary,—
Vex'd like a morning eagle, lost, and weary,   635

(615-16) In the original draft

> O'erspread with crystal vines ; then weeping peas,
> Waving about &c.

(622-3) The draft gives this couplet thus—

> And then the waters, into stubborn streams
> Collecting, mimick'd the wrought rafts and beams,

and in the next line but one reads *dim* for *dusk*.

(628) In place of *jutting* the draft reads successively *massy*, *blackening*, and *bulging*.

(629) *Hid in the dim profound*, according to the draft, which reads *overspread* in the next line but one in place of *far bespread*, and in line 632 *so monstrous strange* for *so huge and strange*.

(633) The draft reads *dizzy* for *hurried*, and in the next line but one *Scared* for *Vex'd*.

And purblind amid foggy, midnight wolds.
But he revives at once : for who beholds
New sudden things, nor casts his mental slough ?
Forth from a rugged arch, in the dusk below,
Came mother Cybele ! alone—alone—   640
In sombre chariot ; dark foldings thrown
About her majesty, and front death-pale,
With turrets crown'd.   Four maned lions hale
The sluggish wheels ; solemn their toothed maws,
Their surly eyes brow-hidden, heavy paws   645
Uplifted drowsily, and nervy tails
Cowering their tawny brushes.   Silent sails

---

(636) The words *damp and* stand cancelled in the finished manuscript before *foggy*.

(639) The draft reads *From out a* $\left\{ \begin{array}{l} dismal \\ beetling \\ gloomy \end{array} \right\}$ *arch* ; and in the

finished manuscript there is the cancelled reading *dark* for *dusk*.

(642-7) In the original draft, there were seven lines in place of
the six of the text, thus—

> About her majesty, and her pale brow
> With turrets crown'd, which forward heavily bow
> Weighing her chin to the breast.   Four lions draw
> The wheels in sluggish time—each toothed maw
> Shut patiently—eyes hid in tawny veils—
> Drooping about their paws, and nervy tails
> Cowering their tufted brushes to the dust.

These were crossed out ; and the passage, revised so as to approach
the final text, was inserted thus—

> About her majesty, and front death-pale
> With turrets crown'd.   Four tawny lions hale
>
> The sluggish wheels ; solemn their $\left\{ \begin{array}{l} closed \\ patient \end{array} \right\}$ maws
>
> Their surly eyes half shut, their heavy paws ·
> Uplifted lazily, and nervy tails
> Vailing their tawny tufts.

In the finished manuscript the passage was written precisely as

This shadowy queen athwart, and faints away
In another gloomy arch.

                    Wherefore delay,
Young traveller, in such a mournful place?   650
Art thou wayworn, or canst not further trace
The diamond path?   And does it indeed end
Abrupt in middle air?   Yet earthward bend
Thy forehead, and to Jupiter cloud-borne
Call ardently!   He was indeed wayworn;   655
Abrupt, in middle air, his way was lost;
To cloud-borne Jove he bowed, and there crost
Towards him a large eagle, 'twixt whose wings,
Without one impious word, himself he flings,
Committed to the darkness and the gloom: 660
Down, down, uncertain to what pleasant doom,
Swift as a fathoming plummet down he fell
Through unknown things; till exhal'd asphodel,
And rose, with spicy fannings interbreath'd,
Came swelling forth where little caves were wreath'd 665
So thick with leaves and mosses, that they seem'd
Large honey-combs of green, and freshly teem'd

---

in the printed text, except that *sleepily* was written in line 646 and
then struck out in favour of *drowsily*.

     (649) *Into* is here struck out in the finished manuscript, and *In*
substituted.

     (657) In the original draft the supernatural machinery for this
transit was entirely different, thus—

> To cloudborne Jove he bent : and there was tost
> Into his grasping hands a silken cord
> At which without a single impious word
> He swung upon it off into the gloom.
> Down, down, uncertain to what pleasant doom,
> Dropt like a fathoming plummet, down he fell
> Through unknown things ; till &c.

With airs delicious.   In the greenest nook
The eagle landed him, and farewell took.

   It was a jasmine bower, all bestrown   670
With golden moss.   His every sense had grown
Ethereal for pleasure; 'bove his head
Flew a delight half-graspable ; his tread
Was Hesperean ; to his capable ears
Silence was music from the holy spheres ;   675
A dewy luxury was in his eyes ;
The little flowers felt his pleasant sighs
And stirr'd them faintly.   Verdant cave and cell
He wander'd through, oft wondering at such swell
Of sudden exaltation : but, " Alas ! "   680
Said he, " will all this gush of feeling pass
Away in solitude?   And must they wane,

(668-71) The draft carries out the idea of the silken cord as follows :

       With airs delicious.   Long he hung about
       Before his nice enjoyment could pick out
       The resting place : but at the last he swung
       Into the greenest cell of all—among
       Dark leaved jasmine : star flower'd and bestrown
       With golden moss.

(674) *Hesperèan*, I presume, not Hespèrean as invariably accented by Milton.   The precise value of *capable* as used here is of
course regulated by past and not by present custom.   In this case
it simply stands for receptive, able to receive, as in *Hamlet* (Act
III, Scene IV)—

           look you how pale he glares,
       His forme and cause conjoyn'd, preaching to stones,
       Would make them capeable.

(679) In the draft—

       He wandered through, with still encreasing swell...

(681) In the draft—

       Said he, " will all these gushing feelings pass...

Like melodies upon a sandy plain,
Without an echo?   Then shall I be left
So sad, so melancholy, so bereft !   685
Yet still I feel immortal !   O my love,
My breath of life, where art thou ?   High above,
Dancing before the morning gates of heaven ?
Or keeping watch among those starry seven,
Old Atlas' children ?   Art a maid of the waters,   690
One of shell-winding Triton's bright-hair'd daughters ?
Or art, impossible ! a nymph of Dian's,
Weaving a coronal of tender scions
For very idleness ?   Where'er thou art,
Methinks it now is at my will to start   695
Into thine arms ; to scare Aurora's train,
And snatch thee from the morning ; o'er the main
To scud like a wild bird, and take thee off
From thy sea-foamy cradle ; or to doff
Thy shepherd vest, and woo thee mid fresh leaves.   700

---

(684) The draft reads *Ah I shall be left...*

(685) Compare the Sonnet *On a Dream*—

> So play'd, so charm'd, so conquer'd, so bereft...

(687-90) Endymion conjectures whether his unknown love is one of the Hours, or one of the nymph Pleione's daughters by Atlas, transferred to heaven as the Pleiades. The draft reads *the starry seven*, and *Art a nymph of the waters*. The finished manuscript has *Art a maid o' the waters*.

(691-2) According to the draft,

> One of shell-winding Triton's floating daughters ?
> Art thou, impossible ! a maid of Dian's,...

(697) In the draft the passage originally stood thus :—

> And snatch thee from among them ; to attain
> The starry hights and find thee ere a breath...

as if the intention had been to refer again to the fourfold conjecture instead of only three of its aspects.

(698) The draft reads *skim* for *scud*.

No, no, too eagerly my soul deceives
Its powerless self : I know this cannot be.
O let me then by some sweet dreaming flee
To her entrancements : hither sleep awhile !
Hither most gentle sleep ! and soothing foil   705
For some few hours the coming solitude."

    Thus spake he, and that moment felt endu'd
With power to dream deliciously ; so wound
Through a dim passage, searching till he found
The smoothest mossy bed and deepest, where   710
He threw himself, and just into the air
Stretching his indolent arms, he took, O bliss !
A naked waist : " Fair Cupid, whence is this ? "
A well-known voice sigh'd, " Sweetest, here am I ! "
At which soft ravishment, with doting cry   715
They trembled to each other.—Helicon !
O fountain'd hill !   Old Homer's Helicon !
That thou wouldst spout a little streamlet o'er
These sorry pages ; then the verse would soar
And sing above this gentle pair, like lark   720

(701-2) In the draft,

    But ah ! too eagerly my soul deceives
    Its mortal self : O since this cannot be,...

(706) The draft reads *With thy quick magic* for *For some few hours.*

(709) In the finished manuscript, *feeling* stands cancelled in favour of *searching.*

(713) The draft reads *Good heavens !* for *Fair Cupid.*

(715) In the draft this line stood thus—

At which each uttering forth $\left\{ \begin{array}{l} \text{an anguish} \\ \text{a wailful} \end{array} \right\}$ cry.

The finished manuscript reads as in the text ; but the first edition has *doating.*

(719-20) The draft reads *this verse* and *the gentle pair,* and in the next line but one *green* for *top.*

Over his nested young : but all is dark
Around thine aged top, and thy clear fount
Exhales in mists to heaven.   Aye, the count
Of mighty Poets is made up ; the scroll
Is folded by the Muses ; the bright roll   725
Is in Apollo's hand : our dazed eyes
Have seen a new tinge in the western skies :
The world has done its duty.   Yet, oh yet,
Although the sun of poesy is set,
These lovers did embrace, and we must weep   730
That there is no old power left to steep
A quill immortal in their joyous tears.
Long time in silence did their anxious fears
Question that thus it was ; long time they lay
Fondling and kissing every doubt away ;   735
Long time ere soft caressing sobs began
To mellow into words, and then there ran
Two bubbling springs of talk from their sweet lips.
" O known Unknown ! from whom my being sips
Such darling essence, wherefore may I not   740
Be ever in these arms ? in this sweet spot
Pillow my chin for ever ? ever press

---

(723) In the draft, *mist*, in the singular.

(725-6) The original reading of the draft was—

$$\text{Is in Apollo's hand : our} \begin{Bmatrix} \text{dazzled} \\ \text{mortal} \end{Bmatrix} \text{eyes...} \qquad \text{the great roll}$$

Time has reversed in favour both of Keats and of some of his contemporaries this verdict that the sun of poetry set with Shakespeare.

(735-6) The draft reads *dreaming* for *every* and *few* for *soft*.

(739) Compare, for mere juxtaposition of words, *Romeo and Juliet*, Act I, Scene V, line 141—

Too early seen unknown, and known too late !

These toying hands and kiss their smooth excess?
Why not for ever and for ever feel
That breath about my eyes?　Ah, thou wilt steal　　745
Away from me again, indeed, indeed—
Thou wilt be gone away, and wilt not heed
My lonely madness.　Speak, delicious fair!
Is—is it to be so?　No!　Who will dare
To pluck thee from me?　And, of thine own will,　　750
Full well I feel thou wouldst not leave me.　Still
Let me entwine thee surer, surer—now
How can we part?　Elysium! who art thou?
Who, that thou canst not be for ever here,
Or lift me with thee to some starry sphere?　　755
Enchantress! tell me by this soft embrace,
By the most soft completion of thy face,
Those lips, O slippery blisses, twinkling eyes,
And by these tenderest, milky sovereignties—
These tenderest, and by the nectar-wine,　　760
The passion "———"O dov'd Ida the divine!

---

(743) The draft reads *languid* for *toying*.

(747-8) Woodhouse notes, apparently from the draft, the variation,

> And there must be a time when thoul't not heed
> My lonely madness—O delicious $\left\{ \begin{array}{l} \text{maid} \\ \text{fair} \end{array} \right\}$.

The finished manuscript and the first edition both read *my
kindest fair!* But the version of the text is from the corrected copy.

(749) In the draft, *What will dare*, and in the next line but one
I know—I feel.

(756-7) The draft gives this couplet thus

> Enchantress! tell me by this mad embrace,
> By the moist languor of thy breathing face...

(760-1) The draft has this couplet as follows—

> These tenderest—and by the breath—the love
> The passion—nectar—Heaven!"———"Jove above!

Endymion! dearest! Ah, unhappy me!
His soul will 'scape us—O felicity!
How he does love me! His poor temples beat
To the very tune of love—how sweet, sweet, sweet.   765
Revive, dear youth, or I shall faint and die;
Revive, or these soft hours will hurry by
In tranced dulness; speak, and let that spell
Affright this lethargy! I cannot quell
Its heavy pressure, and will press at least   770
My lips to thine, that they may richly feast
Until we taste the life of love again.
What! dost thou move? dost kiss? O bliss! O pain!
I love thee, youth, more than I can conceive;
And so long absence from thee doth bereave   775
My soul of any rest : yet must I hence :
Yet, can I not to starry eminence
Uplift thee; nor for very shame can own
Myself to thee :   Ah, dearest, do not groan
Or thou wilt force me from this secrecy,   780
And I must blush in heaven.   O that I
Had done 't already; that the dreadful smiles

The second of these lines originally stood in the finished manuscript
thus—
            The Passion — — — " O Ida the divine !
as if *passion* were meant to scan as a trisyllable, as in many other
cases of similar words in *Endymion*,—*ambrosial* for instance in line
810 ; *Endymion* in lines 823 and 855 of this book; and *intoxication*
in line 502 of Book I ; but Keats has inserted before *Ida* the word
dov'd, not *lov'd* as in the first edition.

    (770) The draft reads *yet* for *and*, and in the next line *'gainst* for
to.

    (774) Cancelled reading from the draft, *Listen to me if Love will
let me*...

    (782) The contraction *done 't* here is a final and deliberate inten-
tion : for although *done it* was printed in the first edition—perhaps

At my lost brightness, my impassion'd wiles,
Had waned from Olympus' solemn height,
And from all serious Gods ; that our delight   785
Was quite forgotten, save of us alone !
And wherefore so asham'd ?   'Tis but to atone
For endless pleasure, by some coward blushes :
Yet must I be a coward !—Horror rushes
Too palpable before me—the sad look   790
Of Jove—Minerva's start—no bosom shook
With awe of purity—no Cupid pinion
In reverence vailed—my crystalline dominion
Half lost, and all old hymns made nullity !
But what is this to love ?   O I could fly   795
With thee into the ken of heavenly powers,
So thou wouldst thus, for many sequent hours,
Press me so sweetly.   Now I swear at once
That I am wise, that Pallas is a dunce— .

---

through Keats having puzzled the printer by writing in the manuscript *do n't*—the printed words are altered to *done't* in the corrected
copy. ⁻

(783) There is a cancelled reading in the draft, *At my dear weakness and...*

(785) The draft reads *Powers* for *Gods* and *my* for *our*, and in the
next line but one *But* for *And.*

(789) In place of *Horror* the draft reads first *The thing*, then
The idea. In the finished manuscript the original reading was *the
horror* ; but *the* is struck out. In the first edition the word was
printed *Honour*, which word Keats habitually spelt without the *u*,
so that in his writing *horror* and *honor* are almost if not quite identical. The correction is made in the copy in my possession ; but
it is not made in Woodhouse's copy though it appears in the longer
list of errata found in some copies. Woodhouse's has only the single-
erratum page.

(793) In the first edition (and as far as I know all others) *veiled*,
but *vailed* in the manuscript, which is obviously right.

(796) The draft reads *starry* for *heavenly.*

Perhaps her love like mine is but unknown—   800
O I do think that I have been alone
In chastity : 'yes, Pallas has been sighing,
While every eve saw me my hair uptying
With fingers cool as aspen leaves.   Sweet love,
I was as vague as solitary dove,   805
Nor knew that nests were built.   Now a soft kiss—
Aye, by that kiss, I vow an endless bliss,
An immortality of passion's thine :
Ere long I will exalt thee to the shine
Of heaven ambrosial ; and we will shade   810
Ourselves whole summers by a river glade ;
And I will tell thee stories of the sky,
And breathe thee whispers of its minstrelsy.
My happy love will overwing all bounds !
O let me melt into thee ; let the sounds   815
Of our close voices marry at their birth ;
Let us entwine hoveringly—O dearth
Of human words ! roughness of mortal speech !
Lispings empyrean will I sometime teach

---

(800) In the draft,

> Does Pallas self not love? she must—she must !

(807) Cancelled reading of the manuscript, *swear* for *vow*.
(813-14) The draft has these two lines thus—

> And breathe thee empyrean minstrelsy.
> O my mad love   ⎫
> My maddened love ⎬ will overwing all bounds !

(815-29) This passage varies considerably in detail from what
was originally written in the draft :—

>   let the sounds
> Of both our voices marry at their birth ;
> Let us entwine inextricably—O dearth
> Of mortal words ! I'll teach thee other speech ;
> Lispings immortal will I sometime teach

Thine honied tongue—lute-breathings, which I gasp   820
To have thee understand, now while I clasp
Thee thus, and weep for fondness—I am pain'd,
Endymion : woe ! woe ! is grief contain'd
In the very deeps of pleasure, my sole life ? "—
Hereat, with many sobs, her gentle strife   825
Melted into a languor.   He return'd
Entranced vows and tears.

                  Ye who have yearn'd
With too much passion, will here stay and pity,
For the mere sake of truth ; as 'tis a ditty
Not of these days, but long ago 'twas told   830
By a cavern wind unto a forest old ;
And then the forest told it in a dream

Thinε honied tongue—Gold-breathings, which I gasp
To have thee understand, now while I clasp

Thee thus, and shed these $\left\{ \begin{array}{l} \text{tears} \\ \text{drops} \end{array} \right\}$—I am pain'd,

Endymion.   There is a grief contain'd
In the very shrine of pleasure, O my life !"
Hereat with fainting sobs her gentle strife
Died into passive languor—he return'd
No answer, saving tears.—Ye who have burn'd
With over passion, here exclaim and pity
Even for the sake of truth ;...

It is perhaps worth while to note the correspondence of thought between the utterance here given to Diana on the subject of the " grief contain'd in the very deeps of pleasure," and that wonderful line of Keats's in the Homer sonnet of 1818,

      There is a budding morrow in midnight,

a line which I have heard competent critics pronounce not only the finest line in Keats's poetry, but one of the finest lines in all poetry.

    (831) Cancelled reading of the manuscript, *Cavern's Mouth* for *cavern wind*.

To a sleeping lake, whose cool and level gleam
A poet caught as he was journeying
To Phœbus' shrine ; and in it he did fling   835
His weary limbs, bathing an hour's space,
And after, straight in that inspired place
He sang the story up into the air,
Giving it universal freedom.   There
Has it been ever sounding for those ears   840
Whose tips are glowing hot.   The legend cheers
Yon centinel stars ; and he who listens to it
Must surely be self-doom'd or he will rue it :
For quenchless burnings come upon the heart,
Made fiercer by a fear lest any part   845
Should be engulphed in the eddying wind.
As much as here is penn'd doth always find
A resting place, thus much comes clear and plain ;
Anon the strange voice is upon the wane—
And 'tis but echo'd from departing sound,   850

---

(833) The draft reads *slumbering* for *sleeping.*
(841) Compare Milton's *Lycidas*—

> But not the praise,
> Phœbus replied, and touch'd my trembling ears ;...

(849-50) The draft reads—

> But after the strange voice is on the wane—
> And 'tis but guess'd from the departing sound,

and in the next line but one *prison'd* for *gentle.* The two lines as
written in the draft make it more absolutely clear than the two lines
as printed that the departure of Diana is divined from the faintly
sounding close of the story to which the poet gave voice.   The birth
of this tale out-does in imaginative delicacy the account of the "sleepy
music" in this Book (lines 358 to 363), though that exceeds this in
compactness.   Keats probably felt that there was quite enough
about the poet's voice, for unless I am much deceived he rejected a
most lovely and elaborate series of comparisons for that voice,—

That the fair visitant at last unwound
Her gentle limbs, and left the youth asleep.—　　852
Thus the tradition of the gusty deep.

---

only inferior, if indeed they are inferior, to the "tradition of the gusty deep" which they would have followed immediately—thus :

Oh ! what a voice is silent.　It was soft
As mountain-echoes, when the winds aloft
(The gentle winds of summer) meet in caves ;
Or when in sheltered places the white waves
Are 'waken'd into music, as the breeze
Dimples and stems the current : or as trees
Shaking their green locks in the days of June :
Or Delphic girls when to the maiden moon
They sang harmonious pray'rs : or sounds that come
(However near) like a faint distant hum
Out of the grass, from which mysterious birth
We guess the busy secrets of the earth.
—Like the low voice of Syrinx, when she ran
Into the forests from Arcadian Pan:
Or sad Œnone's, when she pined away
For Paris, or (and yet 'twas not so gay)
As Helen's whisper when she came to Troy,
Half sham'd to wander with that blooming boy.
Like air-touch'd harps in flowery casements hung ;
Like unto lovers' ears the wild words sung
In garden bowers at twilight: like the sound
Of Zephyr when he takes his nightly round
In May, to see the roses all asleep:
Or like the dim strain which along the deep
The sea-maid utters to the sailors' ear,
Telling of tempests, or of dangers near.
Like Desdemona, who (when fear was strong
Upon her soul) chaunted the willow song,
Swan-like before she perish'd : or the tone
Of flutes upon the waters heard alone :
Like words that come upon the memory
Spoken by friends departed ; or the sigh
A gentle girl breathes when she tries to hide
The love her eyes betray to all beside.

These lines appeared in *The Indicator* for the 19th of January

Now turn we to our former chroniclers.—
Endymion awoke, that grief of hers   855
Sweet paining on his ear : he sickly guess'd
How lone he was once more, and sadly press'd
His empty arms together, hung his head,
And most forlorn upon that widow'd bed
Sat silently.   Love's madness he had known :   860
Often with more than tortured lion's groan
Moanings had burst from him ; but now that rage
Had pass'd away : no longer did he wage
A rough-voic'd war against the dooming stars.
No, he had felt too much for such harsh jars :   865
The lyre of his soul Æolian tun'd
Forgot all violence, and but commun'd
With melancholy thought :   O he had swoon'd
Drunken from pleasure's nipple ; and his love

1820.   See remarks on them in the Preface to this edition of Keats.
It would be really interesting to know whether Shelley had seen the
comparison of this divine voice to "the tone of flutes upon the
waters," when he wrote the much debated passage in *Prometheus
Unbound* (Act II, Scene II, line 38) about the Nightingales' singing,

> Like many a lake-surrounded flute,

which may or may not have been among the "corrections and additions" sent to Mr. and Mrs. Gisborne as late as the end of May 1820.
  (856) Cancelled reading of the manuscript, *in* for *on*.
  (860) The draft reads *Patiently sat* for *Sat silently*.
  (862) In the draft, this line began with the word *Passion* ; and
Complaints and *Plainings* were in turn struck out of the finished
manuscript before the word of the text, *Moanings*, was arrived at.
  (865) The draft gives the line—

$$\text{No, he} \begin{Bmatrix} \text{was} \\ \text{felt} \end{Bmatrix} \text{too divine for such harsh jars.}$$

  (866) In the first edition *Eolian*.   Keats meant to use the diphthong ; but in the manuscript he put the wrong one, *Œ*.
  (868) The draft reads *With thoughts of tenderest birth*.

Henceforth was dove-like.—Loth was he to move   870
From the imprinted couch, and when he did,
'Twas with slow, languid paces, and face hid
In muffling hands.   So temper'd, out he stray'd
Half seeing visions that might have dismay'd
Alecto's serpents; ravishments more keen   875
Than Hermes' pipe, when anxious he did lean
Over eclipsing eyes : and at the last
It was a sounding grotto, vaulted, vast,
O'er studded with a thousand, thousand pearls,
And crimson mouthed shells with stubborn curls,   880
Of every shape and size, even to the bulk
In which whales harbour close, to brood and sulk
Against an endless storm.   Moreover too,

(870-1) In the draft, thus —

Scarcely could he move
From the dear couch.

(873) The draft reads *In muffling arms*, and in the next line
Scarce seeing wonders.

(876) The words *those of* are cancelled in the finished manuscript
before *Herme's* (not *Hermes'*).   The story of Argus seems to have
impressed Keats vividly: see his sonnet, "As Hermes once took to
his feathers light." Probably this vivid impression was derived from
Cary's Dante (*Purgatory*, Canto XXXII), which he certainly read
attentively, and on the fly-leaf of which, by the bye, he wrote that
very sonnet.   He may also have known the story in Ovid's *Metamorphoses* (Book I).

(878) The draft reads *He found* for *It was*.

(879) *And* is here cancelled in favour of *O'er* in the finished
manuscript.

(880) In the draft—

And shells outswelling their faint tinged curls.

(881) Cancelled reading of the manuscript, *hue* for *shape*.

(882) In the finished manuscript and in the first edition *arbour* ;
but although this might have a very far-fetched sense, I do not
think it would be justifiable to restore the reading.

Fish-semblances, of green and azure hue,
Ready to snort their streams. In this cool wonder　885
Endymion sat down, and 'gan to ponder
On all his life : his youth, up to the day
When 'mid acclaim, and feasts, and garlands gay,
He stept upon his shepherd throne: the look
Of his white palace in wild forest nook,　　　　　890
And all the revels he had lorded there :
Each tender maiden whom he once thought fair,
With every friend and fellow-woodlander—
Pass'd like a dream before him. Then the spur
Of the old bards to mighty deeds : his plans　　　895
To nurse the golden age 'mong shepherd clans :
That wondrous night : the great Pan-festival :
His sister's sorrow ; and his wanderings all,
Until into the earth's deep maw he rush'd :
Then all its buried magic, till it flush'd　　　　900
High with excessive love.   "And now," thought he,
" How long must I remain in jeopardy
Of blank amazements that amaze no more ?
Now I have tasted her sweet soul to the core
All other depths are shallow : essences,　　　　905
Once spiritual, are like muddy lees,
Meant but to fertilize my earthly root,
And make my branches lift a golden fruit
Into the bloom of heaven : other light,

---

(884) The draft reads *green and golden hue.*
(895) The draft reads *minstrelsy* instead of *the old bards.*
(897) Cancelled readings from the draft—

　　That wondrous night that wean'd him...
　　That wondrous night : great Pan's high festival.

(899) The draft reads *dim* for *deep.*
(907) The draft reads first *Made* and then *Sent* for *Meant*, and
in the next line *their ripen'd fruit.*

Though it be quick and sharp enough to blight   910
The Olympian eagle's vision, is dark,
Dark as the parentage of chaos.   Hark !
My silent thoughts are echoing from these shells ;
Or they are but the ghosts, the dying swells
Of noises far away ?—list !"—Hereupon   915
He kept an anxious ear.   The humming tone
Came louder, and behold, there as he lay,
On either side outgush'd, with misty spray,
A copious spring ; and both together dash'd
Swift, mad, fantastic round the rocks, and lash'd   920
Among the conchs and shells of the lofty grot,
Leaving a trickling dew.   At last they shot
Down from the ceiling's height, pouring a noise
As of some breathless racers whose hopes poize
Upon the last few steps, and with spent force   925
Along the ground they took a winding course.
Endymion follow'd—for it seem'd that one
Ever pursu'd, the other strove to shun—
Follow'd their languid mazes, till well nigh
He had left thinking of the mystery,—   930
And was now rapt in tender hoverings
Over the vanish'd bliss.   Ah ! what is it sings
His dream away ? What melodies are these ?
They sound as through the whispering of trees,
Not native in such barren vaults.   Give ear !   935

---

(914) This line was written in the draft—

       Or they are subtlest and dying swells.

(917) The word *still* is struck out of the finished manuscript after *louder*.

(920) This line ends with *splash'd* in the draft.

(932) In the draft, this line began with *O'er past and future*. The finished manuscript reads *is't* for *is it*.

"O Arethusa, peerless nymph! why fear
Such tenderness as mine? Great Dian, why,
Why didst thou hear her prayer? O that I
Were rippling round her dainty fairness now,
Circling about her waist, and striving how   940
To entice her to a dive! then stealing in
Between her luscious lips and eyelids thin.
O that her shining hair was in the sun,
And I distilling from it thence to run
In amorous rillets down her shrinking form!   945
To linger on her lilly shoulders, warm
Between her kissing breasts, and every charm
Touch raptur'd!—See how painfully I flow:
Fair maid, be pitiful to my great woe.
Stay, stay thy weary course, and let me lead,   950
A happy wooer, to the flowery mead
Where all that beauty snar'd me."—"Cruel god,
Desist! or my offended mistress' nod
Will stagnate all thy fountains:—teaze me not
With syren words—Ah, have I really got   955
Such power to madden thee? And is it true—
Away, away, or I shall dearly rue
My very thoughts: in mercy then away,
Kindest Alpheus, for should I obey

---

(945) The draft reads—

    Amorous and slow adown her shrinking form!

(947-9) These three lines stood thus in the draft—

    About her { pouting / budding } breasts, and every charm

    Kiss, raptur'd, even to her milky toes.
    O foolish maid be gentle to my woes.

(952) The draft reads *slew* for *snar'd*.
(954) Cancelled reading of the manuscript, *waters* for *fountains*.

My own dear will, 'twould be a deadly bane.   960
O, Oread-Queen! would that thou hadst a pain
Like this of mine, then would I fearless turn
And be a criminal. Alas, I burn,
I shudder—gentle river, get thee hence.
Alpheus! thou enchanter! every sense   965
Of mine was once made perfect in these woods.
Fresh breezes, bowery lawns, and innocent floods,
Ripe fruits, and lonely couch, contentment gave;
But ever since I heedlessly did lave
In thy deceitful stream, a panting glow   970
Grew strong within me: wherefore serve me so,
And call it love?   Alas, 'twas cruelty.
Not once more did I close my happy eye
Amid the thrushes' song. Away! Avaunt!
O 'twas a cruel thing."—"Now thou dost taunt   975
So softly, Arethusa, that I think

---

(960) In the first edition Arethusa's speech is closed at the end of
this line, and taken up again at *Alas, I burn*, in line 363, the intermediate portion being separated from it by independent marks of
quotation, as if spoken by Alpheus; but in the manuscript the one
speech extends from *Cruel God* (952) to *cruel thing* (975); and this
obviously correct arrangement is restored in the copy revised by
Keats.

(964) The draft reads—

    I shudder—for sweet mercy get thee hence.

(966-9) The draft reads *happy* for *perfect*, *shady* for *bowery*, *leafy*
for *lonely*, and *gan* for *did*.

(973) This line ends with *eyes* both in the finished manuscript
and in the first edition; but it is certain that *eye* was the expression
in the poet's mind, for in the draft the line stood thus—

No longer could I close my $\left\{ \begin{array}{l} \text{wearied} \\ \text{sleepless} \end{array} \right\}$ eye.

(974) In the finished manuscript, not *thrush's* but *Thrushes*, without any apostrophe. As Woodhouse records that the draft read
thrushes', it seems safe to adopt that form.

If thou wast playing on my shady brink,
Thou wouldst bathe once again.   Innocent maid!
Stifle thine heart no more; nor be afraid
Of angry powers: there are deities   980
Will shade us with their wings.   Those fitful sighs
'Tis almost death to hear: O let me pour
A dewy balm upon them!—fear no more,
Sweet Arethusa! Dian's self must feel
Sometime these very pangs.   Dear maiden, steal   985
Blushing into my soul, and let us fly
These dreary caverns for the open sky.
I will delight thee all my winding course,
From the green sea up to my hidden source
About Arcadian forests; and will show   990
The channels where my coolest waters flow
Through mossy rocks; where, 'mid exuberant green,
I roam in pleasant darkness, more unseen
Than Saturn in his exile; where I brim
Round flowery islands, and take thence a skim   995
Of mealy sweets, which myriads of bees
Buzz from their honey'd wings: and thou shouldst please
Thyself to choose the richest, where we might

---

(977) In the draft *by* in place of *on*.

(985) In the manuscript, *Some time*, without the final *s* as in the first edition.   I think the insertion of the *s* must have been overlooked by Keats.

(990) The draft reads—

About Arcadia's Plains ; and I will show

and the finished manuscript,

About Arcadian Forests ; and I will shew...

Probably Keats meant to cancel *I*; and it does not appear in his printed edition.

(996) The draft reads *powdery* for *mealy*.

(997) Cancelled reading of the manuscript, *Shake* for *Buzz*.

(998) In the draft, *choose the freshest*.

Be incense-pillow'd every summer night.
Doff all sad fears, thou white deliciousness,   1000
And let us be thus comforted ; unless
Thou couldst rejoice to see my hopeless stream
Hurry distracted from Sol's temperate beam,
And pour to death along some hungry sands."—
" What can I do, Alpheus ?   Dian stands   1005
Severe before me : persecuting fate !
Unhappy Arethusa ! thou wast late
A huntress free in "—At this, sudden fell
Those two sad streams adown a fearful dell.
The Latmian listen'd, but he heard no more,   1010
Save echo, faint repeating o'er and o'er
The name of Arethusa.   On the verge
Of that dark gulph he wept, and said : " I urge
Thee, gentle Goddess of my pilgrimage,
By our eternal hopes, to soothe, to assuage,   1015
If thou art powerful, these lovers' pains ;
And make them happy in some happy plains."

He turn'd—there was a whelming sound—he stept,
There was a cooler light ; and so he kept
Towards it by a sandy path, and lo !   1020
More suddenly than doth a moment go,
The visions of the earth were gone and fled—
He saw the giant sea above his head.

(1004) The draft reads *along hot Afric's sands*, and in the next
line but one *cruel, cruel fate !*

(1016) *Lovers* in the manuscript and in the first edition, without
the apostrophe ; and the speech is not closed with a mark of quotation in either.

(1017) The draft reads *their native plains.*

(1020) Cancelled reading of the finished manuscript, *scanty* for
sandy.

ENDYMION.

BOOK III.

ENDYMION.

BOOK III.

THERE are who lord it o'er their fellow-men
With most prevailing tinsel : who unpen
Their baaing vanities, to browse away
The comfortable green and juicy hay
From human pastures ; or, O torturing fact!　　　　5
Who, through an idiot blink, will see unpack'd
Fire-branded foxes to sear up and singe
Our gold and ripe-ear'd hopes.　With not one tinge
Of sanctuary splendour, not a sight
Able to face an owl's, they still are dight　　　　10
By the blear-ey'd nations in empurpled vests,
And crowns, and turbans.　With unladen breasts,

---

(1) Woodhouse notes that "Keats said, with much simplicity, 'It will be easily seen what I think of the present ministers, by the beginning of the third Book.'" Perhaps the Quarterly Reviewer had heard of that simple saying.

(5) The draft reads *O devilish fact!*—and in the next line *with* for *through*.

Save of blown self-applause, they proudly mount
To their spirit's perch, their being's high account,
Their tiptop nothings, their dull skies, their thrones—   15
Amid the fierce intoxicating tones
Of trumpets, shoutings, and belabour'd drums,
And sudden cannon.   Ah! how all this hums,
In wakeful ears, like uproar past and gone—
Like thunder clouds that spake to Babylon,   20
And set those old Chaldeans to their tasks.—
Are then regalities all gilded masks?
No, there are throned seats unscalable
But by a patient wing, a constant spell,
Or by ethereal things that, unconfin'd,   25
Can make a ladder of the eternal wind,
And poise about in cloudy thunder-tents
To watch the abysm-birth of elements.
Aye, 'bove the withering of old-lipp'd Fate
A thousand Powers keep religious state,   30
In water, fiery realm, and airy bourne;
And, silent as a consecrated urn,
Hold spherey sessions for a season due.
Yet few of these far majesties, ah, few!
Have bar'd their operations to this globe—   35
Few, who with gorgeous pageantry enrobe

---

(19) The draft has *almost* in place of *past and*.
(21-3) The following rejected reading is from the draft:
>   And set those old Chaldeans to their work.—
>   Are then all regal things so gone, so murk?
>   No there are other thrones to mount.
(31-2) The draft yields the rejected couplet—
>   In the several vastnesses of air and fire;
>   And silent, as a corpse upon a pyre.
(34) The draft reads
>   How few of these far majesties, how few!

Our piece of heaven—whose benevolence
Shakes hand with our own Ceres; every sense
Filling with spiritual sweets to plenitude,
As bees gorge full their cells.   And, by the feud   40
'Twixt Nothing and Creation, I here swear,
Eterne Apollo! that thy Sister fair
Is of all these the gentlier-mightiest.
When thy gold breath is misting in the west,
She unobserved steals unto her throne,   45
And there she sits most meek and most alone;
As if she had not pomp subservient;
As if thine eye, high Poet! was not bent
Towards her with the Muses in thine heart;
As if the ministring stars kept not apart,   50
Waiting for silver-footed messages.
O Moon! the oldest shades 'mong oldest trees

(38-9) These two lines stood thus in the draft—

Salutes our native Ceres— $\left\{ \begin{array}{l} \text{and each} \\ \text{every} \end{array} \right\}$ sense

With spiritual honey fills to plenitude...

(41) At the end of this line Keats wrote in the original draft, as if to localize the oath he was recording, "Oxford, Septr. 5."

(42) The word *eterne* seems to be another reminiscence of Spenser: see *Faerie Queene*, Book III, Canto vi, Stanza 47 :

Yet is eterne in mutabilitie,...

(44) The draft reads—

When thy gold hair falls thick about the west.

(49) The draft has *Upon* in place of *Towards*.

(50) This attribution of an active life of ministration to the stars is a recurrence of the idea in Book II, lines 184-5—

by all the stars
That tend thy bidding...

(52) In the draft,

Waiting the oldest shadows $\left\{ \begin{array}{l} \text{'mong} \\ \text{of} \end{array} \right\}$ old trees.

Feel palpitations when thou lookest in :
O Moon ! old boughs lisp forth a holier din
The while they feel thine airy fellowship.   55
Thou dost bless every where, with silver lip
Kissing dead things to life. The sleeping kine,
Couch'd in thy brightness, dream of fields divine :
Innumerable mountains rise, and rise,
Ambitious for the hallowing of thine eyes ;   60
And yet thy benediction passeth not
One obscure hiding-place, one little spot
Where pleasure may be sent : the nested wren
Has thy fair face within its tranquil ken,
And from beneath a sheltering ivy leaf   65
Takes glimpses of thee ; thou art a relief
To the poor patient oyster, where it sleeps
Within its pearly house.—The mighty deeps,
The monstrous sea is thine—the myriad sea !
O Moon ! far-spooming Ocean bows to thee,   70

(56-7) The draft reads—

    Thou dost bless all things—even dead things sip
    A midnight life from thee.

(63) In the draft, *wrought* for *sent* ; and in the next line there is
the cancelled reading, *Quiet behind dark ivy leaves...*
(69) The draft reads—

    The monstrous sea is thine—the monstrous sea !

(70) In the draft *old* occurs in place of *far*. The word *spooming*
for *spuming*, though not ordinarily found in dictionaries, was quite
in Keats's line of reading. Thus Beaumont and Fletcher in *The
Double Marriage* (Act II, Scene 1) have

    Down with the foresail too, we'll spoom before her.

Dryden, in *The Hind and the Panther*, has

    When virtue spooms before a prosperous gale
    My heaving wishes help to fill the sail.

And Tellus feels his forehead's cumbrous load.

Cynthia! where art thou now?   What far abode
Of green or silvery bower doth enshrine
Such utmost beauty?   Alas, thou dost pine
For one as sorrowful : thy cheek is pale   75
For one whose cheek is pale : thou dost bewail
His tears, who weeps for thee.   Where dost thou sigh?
Ah! surely that light peeps from Vesper's eye,
Or what a thing is love! 'Tis She, but lo!
How chang'd, how full of ache, how gone in woe!   80
She dies at the thinnest cloud ; her loveliness
Is wan on Neptune's blue : yet there's a stress
Of love-spangles, just off yon cape of trees,
Dancing upon the waves, as if to please
The curly foam with amorous influence.   85
O, not so idle : for down-glancing thence
She fathoms eddies, and runs wild about

And Brooke, in *Constantia*, has

> The wind fresh blowing from the Syrian shore
> Swift through the floods her spooming vessel bore.

(71) In the manuscript and in the corrected copy, *his*; but *her*
was printed in the first edition, and corrected as an *erratum*,—the
only one in some copies.   The mistake arose through a pencilled
marginal suggestion made in the printer's copy, not in Keats's
writing.

(74) Cancelled reading of the draft, *Thine* for *Such*.

(77-8) In the draft there was a false rhyme here, seen and remedied
in copying out :

> Where art thou Ah
> Surely that light is from the Evening star...

(86-7) The draft shows more than one tentative for this passage,
thus :

> Nor $\left\{ \begin{array}{l} \text{stays it} \\ \text{there sleeps} \end{array} \right\}$ the idleness—but glancing thence...
>
> Nor cradled idly—but down glancing thence...

O'erwhelming water-courses ; scaring out
The thorny sharks from hiding-holes, and fright'ning
Their savage eyes with unaccustom'd lightning.   90
Where will the splendour be content to reach ?
O love ! how potent hast thou been to teach
Strange journeyings !   Wherever beauty dwells,
In gulph or aerie, mountains or deep dells,
In light, in gloom, in star or blazing sun,   95
Thou pointest out the way, and straight 'tis won.
Amid his toil thou gav'st Leander breath ;
Thou leddest Orpheus through the gleams of death ;
Thou madest Pluto bear thin element ;
And now, O winged Chieftain ! thou hast sent   100
A moon-beam to the deep, deep water-world,
To find Endymion.

On gold sand impearl'd
With lilly shells, and pebbles milky white,
Poor Cynthia greeted him, and sooth'd her light
Against his pallid face : he felt the charm   105
To breathlessness, and suddenly a warm
Of his heart's blood : 'twas very sweet ; he stay'd
His wandering steps, and half-entranced laid
His head upon a tuft of straggling weeds,
To taste the gentle moon, and freshening beads,   110

Yet not so idle—for down glancing thence
It mingles and starts about unfathomed...

(89-90) In the draft this couplet reads—

Enormous sharks from hiding-holes, and fright'ning
The whale's large eyes with unaccustomed lightning.

(94-5) The draft reads thus—

In air, or living flame—or magic shells,
In earth, or mist, in star or blazing sun,...

Lash'd from the crystal roof by fishes' tails.
And so he kept, until the rosy veils
Mantling the east, by Aurora's peering hand
Were lifted from the water's breast, and fann'd
Into sweet air; and sober'd morning came   115
Meekly through billows :—when like taper-flame
Left sudden by a dallying breath of air,
He rose in silence, and once more 'gan fare
Along his fated way.

                    Far had he roam'd,
With nothing save the hollow vast, that foam'd,   120
Above, around, and at his feet ; save things
More dead than Morpheus' imaginings :
Old rusted anchors, helmets, breast-plates large
Of gone sea-warriors ; brazen beaks and targe ;
Rudders that for a hundred years had lost   125
The sway of human hand ; gold vase emboss'd
With long-forgotten story, and wherein
No reveller had ever dipp'd a chin
But those of Saturn's vintage ; mouldering scrolls,
Writ in the tongue of heaven, by those souls   130
Who first were on the earth ; and sculptures rude
In ponderous stone, developing the mood
Of ancient Nox ;—then skeletons of man,
Of beast, behemoth, and leviathan,
And elephant, and eagle, and huge jaw   135
Of nameless monster. A cold leaden awe
These secrets struck into him ; and unless
Dian had chac'd away that heaviness,
He might have di'd : but now, with cheered feel,

(128) In the draft, *revellers* for *reveller*.

He onward kept ; wooing these thoughts to steal   140
About the labyrinth in his soul of love.

"What is there in thee, Moon ! that thou shouldst
          move
My heart so potently ?   When yet a child
I oft have dry'd my tears when thou hast smil'd.
Thou seem'dst my sister : hand in hand we went   145
From eve to morn across the firmament.
No apples would I gather from the tree,
Till thou hadst cool'd their cheeks deliciously :
No tumbling water ever spake romance,
But when my eyes with thine thereon could dance :   150
No woods were green enough, no bower divine,
Until thou liftedst up thine eyelids fine :
In sowing time ne'er would I dibble take,
Or drop a seed, till thou wast wide awake ;
And, in the summer tide of blossoming,   155
No one but thee hath heard me blythly sing
And mesh my dewy flowers all the night.
No melody was like a passing spright
If it went not to solemnize thy reign.
Yes, in my boyhood, every joy and pain   160
By thee were fashion'd to the self-same end ;

----

(140) Cancelled reading of the manuscript, *went* for *kept*.

(150) The draft reads *soul* in place of *eyes*.

(156) This line affords a curious instance of waywardness in the
matter of spelling : the last word but one is *blithly* in the first
edition, *blythly* in the finished manuscript, and, fide Woodhouse,
blithely in the draft.   In Book I, line 939, the cognate adjective is
spelt with a *y*, both in manuscript and in first edition ; so that it is
to be presumed that Keats really preferred this orthography, which
is that adopted in *Piers Plowman.*

(159) The draft yields the alternative readings *flew* and *sought* in
place of *went.*

And as I grew in years, still didst thou blend
With all my ardours : thou wast the deep glen ;
Thou wast the mountain-top—the sage's pen—
The poet's harp—the voice of friends—the sun ;   165
Thou wast the river—thou wast glory won ;
Thou wast my clarion's blast—thou wast my steed—
My goblet full of wine—my topmost deed :—
Thou wast the charm of women, lovely Moon !
O what a wild and harmonized tune   170
My spirit struck from all the beautiful !
On some bright essence could I lean, and lull
Myself to immortality : I prest
Nature's soft pillow in a wakeful rest.
But, gentle Orb ! there came a nearer bliss—   175
My strange love came—Felicity's abyss !
She came, and thou didst fade, and fade away—
Yet not entirely ; no, thy starry sway
Has been an under-passion to this hour.
Now I begin to feel thine orby power   180
Is coming fresh upon me : O be kind,
Keep back thine influence, and do not blind
My sovereign vision.—Dearest love, forgive
That I can think away from thee and live !—
Pardon me, airy planet, that I prize   185
One thought beyond thine argent luxuries !
How far beyond ! "   At this a surpris'd start

---

(168) Instead of *topmost* the draft has *highest*.

(170) In the draft, *harmonizing*, and in the next line the alternative readings *sung* and *made* for *struck*.

(176) The draft reads *dear pleasure's own abyss* for *Felicity's abyss*.

(180) The draft reads *orbed* for *orby*.

(183) In the draft, instead of *My sovereign vision*, we read *The vision of my Love*.

Frosted the springing verdure of his heart ;
For as he lifted up his eyes to swear
How his own goddess was past all things fair,   190
He saw far in the concave green of the sea
An old man sitting calm and peacefully.
Upon a weeded rock this old man sat,
And his white hair was awful, and a mat
Of weeds were cold beneath his cold thin feet ;   195
And, ample as the largest winding-sheet,
A cloak of blue wrapp'd up his aged bones,
O'erwrought with symbols by the deepest groans
Of ambitious magic: every ocean-form
Was woven in with black distinctness ; storm,   200
And calm, and whispering, and hideous roar,

---

(188) In the draft thus—

     Blighted the   } flowing river of his heart.
     Stemm'd quick the

(201) This line stands rhymeless in the finished manuscript, as in
the printed text of the first edition ; but in the original draft occurs
the fellow line now restored to the text. Its omission was clearly
an error of transcription, which poet, publisher, and printer alike
failed to discover. The case is similar to that of the long-lost rhyme
in Shelley's *Julian and Maddalo*, only restored in 1877, when the
poet's beautiful little manuscript came into my hands. The following is the passage—

     Fierce yells and howlings and lamentings keen,
     And laughter where complaint had merrier been,
     Moans, shrieks, and curses, and blaspheming prayers
     Accosted us. We climbed the oozy stairs...

The third of these lines was the one lost and recovered. No
doubt in the present case as in that the omission arose in copying,
the sense being complete in each instance without the rhyme. The
only difference is that Keats was his own copyist for the press and
saw his poem in print, while Shelley's only appeared when the poet
was " beyond the stars." Otherwise, the one case perfectly illus-
trates the other.

Quicksand, and whirlpool, and deserted shore,
Were emblem'd in the woof; with every shape
That skims, or dives, or sleeps, 'twixt cape and cape.
The gulphing whale was like a dot in the spell,   205
Yet look upon it, and 'twould size and swell
To its huge self; and the minutest fish
Would pass the very hardest gazer's wish,
And show his little eye's anatomy.
Then there was pictur'd the regality   210
Of Neptune; and the sea nymphs round his state,
In beauteous vassalage, look up and wait.
Beside this old man lay a pearly wand,
And in his lap a book, the which he conn'd
So stedfastly, that the new denizen   215
Had time to keep him in amazed ken,
To mark these shadowings, and stand in awe.

The old man rais'd his hoary head and saw
The wilder'd stranger—seeming not to see,
His features were so lifeless. Suddenly   220
He woke as from a trance; his snow-white brows
Went arching up, and like two magic ploughs
Furrow'd deep wrinkles in his forehead large,
Which kept as fixedly as rocky marge,
Till round his wither'd lips had gone a smile.   225
Then up he rose, like one whose tedious toil
Had watch'd for years in forlorn hermitage,
Who had not from mid-life to utmost age
Eas'd in one accent his o'er-burden'd soul,

---

(206) In the draft—

> Yet look upon it long, 'twould grow and swell...

(226) The draft reads *studious* for *tedious*.

Even to the trees. He rose: he grasp'd his stole,   230
With convuls'd clenches waving it abroad,
And in a voice of solemn joy, that aw'd
Echo into oblivion, he said :—

"Thou art the man!   Now shall I lay my head
In peace upon my watery pillow : now   235
Sleep will come smoothly to my weary brow.
O Jove!   I shall be young again, be young!
O shell-borne Neptune, I am pierc'd and stung
With new-born life!   What shall I do?   Where go,
When I have cast this serpent-skin of woe?—   240
I'll swim to the syrens, and one moment listen
Their melodies, and see their long hair glisten;
Anon upon that giant's arm I'll be,
That writhes about the roots of Sicily :
To northern seas I'll in a twinkling sail,   245
And mount upon the snortings of a whale
To some black cloud ; thence down I'll madly sweep
On forked lightning, to the deepest deep,
Where through some sucking pool I will be hurl'd
With rapture to the other side of the world!   250
O, I am full of gladness!   Sisters three,
I bow full hearted to your old decree!
Yes, every god be thank'd, and power benign,
For I no more shall wither, droop, and pine.
Thou art the man!"   Endymion started back   255
Dismay'd; and, like a wretch from whom the rack

(230) In the finished manuscript, *Not even,—Not* being however crossed through with a pencil.
(240) Cancelled manuscript reading, *Now* for *When.*
(244) It is not clear whether the reference is to Briareus or to Enceladus, since both were supposed to have been imprisoned under Mount Etna.

Tortures hot breath, and speech of agony,
Mutter'd : "What lonely death am I to die
In this cold region ? Will he let me freeze,
And float my brittle limbs o'er polar seas ?   260
Or will he touch me with his searing hand,
And leave a black memorial on the sand ?
Or tear me piece-meal with a bony saw,
And keep me as a chosen food to draw
His magian fish through hated fire and flame ?   265
O misery of hell ! resistless, tame,
Am I to be burnt up ? No, I will shout,
Until the gods through heaven's blue look out!—
O Tartarus ! but some few days agone
Her soft arms were entwining me, and on   270
Her voice I hung like fruit among green leaves :
Her lips were all my own, and—ah, ripe sheaves
Of happiness ! ye on the stubble droop,
But never may be garner'd. I must stoop
My head, and kiss death's foot. Love! love, farewell ! 275
Is there no hope from thee ? This horrid spell
Would melt at thy sweet breath.—By Dian's hind
Feeding from her white fingers, on the wind
I see thy streaming hair ! and now, by Pan,
I care not for this old mysterious man ! "   280

He spake, and walking to that aged form,
Look'd high defiance. Lo ! his heart 'gan warm
With pity, for the grey-hair'd creature wept.
Had he then wrong'd a heart where sorrow kept ?
Had he, though blindly contumelious, brought   285

(266) In the draft, *Oh hell* for *of hell*.
(269) Cancelled reading of the manuscript, *hours* for *days*, and
in the next line but one, *lips* for *voice*.

Rheum to kind eyes, a sting to humane thought,
Convulsion to a mouth of many years?
He had in truth; and he was ripe for tears.
The penitent shower fell, as down he knelt
Before that care-worn sage, who trembling felt   290
About his large dark locks, and faultering spake:

"Arise, good youth, for sacred Phœbus' sake!
I know thine inmost bosom, and I feel
A very brother's yearning for thee steal
Into mine own: for why? thou openest   295
The prison gates that have so long opprest
My weary watching.   Though thou know'st it not,
Thou art commission'd to this fated spot
For great enfranchisement.   O weep no more;
I am a friend to love, to loves of yore: 300
Aye, hadst thou never lov'd an unknown power,
I had been grieving at this joyous hour.
But even now most miserable old,
I saw thee, and my blood no longer cold
Gave mighty pulses: in this tottering case   305
Grew a new heart, which at this moment plays
As dancingly as thine.   Be not afraid,
For thou shalt hear this secret all display'd,
Now as we speed towards our joyous task."

So saying, this young soul in age's mask   310

---

(286) In the finished manuscript, *humane*: in the first edition
human, which must surely be an error undiscovered by Keats.
(291) The draft reads, haltingly, *The youths* in place of *About
his.*
(294) Cancelled reading of the manuscript, *father's* for *brother's.*
(307) The draft reads *As youthfully as thine.*
(309) In the draft, *The while we speed...*

Went forward with the Carian side by side :
Resuming quickly thus ; while ocean's tide
Hung swollen at their backs, and jewel'd sands
Took silently their foot-prints.

                    " My soul stands
Now past the midway from mortality,   315
And so I can prepare without a sigh
To tell thee briefly all my joy and pain.
I was a fisher once, upon this main,
And my boat danc'd in every creek and bay;
Rough billows were my home by night and day,—   320
The sea-gulls not more constant ; for I had
No housing from the storm and tempests mad,
But hollow rocks,—and they were palaces
Of·silent happiness, of slumberous ease :
Long years of misery have told me so.   325
Aye, thus it was one thousand years ago.
One thousand years !—Is it then possible
To look so plainly through them ? to dispel
A thousand years with backward glance sublime ?
To breathe away as 'twere all scummy slime   330
From off a crystal pool, to see its deep,
And one's own image from the bottom peep ?
Yes : now I am no longer wretched thrall,
My long captivity and moanings all
Are but a slime, a thin-pervading scum,   335
The which I breathe away, and thronging come
Like things of yesterday my youthful pleasures.

---

(329) For this line the draft has—

       At one glance back the mistiness of time ?

(337) The draft reads *my first youth's pleasures.*

" I touch'd no lute, I sang not, trod no measures :
I was a lonely youth on desert shores.
My sports were lonely, 'mid continuous roars,   340
And craggy isles, and sea-mew's plaintive cry
Plaining discrepant between sea and sky.
Dolphins were still my playmates ; shapes unseen
Would let me feel their scales of gold and green,
Nor be my desolation ; and, full oft,   345
When a dread waterspout had rear'd aloft
Its hungry hugeness, seeming ready ripe
To burst with hoarsest thunderings, and wipe
My life away like a vast sponge of fate,
Some friendly monster, pitying my sad state,   350
Has div'd to its foundations, gulph'd it down,
And left me tossing safely.   But the crown
Of all my life was utmost quietude :
More did I love to lie in cavern rude,
Keeping in wait whole days for Neptune's voice,   355
And if it came at last, hark, and rejoice !
There blush'd no summer eve but I would steer
My skiff along green shelving coasts, to hear
The shepherd's pipe come clear from aery steep,
Mingled with ceaseless bleatings of his sheep :   360
And never was a day of summer shine,
But I beheld its birth upon the brine :
For I would watch all night to see unfold
Heaven's gates, and Æthon snort his morning gold

---

(342) The draft reads *'twixt the sea and sky* ; and the finished
manuscript reads *atween* for *between*.

(353) In the finished manuscript, *tip-top* instead of *utmost*.

(358) In the finished manuscript, *coast*, not *coasts*.

(364) See Ovid's *Metamorphoses*, Book II (Sandys's Transla-
tion) :

    Meane while the Sunnes swift Horses, hot *Pyröus*,

Wide o'er the swelling streams : and constantly   365
At brim of day-tide, on some grassy lea,
My nets would be spread out, and I at rest.
The poor folk of the sea-country I blest
With daily boon of fish most delicate :
They knew not whence this bounty, and elate   370
Would strew sweet flowers on a sterile beach.

"Why was I not contented ?   Wherefore reach
At things which, but for thee, O Latmian !
Had been my dreary death ?   Fool ! I began
To feel distemper'd longings : to desire   375
The utmost privilege that ocean's sire
Could grant in benediction : to be free
Of all his kingdom.   Long in misery
I wasted, ere in one extremest fit
I plung'd for life or death.   To interknit   380
One's senses with so dense a breathing stuff
Might seem a work of pain ; so not enough
Can I admire how crystal-smooth it felt,
And buoyant round my limbs.   At first I dwelt
Whole days and days in sheer astonishment ;   385
Forgetful utterly of self-intent ;
Moving but with the mighty ebb and flow.
Then, like a new fledg'd bird that first doth show
His spreaded feathers to the morrow chill,
I try'd in fear the pinions of my will.   390

Light *Æthon*, fiery *Phlegon*, bright *Eöus*,
Neighing alowd, inflame the Ayre with heat ;
And, with their thundring hooves, the barriers beate.

(367) Cancelled manuscript reading *outspread* for *spread out*.

(377) In the finished manuscript the word *become* stands cancelled between *to* and *be*.

'Twas freedom! and at once I visited
The ceaseless wonders of this ocean-bed.
No need to tell thee of them, for I see
That thou hast been a witness—it must be—
For these I know thou canst not feel a drouth,   395
By the melancholy corners of that mouth.
So I will in my story straightway pass
To more immediate matter.   Woe, alas!
That love should be my bane!   Ah, Scylla fair!
Why did poor Glaucus ever—ever dare   400
To sue thee to his heart?   Kind stranger-youth!
I lov'd her to the very white of truth,
And she would not conceive it.   Timid thing!
She fled me swift as sea-bird on the wing,
Round every isle, and point, and promontory,   405
From where large Hercules wound up his story
Far as Egyptian Nile.   My passion grew
The more, the more I saw her dainty hue
Gleam delicately through the azure clear :
Until 'twas too fierce agony to bear ;   410
And in that agony, across my grief
It flash'd, that Circe might find some relief—
Cruel enchantress!   So above the water

---

(395) The draft gives this line thus—

For such a drink thou canst not feel a drouth,...

The thought of the melancholy expression of the mouth of one who
has seen "ceaseless wonders" is probably allusive to the portrait
of Dante, foremost of all beholders of "ceaseless wonders."

(406) Whether the reference is to the Pillars of Hercules, the con-
fluence of the Mediterranean and Atlantic, or to the scene of the
Death of Hercules, is not very clear ; but probably *wound up his
story* refers rather to his last labour than to his death on Mount
Œta.

(412) In the draft, *might afford relief.*

I rear'd my head, and look'd for Phœbus' daughter.
Ææa's isle was wondering at the moon:—   415
It seem'd to whirl around me, and a swoon
Left me dead-drifting to that fatal power.

    "When I awoke, 'twas in a twilight bower;
Just when the light of morn, with hum of bees,
Stole through its verdurous matting of fresh trees.   420
How sweet, and sweeter! for I heard a lyre,
And over it a sighing voice expire.
It ceas'd—I caught light footsteps; and anon
The fairest face that morn e'er look'd upon
Push'd through a screen of roses.   Starry Jove!   425
With tears, and smiles, and honey-words she wove
A net whose thraldom was more bliss than all
The range of flower'd Elysium.   Thus did fall
The dew of her rich speech: " Ah! Art awake?
"O let me hear thee speak, for Cupid's sake!   430
" I am so oppress'd with joy!   Why, I have shed
" An urn of tears, as though thou wert cold dead;
" And now I find thee living, I will pour
" From these devoted eyes their silver store,

(415) The draft reads *looking* for *wondering.*
(417) Cancelled reading of the manuscript, *towards* for *to.*
(419) The draft reads *What time* for *Just when.*
(421-2) Cancelled reading of the manuscript—

        How sweet to me! and then I heard a Lyre
        With which a sighing voice.

(425) The draft reads *Mighty* for *Starry.*
(429) The inverted commas before each line of this speech, to mark it as one speech within another, are in the manuscript, but not in the first edition, though carefully inserted in the corrected copy in my possession.
(432) The draft reads *as if* for *as though.*

" Until exhausted of the latest drop,   435
" So it will pleasure thee, and force thee stop
" Here, that I too may live : but if beyond
" Such cool and sorrowful offerings, thou art fond
" Of soothing warmth, of dalliance supreme ;
" If thou art ripe to taste a long love dream ;   440
" If smiles, if dimples, tongues for ardour mute,
" Hang in thy vision like a tempting fruit,
" O let me pluck it for thee."   Thus she link'd
Her charming syllables, till indistinct
Their music came to my o'er-sweeten'd soul ;   445
And then she hover'd over me, and stole
So near, that if no nearer it had been
This furrow'd visage thou hadst never seen.

   " Young man of Latmus ! thus particular
Am I, that thou may'st plainly see how far   450
This fierce temptation went : and thou may'st not
Exclaim, How then, was Scylla quite forgot ?

   " Who could resist ?   Who in this universe ?
She did so breathe ambrosia ; so immerse
My fine existence in a golden clime.   455
She took me like a child of suckling time,

---

(436) In the draft, *would* in place of *will.*
(441) In the draft, *rapture* for *ardour.*
(445-7) The draft reads thus—

   Their music came to my o'ersweeten'd sense
   And then I felt a hovering influence
   A breathing on my forehead.

(449) The first edition reads Latmos ; but the finished manuscript *Latmus*, as at page 14 of the present volume.
(451) The draft reads *that* for *and* ; and the word *and* is wanting in the finished manuscript, so that the line is a syllable short.

And cradled me in roses.   Thus condemn'd,
The current of my former life was stemm'd,
And to this arbitrary queen of sense
I bow'd a tranced vassal : nor would thence   460
Have mov'd, even though Amphion's harp had woo'd
Me back to Scylla o'er the billows rude.
For as Apollo each eve doth devise
A new appareling for western skies ;
So every eve, nay every spendthrift hour   465
Shed balmy consciousness within that bower.
And I was free of haunts umbrageous ;
Could wander in the mazy forest-house
Of squirrels, foxes shy, and antler'd deer,
And birds from coverts innermost and drear   470
Warbling for very joy mellifluous sorrow—
To me new born delights !

                    " Now let me borrow,
For moments few, a temperament as stern
As Pluto's sceptre, that my words not burn
These uttering lips, while I in calm speech tell   475
How specious heaven was changed to real hell.

    " One morn she left me sleeping : half awake
I sought for her smooth arms and lips, to slake
My greedy thirst with nectarous camel-draughts ;
But she was gone.   Whereat the barbed shafts   480
Of disappointment stuck in me so sore,
That out I ran and search'd the forest o'er.

---

(461) In the manuscript, *e'en* for *even*.
(466) The draft reads—
        Shed nectarous Influence within that bower.
(477) Cancelled reading of the manuscript, *day* for *morn*.

Wandering about in pine and cedar gloom
Damp awe assail'd me; for there 'gan to boom
A sound of moan, an agony of sound,   485
Sepulchral from the distance all around.
Then came a conquering earth-thunder, and rumbled
That fierce complain to silence: while I stumbled
Down a precipitous path, as if impell'd.
I came to a dark valley.—Groanings swell'd   490
Poisonous about my ears, and louder grew,
The nearer I approach'd a flame's gaunt blue,
That glar'd before me through a thorny brake.
This fire, like the eye of gordian snake,
Bewitch'd me towards; and I soon was near   495
A sight too fearful for the feel of fear:
In thicket hid I curs'd the haggard scene—
The banquet of my arms, my arbour queen,
Seated upon an uptorn forest root;
And all around her shapes, wizard and brute,   500
Laughing, and wailing, groveling, serpenting,
Showing tooth, tusk, and venom-bag, and sting!
O such deformities! Old Charon's self,
Should he give up awhile his penny pelf,
And take a dream 'mong rushes Stygian,   505
It could not be so phantasy'd. Fierce, wan,
And tyrannizing was the lady's look,

---

(483) The contraction *Wand'ring* occurs here in the finished
manuscript.

(495) In the draft, *Drew me towards it*, showing that *towards*
was used as a dissyllable; so that I fear *it* was advisedly cancelled
in revising the line.

(498) Woodhouse notes, presumably from the draft, the variation—

My beautiful rose bud, my arbour Queen,

and in the next line but one *about* for *around*.

As over them a gnarled staff she shook.
Oft-times upon the sudden she laugh'd out,
And from a basket empty'd to the rout   510
Clusters of grapes, the which they raven'd quick
And roar'd for more; with many a hungry lick
About their shaggy jaws.   Avenging, slow,
Anon she took a branch of mistletoe,
And empty'd on't a black dull-gurgling phial: 515
Groan'd one and all, as if some piercing trial
Was sharpening for their pitiable bones.
She lifted up the charm: appealing groans
From their poor breasts went sueing to her ear
In vain; remorseless as an infant's bier   520
She whisk'd against their eyes the sooty oil.
Whereat was heard a noise of painful toil,
Increasing gradual to a tempest rage,
Shrieks, yells, and groans of torture-pilgrimage;
Until their grieved bodies 'gan to bloat   525
And puff from the tail's end to stifled throat:
Then was appalling silence: then a sight
More wildering than all that hoarse affright;
For the whole herd, as by a whirlwind writhen,
Went through the dismal air like one huge Python   530
Antagonizing Boreas,—and so vanish'd.
Yet there was not a breath of wind: she banish'd
These phantoms with a nod.   Lo! from the dark
Came waggish fauns, and nymphs, and satyrs stark,
With dancing and loud revelry,—and went   535
Swifter than centaurs after rapine bent.—
Sighing an elephant appear'd and bow'd

---

(537) The draft reads *For a large Elephant*; and in the finished
manuscript the line begins with *Seeing*, instead of *Sighing* as in the
printed book.

Before the fierce witch, speaking thus aloud
In human accent: "Potent goddess! chief
" Of pains resistless! make my being brief,   540
" Or let me from this heavy prison fly :
" Or give me to the air, or let me die !
" I sue not for my happy crown again ;
" I sue not for my phalanx on the plain ;
" I sue not for my lone, my widow'd wife ;   545
" I sue not for my ruddy drops of life,
" My children fair, my lovely girls and boys!
" I will forget them ; I will pass these joys ;
" Ask nought so heavenward, so too—too high :
" Only I pray, as fairest boon, to die,   550
. " Or be deliver'd from this cumbrous flesh,
" From this gross, detestable, filthy mesh,
" And merely given to the cold bleak air.
" Have mercy, Goddess!   Circe, feel my prayer!"

---

(539) In the draft this line stands thus—

With human voice : O potent goddess ! chief...

The inverted commas before each line to mark this speech within speech are in the finished manuscript as in the case of Circe's speech (line 429); but in this instance Keats does not seem to have noticed, when correcting the printed book, that the manuscript had been departed from here also.

(540) The draft gives spells and charms as alternative readings for pains.

(545-8) The draft reads as follows—

I sue not for my lonely, my dear wife,
I sue not for my hearts blood drops of life,
My sweetest babes, my lovely girls and boys,
Ah, likely they are dead—I pass these joys...

(554) At this point the draft reads thus—

Have mercy goddess ! feel oh feel my prayer.
Pity great Circe ! "—Nor sight nor syllable
Saw I or heard I more of this sick spell.

"That curst magician's name fell icy numb   555
Upon my wild conjecturing : truth had come
Naked and sabre-like against my heart.
I saw a fury whetting a death-dart ;
And my slain spirit, overwrought with fright,
Fainted away in that dark lair of night.   560
Think, my deliverer, how desolate
My waking must have been ! disgust, and hate,
And terrors manifold divided me
A spoil amongst them. I prepar'd to flee
Into the dungeon core of that wild wood :   565
I fled three days—when lo ! before me stood
Glaring the angry witch. O Dis, even now,
A clammy dew is beading on my brow,
At mere remembering her pale laugh, and curse.
"Ha! ha! Sir Dainty ! there must be a nurse   570
" Made of rose leaves and thistledown, express,
" To cradle thee my sweet, and lull thee : yes,
" I am too flinty-hard for thy nice touch :
" My tenderest squeeze is but a giant's clutch.
" So, fairy-thing, it shall have lullabies   575
" Unheard of yet ; and it shall still its cries
" Upon some breast more lilly-feminine.
" Oh, no—it shall not pine, and pine, and pine

---

(560) In the draft, *dull realm* for *dark lair*.

(567) In the finished manuscript we read *e'en* for *even*.

(569) In the manuscript, *remembring*.

(570) This line begins with *Ah, Ah,* in the finished manuscript, and Woodhouse notes, in apparent allusion to the draft, " formerly *O! O!*" The inverted commas before each line again occur both in the manuscript and in the corrected copy of the first edition, but were not printed in that edition.

(575) The draft reads *tender* for *fairy*.

(577) In the draft, *zephyr* in place of *lilly*, and in the next line but one, *little* for *trifling*.

" More than one pretty, trifling thousand years ;
" And then 'twere pity, but fate's gentle shears   580
" Cut short its immortality.   Sea-flirt !
" Young dove of the waters ! truly I'll not hurt
" One hair of thine : see how I weep and sigh,
" That our heart-broken parting is so nigh.
" And must we part ?   Ah, yes, it must be so.   585
" Yet ere thou leavest me in utter woe,
" Let me sob over thee my last adieus,
" And speak a blessing : Mark me !   Thou hast thews
" Immortal, for thou art of heavenly race :
" But such a love is mine, that here I chace   590
" Eternally away from thee all bloom
" Of youth, and destine thee towards a tomb.
" Hence shalt thou quickly to the watery vast ;
" And there, ere many days be overpast,
" Disabled age shall seize thee ; and even then   595
" Thou shalt not go the way of aged men ;
" But live and wither, cripple and still breathe
" Ten hundred years : which gone, I then bequeath
" Thy fragile bones to unknown burial.
" Adieu, sweet love, adieu !"—As shot stars fall,   600
She fled ere I could groan for mercy.   Stung
And poison'd was my spirit : despair sung
A war-song of defiance 'gainst all hell.
A hand was at my shoulder to compel

(581-3) The draft gives this passage thus—

Great Jove
What fury of the three could harm this dove
Dear youth ! see how I weep, hear how I sigh...

in which *Great Jove* is certainly preferable to *Sea-flirt !*
(588) The finished manuscript reads *Thou hadst thews.*
(595) The word *even* is contracted to *e'en* in the finished manuscript.

My sullen steps ; another 'fore my eyes   605
Mov'd on with pointed finger.   In this guise
Enforced, at the last by ocean's foam
I found me ; by my fresh, my native home.
Its tempering coolness, to my life akin,
Came salutary as I waded in ;   610
And, with a blind voluptuous rage, I gave
Battle to the swollen billow-ridge, and drave
Large froth before me, while there yet remain'd
Hale strength, nor from my bones all marrow drain'd.

"Young lover, I must weep—such hellish spite   615
With dry cheek who can tell ?   While thus my might
Proving upon this element, dismay'd,
Upon a dead thing's face my hand I laid ; '
I look'd—'twas Scylla!   Cursed, cursed Circe !
O vulture-witch, hast never heard of mercy ?   620
Could not thy harshest vengeance be content,
But thou must nip this tender innocent
Because I lov'd her ?—Cold, O cold indeed
Were her fair limbs, and like a common weed
The sea-swell took her hair.   Dead as she was   625

---

(612) The past tense *drave*, common enough in Elizabethan literature, is probably another Spenserian memory : thus, in *The Faerie
Queene*, Book I, Canto ix, stanza 33, we have—

> the ghastly Owle,
> Shrieking his balefull note, which ever drave
> Far from that haunt all other chearefull fowle.

(620) In the finished manuscript, *hast* was written originally ;
but *hadst* is written over it in pencil, though this seemingly more
correct inflection was not adopted in the printed book or restored in
the corrected copy.

(621) In the finished manuscript,

> Was not thine harshest Avengeance content,

but in the first edition the line stands as in the text.

I clung about her waist, nor ceas'd to pass
Fleet as an arrow through unfathom'd brine,
Until there shone a fabric crystalline,
Ribb'd and inlaid with coral, pebble, and pearl.
Headlong I darted; at one eager swirl   630
Gain'd its bright portal, enter'd, and behold!
'Twas vast, and desolate, and icy-cold;
And all around—But wherefore this to thee
Who in few minutes more thyself shalt see?—
I left poor Scylla in a niche and fled.   635
My fever'd parchings up, my scathing dread
Met palsy half way: soon these limbs became
Gaunt, wither'd, sapless, feeble, cramp'd, and lame.

"Now let me pass a cruel, cruel space,
Without one hope, without one faintest trace   640
Of mitigation, or redeeming bubble
Of colour'd phantasy; for I fear 'twould trouble
Thy brain to loss of reason: and next tell
How a restoring chance came down to quell
One half of the witch in me.

             "On a day,   645
Sitting upon a rock above the spray,
I saw grow up from the horizon's brink
A gallant vessel: soon she seem'd to sink
Away from me again, as though her course
Had been resum'd in spite of hindering force—   650

---

(626) In the draft—
    I clung about her waist and dived nor ceas'd to pass...

(644) In the finished manuscript the word *small* is cancelled before *restoring*.

(650) In the draft this line reads—
    She would resume in spite of adverse force.

So vanish'd : and not long, before arose
Dark clouds, and muttering of winds morose.
Old Æolus would stifle his mad spleen,
But could not : therefore all the billows green
Toss'd up the silver spume against the clouds.　　655
The tempest came : I saw that vessel's shrouds
In perilous bustle ; while upon the deck
Stood trembling creatures.　I beheld the wreck ;
The final gulphing ; the poor struggling souls :
I heard their cries amid loud thunder-rolls.　　660
O they had all been sav'd but crazed eld
Annull'd my vigorous cravings : and thus quell'd
And curb'd, think on't, O Latmian ! did I sit
Writhing with pity, and a cursing fit
Against that hell-born Circe.　The crew had gone,　665
By one and one, to pale oblivion ;
And I was gazing on the surges prone,
With many a scalding tear and many a groan,
When at my feet emerg'd an old man's hand,
Grasping this scroll, and this same slender wand.　　670
I knelt with pain—reach'd out my hand—had grasp'd
These treasures—touch'd the knuckles—they unclasp'd—
I caught a finger : but the downward weight
O'erpowered me—it sank.　Then 'gan abate
The storm, and through chill aguish gloom outburst　675
The comfortable sun.　I was athirst
To search the book, and in the warming air
Parted its dripping leaves with eager care.
Strange matters did it treat of, and drew on
My soul page after page, till well-nigh won　　680

---

(653) *Œolus* in the manuscript, *Eolus* in the first edition.
(655) In the finished manuscript, *their silver spume*, not *the*.
(678) The draft reads *Unfolded its damp leaves*.

Into forgetfulness ; when, stupefied,
I read these words, and read again, and tried
My eyes against the heavens, and read again.
O what a load of misery and pain
Each Atlas-line bore off!—a shine of hope   685
Came gold around me, cheering me to cope
Strenuous with hellish tyranny.   Attend !
For thou hast brought their promise to an end.

" In the wide sea there lives a forlorn wretch,
Doom'd with enfeebled carcase to outstretch   690
His loath'd existence through ten centuries,
And then to die alone.   Who can devise
A total opposition ?   No one.   So
One million times ocean must ebb and flow,
And he oppressed.   Yet he shall not die,   695
These things accomplish'd :—If he utterly
Scans all the depths of magic, and expounds
The meanings of all motions, shapes, and sounds ;
If he explores all forms and substances
Straight homeward to their symbol-essences ;   700
He shall not die.   Moreover, and in chief,
He must pursue this task of joy and grief
Most piously ;—all lovers tempest-tost,
And in the savage overwhelming lost,
He shall deposit side by side, until   705

(685-6) The draft reads—
          sweet rays of hope
   Glanc'd round me cheering me at once to cope...

(689) The word *Listen* stands in the finished manuscript at the beginning of this line, making an Alexandrine of it ; but it is struck through with a pencil.

(697) In the draft this line begins with *Sounds* instead of *Scans.*

(702) The draft reads *heaviest grief* for *joy and grief.*

Time's creeping shall the dreary space fulfil:
Which done, and all these labours ripened,
A youth, by heavenly power lov'd and led,
Shall stand before him; whom he shall direct
How to consummate all. The youth elect   710
Must do the thing, or both will be destroy'd."—

"Then," cried the young Endymion, overjoy'd,
"We are twin brothers in this destiny!
Say, I intreat thee, what achievement high
Is, in this restless world, for me reserv'd.   715
What! if from thee my wandering feet had swerv'd,
Had we both perish'd?"—"Look!" the sage reply'd,
"Dost thou not mark a gleaming through the tide,
Of diverse brilliances? 'tis the edifice
I told thee of, where lovely Scylla lies;   720
And where I have enshrined piously
All lovers, whom fell storms have doom'd to die
Throughout my bondage." Thus discoursing, on
They went till unobscur'd the porches shone;
Which hurryingly they gain'd, and enter'd straight.   725
Sure never since king Neptune held his state
Was seen such wonder underneath the stars.
Turn to some level plain where haughty Mars
Has legion'd all his battle; and behold
How every soldier, with firm foot, doth hold   730
His even breast: see, many steeled squares,
And rigid ranks of iron—whence who dares
One step? Imagine further, line by line,

----

(719) The first edition reads *divers*; but the manuscript reads *diverse*, the final *e* being crossed through with a pencil: probably this was one of the changes made by Taylor which Keats did not approve; for *diverse* gives the more characteristic sense.

These warrior thousands on the field supine :—
So in that crystal place, in silent rows,   735
Poor lovers lay at rest from joys and woes.—
The stranger from the mountains, breathless, trac'd
Such thousands of shut eyes in order plac'd ;
Such ranges of white feet, and patient lips
All ruddy,—for here death no blossom nips.   740
He mark'd their brows and foreheads ; saw their hair
Put sleekly on one side with nicest care ;
And each one's gentle wrists, with reverence,
Put cross-wise to its heart.

                              " Let us commence,"
Whisper'd the guide, stuttering with joy, " even now."
He spake, and, trembling like an aspen-bough,   746
Began to tear his scroll in pieces small,
Uttering the while some mumblings funeral.
He tore it into pieces small as snow
That drifts unfeather'd when bleak northerns blow ;   750
And having done it, took his dark blue cloak
And bound it round Endymion : then struck
His wand against the empty air times nine.—
" What more there is to do, young man, is thine :
But first a little patience ; first undo   755

---

(744) The words *Let us commence, Whisper'd the guide, stuttering with joy, even now* are enclosed in inverted commas as one speech in the first edition ; and the manuscript reads similarly except that it has *e'en* for *even*.

(750) The draft reads *all shatter'd* for *unfeather'd*.

(751) In the manuscript, *having don't, he took*, instead of *having done it, took*.

(752) In the manuscript Keats perfects his rhyme here by using *stroke* as the past tense of *strike* ; but the word is *struck* in his printed text.

(753) The draft reads *at something in the air*.

This tangled thread, and wind it to a clue.
Ah, gentle! 'tis as weak as spider's skein ;
And shouldst thou break it—What, is it done so clean ?
A power overshadows thee ! O, brave !
The spite of hell is tumbling to its grave.   760
Here is a shell ; 'tis pearly blank to me,
Nor mark'd with any sign or charactery—
Canst thou read aught ? O read for pity's sake !
Olympus ! we are safe ! Now, Carian, break
This wand against yon lyre on the pedestal."   765

'Twas done : and straight with sudden swell and fall
Sweet music breath'd her soul away, and sigh'd
A lullaby to silence.—"Youth ! now strew
These minced leaves on me, and passing through
Those files of dead, scatter the same around,   770
And thou wilt see the issue."—'Mid the sound
Of flutes and viols, ravishing his heart,
Endymion from Glaucus stood apart,
And scatter'd in his face some fragments light.
How lightning-swift the change ! a youthful wight   775
Smiling beneath a coral diadem,
Out-sparkling sudden like an upturn'd gem,
Appear'd, and, stepping to a beauteous corse,
Kneel'd down beside it, and with tenderest force

---

(756) In the manuscript *clew* for *clue*.

(758) The words *is it* are contracted here to *is't* in the manuscript.

(767) There is nothing in the finished manuscript to indicate how this line came to lose its fellow, if it ever had one ; and Woodhouse notes nothing from the draft bearing on that point. There is perhaps a reminiscence here of William Chamberlayne, in whose *Pharonnida* (Book III, Canto iii, page 51 of the second volume of the 1820 edition) we have—

          The glad birds had sung
   A lullaby to night,...

Press'd its cold hand, and wept,—and Scylla sigh'd ! 780
Endymion, with quick hand, the charm apply'd—
The nymph arose : he left them to their joy,
And onward went upon his high employ,
Showering those powerful fragments on the dead.
And, as he pass'd, each lifted up its head,   785
As doth a flower at Apollo's touch.
Death felt it to his inwards : 'twas too much :
Death fell a weeping in his charnel-house.
The Latmian persever'd along, and thus   ˙
All were re-animated.   There arose   790
A noise of harmony, pulses and throes
Of gladness in the air—while many, who
Had died in mutual arms devout and true,
Sprang to each other madly ; and the rest
Felt a high certainty of being blest.   795
They gaz'd upon Endymion.   Enchantment
Grew drunken, and would have its head and bent.
Delicious symphonies, like airy flowers,
Budded, and swell'd, and, full-blown, shed full showers
Of light, soft, unseen leaves of sounds divine.   800
The two deliverers tasted a pure wine
Of happiness, from fairy-press ooz'd out.
Speechless they ey'd each other, and about

---

(787) The draft reads *at* for *to*.

(791) The draft reads *A hum, a harmony*. Compare the reading
of the text with *Sleep and Poetry*—

> The fervid choir that lifted up a noise
> Of harmony,...

(795) The draft reads *sweet* for *high*.

(796) The variation *Ravishment* for *Enchantment* stands cancelled
in the finished manuscript.

(802) The draft reads

> Of happiness, not from earthly grapes press'd out.

The fair assembly wander'd to and fro,
Distracted with the richest overflow   805
Of joy that ever pour'd from heaven.

————" Away !"
Shouted the new born god ; " Follow, and pay
Our piety to Neptunus supreme ! "—
Then Scylla, blushing sweetly from her dream,
They led on first, bent to her meek surprise,   810
Through portal columns of a giant size,
Into the vaulted, boundless emerald.
Joyous all follow'd, as the leader call'd,
Down marble steps ; pouring as easily
As hour-glass sand,—and fast, as you might see   815
Swallows obeying the south summer's call,
Or swans upon a gentle waterfall.

   Thus went that beautiful multitude, nor far,
Ere from among some rocks of glittering spar,
Just within ken, they saw descending thick   820
Another multitude.   Whereat more quick
Mov'd either host.   On a wide sand they met,
And of those numbers every eye was wet ;
For each their old love found.   A murmuring rose,
Like what was never heard in all the throes   825
Of wind and waters : 'tis past human wit
To tell ; 'tis dizziness to think of it.

   This mighty consummation made, the host
Mov'd on for many a league ; and gain'd, and lost
Huge sea-marks ; vanward swelling in array,   830

---

(811) *Though* stands for *Through* both in the finished manuscript
and in the first edition.

And from the rear diminishing away,—
Till a faint dawn surpris'd them. Glaucus cry'd,
"Behold! behold, the palace of his pride!
God Neptune's palaces!" With noise increas'd,
They shoulder'd on towards that brightening east.   835
At every onward step proud domes arose
In prospect,—diamond gleams, and golden glows
Of amber 'gainst their faces levelling.
Joyous, and many as the leaves in spring,
Still onward; still the splendour gradual swell'd.   840
Rich opal domes were seen, on high upheld
By jasper pillars, letting through their shafts
A blush of coral. Copious wonder-draughts
Each gazer drank; and deeper drank more near:
For what poor mortals fragment up, as mere   845
As marble was there lavish, to the vast
Of one fair palace, that far far surpass'd,

(832-40) In the draft this passage reads thus :

    Till a faint dawning bloom'd—and Glaucus cried,
    " Behold ! behold, the palace of his pride !
    Of God Neptunus pride." With hum increased
    The host moved on towards that brightening east.
    And as it moved along proud domes arose
    In prospect,—diamond gleams, and golden glows
    Of amber leveling against their faces.
    With expectation high, and hurried paces
    Still onward ; &c.

The word *hum* instead of *noise* in line 834 was repeated in the
finished manuscript, which reads otherwise like the printed text.

(845) Cancelled reading of the manuscript, *treasure up* for *fragment up*. The use of the word *mere* here, though peculiar, is not
without authority, "trifling" and "common" being among the
equivalents given by Ash.

(847) The draft reads—

    Of one fair palace, that to nothing cast...

and in the finished manuscript we have the reading *as far* struck
out in favour of *far far*.

Even for common bulk, those olden three,
Memphis, and Babylon, and Nineveh.

As large, as bright, as colour'd as the bow　　　850
Of Iris, when unfading it doth show
Beyond a silvery shower, was the arch
Through which this Paphian army took its march,
Into the outer courts of Neptune's state :
Whence could be seen, direct, a golden gate,　　　855
To which the leaders sped ; but not half raught
Ere it burst open swift as fairy thought,
And made those dazzled thousands veil their eyes
Like callow eagles at the first sunrise.
Soon with an eagle nativeness their gaze　　　860
Ripe from hue-golden swoons took all the blaze,
And then, behold ! large Neptune on his throne
Of emerald deep : yet not exalt alone ;
At his right hand stood winged Love, and on
His left sat smiling Beauty's paragon.　　　865

Far as the mariner on highest mast
Can see all round upon the calmed vast,
So wide was Neptune's hall : and as the blue

(859-61) This simile must surely be a reminiscence of Perrin's *Fables Amusantes* or some similar book used in Mr. Clarke's School. I remember the Fable of the old eagle and her young stood first in the book I used at school.　The draft gives line 860 thus—

But soon like eagles natively their gaze...

(864-5) This couplet reads as follows in the draft :

At his right hand stood winged Love, elate
And on his left Love's fairest mother sate.

This reading leaves no doubt, if indeed there was any before, as to the identity of " smiling Beauty's paragon."

Doth vault the waters, so the waters drew
Their doming curtains, high, magnificent,　　　870
Aw'd from the throne aloof;—and when storm-rent
Disclos'd the thunder-gloomings in Jove's air;
But sooth'd as now, flash'd sudden everywhere,
Noiseless, sub-marine cloudlets, glittering
Death to a human eye : for there did spring　　　875
From natural west, and east, and south, and north,
A light as of four sunsets, blazing forth
A gold-green zenith 'bove the Sea-God's head.
Of lucid depth the floor, and far outspread
As breezeless lake, on which the slim canoe　　　880
Of feather'd Indian darts about, as through
The delicatest air : air verily,
But for the portraiture of clouds and sky :
This palace floor breath-air,—but for the amaze
Of deep-seen wonders motionless,—and blaze　　　885
Of the dome pomp, reflected in extremes,
Globing a golden sphere.

　　　　　　　　They stood in dreams
Till Triton blew his horn.　The palace rang;
The Nereids danc'd ; the Syrens faintly sang ;
And the great Sea-King bow'd his dripping head.　　　890
Then Love took wing, and from his pinions shed
On all the multitude a nectarous dew.
The ooze-born Goddess beckoned and drew
Fair Scylla and her guides to conference ;
And when they reach'd the throned eminence　　　895
She kist the sea-nymph's cheek,—who sat her down

---

(869) Originally an Alexandrine, reading *canopy* for *vault*, but
corrected in the manuscript.
　(889) The draft reads *sweetly* for *faintly*.

A toying with the doves.   Then,—" Mighty crown
And sceptre of this kingdom ! " Venus said,
" Thy vows were on a time to Nais paid :
Behold ! "—   Two copious tear-drops instant fell   900
From the God's large eyes ; he smil'd delectable,
And over Glaucus held his blessing hands.—
" Endymion !   Ah ! still wandering in the bands
Of love ?   Now this is cruel.   Since the hour
I met thee in earth's bosom, all my power   905
Have I put forth to serve thee.   What, not yet
Escap'd from dull mortality's harsh net ?
A little patience, youth ! 'twill not be long,
Or I am skilless quite : an idle tongue,
A humid eye, and steps luxurious,   910
Where these are new and strange, are ominous.
Aye, I have seen these signs in one of heaven,
When others were all blind ; and were I given
To utter secrets, haply I might say
Some pleasant words :—but Love will have his day.   915
So wait awhile expectant.   Pr'ythee soon,
Even in the passing of thine honey-moon,
Visit thou my Cythera : thou wilt find
Cupid well-natured, my Adonis kind ;

---

(899) Glaucus was the son of Nais (one of the Oceanides) by
Magnes.

(903) In the manuscript, *wandring*.

(907) The draft reads *rough* for *harsh*.

(913) The draft reads *When others' sight was blind*; and in the
next line but one *honey* for *pleasant*.

(917) In the finished manuscript, *even* is contracted to *e'en*.

(918-19) Woodhouse, apparently following the draft, gives this
couplet thus :

        Visit thou my Cithera : thou wilt find
        Cupid a treasure, my Adonis kind ;

and I presume there can be no doubt that the reading of the finished

And pray persuade with thee—Ah, I have done,   920
All blisses be upon thee, my sweet son ! "—
Thus the fair goddess : while Endymion
Knelt to receive those accents halcyon.

Meantime a glorious revelry began
Before the Water-Monarch.   Nectar ran   925
In courteous fountains to all cups outreach'd ;
And plunder'd vines, teeming exhaustless, pleach'd
New growth about each shell and pendent lyre ;
The which, in disentangling for their fire,
Pull'd down fresh foliage and coverture   930
For dainty toying.   Cupid, empire-sure,
Flutter'd and laugh'd, and oft-times through the throng
Made a delighted way.   Then dance, and song,
And garlanding grew wild ; and pleasure reign'd.
In harmless tendril they each other chain'd,   935
And strove who should be smother'd deepest in
Fresh crush of leaves.

               O 'tis a very sin
For one so weak to venture his poor verse
In such a place as this.   O do not curse,
High Muses ! let him hurry to the ending.   940

----

manuscript and all printed editions, *Visit my Cytherea*, was the
result of an error of transcription.   The reference is unquestionably
to the island Cythera.

(922) The draft has *blithe* in place of *fair*.
(930) In the draft, *full* instead of *fresh*.
(934-5) The draft reads thus—

                    and wildness reigns.
          They bound each other up in tendril chains...

(937) In the draft, *crushing*, not *crush of*.

All suddenly were silent.   A soft blending
Of dulcet instruments came charmingly ;
And then a hymn.

"KING of the stormy sea !
Brother of Jove, and co-inheritor
Of elements !   Eternally before   945
Thee the waves awful bow.   Fast, stubborn rock,
At thy fear'd trident shrinking, doth unlock
Its deep foundations, hissing into foam.
All mountain-rivers, lost in the wide home
Of thy capacious bosom, ever flow.   950
Thou frownest, and old Æolus thy foe
Skulks to his cavern, 'mid the gruff complaint
Of all his rebel tempests.   Dark clouds faint
When, from thy diadem, a silver gleam
Slants over blue dominion.   Thy bright team   955
Gulphs in the morning light, and scuds along

---

(945) This passage was written thus—
Eternally in awe
Of thee the Waves bow down.
The reading of the text is inserted with a pencil in the finished
manuscript.
(949-50) In the draft these two lines were written and pointed thus—
A thousand rivers, lost in the wide home
Of thy capacious bosom, ever flow.
And in the finished manuscript also there is a comma after *bosom*
and none after *lost*.   This is clearly sufficient evidence on which to
reject the punctuation of the first and other printed editions, which
place a comma after *lost* and none after *bosom*.
(954-6) The draft reads—
When thy bright diadem a silver gleam
O'er blue dominion starts.   Thy finny team
Snorts in the morning light, and sends along...
Compare *Hyperion*, Book II, Line 236—
I saw him on the calmed waters scud,...

To bring thee nearer to that golden song
Apollo singeth, while his chariot
Waits at the doors of heaven.   Thou art not
For scenes like this: an empire stern hast thou ;   960
And it hath furrow'd that large front : yet now,
As newly come of heaven, dost thou sit
To blend and interknit
Subdued majesty with this glad time.
O shell-borne King sublime !   965
We lay our hearts before thee evermore—
We sing, and we adore !

   " Breathe softly, flutes ;
Be tender of your strings, ye soothing lutes ;
Nor be the trumpet heard ! O vain, O vain ;   970
Not flowers budding in an April rain,
Nor breath of sleeping dove, nor river's flow,—
No, nor the Æolian twang of Love's own bow,
Can mingle music fit for the soft ear
Of goddess Cytherea !   975
Yet deign, white Queen of Beauty, thy fair eyes
On our souls' sacrifice.

   " Bright-winged Child !
Who has another care when thou hast smil'd ?
Unfortunates on earth, we see at last   980
All death-shadows, and glooms that overcast

---

(960) The manuscript shows a cancelled reading, *these* for *this.*
(962) Woodhouse notes, presumably from the draft, the variation—
          Like a young child of heaven, dost thou sit...

(979) The draft reads—
          Who is not full of heaven when thou hast smil'd ?

Our spirits, fann'd away by thy light pinions.
O sweetest essence! sweetest of all minions!
God of warm pulses, and dishevell'd hair,
And panting bosoms bare!　　　　　　　　　985
Dear unseen light in darkness! eclipser
Of light in light! delicious poisoner!
Thy venom'd goblet will we quaff until
We fill—we fill!
And by thy Mother's lips————"

　　　　　　　　Was heard no more　　990
For clamour, when the golden palace door
Opened again, and from without, in shone
A new magnificence.　On oozy throne
Smooth-moving came Oceanus the old,
To take a latest glimpse at his sheep-fold,　　995
Before he went into his quiet cave
To muse for ever—Then a lucid wave,
Scoop'd from its trembling sisters of mid-sea,
Afloat, and pillowing up the majesty
Of Doris, and the Ægean seer, her spouse—　　1000
Next, on a dolphin, clad in laurel boughs,
Theban Amphion leaning on his lute:
His fingers went across it—All were mute
To gaze on Amphitrite, queen of pearls,
And Thetis pearly too.—

　　　　　　　The palace whirls　　1005
Around giddy Endymion; seeing he

———————————————————————

(983) In the draft—

　　　O sweetest essence of all sweetest minions!

(1000) Nereus, the son of Oceanus, who espoused his sister Doris, and had by her fifty daughters, the Nereides.

Was there far strayed from mortality.
He could not bear it—shut his eyes in vain ;
Imagination gave a dizzier pain.
"O I shall die ! sweet Venus, be my stay !   1010
Where is my lovely mistress ?   Well-away !
I die—I hear her voice—I feel my wing—"
At Neptune's feet he sank.   A sudden ring
Of Nereids were about him, in kind strife
To usher back his spirit into life :   1015
But still he slept.   At last they interwove
Their cradling arms, and purpos'd to convey
Towards a crystal bower far away.

Lo ! while slow carried through the pitying crowd,
To his inward senses these words spake aloud ;   1020

(1007) The draft gives this line thus—

    Was there, a stray lamb from mortality.

(1012) This line reads thus in the draft—

    I die—love calls me hence "—thus muttering...

(1015) After this line are the four following in the draft—

    They gave him nectar—shed bright drops, and strove
    Long time in vain.   At last they interwove
    Their cradling arms, and carefully conveyed
    His body towards a quiet bowery shade.

Perhaps the last three words were found inappropriate to the sub-
marine scenery and thus led to the loss of the rhyme.   In the
finished manuscript, after *Their cradling arms, and*, Keats had
written *did his*, probably meaning to complete the line with some
such expression as *body move* ; but he struck *did his* out and wrote
carried him, then cancelled that, and supplied the reading of the
text.   Were it not for the greater propriety of the *crystal bower*,
there would be a strong temptation to restore the reading of the
draft, merely substituting *crystal* for *bowery*.

(1019) Cancelled readings, *parting crowd* for *pitying crowd* in
the draft, and *throng* for *crowd* in the finished manuscript.

Written in star-light on the dark above :
Dearest Endymion! my entire love!
How have I dwelt in fear of fate : 'tis done—
Immortal bliss for me too hast thou won.
Arise then! for the hen-dove shall not hatch   1025
Her ready eggs, before I'll kissing snatch
Thee into endless heaven. Awake! awake!

   The youth at once arose: a placid lake
Came quiet to his eyes ; and forest green,
Cooler than all the wonders he had seen,   1030
Lull'd with its simple song his fluttering breast.
How happy once again in grassy nest !

  (1022) The draft reads *my own entire love!*
  (1026) The draft reads *madly* for *kissing.*
  (1032) At the end of this Book Keats wrote in the draft, " Oxf : Sept. 26 ".

ENDYMION.

BOOK IV.

ENDYMION.

BOOK IV.

MUSE of my native land! loftiest Muse!
O first-born on the mountains! by the hues
Of heaven on the spiritual air begot :
Long didst thou sit alone in northern grot,
While yet our England was a wolfish den ;   5
Before our forests heard the talk of men ;
Before the first of Druids was a child ;—
Long didst thou sit amid our regions wild
Rapt in a deep prophetic solitude.
There came an eastern voice of solemn mood :—   10
Yet wast thou patient.   Then sang forth the Nine,
Apollo's garland :—yet didst thou divine

---

(2) This line originally began with *O Mountain-born* in the
draft, where also *while* stands cancelled in favour of *by*.

(6) The draft reads *voice* for *talk*, and in line 7 *babe* for *child*.

(10) Cancelled reading of the manuscript, *an hebrew voice*.

(11) The draft reads *those nine*.   The references to the Hebrew,
Greek, Roman, and Italian literatures are scarcely as clear and
pointed as might have been expected from Keats.

Such home-bred glory, that they cry'd in vain,
" Come hither, Sister of the Island ! "   Plain
Spake fair Ausonia ; and once more she spake   15
A higher summons :—still didst thou betake
Thee to thy native hopes.   O thou hast won
A full accomplishment !   The thing is done,
Which undone, these our latter days had risen
On barren souls.   Great Muse, thou know'st what prison,
Of flesh and bone, curbs, and confines, and frets   21
Our spirit's wings : despondency besets
Our pillows ; and the fresh to-morrow morn
Seems to give forth its light in very scorn
Of our dull, uninspir'd, snail-paced lives.   25
Long have I said, how happy he who shrives
To thee !   But then I thought on poets gone,
And could not pray :—nor can I now—so on
I move to the end in lowliness of heart.——

" Ah, woe is me ! that I should fondly part   30
From my dear native land !   Ah, foolish maid !
Glad was the hour, when, with thee, myriads bade
Adieu to Ganges and their pleasant fields !

---

(13) In the finished manuscript, *in vain they cry'd.*
(14) The draft gives *from the Island.*
(16) The draft reads *In self surpassing summons.*
(17) Originally an Alexandrine, in both the manuscripts—

   Thee to thyself and to thy hopes. O thou hast won—

but altered in the second manuscript so as to correspond with the
text.
(19) In the draft, thus—

   Which wanting all these latter days had dawnd...

(20) The draft reads *Oh Muse,* not *Great Muse.*
(31) The draft reads *With* for *From.*

To one so friendless the clear freshet yields
A bitter coolness; the ripe grape is sour: 35
Yet I would have, great gods! but one short hour
Of native air—let me but die at home."

   Endymion to heaven's airy dome
Was offering up a hecatomb of vows,
When these words reach'd him. Whereupon he bows 40
His head through thorny-green entanglement
Of underwood, and to the sound is bent,
Anxious as hind towards her hidden fawn.

   " Is no one near to help me? No fair dawn
Of life from charitable voice? No sweet saying   45
To set my dull and sadden'd spirit playing?
No hand to toy with mine? No lips so sweet
That I may worship them? No eyelids meet
To twinkle on my bosom? No one dies
Before me, till from these enslaving eyes   50
Redemption sparkles!—I am sad and lost."

(34-6) In the draft lines 34 and 36 read thus—

   Where no friends are, the very freshet yields...
   Then take my life, great Gods ! for one short hour...

In the finished manuscript this last line originally began with
And, which is struck out and replaced by *Yet*.

(41-2) Cancelled readings from the draft—

                            thro' ever rough entanglement
   In the { thick / briar'd } wood...

(45) The draft reads *hope* for *life* ; but neither manuscript affords
any help to this ailing line.

(48-54) In place of this passage the draft has the following :

                   No eyelids meet
   To twinkle on my bosom ! false ! 'twas false
   They said how beautiful I was ! who calls

Thou, Carian lord, hadst better have been tost
Into a whirlpool. Vanish into air,
Warm mountaineer! for canst thou only bear
A woman's sigh alone and in distress?   55
See not her charms!   Is Phœbe passionless?
Phœbe is fairer far—O gaze no more :—
Yet if thou wilt behold all beauty's store,
Behold her panting in the forest grass !
Do not those curls of glossy jet surpass   60
For tenderness the arms so idly lain
Amongst them?   Feelest not a kindred pain,
To see such lovely eyes in swimming search
After some warm delight, that seems to perch
Dovelike in the dim cell lying beyond   65
Their upper lids?—Hist !

                         " O for Hermes' wand,
To touch this flower into human shape !
That woodland Hyacinthus could escape
From his green prison, and here kneeling down
Call me his queen, his second life's fair crown !   70
Ah me, how I could love !—My soul doth melt

———————————————————

Me now divine?   Who now kneels down and dies
Before me till from these enslaving eyes
Redemption sparkles.   Ah me how sad I am !
Of all the poisons sent to make us mad
Of all death's overwhelmings "—Stay Beware
Young Mountaineer !

I presume it was intended to read *Ah me how I am sad!*
   (55) In the draft—

       A woman's sigh in the luxury of distress?

   (63) The draft reads *fruitless* for *swimming.*
   (70) According to the draft, *living's crown.*

For the unhappy youth—Love! I have felt
So faint a kindness, such a meek surrender
To what my own full thoughts had made too tender,
That but for tears my life had fled away!—   75
Ye deaf and senseless minutes of the day,
And thou, old forest, hold ye this for true,
There is no lightning, no authentic dew
But in the eye of love: there's not a sound,
Melodious howsoever, can confound   80
The heavens and earth in one to such a death
As doth the voice of love: there's not a breath
Will mingle kindly with the meadow air,
Till it has panted round, and stolen a share
Of passion from the heart!"—

                                    Upon a bough   85
He leant, wretched.   He surely cannot now

(72-3) The draft reads these two lines thus :

> After some beauteous youth—Who, who hath felt
> So warm a faintness, such a meek surrender...

and there is a cancelled opening for line 73, *As I do now.*

(74) In the draft, *fair* for *full.*

(76-7) The draft reads as follows :

> Sweet shadow, be distinct awhile and stay
> While I speak to thee—trust me it is true...

(79) Cancelled reading of the manuscript, *a Lover's eye* instead of *the eye of Love.*

(82) The draft reads, correspondingly with the cancelled reading of the finished manuscript in line 79,

> As will a lover's voice : there's not a breath...

(85) The draft has the following passage at this point :

> Of passion from the heart—Where love is not
> Only is solitude—poor shadow ! what
> I say thou hearest not ! away begone

Thirst for another love : O impious,
That he can even dream upon it thus !—
Thought he, "Why am I not as are the dead,
Since to a woe like this I have been led   90
Through the dark earth, and through the wondrous sea?
Goddess ! I love thee not the less: from thee
By Juno's smile I turn not—no, no, no—
While the great waters are at ebb and flow.—
I have a triple soul ! O fond pretence—   95
For both, for both my love is so immense,
I feel my heart is cut for them in twain."

   And so he groan'd, as one by beauty slain.
The lady's heart beat quick, and he could see
Her gentle bosom heave tumultuously.   100
He sprang from his green covert : there she lay,

 And leave me prythee with my grief alone ! "
 The Latmian lean'd his arm upon a bough,
 A wretched mortal : what can he do now ?
 Must he another Love ? O impious...

(89-91) In the finished manuscript, the note of interrogation is at
the end of line 89 and a full-stop at the end of line 91.
 (92) The draft reads *Mine own* for *Goddess.*
 (94) At this point the draft shows the following variation :

 While the fair moon gives light, or rivers flow
 My adoration of thee is yet pure
 As infants prattling.   How is this—why sure
 I have a tripple soul !

 (97) In the first edition this line is—

 I feel my heart is cut in twain for them.

And it is left so in the corrected copy.   It was originally written so
in the finished manuscript, where, however, the inversion of the last
four words is directed in pencil, so that the right reading, that of
the text, must have been lost through a series of oversights.

Sweet as a muskrose upon new-made hay ;
With all her limbs on tremble, and her eyes
Shut softly up alive.   To speak he tries.
"Fair damsel, pity me! forgive that I   105
Thus violate thy bower's sanctity !
O pardon me, for I am full of grief—
Grief born of thee, young angel ! fairest thief!
Who stolen hast away the wings wherewith
I was to top the heavens.   Dear maid, sith   110
Thou art my executioner, and I feel
Loving and hatred, misery and weal,
Will in a few short hours be nothing to me,
. And all my story that much passion slew me ;
Do smile upon the evening of my days :   115
And, for my tortur'd brain begins to craze,
Be thou my nurse ; and let me understand
How dying I shall kiss that lilly hand.—
Dost weep for me ?   Then should I be content.
Scowl on, ye fates ! until the firmament   120
Outblackens Erebus, and the full-cavern'd earth
Crumbles into itself.   By the cloud girth
Of Jove, those tears have given me a thirst
To meet oblivion."—As her heart would burst
The maiden sobb'd awhile, and then reply'd :   125
"Why must such desolation betide
As that thou speak'st of ?   Are not these green nooks

---

(104) Here again the draft is fuller,—thus :

> Shut softly up alive—Ye harmonies
> Ye tranced visions—ye flights ideal
> Nothing are ye to life so dainty real
> O Lady pity me !

(127) In this line we read *speakst* in the finished manuscript, but *speakest* in the first edition.

Empty of all misfortune ? Do the brooks
Utter a gorgon voice ? Does yonder thrush,
Schooling its half-fledg'd little ones to brush   130
About the dewy forest, whisper tales ?—
Speak not of grief, young stranger, or cold snails
Will slime the rose to night.   Though if thou wilt,
Methinks 'twould be a guilt—a very guilt—
Not to companion thee, and sigh away   135
The light—the dusk—the dark—till break of day ! "
" Dear lady," said Endymion, " 'tis past :

---

(128) For this choice use of the word *empty*, compare Shakespeare,
Love's Labour's Lost, Act V, Scene II, line 878 :

> And I shall find you empty of that fault,...

(136) After this line the speech of Phœbe still goes on in the
draft ; and Endymion's answer varies,—thus :

> Canst thou do so ? Is there no balm, no cure
> Could not a beckoning Hebe soon allure
> Thee into Paradise ? What sorrowing
> So weighs thee down what utmost woe could bring
> This madness—Sit thee down by me, and ease
> Thine heart in whispers—haply by degrees
> I may find out some soothing medicine."—
> " Dear Lady," said Endymion, " I pine
> I die—the tender accents thou hast spoken
> Have finish'd all—my heart is lost and broken.
> That I may pass in patience still speak :
> Let me have music dying, and I seek
> No more delight—I bid adieu to all.
> Didst thou not after other climates call
> And murmur about Indian streams—now, now—
> I listen, it may save me—O my vow—
> Let me have music dying ! " The ladye
> Sitting beneath the midmost forest tree
> With tears of pity sang this roundelay—

It will be remembered that this antiquated use of the word *lad̃ye*
was defended by Coleridge both in theory and in practice. See the
Ballad of *The Dark Ladye*.

I love thee! and my days can never last.
That I may pass in patience still speak :
Let me have music dying, and I seek   140
No more delight—I bid adieu to all.
Didst thou not after other climates call,
And murmur about Indian streams ?"—Then she,
Sitting beneath the midmost forest tree,
For pity sang this roundelay——   145

          " O Sorrow,
          Why dost borrow
The natural hue of health, from vermeil lips ?—
          To give maiden blushes
          To the white rose bushes ?   150
Or is't thy dewy hand the daisy tips ?

          " O Sorrow,
          Why dost borrow
The lustrous passion from a falcon-eye ?—
          To give the glow-worm light ?   155
          Or, on a moonless night,
To tinge, on syren shores, the salt sea-spry ?

---

(151) In the first edition *is it* ; but *is't* in the manuscript and in
the corrected copy.

(154) The draft reads *lover's eye* for *falcon-eye*.

(157) Keats has been supposed to have invented the variant *spry*
for *spray* for convenience of rhyming, just as Shelley has been
accused of inventing for like reasons the word *uprest*, for example,
in *Laon and Cythna*, Canto III, Stanza xxi. Sandys, the translator
of Ovid, may not be a very good authority ; but he is not improbably
Keats's authority for *spry*, and will certainly do in default of a
better. The following couplet is from Sandys's Ovid (Book XI,
verses 498-9) :

Now tossing Seas appeare to touch the sky,
And wrap their curles in clouds, frotht with their spry.

"O Sorrow,
  Why dost borrow
The mellow ditties from a mourning tongue ?—   160
  To give at evening pale
  Unto the nightingale,
That thou mayst listen the cold dews among ?

"O Sorrow,
  Why dost borrow   165
Heart's lightness from the merriment of May ?—
  A lover would not tread
  A cowslip on the head,
Though he should dance from eve till peep of day—
  Nor any drooping flower   170
  Held sacred for thy bower,
Wherever he may sport himself and play.

" To Sorrow,
  I bade good-morrow,
And thought to leave her far away behind ;   175
  But cheerly, cheerly,
  She loves me dearly ;
She is so constant to me, and so kind :
  I would deceive her
  And so leave her,   180
But ah ! she is so constant and so kind.

"Beneath my palm trees, by the river side,
I sat a weeping : in the whole world wide

---

(172) The draft reads *However* for *Wherever*.
(174) In the finished manuscript, *bad* : in the first edition, *bade*.
(181) The draft reads this line thus—

    But ah ! she is too constant and too kind.

There was no one to ask me why I wept,—
　　　And so I kept　　　　　　　　　　185
Brimming the water-lilly cups with tears
　　　Cold as my fears.

" Beneath my palm trees, by the river side,
I sat a weeping : what enamour'd bride,
Cheated by shadowy wooer from the clouds,　　190
　　　But hides and shrouds
Beneath dark palm trees by a river side ?

" And as I sat, over the light blue hills
There came a noise of revellers : the rills
Into the wide stream came of purple hue—　　195
　　　'Twas Bacchus and his crew !
The earnest trumpet spake, and silver thrills
From kissing cymbals made a merry din—
　　　'Twas Bacchus and his kin !
Like to a moving vintage down they came,　　200
Crown'd with green leaves, and faces all on flame ;
All madly dancing through the pleasant valley,
　　　To scare thee, Melancholy !
O then, O then, thou wast a simple name !
And I forgot thee, as the berried holly　　205
By shepherds is forgotten, when, in June,
Tall chesnuts keep away the sun and moon :—
　　　I rush'd into the folly !

" Within his car, aloft, young Bacchus stood,
Trifling his ivy-dart, in dancing mood,　　210

----

(187) In the draft, *Chill'd with strange fears.*
(190) The draft gives *lover* for *wooer.*
(202-3) The draft reads *down* for *through* and *my* for *thee.*
(207) In the draft *Beeches* instead of *chesnuts.*

With sidelong laughing;
And little rills of crimson wine imbru'd
His plump white arms, and shoulders, enough white
    For Venus' pearly bite:
And near him rode Silenus on his ass,   215
Pelted with flowers as he on did pass
    Tipsily quaffing.

"Whence came ye, merry Damsels! whence came ye!
So many, and so many, and such glee?
Why have ye left your bowers desolate,   220
    Your lutes, and gentler fate?—
'We follow Bacchus! Bacchus on the wing,
    A conquering!
Bacchus, young Bacchus! good or ill betide,
We dance before him thorough kingdoms wide:—   225
Come hither, lady fair, and joined be
    To our wild minstrelsy!'

"Whence came ye, jolly Satyrs! whence came ye!
So many, and so many, and such glee?
Why have ye left your forest haunts, why left   230
    Your nuts in oak-tree cleft?—
'For wine, for wine we left our kernel tree;
For wine we left our heath, and yellow brooms,
    And cold mushrooms;
For wine we follow Bacchus through the earth;   235

(212-13) The draft reads *streaks* for *rills* and *dainty* for *enough*.
(214) In the draft, *For any pearly bite.*
(221) An additional line comes between 221 and 222 in the draft—

    We follow Bacchus from a far country.

(225) The draft reads *beside* for *before.*
(232) The draft reads *forest meat* for *kernel tree.*

Great God of breathless cups and chirping mirth !—
Come hither, lady fair, and joined be
　　　To our mad minstrelsy ! '

" Over wide streams and mountains great we went,
And, save when Bacchus kept his ivy tent,　　　240
Onward the tiger and the leopard pants,
　　　With Asian elephants :
Onward these myriads—with song and dance,
With zebras striped, and sleek Arabians' prance,
Web-footed alligators, crocodiles,　　　245
Bearing upon their scaly backs, in files,
Plump infant laughers mimicking the coil
Of seamen, and stout galley-rowers' toil :
With toying oars and silken sails they glide,
　　　Nor care for wind and tide.　　　250

" Mounted on panthers' furs and lions' manes,
From rear to van they scour about the plains ;
A three days' journey in a moment done :
And always, at the rising of the sun,
About the wilds they hunt with spear and horn,　　　255
　　　On spleenful unicorn.

" I saw Osirian Egypt kneel adown
　　　Before the vine-wreath crown !
I saw. parch'd Abyssinia rouse and sing
　　　To the silver cymbals' ring !　　　260
I saw the whelming vintage hotly pierce

---

(236) The draft has *endless* for *chirping*.
(247) This line reads as follows in the draft—
　　　Arch infant crews in mimic of the coil...
(254) The draft reads *alway* without the *s*.

Old Tartary the fierce!
The kings of Inde their jewel-sceptres vail,
And from their treasures scatter pearled hail;
Great Brahma from his mystic heaven groans,   265
      And all his priesthood moans;
Before young Bacchus' eye-wink turning pale.—
Into these regions came I following him,
Sick hearted, weary—so I took a whim
To stray away into these forests drear   270
      Alone, without a peer:
And I have told thee all thou mayest hear.

      "Young stranger!
      I've been a ranger
In search of pleasure throughout every clime: 275
      Alas, 'tis not for me!
      Bewitch'd I sure must be,
To lose in grieving all my maiden prime.

      "Come then, Sorrow!
      Sweetest Sorrow!   280
Like an own babe I nurse thee on my breast:
      I thought to leave thee
      And deceive thee,
But now of all the world I love thee best.

---

(263) The draft reads *jewel'd sceptres*.

(267) At this point the following line is cancelled in the draft:

    All city gates were opened to his pomp.

(272) The biblical dissyllabic form *mayest* is clearly used by deliberate preference, for the line originally stood thus in the draft:

    And I have told thee all that thou canst hear.

(277) In the draft, *Bewitch'd must I sure be*.

"There is not one,   285
   No, no, not one
But thee to comfort a poor lonely maid ;
   Thou art her mother,
   And her brother,
Her playmate, and her wooer in the shade."   290

   O what a sigh she gave in finishing,
And look, quite dead to every worldly thing !
Endymion could not speak, but gaz'd on her ;
And listened to the wind that now did stir
About the crisped oaks full drearily,   295
Yet with as sweet a softness as might be
Remember'd from its velvet summer song.
At last he said : "Poor lady, how thus long
Have I been able to endure that voice ?
Fair Melody ! kind Syren ! I've no choice ;   300
I must be thy sad servant evermore :
I cannot choose but kneel here and adore.
Alas, I must not think—by Phœbe, no !
Let me not think, soft Angel ! shall it be so ?
Say, beautifullest, shall I never think ?   305
O thou could'st foster me beyond the brink
Of recollection ! make my watchful care
Close up its bloodshot eyes, nor see despair !
Do gently murder half my soul, and I

(291-2) The draft reads *Sob* for *sigh*, and begins line 292 with
And look'd quite dead.

(297) The gentleness of summer wind seems to have been a
cherished idea with Keats. Compare *Sleep and Poetry*, line 1—

   What is more gentle than a wind in summer ?

(304) In the finished manuscript, *shall't* for *shall it*.

Shall feel the other half so utterly!—   310
I'm giddy at that cheek so fair and smooth ;
O let it blush so ever! let it soothe
My madness! let it mantle rosy-warm[1]
With the tinge of love, panting in safe alarm.—
This cannot be thy hand, and yet it is ;   315
And this is sure thine other softling—this
Thine own fair bosom, and I am so near!
Wilt fall asleep? O let me sip that tear !
And whisper one sweet word that I may know
This is this world—sweet dewy blossom ! "—*Woe!* 320
Woe! Woe to that Endymion! Where is he?—
Even these words went echoing dismally
Through the wide forest—a most fearful tone,
Like one repenting in his latest moan ;
And while it died away a shade pass'd by,   325
As of a thunder cloud. When arrows fly
Through the thick branches, poor ring-doves sleek forth
Their timid necks and tremble ; so these both
Leant to each other trembling, and sat so
Waiting for some destruction—when lo,   330
Foot-feather'd Mercury appear'd sublime
Beyond the tall tree tops ; and in less time
Than shoots the slanted hail-storm, down he dropt
Towards the ground ; but rested not, nor stopt

(310-16) The draft reads thus at this point :

    That—oh how beautiful—how giddy smooth !
    Blush so for ever ! let those glances soothe
    My madness for did I no mercy spy
    Dear lady I should shudder and then die.
    This cannot be thy hand—and yet it is
    And this thine other softling—and is this
    Thine own fair bosom, and am I so near ?

One moment from his home : only the sward   335
He with his wand light touch'd, and heavenward
Swifter than sight was gone—even before
The teeming earth a sudden witness bore
Of his swift magic.   Diving swans appear
Above the crystal circlings white and clear ;   340
And catch the cheated eye in wide surprise,
How they can dive in sight and unseen rise—
So from the turf outsprang two steeds jet-black,
Each with large dark blue wings upon his back.
The youth of Caria plac'd the lovely dame   345
On one, and felt himself in spleen to tame
The other's fierceness.   Through the air they flew,
High as the eagles.   Like two drops of dew
Exhal'd to Phœbus' lips, away they are gone,
Far from the earth away—unseen, alone,   350
Among cool clouds and winds, but that the free,
The buoyant life of song can floating be
Above their heads, and follow them untir'd.—
Muse of my native land, am I inspir'd ?
This is the giddy air, and I must spread   355
Wide pinions to keep here ; nor do I dread
Or height, or depth, or width, or any chance
Precipitous : I have beneath my glance
Those towering horses and their mournful freight.

---

(341) In the first edition *wild surprise* ; and no change is made
here in the corrected copy ; but *wide*, the word in both the manuscripts, is so far more characteristic that *wild* may be concluded to
have passed through an oversight.

(343) The draft reads *coal black.*

(349) In the manuscript, *they're* for *they are.*   Compare Donne,
1st Satyre,

> At last his love he in a window spies,
> And, like light dew exhaled, he flings from me.

Could I thus sail, and see, and thus await   360
Fearless for power of thought, without thine aid ?—

There is a sleepy dusk, an odorous shade
From some approaching wonder, and behold
Those winged steeds, with snorting nostrils bold
Snuff at its faint extreme, and seem to tire,   365
Dying to embers from their native fire !

There curl'd a purple mist around them ; soon,
It seem'd as when around the pale new moon
Sad Zephyr droops the clouds like weeping willow :
'Twas Sleep slow journeying with head on pillow.   370
For the first time, since he came nigh dead born
From the old womb of night, his cave forlorn
Had he left more forlorn ; for the first time,
He felt aloof the day and morning's prime—
Because into his depth Cimmerian   375
There came a dream, showing how a young man,
Ere a lean bat could plump its wintery skin,
Would at high Jove's empyreal footstool win
An immortality, and how espouse
Jove's daughter, and be reckon'd of his house.   380
Now was he slumbering towards heaven's gate,
That he might at the threshold one hour wait
To hear the marriage melodies, and then
Sink downward to his dusky cave again.

(366) In the draft—
        Seeming but embers to their former fire.
(367-8) The draft reads *comes* for *curl'd* and *half moon* for *new moon*.
(370) In the draft, *voyaging*, not *journeying*.
(384) The draft gives this line thus—
        Betake him downward to his cave again.

His litter of smooth semilucent mist,   385
Diversely ting'd with rose and amethyst,
Puzzled those eyes that for the centre sought ;
And scarcely for one moment could be caught
His sluggish form reposing motionless.
Those two on winged steeds, with all the stress   390
Of vision search'd for him, as one would look
Athwart the sallows of a river nook
To catch a glance at silver throated eels,—
Or from old Skiddaw's top, when fog conceals
His rugged forehead in a mantle pale,   395
With an eye-guess towards some pleasant vale
Descry a favourite hamlet faint and far.

These raven horses, though they foster'd are
Of earth's splenetic fire, dully drop
Their full-vein'd ears, nostrils blood wide, and stop ;   400
Upon the spiritless mist have they outspread
Their ample feathers, are in slumber dead,—
And on those pinions, level in mid air,
Endymion sleepeth and the lady fair.
Slowly they sail, slowly as icy isle   405
Upon a calm sea drifting : and meanwhile
The mournful wanderer dreams.   Behold ! he walks
On heaven's pavement ; brotherly he talks
To divine powers : from his hand full fain
Juno's proud birds are pecking pearly grain :   410
He tries the nerve of Phœbus' golden bow,

---

(385) In the draft, *pale* for *smooth*.
(387-8) The draft reads *Puzzled the eyes* and *scarcely one short moment*.
(394) The draft has *front* instead of *top*.
(401) The draft reads *air* for *mist* ; and in the finished manuscript the word was first written *mists*.

And asketh where the golden apples grow :
Upon his arm he braces Pallas' shield,
And strives in vain to unsettle and wield
A Jovian thunderbolt : arch Hebe brings   415
A full-brimm'd goblet, dances lightly, sings
And tantalizes long ; at last he drinks,
And lost in pleasure at her feet he sinks,
Touching with dazzled lips her starlight hand.
He blows a bugle,—an ethereal band   420
Are visible above : the Seasons four,—
Green-kyrtled Spring, flush Summer, golden store
In Autumn's sickle, Winter frosty hoar,
Join dance with shadowy Hours ; while still the blast,
In swells unmitigated, still doth last   425
To sway their floating morris. "Whose is this ?
Whose bugle ?" he inquires : they smile—"O Dis !
Why is this mortal here ? Dost thou not know
Its mistress' lips ? Not thou ?—'Tis Dian's : lo !
She rises crescented !" He looks, 'tis she,   430

---

(418) In the draft—

    With pleasure at her knees he swoons and sinks.

(420) This line stands thus (an Alexandrine) in the draft :

    He takes a bugle blows it, an aerial band...

(421) In the draft, *o'erhead* for *above.*

(424) In the draft, *with the shadowy Hours* ; and the next line
stands thus (another Alexandrine)—

    Echoed in swells unmitigated, still doth last.

(428) The draft reads *a mortal.*

(429-30) In both manuscripts the preceding line stands rhymeless,
and these two stand thus—

    Its Mistress' Lips? Not thou? Ah, Ah, Ah, Ah !
    'Tis Dian's, here she comes, look out afar,

so that by the withdrawal of one line two very noticeable flaws were
remedied. In line 430, the finished manuscript has a cancelled
reading *look'd* for *looks.*

His very goddess : good-bye earth, and sea,
And air, and pains, and care, and suffering ;
Good-bye to all but love !   Then doth he spring
Towards her, and awakes—and, strange, o'erhead,
Of those same fragrant exhalations bred,   435
Beheld awake his very dream : the gods
Stood smiling ; merry Hebe laughs and nods ;
And Phœbe bends towards him crescented.
O state perplexing !   On the pinion bed,
Too well awake, he feels the panting side   440
Of his delicious lady.   He who died
For soaring too audacious in the sun,
When that same treacherous wax began to run,
Felt not more tongue-tied than Endymion.
His heart leapt up as to its rightful throne,   445
To that fair shadow'd passion puls'd its way—
Ah, what perplexity !   Ah, well a day !
So fond, so beauteous was his bed-fellow,
He could not help but kiss her : then he grew
Awhile forgetful of all beauty save   450
Young Phœbe's, golden hair'd ; and so 'gan crave

---

(432) The draft reads *cares*.

(442-4) The draft reads as follows :

> Because in sunshine treacherous wax would melt,
> Even at the fatal melting thereof, felt
> Not more tongue-tied than did Endymion.

In the finished manuscript the reading is that of the text ; and line
443 clearly begins with *When* : in the first edition it begins with
Where ; but, though no alteration is here made in the corrected
copy, the manuscript, supported as it is by the sense of the passage
as given in the draft, must rule the text.

(449) This line reads thus in the draft—

> He could not help but kiss—then did he grow...

but the finished manuscript gives the reading of the text.

Forgiveness : yet he turn'd once more to look
At the sweet sleeper,—all his soul was shook,—
She press'd his hand in slumber ; so once more
He could not help but kiss her and adore.   455
At this the shadow wept, melting away.
The Latmian started up : " Bright goddess, stay !
Search my most hidden breast !   By truth's own tongue,
I have no dædale heart : why is it wrung
To desperation ?   Is there nought for me,   460
Upon the bourn of bliss, but misery ? "

      These words awoke the stranger of dark tresses :
Her dawning love-look rapt Endymion blesses
With 'haviour soft.   Sleep yawn'd from underneath.
" Thou swan of Ganges, let us no more breathe   465
This murky phantasm ! thou contented seem'st
Pillow'd in lovely idleness, nor dream'st
What horrors may discomfort thee and me.
Ah, shouldst thou die from my heart-treachery !—
Yet did she merely weep—her gentle soul   470
Hath no revenge in it : as it is whole
In tenderness, would I were whole in love !

---

(455) The draft reads *kiss, kiss and adore.*

(458) Cancelled reading of the finished manuscript, *most inmost* for *most hidden.*

(461) In the first edition, *bourne,* with a final *e* ; but the manuscript reads *bourn.*

(462-3) The draft reads *lady* for *stranger* and *love-glance* for *love-look.*

(464) The contraction *'haviour,* it will be remembered, is of common Elizabethan use.   Compare *Romeo and Juliet,* Act II, Scene II, lines 98-9 :

> In truth, fair Montague, I am too fond,
> And therefore thou mayst think my 'haviour light.

(465) In the draft, *Thou wandering fair one.*

Can I prize thee, fair maid, all price above,
Even when I feel as true as innocence?
I do, I do.—What is this soul then? Whence 475
Came it? It does not seem my own, and I
Have no self-passion or identity.
Some fearful end must be : where, where is it?
By Nemesis, I see my spirit flit
Alone about the dark—Forgive me, sweet : 480
Shall we away?" He rous'd the steeds : they beat
Their wings chivalrous into the clear air,
Leaving old Sleep within his vapoury lair.

The good-night blush of eve was waning slow,
And Vesper, risen star, began to throe 485
In the dusk heavens silverly, when they
Thus sprang direct towards the Galaxy.
Nor did speed hinder converse soft and strange—
Eternal oaths and vows they interchange,
In such wise, in such temper, so aloof 490
Up in the winds, beneath a starry roof,
So witless of their doom, that verily
'Tis well nigh past man's search their hearts to see ;

---

(483) The draft reads—

> Leaving old Sleep to sail in vapoury lair.

(484-7) These four lines stand thus in the draft :

> The good-night hush of eve was waning slow,
> And Vesper's timid pulse began to throe
> In the dusk heavens silverly, when they
> Thus sprang direct up to the Galaxy.

The finished manuscript corresponds with the text; but in the printed book the word *silvery* for *silverly* slipped in, and so the passage has been printed ever since. There can be no doubt that *silverly* was the word intended.

(492) The draft reads *witless of all things*.

Whether they wept, or laugh'd, or griev'd, or toy'd—
Most like with joy gone mad, with sorrow cloy'd.   495

    Full facing their swift flight, from ebon streak,
The moon put forth a little diamond peak,
No bigger than an unobserved star,
Or tiny point of fairy scymetar ;
Bright signal that she only stoop'd to tie   500
Her silver sandals, ere deliciously
She bow'd into the heavens her timid head.
Slowly she rose, as though she would have fled,
While to his lady meek the Carian turn'd,
To mark if her dark eyes had yet discern'd   505
This beauty in its birth—Despair ! despair !
He saw her body fading gaunt and spare
In the cold moonshine.   Straight he seiz'd her wrist ;
It melted from his grasp : her hand he kiss'd,
And, horror ! kiss'd his own—he was alone.   510
Her steed a little higher soar'd, and then
Dropt hawkwise to the earth.

              There lies a den,
Beyond the seeming confines of the space

---

(495) In the draft there are two cancelled readings, *Until* and
Haply, in place of *Most like* ; and *woe* stands in the place of *joy*.
  (505-10) In the draft, this passage stands thus :

        To mark if her dark eyes slept or discern'd
        Such beauty being born—Despair ! despair!
        He saw her body faded gaunt and spare
        In the cold moonshine.   Straight her wrist he seized
        It melted from his grasp—his lips were teazed
        To madness for his——

In the finished manuscript there is no variation from the printed
text to account for the loss of a rhyme.
  (513) In the draft this line stands thus—

        Of misery beyond the seeming confines of the space...

Made for the soul to wander in and trace
Its own existence, of remotest glooms.   515
Dark regions are around it, where the tombs
Of buried griefs the spirit sees, but scarce
One hour doth linger weeping, for the pierce
Of new-born woe it feels more inly smart:
And in these regions many a venom'd dart   520
At random flies; they are the proper home
Of every ill : the man is yet to come
Who hath not journeyed in this native hell.
But few have ever felt how calm and well
Sleep may be had in that deep den of all.   525
There anguish does not sting ; nor pleasure pall :
Woe-hurricanes beat ever at the gate,
Yet all is still within and desolate.
Beset with plainful gusts, within ye hear
No sound so loud as when on curtain'd bier   530
The death-watch tick is stifled.   Enter none
Who strive therefore : on the sudden it is won.
Just when the sufferer begins to burn,
Then it is free to him ; and from an urn,
Still fed by melting ice, he takes a draught—   535
Young Semele such richness never quaft .
In her maternal longing ! Happy gloom !
Dark Paradise ! where pale becomes the bloom

---

(518) The draft reads *lingers* for *doth linger*, so as to force the word *hour* into service as a dissyllable.

(520) In the draft, *a random dart*.

(522) The draft reads *that soul* for *the man*.

(526-7) The draft reads thus :

> There anguish stings not—sweetness cannot pall :
> Dark hurricanes of woe beat ever at the gate,...

(531) The draft has *muffled* in place of *stifled*.

(534) The draft reads *This den is free to him*.

Of health by due; where silence dreariest
Is most articulate; where hopes infest;   540
Where those eyes are the brightest far that keep
Their lids shut longest in a dreamless sleep.
O happy spirit-home! O wondrous soul!
Pregnant with such a den to save the whole
In thine own depth.   Hail, gentle Carian!   545
For, never since thy griefs and woes began,
Hast thou felt so content: a grievous feud
Hath led thee to this Cave of Quietude.
Aye, his lull'd soul was there, although upborne
With dangerous speed: and so he did not mourn   550
Because he knew not whither he was going.
So happy was he, not the aerial blowing
Of trumpets at clear parley from the east
Could rouse from that fine relish, that high feast.

---

(539) The curious expression *Of health by due,* unmistakably so
written in the finished manuscript and printed in the first edition,
is represented in the draft by *The rightful tinge of health.* We
may therefore presume that *by due* is used as an equivalent for *by
right.*

(542) The draft reads *close* for *shut.*

(546) In the draft, *griefs and joys.*

(548) In the first edition, *Hath let*; but *led* in both manuscripts.

(550) In the draft this line reads thus :

With dangerous speed : nor did he sigh and mourn...

In the finished manuscript it was written thus :

On dangerous Winds : and so he did not mourn...

and then changed so as to correspond with the text.

(554) At this point the draft reads as follows :—

Could rouse { him from that / from } inward feast—and yet to hear't
'Twas like a gift of Prophecy—alert
The feather'd horse he snorted with alarm
And towards it flapp'd away—Alas no charm...

They stung the feather'd horse : with fierce alarm   555
He flapp'd towards the sound.   Alas, no charm
Could lift Endymion's head, or he had view'd
A skyey mask, a pinion'd multitude,—
And silvery was its passing : voices sweet
Warbling the while as if to lull and greet   560
The wanderer in his path.   Thus warbled they,
While past the vision went in bright array.

"Who, who from Dian's feast would be away?
For all the golden bowers of the day
Are empty left ?   Who, who away would be   565
From Cynthia's wedding and festivity ?
Not Hesperus : lo! upon his silver wings
He leans away for highest heaven and sings,
Snapping his lucid fingers merrily !—
Ah, Zephyrus ! art here, and Flora too !   570
Ye tender bibbers of the rain and dew,
Young playmates of the rose and daffodil,   ·
Be careful, ere ye enter in, to fill
      Your baskets high
With fennel green, and balm, and golden pines,   575
Savory, latter-mint, and columbines,

---

(563) The draft reads thus :

    Who, who would absent be from Dian's feast
    For all the golden chambers of the East
    Are empty left ?   Who, who away would be
    From Cynthia's wedding and festivity?
      Who, who would be ?

(569) The draft has two additional lines after this one,

    He stay behind—he glad of lazy plea ?
      Not he ! not he !

(573) The draft reads this line thus :—

    Mind ere ye enter in to oppress and fill...

Cool parsley, basil sweet, and sunny thyme ;
Yea, every flower and leaf of every clime,
All gather'd in the dewy morning : hie
    Away ! fly, fly !—   580
Crystalline brother of the belt of heaven,
Aquarius ! to whom king Jove has given
Two liquid pulse streams 'stead of feather'd wings,
Two fan-like fountains,—thine illuminings
    For Dian play :   585
Dissolve the frozen purity of air ;
Let thy white shoulders silvery and bare
Show cold through watery pinions ; make more bright
The Star-Queen's crescent on her marriage night :
    Haste, haste away !—   590
Castor has tam'd the planet Lion, see !
And of the Bear has Pollux mastery :
A third is in the race ! who is the third,
Speeding away swift as the eagle bird ?
    The ramping Centaur !   595
The Lion's mane's on end : the Bear how fierce !
The Centaur's arrow ready seems to pierce
Some enemy : far forth his bow is bent
Into the blue of heaven.   He'll be shent,

(576-7) The word *early* is cancelled in the finished manuscript
before *latter mint* ; and line 577 reads in the draft—

    Cool parsley, dripping cresses, sunny thyme.

(584) This was originally a short line consisting of the words
Thine illuminings alone.   The whole stanza, lines 581 to 590, was
sent by Keats to his friend Baily for his " vote, pro or con ", in a
letter dated the 22nd of November 1817.   The curious may see the
passage as given in the letter in the present edition with its slight
variations of spelling and capitalling, and its *hath* for *has* in
line 582.

(589) The draft reads *Night-Queen's* for *Star-Queen's*.

(593) The draft reads *Ay three are in the race !*

Pale unrelentor,   600
When he shall hear the wedding lutes a playing.—
Andromeda ! sweet woman ! why delaying
So timidly among the stars : come hither !
Join this bright throng, and nimbly follow whither
     They all are going.   605
Danae's Son, before Jove newly bow'd,
Has wept for thee, calling to Jove aloud.
Thee, gentle lady, did he disenthral :
Ye shall for ever live and love, for all
     Thy tears are flowing.—   610
By Daphne's fright, behold Apollo !—"

                   More
Endymion heard not : down his steed him bore,
Prone to the green head of a misty hill.

    His first touch of the earth went nigh to kill.
"Alas !" said he, " were I but always borne   615
Through dangerous winds, had but my footsteps worn
A path in hell, for ever would I bless
Horrors which nourish an uneasiness
For my own sullen conquering : to him
Who lives beyond earth's boundary, grief is dim,   620
Sorrow is but a shadow : now I see
The grass ; I feel the solid ground—Ah, me !

(607-8) The draft reads—
            calling to Jove aloud
    For thee—thee gentle did he disenthrall.
    (622) In the draft, this line is—
    The real grass, the solid ground—Ah, me !
but in the finished manuscript it is an Alexandrine—
    The real grass ; I feel the solid ground—Ah, me !
The reading of the text is that of the first edition.

It is thy voice—divinest! Where?—who? who
Left thee so quiet on this bed of dew?
Behold upon this happy earth we are;   625
Let us aye love each other; let us fare
On forest-fruits, and never, never go
Among the abodes of mortals here below,
Or be by phantoms dup'd.   O destiny!
Into a labyrinth now my soul would fly,   630
But with thy beauty will I deaden it.
Where didst thou melt to?   By thee will I sit
For ever: let our fate stop here—a kid
I on this spot will offer: Pan will bid
Us live in peace, in love and peace among   635
His forest wildernesses.   I have clung
To nothing, lov'd a nothing, nothing seen
Or felt but a great dream!   O I have been
Presumptuous against love, against the sky,
Against all elements, against the tie   640
Of mortals each to each, against the blooms
Of flowers, rush of rivers, and the tombs
Of heroes gone!   Against his proper glory
Has my own soul conspired: so my story
Will I to children utter, and repent.   645

---

(624) The draft has *safe upon* for *quiet on.*
(629-30) This couplet stands thus in the draft :—

> Or be by phantoms duped.   Alas! alas!
> Into a labyrinth now my soul would pass,...

(632) The finished manuscript and the first edition read *too* for
to ; but as the question is repeated in line 668 in the words *Whither
didst melt,* there can be no possible doubt as to the right reading.
(641-3) The draft reads—

> Of mortals to each other, against the blooms
> Of roses, rush of rivers, and the tombs
> Of heroes gone !   Against its proper glory...

There never liv'd a mortal man, who bent
His appetite beyond his natural sphere,
But starv'd and died.   My sweetest Indian, here,
Here will I kneel, for thou redeemed hast
My life from too thin breathing : gone and past   650
Are cloudy phantasms.   Caverns lone, farewell !
And air of visions, and the monstrous swell
Of visionary seas !   No, never more
Shall airy voices cheat me to the shore
Of tangled wonder, breathless and aghast.   655
Adieu, my daintiest Dream ! although so vast
My love is still for thee.   The hour may come
When we shall meet in pure elysium.
On earth I may not love thee ; and therefore
Doves will I offer up, and sweetest store   660
All through the teeming year : so thou wilt shine
On me, and on this damsel fair of mine,
And bless our simple lives.   My Indian bliss !
My river-lilly bud ! one human kiss !
One sigh of real breath—one gentle squeeze,   665

---

(646) The draft has the word *Has* instead of *There*.
(649) In the finished manuscript this line stands thus :—

    Will I kneel, for thou redeemed hast...

(650) Woodhouse notes the following variation, presumably from the draft :—

    My spirit from too thin a breath—gone and past...

(653) Woodhouse notes the variation *No more, no more.* See Book II, line 199 *et seq.*, for the explanation of this speech of Endymion's.
(656) Woodhouse notes the variation *how vast, how vast.*
(660) Woodhouse notes the variation *I offer thee.*
(661) Cancelled reading of the finished manuscript, *smile* for *shine.*
(664) Woodhouse notes the variation *mortal* for *human.*

Warm as a dove's nest among summer trees,
And warm with dew at ooze from living blood !
Whither didst melt ?   Ah, what of that !—all good
We'll talk about—no more of dreaming.—Now,
Where shall our dwelling be ?   Under the brow   670
Of some steep mossy hill, where ivy dun
Would hide us up, although spring leaves were none ;
And where dark yew trees, as we rustle through,
Will drop their scarlet berry cups of dew ?
O thou wouldst joy to live in such a place ;   675
Dusk for our loves, yet light enough to grace
Those gentle limbs on mossy bed reclin'd :
For by one step the blue sky shouldst thou find,
And by another, in deep dell below,
See, through the trees, a little river go   680
All in its mid-day gold and glimmering.
Honey from out the gnarled hive I'll bring,
And apples, wan with sweetness, gather thee,—
Cresses that grow where no man may them see,
And sorrel untorn by the dew-claw'd stag :   685

---

(666) An imagination in which Hunt would have found it difficult to discover the reality ; but probably Keats had never seen the miserable platform of dry twigs that serves for " a dove's nest among summer trees."

(670) Endymion's imaginary home and employments as pictured in the next fifty lines may be compared with Shelley's Ægean island described so wonderfully in *Epipsychidion*.   Both passages are thoroughly characteristic ; and they show the divergence between the modes of thought and sentiment of the two men in a very marked way.

(680) In the draft,

> See, through the trees, a river at its flow...

(682) The draft reads *nest* for *hive*.

(685) The dew-claw is the small process at the back of the leg above the foot.

Pipes will I fashion of the syrinx flag,
That thou mayst always know whither I roam,
When it shall please thee in our quiet home
To listen and think of love.   Still let me speak ;
Still let me dive into the joy I seek,—   690
For yet the past doth prison me.   The rill,
Thou haply mayst delight in, will I fill
With fairy fishes from the mountain tarn,
And thou shalt feed them from the squirrel's barn.
Its bottom will I strew with amber shells,   695
And pebbles blue from deep enchanted wells.
Its sides I'll plant with dew-sweet eglantine,
And honeysuckles full of clear bee-wine.
I will entice this crystal rill to trace
Love's silver name upon the meadow's face.   700
I'll kneel to Vesta, for a flame of fire ;
And to god Phœbus, for a golden lyre ;
To Empress Dian, for a hunting spear ;
To Vesper, for a taper silver-clear,
That I may see thy beauty through the night ;   705
To Flora, and a nightingale shall light
Tame on thy finger ; to the River-gods,
And they shall bring thee taper fishing-rods

---

(688) The draft reads *That thou by ear mayst know.*
(691) In the draft, *For yet the past doth weigh me down.*
(693-4) The draft reads *tarns* and *barns.*
(697) In the finished manuscript, *I plant,*—not *I'll plant.*
(699) Cancelled readings of the manuscript,

> Aye, } I will make this crystal rillet trace.
> And

(700) After this line there is a couplet in the finished manuscript, which does not appear in the printed book,—

> And by it shalt thou sit and sing, hey nonny !
> While doves coo to thee for a little honey.

Of gold, and lines of Naiads' long bright tress.
Heaven shield thee for thine utter loveliness!　　　　710
Thy mossy footstool shall the altar be
'Fore which I'll bend, bending, dear love, to thee:
Those lips shall be my Delphos, and shall speak
Laws to my footsteps, colour to my cheek,
Trembling or stedfastness to this same voice,　　　　715
And of three sweetest pleasurings the choice:
And that affectionate light, those diamond things,
Those eyes, those passions, those supreme pearl springs,
Shall be my grief, or twinkle me to pleasure.
Say, is not bliss within our perfect seisure?　　　　720
O that I could not doubt!"

　　　　　　　　　　The mountaineer
Thus strove by fancies vain and crude to clear
His briar'd path to some tranquillity.
It gave bright gladness to his lady's eye,
And yet the tears she wept were tears of sorrow;　　　725
Answering thus, just as the golden morrow

---

(709) The draft reads *with* for *and*.

(716) This line originally began with the words *And the most velvet*, which are struck out in the finished manuscript. Woodhouse notes, doubtless from the draft, the line—

　　　And the most velvet peaches to my choice.

(720) The draft reads *Is not, then, bliss* &c.

(721) In the first edition there is a note of interrogation after *doubt*; but a note of exclamation stands there both in the manuscript and in the corrected copy.

(723) The draft reads *The* for *His*.

(724-5) At the end of the book containing the draft, Keats wrote, apparently as a memorandum for this passage, the two lines—

　　　There was rejoicing in his Lady's eye
　　　And yet the tears she wept were tears of sorrow.

(726) The draft has *what time* for *just as*.

Beam'd upward from the vallies of the east :
"O that the flutter of this heart had ceas'd,
Or the sweet name of love had pass'd away.
Young feather'd tyrant ! by a swift decay 730
Wilt thou devote this body to the earth :
And I do think that at my very birth
I lisp'd thy blooming titles inwardly ;
For at the first, first dawn and thought of thee,
With uplift hands I blest the stars of heaven. 735
Art thou not cruel ? Ever have I striven
To think thee kind, but ah, it will not do !
When yet a child, I heard that kisses drew
Favour from thee, and so I kisses gave
To the void air, bidding them find out love : 740
But when I came to feel how far above
All fancy, pride, and fickle maidenhood,
All earthly pleasure, all imagin'd good,
Was the warm tremble of a devout kiss,—
Even then, that moment, at the thought of this, 745
Fainting I fell into a bed of flowers,
And languish'd there three days. Ye milder powers,
Am I not cruelly wrong'd ? Believe, believe

---

(734) The draft reads *thought and dawn* instead of *dawn and thought.*

(739) In the finished manuscript, this line ends with *so I gave gave,* as if one *gave* were an accidental repetition instead of the right word ; and indeed the word *kisses* is inserted in pencil in the margin as a substitute for the first *gave.* Nevertheless the first edition reads *so I gave and gave* ; but the reading of the text is supplied in the corrected copy. It is surprising that Keats did not discover the rhymelessness of this line and of line 758, or the bad rhyme of lines 754 and 755.

(743) Cancelled reading of the manuscript, *Was* for the initial *All* in this line.

(748) Cancelled reading of the manuscript, *serv'd* for *wrong'd.*

Me, dear Endymion, were I to weave
With my own fancies garlands of sweet life,   750
Thou shouldst be one of all.   Ah, bitter strife !
I may not be thy love :   I am forbidden—
Indeed I am—thwarted, affrighted, chidden,
By things I trembled at, and gorgon wrath.
Twice hast thou ask'd whither I went : henceforth   755
Ask me no more !   I may not utter it,
Nor may I be thy love.   We might commit
Ourselves at once to vengeance ; we might die ;
We might embrace and die : voluptuous thought !
Enlarge not to my hunger, or I'm caught   760
In trammels of perverse deliciousness.
No, no, that shall not be : thee will I bless,
And bid a long adieu."

          The Carian
No word return'd : both lovelorn, silent, wan,
Into the vallies green together went.   765
Far wandering, they were perforce content
To sit beneath a fair lone beechen tree ;
Nor at each other gaz'd, but heavily
Por'd on its hazle cirque of shedded leaves.

      Endymion ! unhappy ! it nigh grieves   770
Me to behold thee thus in last extreme :

(749-51) The draft has the following variation :—

                         were I to weave
          My own imaginations to sweet life
          Thou would'st o'ertop them all.

(754) In the draft, *tremble*, not *trembled*.
(766) This line begins in the draft with *Long* instead of *Far*.
(769) The draft reads *carpet of shed leaves* instead of *cirque of
shedded leaves.*

Ensky'd ere this, but truly that I deem
Truth the best music in a first-born song.
Thy lute-voic'd brother will I sing ere long,
And thou shalt aid—hast thou not aided me?   775
Yes, moonlight Emperor! felicity
Has been thy meed for many thousand years;
Yet often have I, on the brink of tears,
Mourn'd as if yet thou wert a forester;—
Forgetting the old tale.

            He did not stir   780
His eyes from the dead leaves, or one small pulse
Of joy he might have felt.   The spirit culls
Unfaded amaranth, when wild it strays
Through the old garden-ground of boyish days.
A little onward ran the very stream   785
By which he took his first soft poppy dream;
And on the very bark 'gainst which he leant
A crescent he had carv'd, and round it spent
His skill in little stars.   The teeming tree
Had swollen and green'd the pious charactery,   790
But not ta'en out.   Why, there was not a slope
Up which he had not fear'd the antelope;

---

(772) In the draft—

    That hadst been high ere this, but that I deem...

(774) Another allusion to the poetic scheme of which the sumptuous fragment *Hyperion* is the unachieved result.

(778) The draft reads—

    Yet often have I, mid some foolish tears,...

(783) The draft has *perchance* in place of *wild*, so as to make *amaranth* scan as a dissyllable.

(791-2) The draft reads *effaced* for *ta'en out* and *chaced* for *fear'd*, which is of course used in its old sense of *frightened*.

And not a tree, beneath whose rooty shade
He had not with his tamed leopards play'd :
Nor could an arrow light, or javelin,   795
Fly in the air where his had never been—
And yet he knew it not.

                    O treachery !
Why does his lady smile, pleasing her eye
With all his sorrowing ?   He sees her not.
But who so stares on him ?   His sister sure !   800
Peona of the woods !—Can she endure—
Impossible—how dearly they embrace !
His lady smiles ; delight is in her face ;
It is no treachery.

                    " Dear brother mine !
Endymion, weep not so !   Why shouldst thou pine   805
When all great Latmus so exalt will be ?
Thank the great gods, and look not bitterly ;
And speak not one pale word, and sigh no more.
Sure I will not believe thou hast such store
Of grief, to last thee to my kiss again.   810

---

(794) Woodhouse notes, presumably from the draft, the variation *jessied falcons* for *tamed leopards*.

(799) The finished manuscript does not help us to the missing rhyme ; and Woodhouse notes nothing from the draft here, though against line 801 he records what is doubtless a variation from the draft, *Peona kind and fair*.

(805) Woodhouse notes the variation *Dear Endy: weep*, &c., which I should not like to accept literally without seeing the original.

(806) Here again as in Book III, line 449, the first edition reads *Latmos* though the manuscript reads *Latmus*.

(808) Another variation noted by Woodhouse is *nor sigh once more* for *and sigh no more*.

Thou surely canst not bear a mind in pain,
Come hand in hand with one so beautiful.
Be happy both of you ! for I will pull
The flowers of autumn for your coronals.
Pan's holy priest for young Endymion calls ;   815
And when he is restor'd, thou, fairest dame,
Shalt be our queen.   Now, is it not a shame
To see ye thus,—not very, very sad ?
Perhaps ye are too happy to be glad :
O feel as if it were a common day ;   820
Free-voic'd as one who never was away.
No tongue shall ask, whence come ye ? but ye shall
Be gods of your own rest imperial.
Not even I, for one whole month, will pry
Into the hours that have pass'd us by,   825
Since in my arbour I did sing to thee.
O Hermes ! on this very night will be

---

(811) At this point Woodhouse gives the following passage, which
is doubtless from the draft :—

> Were this sweet damsel like a long neck'd crane
> Or an old rocking barn owl half asleep
> Some reason would there be for thee to keep
> So dull-eyed—but thou knowst she's beautiful
> Yes, Yes ! and thou dost love her well—I'll pull...

(815) Woodhouse notes the variation *Great Pan's high priest.*
(816) Woodhouse notes the variation—

> This Shepherd Prince restor'd, thou, fairest dame,...

(819) Woodhouse notes the following two variants of this line,—
one expressly from the draft and the other presumably from the
same source :

> (1) Perhaps ye feel too much joy—too overglad :
> (2) Perhaps ye are too glad, too overglad.

(825) The draft reads *Into the long hours*, so as to avoid the
necessity for scanning *hours* as a dissyllable.
(827) In the draft thus—

> Why ! hark ye ! on this very eve will be...

A hymning up to Cynthia, queen of light ;
For the soothsayers old saw yesternight
Good visions in the air,—whence will befal,   830
As say these sages, health perpetual
To shepherds and their flocks ; and furthermore,
In Dian's face they read the gentle lore :
Therefore for her these vesper-carols are.
Our friends will all be there from nigh and far.   835
Many upon thy death have ditties made ;
And many, even now, their foreheads shade
With cypress, on a day of sacrifice.
New singing for our maids shalt thou devise,
And pluck the sorrow from our huntsmen's brows.   840
Tell me, my lady-queen, how to espouse
This wayward brother to his rightful joys !
His eyes are on thee bent, as thou didst poise
His fate most goddess-like.   Help me, I pray,
To lure—Endymion, dear brother, say   845
What ails thee ? "   He could bear no more, and so
Bent his soul fiercely like a spiritual bow,
And twang'd it inwardly, and calmly said :
" I would have thee my only friend, sweet maid !
My only visitor ! not ignorant though,   850
That those deceptions which for pleasure go
'Mong men, are pleasures real as real may be :
But there are higher ones I may not see,
If impiously an earthly realm I take.
Since I saw thee, I have been wide awake   855
Night after night, and day by day, until
Of the empyrean I have drunk my fill.
Let it content thee, Sister, seeing me

---

(840) The draft has *cypress* for *sorrow.*
(853) In the draft, *But I have* &c.

More happy than betides mortality.
A hermit young, I'll live in mossy cave,   860
Where thou alone shalt come to me, and lave
Thy spirit in the wonders I shall tell.
Through me the shepherd realm shall prosper well;
For to thy tongue will I all health confide.
And, for my sake, let this young maid abide   865
With thee as a dear sister.   Thou alone,
Peona, mayst return to me.   I own
This may sound strangely : but when, dearest girl,
Thou seest it for my happiness, no pearl
Will trespass down those cheeks.   Companion fair! 870
Wilt be content to dwell with her, to share
This sister's love with me?"   Like one resign'd
And bent by circumstance, and thereby blind
In self-commitment, thus that meek unknown :
"Aye, but a buzzing by my ears has flown,   875
Of jubilee to Dian :—truth I heard?
Well then, I see there is no little bird,
Tender soever, but is Jove's own care.
Long have I sought for rest, and, unaware,

---

(862) Woodhouse notes the variation *will* for *shall*.

(866) Woodhouse notes the variation *With thee ev'n as a sister*.

(874) Woodhouse notes the variation *mild* for *meek*.

(876) This line ends with a note of exclamation in the first edition, but with a note of interrogation both in the finished manuscript and in the corrected copy.   Woodhouse does not cite the draft on this point.

(877-8) A curious importation from Hebrew theology into a subject from Greek mythology.   Compare St. Matthew, X, 29 : "Are not two sparrows sold for a farthing? and one of them shall not fall on the ground without your Father."   Or, as made familiar to our childhood by the popular hymn-wright,—

A little sparrow cannot fall,
Unnoticed, Lord, by Thee.

Behold I find it! so exalted too!   880
So after my own heart! I knew, I knew
There was a place untenanted in it:
In that same void white Chastity shall sit,
And monitor me nightly to lone slumber.
With sanest lips I vow me to the number   885
Of Dian's sisterhood; and, kind lady,
With thy good help, this very night shall see
My future days to her fane consecrate."

As feels a dreamer what doth most create
His own particular fright, so these three felt: 890
Or like one who, in after ages, knelt
To Lucifer or Baal, when he'd pine
After a little sleep: or when in mine
Far under-ground, a sleeper meets his friends
Who know him not.   Each diligently bends   895
Towards common thoughts and things for very fear;
Striving their ghastly malady to cheer,
By thinking it a thing of yes and no,
That housewives talk of.   But the spirit-blow
Was struck, and all were dreamers.   At the last   900
Endymion said: " Are not our fates all cast?
Why stand we here? Adieu, ye tender pair!
Adieu!"   Whereat those maidens, with wild stare,
Walk'd dizzily away.   Pained and hot
His eyes went after them, until they got   905
Near to a cypress grove, whose deadly maw,

---

(882) Woodhouse notes the variation *void* for *place*.
(888-9) The draft reads *in* for *to* and *can* for *doth*.
(892) In the draft, *at strife* in place of *he'd pine*.
(904) The draft reads *patiently* for *dizzily*.
(906) In the draft, *shade* for *maw*.

In one swift moment, would what then he saw
Engulph for ever. " Stay !" he cried, "ah, stay !
Turn, damsels ! hist! one word I have to say.
Sweet Indian, I would see thee once again. 910
It is a thing I dote on : so I'd fain,
Peona, ye should hand in hand repair
Into those holy groves, that silent are
Behind great Dian's temple.   I'll be yon,
At vesper's earliest twinkle—they are gone— 915
But once, once, once again—"   At this he press'd
His hands against his face, and then did rest
His head upon a mossy hillock green,
And so remain'd as he a corpse had been
All the long day ; save when he scantly lifted 920
His eyes abroad, to see how shadows shifted
With the slow move of time,—sluggish and weary
Until the poplar tops, in journey dreary,
Had reach'd the river's brim.   Then up he rose,
And, slowly as that very river flows, 925
Walk'd towards the temple grove with this lament :
" Why such a golden eve ? The breeze is sent
Careful and soft, that not a leaf may fall
Before the serene father of them all

(918-22) In the draft this passage stands thus :—

> His hands upon a pillow of green moss
> And so remained without impatient toss
> All the day long—save when he scantly lifted
> His eyes abroad, to see how shadows shifted,
> And note the weary time.—Ah weary, weary,...

The word *hands* in line 918 was probably a mere slip.
 (926-7) Woodhouse gives, presumably from the draft, the couplet,

> Walk'd towards the temple grove lamenting " O
> " Why such a golden eve ? The breezes blow,...

Bows down his summer head below the west.   930
Now am I of breath, speech, and speed possest,
But at the setting I must bid adieu
To her for the last time.   Night will strew
On the damp grass myriads of lingering leaves,
And with them shall I die ; nor much it grieves   935
To die, when summer dies on the cold sward.
Why, I have been a butterfly, a lord
Of flowers, garlands, love-knots, silly posies,
Groves, meadows, melodies, and arbour roses ;
My kingdom's at its death, and just it is   940
That I should die with it : so in all this
We miscall grief, bale, sorrow, heartbreak, woe,
What is there to plain of ?   By Titan's foe
I am but rightly serv'd."   So saying, he
Tripp'd lightly on, in sort of deathful glee ;   945
Laughing at the clear stream and setting sun,
As though they jests had been : nor had he done
His laugh at nature's holy countenance,
Until that grove appear'd, as if perchance,
And then his tongue with sober seemlihed   950
Gave utterance as he enter'd : " Ha ! I said,
" King of the butterflies ; but by this gloom,

---

(933) This line, though possibly corrupt, stands thus in the finished manuscript and in Keats's edition. Woodhouse does not bring the draft in evidence.

(934) In the manuscript, *ling'ring* for *lingering*.

(949-50) In the draft—

> Until he saw that grove, as if perchance,
> And then his soul was changed...

(951) The inverted commas are closed after *Ha !* in the first edition ; but it is not so in the manuscript ; and the matter is set right in the corrected copy.

And by old Rhadamanthus' tongue of doom,
This dusk religion, pomp of solitude,
And the Promethean clay by thief endued,   955
By old Saturnus' forelock, by his head
Shook with eternal palsy, I did wed
Myself to things of light from infancy ;
And thus to be cast out, thus lorn to die,
Is sure enough to make a mortal man   960
Grow impious."   So he inwardly began
On things for which no wording can be found ;
Deeper and deeper sinking, until drown'd
Beyond the reach of music : for the choir
Of Cynthia he heard not, though rough briar   965
Nor muffling thicket interpos'd to dull
The vesper hymn, far swollen, soft and full,
Through the dark pillars of those sylvan aisles.
He saw not the two maidens, nor their smiles,
Wan as primroses gather'd at midnight   970
By chilly finger'd spring.   " Unhappy wight !
Endymion !" said Peona, " we are here !
What wouldst thou ere we all are laid on bier ?"
Then he embrac'd her, and his lady's hand

---

(955) Cancelled reading of the manuscript, *And by Promethean...*
This was probably rejected to get rid of the repetition of the word *by*.

(956) The draft reads *And by old Saturn's single forelock...*

(967) The draft reads *prelude* for *vesper*.

(968) It is worth noting that, when writing out the fair copy,
Keats made three several attempts to spell this word *aisles* rightly,
having first written it *isles*, then *ailes* and lastly *aisles*.

(974-7) The draft reads as follows :—

> Her brother kiss'd her, and his lady's hand
> Saying, " Sweet sister I would have command,
> If it were heaven's will, on our sad fate."
> Then that dark-tressed stranger stood elate...

Press'd, saying : " Sister, I would have command,   975
If it were heaven's will, on our sad fate."
At which that dark-ey'd stranger stood elate
And said, in a new voice, but sweet as love,
To Endymion's amaze : " By Cupid's dove,
And so thou shalt ! and by the lilly truth   980
Of my own breast thou shalt, beloved youth ! "
And as she spake, into her face there came
Light, as reflected from a silver flame :
Her long black hair swell'd ampler, in display
Full golden ; in her eyes a brighter day   985
Dawn'd blue and full of love.   Aye, he beheld
Phœbe, his passion ! joyous she upheld
Her lucid bow, continuing thus : " Drear, drear
Has our delaying been ; but foolish fear
Withheld me first ; and then decrees of fate ;   990
And then 'twas fit that from this mortal state
Thou shouldst, my love, by some unlook'd for change
Be spiritualiz'd.   Peona, we shall range
These forests, and to thee they safe shall be
As was thy cradle ; hither shalt thou flee   ·   995
To meet us many a time."   Next Cynthia bright
Peona kiss'd, and bless'd with fair good night :
Her brother kiss'd her too, and knelt adown
Before his goddess, in a blissful swoon.
She gave her fair hands to him, and behold,   1000

(984-6) In the draft thus :—

> Her long black hair swell'd ampler, while it turned
> Golden—and her eyes of jet dawned forth a brighter day
> Blue—blue—and full of love.

(997-8) In the finished manuscript the word *kist* occurs twice in
these two lines instead of *kiss'd* as in the first edition ; but *bless'd*
is not similarly transformed to *blest*.

Before three swiftest kisses he had told,
They vanish'd far away!—Peona went
Home through the gloomy wood in wonderment.

THE END.

(1003) At the end of the draft Keats wrote " Burford Bridge
Nov. 28. 1817—".

The imprint of *Endymion* is as follows :—

T. Miller, Printer, Noble Street, Cheapside.

APPENDIX TO VOLUME I.

CONTENTS OF THE APPENDIX.

I.

REVIEW OF KEATS'S

FIRST VOLUME OF POEMS (1817)

WRITTEN BY LEIGH HUNT

and published in *The Examiner* for the 1st of June
and the 6th and 13th of July 1817.

THIS is the production of the young writer, whom we had
the pleasure of announcing to the public a short time
since, and several of whose Sonnets have appeared meanwhile in the *Examiner* with the signature of J. K. From
these and stronger evidences in the book itself, the readers
will conclude that the author and his critic are personal
friends; and they are so,—made however, in the first
instance, by nothing but his poetry, and at no greater
distance of time than the announcement above-mentioned.
We had published one of his Sonnets in our paper, with-

Hunt refers in the opening sentence to an article entitled "Young
Poets", which had appeared in *The Examiner* for the 1st of December 1816. "The last of these young aspirants whom we have
met with ", he says, " and who promise to help the new school to
revive Nature and

To put a spirit of youth in every thing,—

is, we believe, the youngest of them all. His name is John Keats.
He has not yet published anything except in a newspaper ; but a
set of his manuscripts was handed us the other day, and fairly surprised us with the truth of their ambition, and ardent grappling with
Nature ". Hunt then prints the sonnet on Chapman's Homer, with

out knowing more of him than any other anonymous correspondent; but at the period in question, a friend brought us one morning some copies of verses, which he said were from the pen of a youth. We had not been led, generally speaking, by a good deal of experience in these matters, to expect pleasure from introductions of the kind, so much as pain; but we had not read more than a dozen lines, when we recognized "a young poet indeed."

7   It is no longer a new observation, that poetry has of late years undergone a very great change, or rather, to speak properly, poetry has undergone no change, but something which was not poetry has made way for the return of something which is. The school which existed till lately since the restoration of Charles the 2d, was rather a school of wit and ethics in verse, than any thing else; nor was the verse, with the exception of Dryden's, of the best order. The authors, it is true, are to be held in great honour. Great wit there certainly was, excellent satire, excellent sense, pithy sayings; and Pope distilled as much real poetry as could be got from the drawing-room world in which the art then lived,—from the flowers and luxuries of artificial life,—into that exquisite little toilet-bottle of essence, the *Rape of the Lock*. But there was little imagination, of a higher order, no intense feeling of nature, no sentiment, no real music or variety. Even the writers who gave evidences meanwhile of a truer

the further remarks quoted at page 78 of the present volume. The sonnet which had been published in *The Examiner* before Hunt's introduction to the "set of manuscripts" was that given at page 71 of the present volume. Those published between the 1st of December 1816 and the 1st of June 1817 in *The Examiner* were the sonnets to Kosciusko, "After dark vapors", on the Elgin Marbles and to Haydon, and on *The Floure and the Lefe*.

poetical faculty, Gray, Thomson, Akenside, and Collins himself, were content with a great deal of second-hand workmanship, and with false styles made up of other languages and a certain kind of inverted cant. It has been thought that Cowper was the first poet who re-opened the true way to nature and a natural style; but we hold this to be a mistake, arising merely from certain negations on the part of that amiable but by no means powerful writer. Cowper's style is for the most part as inverted and artificial as that of the others; and we look upon him to have been by nature not so great a poet as Pope: but Pope, from certain infirmities on his part, was thrown into the society of the world, and thus had to get what he could out of an artificial sphere :—Cowper, from other and more distressing infirmities, (which by the way the wretched superstition that undertook to heal, only burnt in upon him) was confined to a still smaller though more natural sphere, and in truth did not much with it, though quite as much perhaps as was to be expected from an organization too sore almost to come in contact with any thing.

It was the Lake Poets in our opinion (however grudgingly we say it, on some accounts) that were the first to revive a true taste for nature; and like most Revolutionists, especially of the cast which they have since turned out to be, they went to an extreme, calculated rather at first to make the readers of poetry disgusted with originality and adhere with contempt and resentment to their magazine common-places. This had a bad effect also in the way of re-action; and none of those writers have ever since been able to free themselves from certain stubborn affectations, which having been ignorantly confounded by others with the better part of them, have been retained by their self-love with a still less pardonable want of wisdom. The greater part indeed of the poetry of Mr. Southey, a weak man in all respects, is really made up of little else. Mr. Coleridge still trifles with his poetical as he has done with his metaphysical talent. Mr. Lamb, in our opinion, has a more real tact of humanity, a modester, Shakspearean wisdom, than any of them ; and had he written more, might have delivered the school victoriously from all its defects. But it is Mr. Wordsworth who has advanced it the most, and who in spite of some morbidities as well as mistaken theories in other respects, has opened upon us a fund of thinking and imagination, that ranks him as the successor of the true and abundant poets of the older time. Poetry, like Plenty, should be represented with a cornucopia, but it should be a real one ; not swelled out and insidiously *optimized* at the top, like Mr. Southey's stale strawberry baskets, but fine and full to the depth, like a heap from the vintage. Yet from the time of Milton till lately, scarcely a tree had been planted that could be called a poet's own. People got shoots from France, that ended in nothing but a little barren wood, from which they made flutes for young gentlemen and fan-sticks for ladies. The rich and enchanted ground of real poetry, fertile with all that English succulance could produce, bright with all that Italian sunshine could lend, and haunted with exquisite humanities, had become invisible to mortal eyes like the garden of Eden :—

And from that time those Graces were not found.

THESE Graces, however, are re-appearing ; and one of the greatest evidences is the little volume before us ; for the work is not one of mere imitation, or a compilation of ingenious and promising thihgs that merely announce better, and that after all might only help to keep up a bad system ; but here is a young poet giving himself up to his own impressions, and revelling in real poetry for it's own sake. He has had his advantages, because others have cleared the way into those happy bowers ; but it shews the strength of his natural tendency, that he has not been turned aside by the lingering enticements of a former system, and by the self-love which interests others in enforcing them. We do not, of course, mean to say, that Mr. Keats has as much talent as he will have ten years hence, or that there are no imitations in his book, or that he does not make mistakes common to inexperience ;—the reverse is inevitable at his time of life. In proportion to our ideas, or impressions of the images of things, must be our acquaintance with the things themselves. But our author has all the sensitiveness of temperament requisite to receive these impressions ; and wherever he has turned hitherto, he has evidently felt them deeply.

The very faults indeed of Mr. Keats arise from a passion for beauties, and a young impatience to vindicate them ; and as we have mentioned these, we shall refer to them at once. They may be comprised in two ;—first, a tendency to notice every thing too indiscriminately and without an eye to natural proportion and effect ; and second, a sense of the proper variety of versification without a due consideration of its principles.

The former error is visible in several parts of the book, but chiefly though mixed with great beauties in the Epistles, and more between pages 28 and 47,[1] where are collected the author's earliest pieces, some of which, we think, might have been omitted, especially the string of magistrate-interrogatories about a shell and a copy of

---

[1] That is to say, the poems occupying pages 26 to 39 of the present volume.

verses. See also (p. 61) [1] a comparison of wine poured out in heaven to the appearance of a falling star, and (p. 62) [2] the sight of far-seen fountains in the same region to "silver streaks across a dolphin's fin." It was by thus giving way to every idea that came across him, that Marino, a man of real poetical fancy, but no judgment, corrupted the poetry of Italy; a catastrophe, which however we by no means anticipate from our author, who with regard to this point is much more deficient in age than in good taste. We shall presently have to notice passages of a reverse nature, and these are by far the most numerous. But we warn him against a fault, which is the more tempting to a young writer of genius, inasmuch as it involves something so opposite to the contented commonplace and vague generalities of the late school of poetry. There is a super-abundance of detail, which, though not so wanting, of course, in power of perception, is as faulty and unseasonable sometimes as common-place. It depends upon circumstances, whether we are to consider ourselves near enough, as it were, to the subject we are describing to grow microscopical upon it. A person basking in a landscape for instance, and a person riding through it, are in two very different situations for the exercise of their eyesight; and even where the license is most allowable, care must be taken not to give to small things and great, to nice detail and to general feeling, the same proportion of effect. Errors of this kind in poetry answer to a want of perspective in painting, and of a due distribution of light and shade. To give an excessive instance in the former art, there was Denner, who copied faces to a nicety amounting to a horrible want of it, like

---

[1] Page 48 of this volume.
[2] Page 49 of this volume.

Brobdignagian visages encountered by Gulliver; and who, according to the facetious Peter Pindar,

> Made a bird's beak appear at twenty mile.

And the same kind of specimen is afforded in poetry by Darwin, a writer now almost forgotten and deservedly, but who did good in his time by making unconscious caricatures of all the poetical faults in vogue, and flattering himself that the sum total went to the account of his original genius. Darwin would describe a dragon-fly and a lion in the same terms of proportion. You did not know which he would have scrambled from the sooner. His pictures were like the two-penny sheets which the little boys buy, and in which you see J Jackdaw and K King, both of the same dimensions.

Mr. Keats's other fault, the one in his versification, arises from a similar cause,—that of contradicting overzealously the fault on the opposite side. It is this which provokes him now and then into mere roughnesses and discords for their own sake, not for that of variety and contrasted harmony. We can manage, by substituting a greater feeling for a smaller, a line like the following:—

> I shall roll on the grass with two-fold ease ;—

but by no contrivance of any sort can we prevent this from jumping out of the heroic measure into mere rhythmicality,—

> How many bards gild the lapses of time !

We come now however to the beauties; and the reader will easily perceive that they not only outnumber the faults a hundred fold, but that they are of a nature decidedly opposed to what is false and inharmonious. Their characteristics indeed are a fine ear, a fancy and imagination at will, and an intense feeling of external

beauty in it's most natural and least expressible simplicity.

We shall give some specimens of the least beauty first,
and conclude with a noble extract or two that will shew
the second, as well as the powers of our young poet in
general. The harmony of his verses will appear throughout.

The first poem consists of a piece of luxury in a rural
spot, ending with an allusion to the story of Endymion,
and to the origin of other lovely tales of mythology, on
the ground suggested by Mr. Wordsworth in a beautiful
passage of his *Excursion.* Here, and in the other largest
poem, which closes the book, Mr. Keats is seen to his
best advantage, and displays all that fertile power of association and imagery which constitutes the abstract poetical faculty as distinguished from every other. He wants
age for a greater knowledge of humanity, but evidences
of this also bud forth here and there.—To come however
to our specimens :—

The first page of the book presents us with a fancy,
founded, as all beautiful fancies are, on a strong sense of
what really exists or occurs. He is speaking of

A gentle Air in Solitude.

There crept
A little noiseless noise among the leaves,
Born of the very sigh that silence heaves.

Young Trees.

There too should be
The frequent chequer of a youngling tree,
That with a score of light green brethren shoots
From the quaint mossiness of aged roots :
Round which is heard a spring-head of clear waters.

Any body who has seen a throng of young beeches, furnishing those natural clumpy seats at the root, must

recognise the truth and grace of this description. The remainder of this part of the poem, especially from—

> Open afresh your round of starry folds,
> Ye ardent marigolds !—

down to the bottom of page 5, affords an exquisite proof of close observation of nature as well as the most luxuriant fancy.

The Moon.

> Lifting her silver rim
> Above a cloud, and with a gradual swim
> Coming into the blue with all her light.

Fir Trees.

> Fir trees grow around,
> Aye dropping their hard fruit upon the ground.

This last line is in the taste of the Greek simplicity.

A starry Sky.

> The dark silent blue
> With all it's diamonds trembling through and through.

Sound of a Pipe.

> And some are hearing eagerly the wild
> Thrilling liquidity of dewy piping.

The *Specimen of an Induction to a Poem,* and the frag-- ment of the Poem itself entitled *Calidore,* contain some very natural touches on the human side of things; as when speaking of a lady who is anxiously looking out on the top of a tower for her defender, he describes her as one

> Who cannot feel for cold her tender feet ;

and when Calidore has fallen into a fit of amorous ab- straction, he says that

> —— The kind voice of good Sir Clerimond
> Came to his ear, as something from beyond
> His present being.

THE Epistles, the Sonnets, and indeed the whole of the

book, contain strong evidences of warm and social feelings, but particularly the Epistle to Charles Cowden
Clarke, and the Sonnet to his own Brothers, in which the
"faint cracklings" of the coal-fire are said to be

> Like whispers of the household gods that keep
> A gentle empire o'er fraternal souls.

The Epistle to Mr. Clarke is very amiable as well as
poetical, and equally honourable to both parties,—to the
young writer who can be so grateful towards his teacher,
and to the teacher who had the sense to perceive his
genius, and the qualities to call forth his affection. It
consists chiefly of recollections of what his friend had
pointed out to him in poetry and in general taste; and
the lover of Spenser will readily judge of his preceptor's
qualifications, even from a single triplet, in which he is
described, with a deep feeling of simplicity, as one

> Who had beheld Belphœbe in a brook,
> And lovely Una in a leafy nook,
> And Archimago leaning o'er his book.

The Epistle thus concludes:—

Picture of Companionship.

> But many days have past—
> Since I have walked with you through shady lanes,
> That freshly terminate in open plains,
>   *   *   *   *   *
> In those still moments I have wished you joys
> That well you know to honour :—"Life's very toys
> With him," said I, "will take a pleasant charm ;
> It cannot be that ought will work him harm." [1]

And we can only add, without any disrespect to the graver
warmth of our young poet, that if Ought attempted it,

---

[1] I have omitted ten lines from Hunt's quotation ; but see page
57.

Ought would find he had stout work to do with more than one person.

The following passage in one of the Sonnets passes, with great happiness, from the mention of physical associations to mental; and concludes with a feeling which must have struck many a contemplative mind, that has found the sea-shore like a border, as it were, of existence. He is speaking of

The Ocean.

The Ocean with it's vastness, it's blue green,
It's ships, it's rocks, it's caves,—it's hopes, it's fears,—
It's voice mysterious, which whoso hears
Must think on what will be, and what has been.

We have read somewhere the remark of a traveller, who said that when he was walking alone at night-time on the sea-shore, he felt conscious of the earth, not as the common every day sphere it seems, but as one of the planets, rolling round with him in the mightiness of space. The same feeling is common to imaginations that are not in need of similar local excitements.

The best poem is certainly the last and longest, entitled *Sleep and Poetry.* It originated in sleeping in a room adorned with busts and pictures, and is a striking specimen of the restlessness of the young poetical appetite, obtaining its food by the very desire of it, and glancing for fit subjects of creation " from earth to heaven." Nor do we like it the less for an impatient, and as it may be thought by some, irreverend assault upon the late French school of criticism and monotony, which has held poetry chained long enough to render it somewhat indignant when it has got free.

The following ardent passage is highly imaginative :—

An Aspiration after Poetry.

O Poesy ! for thee I grasp my pen
That am not yet a glorious denizen

Of thy wide heaven ; yet, to my ardent prayer,
Yield from thy sanctuary some clear air, &c. [1]

Mr. Keats takes an opportunity, though with very different feelings towards the school than he has exhibited
towards the one above-mentioned, to object to the mor-
bidity that taints the productions of the Lake Poets.
They might answer perhaps, generally, that they chuse
to grapple with what is unavoidable, rather than pretend
to be blind to it ; but the more smiling Muse may reply,
that half of the evils alluded to are produced by brooding
over them ; and that it is much better to strike at as
many *causes* of the rest as possible, than to pretend to be
satisfied with them in the midst of the most evident
dissatisfaction.

Happy Poetry Preferred.

These things are doubtless : yet in truth we've had
Strange thunders from the potency of song ;
Mingled indeed with what is sweet and strong,
From majesty : but in clear truth the themes
Are ugly cubs, the Poets Polyphemes
Disturbing the grand sea. A drainless shower
Of light is poesy ; 'tis the supreme of power ;
'Tis might half slumb'ring on its own right arm.
The very archings of her eye-lids charm
A thousand willing agents to obey.
And still she governs with the mildest sway :
But strength alone though of the Muses born
Is like a fallen angel ; trees uptorn,
Darkness, and worms, and shrouds, and sepulchres
Delight it ; for it feeds upon the burrs
And thorns of life ; forgetting the great end
Of poesy, that it should be a friend
To soothe the cares, and lift the thoughts of man.

---

[1] Hunt, it will be seen, took the liberty of compressing his quotation by silently omitting seven lines and piecing two fragments of
lines. He continued the quotation for twenty-eight lines more : see
pages 90 and 91.

We conclude with the beginning of the paragraph which follows this passage, and which contains an idea of as lovely and powerful a nature in embodying an abstraction, as we ever remember to have seen put into words :—

> Yet I rejoice : a myrtle fairer than
> E'er grew in Paphos, from the bitter weeds
> Lift's it's sweet head into the air, *and feeds*
> *A silent space with ever sprouting green.*

Upon the whole, Mr. Keats's book cannot be better described than in a couplet written by Milton when he too was young, and in which he evidently alludes to himself. It is a little luxuriant heap of

> Such sights as youthful poets dream
> On summer eves by haunted stream.

II.

FOUR SONNETS FROM LEIGH HUNT'S FOLIAGE.

To JOHN KEATS.

'Tis well you think me truly one of those,
Whose sense discerns the loveliness of things ;
For surely as I feel the bird that sings
Behind the leaves, or dawn as it up grows,
Or the rich bee rejoicing as he goes,
Or the glad issue of emerging springs,
Or overhead the glide of a dove's wings,
Or turf, or trees, or, midst of all, repose.
And surely as I feel things lovelier still,
The human look, and the harmonious form
Containing woman, and the smile in ill,
And such a heart as Charles's,[1] wise and warm,—
As surely as all this, I see, ev'n now,
Young Keats, a flowering laurel on your brow.

Although it may not be strictly relevant, it will interest some readers to know that these sonnets are transcribed for the present appendix from Keats's own copy of *Foliage; or Poems Original and Translated, by Leigh Hunt* (1818), bearing upon the title-page, in Hunt's beautiful writing, the words "John Keats from his affectionate friend the Author." Keats gave the book to Miss Brawne ; and it is now in my possession.

[1] Hunt notes "Charles C. C. [Cowden Clarke], a mutual friend."

ON RECEIVING A CROWN OF IVY FROM THE SAME.

A crown of ivy! I submit my head
To the young hand that gives it,—young, 'tis true,
But with a right, for 'tis a poet's too.
How pleasant the leaves feel! and how they spread
With their broad angles, like a nodding shed
Over both eyes! and how complete and new,
As on my hand I lean, to feel them strew
My sense with freshness,—Fancy's rustling bed!
Tress-tossing girls, with smell of flowers and grapes
Come dancing by, and downward piping cheeks,
And up-thrown cymbals, and Silenus old
Lumpishly borne, and many trampling shapes,—
And lastly, with his bright eyes on her bent,
Bacchus,—whose bride has of his hand fast hold.

ON THE SAME.

It is a lofty feeling, yet a kind,
Thus to be topped with leaves ;—to have a sense
Of honour-shaded thought,—an influence
As from great Nature's fingers, and be twined
With her old, sacred, verdurous ivy-bind,
As though she hallowed with that sylvan fence
A head that bows to her benevolence,
Midst pomp of fancied trumpets in the wind.
'Tis what's within us crowned. And kind and great
Are all the conquering wishes it inspires,—
Love of things lasting, love of the tall woods,
Love of love's self, and ardour for a state
Of natural good befitting such desires,
Towns without gain, and haunted solitudes.

VOL. I.   A A

TO THE GRASSHOPPER AND THE CRICKET.

Green little vaulter in the sunny grass
Catching your heart up at the feel of June,
Sole voice that's heard amidst the lazy noon,
When ev'n the bees lag at the summoning brass;
And you, warm little housekeeper, who class
With those who think the candles come too soon,
Loving the fire, and with your tricksome tune
Nick the glad silent moments as they pass;
Oh sweet and tiny cousins, that belong,
One to the fields, the other to the hearth,
Both have your sunshine; both though small are strong
At your clear hearts; and both were sent on earth
To sing in thoughtful ears this natural song,—
In doors and out, summer and winter, Mirth.

30th December, 1816.

III.

SONNET

WRITTEN ON THE BLANK LEAF OF KEATS'S POEMS (1817) BY CHARLES OLLIER.

Keats I admire thine upward daring Soul,
  Thine eager grasp at immortality
  I deem within thy reach ;—rejoic'd I see
Thee spurn, with brow serene, the gross controul
Of circumstance, while o'er thee visions roll
  In radiant pomp of lovely Poesy!
  She points to blest abodes where spirits free
Feed on her smiles and her great name extol.—
Still shall the pure flame bright within thee burn
  While nature's voice alone directs thy mind ;
Who bids thy speculation inward turn
  Assuring thee her transcript thou shalt find.
Live her's—live freedom's friend—so round thine urn
  The oak shall with thy laurels be entwin'd.

I have no evidence of the authorship of this sonnet beyond the hand-writing ; but I have no doubt about its being the writing of Charles Ollier. The sonnet is dated the 2nd of March 1817, and represents a far pleasanter phase of Keats's connexion with his first publisher than that represented by the next appendix.

IV.

LETTER FROM MESSRS. C. & J. OLLIER TO GEORGE KEATS CONCERNING KEATS'S POEMS (1817)

reprinted from *The Athenæum* for the 7th of June 1873.

Sir,—We regret that your brother ever requested us to publish his book, or that our opinion of its talent should have led us to acquiesce in undertaking it. We are, however, much obliged to you for relieving us from the unpleasant necessity of declining any further connexion with it, which we must have done, as we think the curiosity is satisfied, and the sale has dropped. By far the greater number of persons who have purchased it from us have found fault with it in such plain terms, that we have in many cases offered to take the book back rather than be annoyed with the ridicule which has, time after time, been showered upon it. In fact, it was only on Saturday last that we were under the mortification of having our own opinion of its merits flatly contradicted by a gentleman, who told us he considered it ' no better than a take in.' These are unpleasant imputations for any one in business to labour under, but we should have borne them and concealed their existence from you had not the style of your note shewn us that such delicacy would be quite thrown away. We shall take means without delay for ascertaining the number of copies on hand, and you shall be informed accordingly. Your most, &c.

C. & J. Ollier.

3, Welbeck Street, 29th April, 1817.

V.

REVIEW OF ENDYMION

PUBLISHED IN THE QUARTERLY REVIEW.

R EVIEWERS have been sometimes accused of not
reading the works which they affected to criticise.
On the present occasion we shall anticipate the author's
complaint, and honestly confess that we have not read
his work. Not that we have been wanting in our duty
—far from it—indeed, we have made efforts almost as
superhuman as the story itself appears to be, to get
through it ; but with the fullest stretch of our persever-
ance, we are forced to confess that we have not been able
to struggle beyond the first of the four books of which
this Poetic Romance consists. We should extremely
lament this want of energy, or whatever it may be, on
our parts, were it not for one consolation—namely, that
we are no better acquainted with the meaning of the
book through which we have so painfully toiled, than we
are with that of the three which we have not looked
into.

It is not that Mr. Keats, (if that be his real name, for

This is the review immortalized, as far as things hateful can be,
by Shelley in his *Adonais*. It is a curiously unimportant production ; but it is well that it should be in evidence. It appeared
in No. XXXVII of the review, headed " April, 1818 " on page 1,
but described on the wrapper as " published in September, 1818 ".

we almost doubt that any man in his senses would put his real name to such a rhapsody,) it is not, we say, that the author has not powers of language, rays of fancy, and gleams of genius—he has all these ; but he is unhappily a disciple of the new school of what has been somewhere called Cockney poetry ; which may be defined to consist of the most incongruous ideas in the most uncouth language.

Of this school, Mr. Leigh Hunt, as we observed in a former Number, aspires to be the hierophant. Our readers will recollect the pleasant recipes for harmonious and sublime poetry which he gave us in his preface to 'Rimini,' and the still more facetious instances of his harmony and sublimity in the verses themselves ; and they will recollect above all the contempt of Pope, Johnson, and such like poetasters and pseudo-critics, which so forcibly contrasted itself with Mr. Leigh Hunt's self-complacent approbation of

> —— 'all the things itself had wrote,
> Of special merit though of little note.'

This author is a copyist of Mr. Hunt ; but he is more unintelligible, almost as rugged, twice as diffuse, and ten times more tiresome and absurd than his prototype, who, though he impudently presumed to seat himself in the chair of criticism, and to measure his own poetry by his own standard, yet generally had a meaning. But Mr. Keats had advanced no dogmas which he was bound to support by examples ; his nonsense therefore is quite gratuitous ; he writes it for its own sake, and, being bitten by Mr. Leigh Hunt's insane criticism, more than rivals the insanity of his poetry.

Mr. Keats's preface hints that his poem was produced under peculiar circumstances.

'Knowing within myself (he says) the manner in which this Poem has been produced, it is not without a feeling of regret that I make it public.—What manner I mean, will be *quite clear* to the reader, who must soon perceive great inexperience, immaturity, and every error denoting a feverish attempt, rather than a deed accomplished.'—*Preface*, p. vii.

We humbly beg his pardon, but this does not appear to us to be *quite so clear*—we really do not know what he means—but the next passage is more intelligible.

'The two first books, and indeed the two last, I feel sensible are not of such completion as to warrant their passing the press.'—*Preface*, p. vii.

Thus 'the two first books' are, even in his own judgment, unfit to appear, and 'the two last' are, it seems, in the same condition—and as two and two make four, and as that is the whole number of books, we have a clear and, we believe, a very just estimate of the entire work.

Mr. Keats, however, deprecates criticism on this 'immature and feverish work' in terms which are themselves sufficiently feverish ; and we confess that we should have abstained from inflicting upon him any of the tortures of the *'fierce hell'* of criticism, which terrify his imagination, if he had not begged to be spared in order that he might write more; if we had not observed in him a certain degree of talent which deserves to be put in the right way, or which, at least, ought to be warned of the wrong ; and if, finally, he had not told us that he is of an age and temper which imperiously require mental discipline.

Of the story we have been able to make out but little ; it seems to be mythological, and probably relates to the loves of Diana and Endymion ; but of this, as the scope of the work has altogether escaped us, we cannot speak with any degree of certainty ; and must therefore content ourselves with giving some instances of its diction and

versification :—and here again we are perplexed and
puzzled.—At first it appeared to us, that Mr. Keats had
been amusing himself and wearying his readers with an
immeasurable game at *bouts-rimés;* but, if we recollect
rightly, it is an indispensable condition at this play, that
the rhymes when filled up shall have a meaning ; and
our author, as we have already hinted, has no meaning.
He seems to us to write a line at random, and then he
follows not the thought excited by this line, but that
suggested by the *rhyme* with which it concludes.   There
is hardly a complete couplet inclosing a complete idea in
the whole book. He wanders from one subject to another,
from the association, not of ideas but of sounds, and the
work is composed of hemistichs which, it is quite evident,
have forced themselves upon the author by the mere
force of the catchwords on which they turn.

We shall select, not as the most striking instance, but
as that least liable to suspicion, a passage from the
opening of the poem.

———— 'Such the sun, the moon,
Trees old and young, sprouting a shady boon
For simple sheep ; and such are daffodils
With the green world they live in ; and clear rills
That for themselves a cooling covert make
'Gainst the hot season ; the mid forest brake,
Rich with a sprinkling of fair musk-rose blooms :
And such too is the grandeur of the dooms
We have imagined for the mighty dead; &c. &c.'—pp. 3, 4.

Here it is clear that the word, and not the idea, *moon*
produces the simple sheep and their shady *boon,* and that
' the *dooms* of the mighty dead' would never have intruded
themselves but for the '*fair musk-rose blooms.*'
Again.

' For 'twas the morn : Apollo's upward fire
Made every eastern cloud a silvery pyre

Of brightness so unsullied, that therein
A melancholy spirit well might win
Oblivion, and melt out his essence fine
Into the winds : rain-scented eglantine
Gave temperate sweets to that well-wooing sun ;
The lark was lost in him ; cold springs had run
To warm their chilliest bubbles in the grass ;
Man's voice was on the mountains ; and the mass
Of nature's lives and wonders puls'd tenfold,
To feel this sun-rise and its glories old.'—p. 8.

Here Apollo's *fire* produces a *pyre*, a silvery pyre of clouds, *wherein* a spirit might *win* oblivion and melt his essence *fine*, and scented *eglantine* gives sweets to the *sun*, and cold springs had *run* into the *grass*, and then the pulse of the *mass* pulsed *tenfold* to feel the glories *old* of the new-born day, &c.

One example more.

' Be still the unimaginable lodge
For solitary thinkings ; such as dodge
Conception to the very bourne of heaven,
Then leave the naked brain : be still the leaven,
That spreading in this dull and clodded earth
Gives it a touch ethereal—a new birth.'—p. 17.

Lodge, dodge—heaven, leaven—earth, birth; such, in six words, is the sum and substance of six lines.

We come now to the author's taste in versification. He cannot indeed write a sentence, but perhaps he may be able to spin a line. Let us see. The following are specimens of his prosodial notions of our English heroic metre.

' Dear as the temple's self, so does the moon,
The passion poesy, glories infinite.'—p. 4.

' So plenteously all weed-hidden roots.'—p. 6.

' Of some strange history, potent to send.'—p. 18.

' Before the deep intoxication.'—p. 27.

' Her scarf into a fluttering pavilion.'—p. 33.

'The stubborn canvass for my voyage prepared——.'—p. 39.

' " Endymion ! the cave is secreter
Than the isle of Delos.   Echo hence shall stir
No sighs but sigh-warm kisses, or light noise
Of thy combing hand, the while it travelling cloys
And trembles through my labyrinthine hair." '—p. 48.

By this time our readers must be pretty well satisfied as to the meaning of his sentences and the structure of his lines : we now present them with some of the new words with which, in imitation of Mr. Leigh Hunt, he adorns our language.

We are told that 'turtles *passion* their voices,' (p. 15) ; that 'an arbour was *nested*,' (p. 23) ; and a lady's locks '*gordian'd* up,' (p. 32) ; and to supply the place of the nouns thus verbalized Mr. Keats, with great fecundity, spawns new ones; such as 'men-slugs and human *serpentry*,' (p. 41) ; the '*honey-feel* of bliss,' (p. 45) ; 'wives prepare *needments*,' (p. 13)—and so forth.

Then he has formed new verbs by the process of cutting off their natural tails, the adverbs, and affixing them to their foreheads ; thus, 'the wine out-sparkled,' (p. 10) ; the 'multitude up-followed,' (p. 11) ; and 'night up-took,' (p. 29). 'The wind up-blows,' (p. 32) ; and the 'hours are down-sunken,' (p. 36.)

But if he sinks some adverbs in the verbs he compensates the language with adverbs and adjectives which he separates from the parent stock.   Thus, a lady 'whispers *pantingly* and close,' makes '*hushing* signs,' and steers her skiff into a '*ripply* cove,' (p. 23) ; a shower falls '*refreshfully*,' (45) ; and a vulture has a '*spreaded* tail,' (p. 44.)

But enough of Mr. Leigh Hunt and his simple neophyte.—If any one should be bold enough to purchase this 'Poetic Romance,' and so much more patient, than ourselves, as to get beyond the first book, and so much more fortunate as to find a meaning, we entreat him to make us acquainted with his success ; we shall then return to the task which we now abandon in despair, and endeavour to make all due amends to Mr. Keats and to our readers.

VI.

REVIEW OF ENDYMION AND LAMIA &c.

PUBLISHED IN THE EDINBURGH REVIEW.

WE had never happened to see either of these volumes till very lately—and have been exceedingly struck with the genius they display, and the spirit of poetry which breathes through all their extravagance. That imitation of our older writers, and especially of our older dramatists, to which we cannot help flattering ourselves that we have somewhat contributed, has brought on, as it were, a second spring in our poetry ;—and few of its blossoms are either more profuse of sweetness or richer in promise, than this which is now before us. Mr Keats, we understand, is still a very young man ; and his whole works, indeed, bear evidence enough of the fact. They are full of extravagance and irregularity, rash attempts at originality, interminable wanderings, and excessive obscurity. They manifestly require, therefore, all the indulgence that can be claimed for a first attempt :—but we think it no less plain that they deserve it ; for they are flushed all over with the rich lights of fancy, and so coloured and bestrewn with the flowers of poetry, that

---

This review appeared in No. LXVII of *The Edinburgh Review*, that for August 1820, and was reprinted in Jeffrey's collected essays. As it is almost entirely about *Endymion*, I give it all here, instead of reserving some portion of it for the Appendix to Volume II, which contains the poems published in the *Lamia* volume.

even while perplexed and bewildered in their labyrinths, it is impossible to resist the intoxication of their sweetness, or to shut our hearts to the enchantments they so lavishly present. The models upon which he has formed himself, in the Endymion, the earliest and by much the most considerable of his poems, are obviously the Faithful Shepherdess of Fletcher, and the Sad Shepherd of Ben Jonson ;—the exquisite metres and inspired diction of which he has copied with great boldness and fidelity —and, like his great originals, has also contrived to impart to the whole piece that true rural and poetical air which breathes only in them and in Theocritus—which is at once homely and majestic, luxurious and rude, and sets before us the genuine sights and sounds and smells of the country, with all the magic and grace of Elysium. His subject has the disadvantage of being mythological ; and in this respect, as well as on account of the raised and rapturous tone it consequently assumes, his poetry may be better compared perhaps to the Comus and the Arcades of Milton, of which, also, there are many traces of imitation. The great distinction, however, between him and these divine authors, is, that imagination in them is subordinate to reason and judgment, while, with him, it is paramount and supreme—that their ornaments and images are employed to embellish and recommend just sentiments, engaging incidents, and natural characters, while his are poured out without measure or restraint, and with no apparent design but to unburden the breast of the author, and give vent to the overflowing vein of his fancy. The thin and scanty tissue of his story is merely the light frame work on which his florid wreaths are suspended ; and while his imaginations go rambling and entangling themselves everywhere, like wild honeysuckles, all idea of sober reason, and plan, and consist-

ency, is utterly forgotten, and are 'strangled in their
waste fertility.' A great part of the work indeed, is
written in the strangest and most fantastical manner that
can be imagined. It seems as if the author had ventured everything that occurred to him in the shape of a
glittering image or striking expression—taken the first
word that presented itself to make up a rhyme, and then
made that word the germ of a new cluster of images—a
hint for a new excursion of the fancy—and so wandered
on, equally forgetful whence he came, and heedless
whither he was going, till he had covered his pages with
an interminable arabesque of connected and incongruous
figures, that multiplied as they extended, and were only
harmonized by the brightness of their tints, and the
graces of their forms.   In this rash and headlong career
he has of course many lapses and failures.   There is no
work, accordingly, from which a malicious critic could
cull more matter for ridicule, or select more obscure, un-
natural, or absurd passages.   But we do not take *that* to
be our office ;—and just beg leave, on the contrary, to
say, that any one who, on this account, would represent
the whole poem as despicable, must either have no notion
of poetry, or no regard to truth.

It is, in truth, at least as full of genius as of absurdity;
and he who does not find a great deal in it to admire and
to give delight, cannot in his heart see much beauty in the
two exquisite dramas to which we have already alluded,
or find any great pleasure in some of the finest creations of
Milton and Shakespeare.   There are very many such
persons, we verily believe, even among the reading and
judicious part of the community—correct scholars we
have no doubt many of them, and, it may be, very classical composers in prose and in verse—but utterly ignorant of the true genius of English poetry, and incapable

of estimating its appropriate and most exquisite beauties. With that spirit we have no hesitation in saying that Mr K. is deeply imbued—and of those beauties he has presented us with many striking examples. We are very much inclined indeed to add, that we do not know any book which we would sooner employ as a test to ascertain whether any one had in him a native relish for poetry, and a genuine sensibility to its intrinsic charm. The greater and more distinguished poets of our country have so much else in them to gratify other tastes and propensities, that they are pretty sure to captivate and amuse those to whom their poetry is but an hindrance and obstruction, as well as those to whom it constitutes their chief attraction. The interest of the stories they tell—the vivacity of the characters they delineate—the weight and force of the maxims and sentiments in which they abound—the very pathos and wit and humour they display, which may all and each of them exist apart from their poetry and independent of it, are quite sufficient to account for their popularity, without referring much to that still higher gift, by which they subdue to their enchantments those whose souls are attuned to the finer impulses of poetry. It is only where those other recommendations are wanting, or exist in a weaker degree, that the true force of the attraction, exercised by the pure poetry with which they are so often combined, can be fairly appreciated—where, without much incident or many characters, and with little wit, wisdom, or arrangement, a number of bright pictures are presented to the imagination, and a fine feeling expressed of those mysterious relations by which visible external things are assimilated with inward thoughts and emotions, and become the images and exponents of all passions and affections. To an unpoetical

reader such passages always appear mere raving and absurdity—and to this censure a very great part of the
volume before us will certainly be exposed, with this class
of readers. Even in the judgment of a fitter audience,
however, it must, we fear, be admitted, that, besides the
riot and extravagance of his fancy, the scope and sub-
stance of Mr K.'s poetry is rather too dreary and ab-
stracted to excite the strongest interest, or to sustain the
attention through a work of any great compass or extent.
He deals too much with shadowy and incomprehensible
beings, and is too constantly rapt into an extramundane
Elysium, to command a lasting interest with ordinary
mortals—and must employ the agency of more varied
and coarser emotions, if he wishes to take rank with the
seducing poets of this or of former generations. There
is something very curious too, we think, in the way in
which he, and Mr Barry Cornwall also, have dealt with
the Pagan mythology, of which they have made so much
use in their poetry. Instead of presenting its imaginary
persons under the trite and vulgar traits that belong to
them in the ordinary systems, little more is borrowed
from these than the general conception of their conditions
and relations ; and an original character and distinct individuality is bestowed upon them, which has all the
merit of invention, and all the grace and attraction of the
fictions on which it is engrafted. The antients, though
they probably did not stand in any great awe of their
deities, have yet abstained very much from any minute
or dramatic representation of their feelings and affections.
In Hesiod and Homer, they are coarsely delineated by
some of their actions and adventures, and introduced to
us merely as the agents in those particular transactions ;
while in the Hymns, from those ascribed to Orpheus and
Homer, down to those of Callimachus, we have little but

pompous epithets and invocations, with a flattering com-
memoration of their most famous exploits—and are never
allowed to enter into their bosoms, or follow out the train
of their feelings, with the presumption of our human
sympathy. Except the love-song of the Cyclops to his
Sea Nymph in Theocritus—the Lamentation of Venus
for Adonis in Moschus—and the more recent Legend of
Apuleius, we scarcely recollect a passage in all the writings of antiquity in which the passions of an immortal
are fairly disclosed to the scrutiny and observation of
men. The author before us, however, and some of his
contemporaries, have dealt differently with the subject;
—and, sheltering the violence of the fiction under the
ancient traditionary fable, have created and imagined an
entire new set of characters, and brought closely and
minutely before us the loves and sorrows and perplexities
of beings, with whose names and supernatural attributes
we had long been familiar, without any sense or feeling
of their personal character. We have more than doubts
of the fitness of such personages to maintain a perma-
nent interest with the modern public;—but the way in
which they are here managed, certainly gives them the
best chance that now remains for them; and, at all
events, it cannot be denied that the effect is striking
and graceful. But we must now proceed to our extracts.

The first of the volumes before us is occupied with the
loves of Endymion and Diana—which it would not be
very easy, and which we do not at all intend to analyze
in detail. In the beginning of the poem, however, the
Shepherd Prince is represented as having had strange
visions and delirious interviews with an unknown and
celestial beauty; soon after which, he is called on to pre-
side at a festival in honour of Pan; and his appearance
in the procession is thus described.

> His youth was fully blown,
> Showing like Ganymede to manhood grown ;
> And, for those simple times, his garments were
> A chieftain king's : beneath his breast, half bare,
> Was hung a silver bugle, and between
> His nervy knees there lay a boar-spear keen.
> A smile was on his countenance ; he seem'd,
> To common lookers on, like one who dream'd
> Of idleness in groves Elysian :
> But there were some who feelingly could scan
> A lurking trouble in his nether lip,
> And see that oftentimes the reins would slip
> Through his forgotten hands. pp. 11, 12.

There is then a choral hymn addressed to the sylvan
deity, which appears to us to be full of beauty ; and reminds us, in many places, of the finest strains of Sicilian
or English poetry.   A part of it is as follows.

> O THOU, whose mighty palace roof doth hang &c.[1]

The enamoured youth sinks into insensibility in the
midst of the solemnity, and is borne apart and revived
by the care of his sister ; and, opening his heavy eyes in
her arms, says—

> I feel this thine endearing love
> All through my bosom : thou art as a dove
> Trembling its closed eyes and sleeked wings
> About me ; and the pearliest dew not brings
> Such morning incense from the fields of May,
> As do those brighter drops that twinkling stray
> From those kind eyes.   Then think not thou
> That, any longer, I will pass my days
> Alone and sad.[2]

---

[1] The extract given here consists of lines 232 to 241 and 247 to
286 of Book I.   See pages 132 to 135.

[2] The quotation is given in full thus far as an example of the kind
of thing that a " friendly critic " permitted himself in 1820.   It will
be seen that the text is entirely altered after the word *eyes*.   The
quotation extended twenty lines further, ending with *So mournful
strange* in line 497 of Book I.   See pages 145 and 146.

He then tells her all the story of his love and madness; and is afterwards led away by butterflies to the
haunts of Naiads, and by them sent down into enchanted
caverns, where he sees Venus and Adonis, and great
flights of Cupids, and wanders over diamond terraces
among beautiful fountains and temples and statues, and
all sorts of fine and strange things. All this is very
fantastical : But there are splendid pieces of description,
and a sort of wild richness on the whole. We cull a few
little morsels. This is the picture of the sleeping
Adonis.

> In midst of all, there lay a sleeping youth
> Of fondest beauty. Sideway his face repos'd
> On one white arm, and tenderly unclos'd,
> By tenderest pressure, a faint damask mouth, &c.[1]

There is another and more classical sketch of Cybele.[2]
In the midst of all these spectacles, he has, we do not
very well know how, a ravishing interview with his unknown goddess; and, when she melts away from him,
he finds himself in a vast grotto, where he overhears the
courtship of Alpheus and Arethusa, and, as they elope
together, discovers that the grotto has disappeared, and
that he is at the bottom of the sea, under the transparent arches of its naked waters. The following is
abundantly extravagant; but comes of no ignoble lineage, nor shames its high descent.

> Far had he roam'd,
> With nothing save the hollow vast, that foam'd

---

[1] Compare this also with the original at pages 196 and 197. The
quotation goes on nine lines further, ending with line 414, Book II;
and then comes the passage from *Hard by* (line 418) to the end of
line 427 (page 198).

[2] Lines 639 to 649 (pages 209 and 210) are here quoted.

>   Above, around, and at his feet ; save things
>   More dead than Morpheus' imaginings : &c.[1]

There he finds antient Glaucus enchanted by Circe—
hears his wild story—and goes with him to the deli-
verance and restoration of thousands of drowned lovers,
whose bodies were piled and stowed away in a large sub-
marine palace.   When this feat is happily performed, he
finds himself again on dry ground, with woods and waters
around him ; and cannot help falling desperately in love
with a beautiful damsel whom he finds there pining for
some such consolations, and who tells a long story of her
having come from India in the train of Bacchus, and
having strayed away from him into that forest :—so they
vow eternal fidelity, and are wafted up to heaven on
flying horses, on which they sleep and dream among the
stars ;—and then the lady melts away, and he is again
alone upon the earth ; but soon rejoins his Indian love,
and agrees to give up his goddess, and live only for her :
But she refuses, and says she is resolved to devote herself to the service of Diana ; and when she goes to de-
dicate herself, she turns out to be the goddess in a new
shape, and exalts her lover with her to a blest immortality.

We have left ourselves room to say but little of the
second volume, which is of a more miscellaneous character.   Lamia is a Greek antique story, in the measure
and taste of Endymion.   Isabella is a paraphrase of the
same tale of Boccacio, which Mr Cornwall has also imitated under the title of 'a Sicilian Story.'   It would be
worth while to compare the two imitations ; but we have
no longer time for such a task.   Mr K. has followed his

---

[1] This is duly followed by the fourteen descriptive lines that follow it in the text, down to *monster*.   See page 239.

original more closely, and has given a deep pathos to
several of his stanzas. The widowed bride's discovery
of the murdered body is very strikingly given.

> Soon she turn'd up a soiled glove, whereon
>   Her silk had play'd in purple phantasies,
> She kiss'd it with a lip more chill than stone,
>   And put it in her bosom, where it dries.
> Then 'gan she work again ; nor stay'd her care,
> But to throw back at times her veiling hair.
>
> That old nurse stood beside her wondering,
>   Until her heart felt pity to the core
> At sight of such a dismal labouring,
>   And so she kneeled, with her locks all hoar,
> And put her lean hands to the horrid thing :
>   Three hours they labour'd at this travail sore ;
> At last they felt the kernel of the grave, &c.[1]

The following lines from an ode to a Nightingale, are
equally distinguished for harmony and feeling.

> O for a beaker full of the warm South,
>   Full of the true, the blushful Hippocrene,
>   With beaded bubbles winking at the brim,
>   And purple-stained mouth ;
>   That I might drink, and leave the world unseen,
>   And with thee fade away into the forest dim :
> Fade far away, dissolve, and quite forget
>   What thou among the leaves hast never known,
> The weariness, the fever, and the fret
>   · Here, where men sit and hear each other groan ;
> Where palsy shakes a few, sad, last grey hairs,
>   Where youth grows pale, and spectre-thin, and dies;
>   Where but to think is to be full of sorrow
>   And leaden-eyed despairs.
> The voice I hear this passing night was heard
>   In ancient days by emperor and clown :
> Perhaps the self-same song that found a path

---

[1] I retain thus much of the extract as a fine example of the art of
quoting murderously with the best intentions. Stanzas LI and LII
were also given here.

Through the sad heart of Ruth, when, sick for home,
  She stood in tears amid the alien corn ;
    The same that oft-times hath
Charm'd magic casements, opening on the foam
  Of perilous seas, in faery lands forlorn.[1]

We must close our extracts with the following lively lines to Fancy.

O sweet Fancy ! let her loose ; &c.[2]

There is a fragment of a projected Epic, entitled ' Hyperion,' on the expulsion of Saturn and the Titanian deities by Jupiter and his younger adherents, of which we cannot advise the completion : For, though there are passages of some force and grandeur, it is sufficiently obvious, from the specimen before us, that the subject is too far removed from all the sources of human interest, to be successfully treated by any modern author. Mr Keats has unquestionably a very beautiful imagination, and a great familiarity with the finest diction of English poetry ; but he must learn not to misuse or misapply these advantages ; and neither to waste the good gifts of nature and study on intractable themes, nor to luxuriate too recklessly on such as are more suitable.

---

[1] It is to be observed that, wishing to give no more of stanza 3 after the eighth line, the reviewer places a full-stop instead of a comma at *despairs*, and calmly passes on to the third line of stanza 7 without any indication of a break.

[2] The lines quoted are 9 to 24 and 39 to 66.

END OF VOLUME I.

CHISWICK PRESS: C. WHITTINGHAM AND CO. TOOKS COURT, CHANCERY LANE.

www.ingramcontent.com/pod-product-compliance
Lightning Source LLC
Chambersburg PA
CBHW021337110726
47900CB00005B/1504